# The Last Place

*Also by Laura Lippman
in Large Print:*

The Sugar House

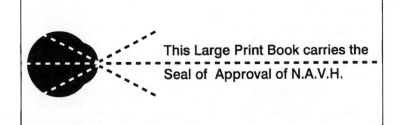

This Large Print Book carries the
Seal of Approval of N.A.V.H.

# The
# Last
# Place

*Laura Lippman*

Published in 2003 by arrangement with William Morrow, an imprint of HarperCollins Publishers, Inc.

Wheeler Large Print Hardcover Series.

The text of this Large Print edition is unabridged.
Other aspects of the book may vary from the original edition.

Set in 16 pt. Plantin by Ramona A. Watson.

Printed in the United States on permanent paper.

**Library of Congress Cataloging-in-Publication Data**

Lippman, Laura, 1959–
    The last place / Laura Lippman.
      p. cm.
    ISBN 1-58724-417-9 (lg. print : hc : alk. paper)
    1. Monaghan, Tess (Fictitious character) — Fiction.
2. Women private investigators — Maryland — Baltimore —
Fiction.   3. Baltimore (Md.) — Fiction.   4. Serial murders —
Fiction.   5. Maryland — Fiction.   6. Large type books.
I. Title.
PS3562.I586L37 2003
   813′.6—dc21                          2003041135

*In memory of my grandparents —*
*Louise Deaver Lippman*
*and Theodore Lippman*
*Mary Julia Moore Mabry*
*and E. Speer Mabry Jr.*

Ripe plums are falling,
Now there are only seven,
May a fine lover come for me,
Now while there's still time.
Ripe plums are falling,
Now there are only three,
May a fine lover come for me,
While there's still time.
Ripe plums are falling,
I lay them in a shuttle basket,
May a fine lover come for me.
Tell me his name.

— CONFUCIUS

# Acknowledgments

Thanks to the stalwarts (Joan Jacobson, Vicky Bijur, Carrie Feron) and some new technical advisers — particularly Dr. Mark S. Komrad, Heather Dewar, and Tom Horton. I could not have written this book without the guidance of Tom's *An Island Out of Time*, which helped me create the mythical island that appears here. It should be noted that Father Andrew White is a real person and he did keep journals on his trip to the New World, but he never described Notting Island, for it exists only in my imagination. This is a work of fiction.

This book was written during what proved to be my final year at the Baltimore *Sun*, and I want to include here the dedication that Rafael Alvarez was not allowed to use in *Storyteller*, a collection of his newspaper pieces published by the *Sun* in 2001: Thank you to the Washington-Baltimore Newspaper Guild for allowing Rafael, me, and thousands of other workers — past, present, and future — to earn a living wage.

He begins his day on the water. The way his father did. The way she does.

Not that he can quite admit to himself that he has come here to see her this morning. He has legitimate reasons to be on this idling motorboat as day breaks. He smiles at his own turn of phrase: legitimate reasons. Legitimate. A funny word, when applied to his life, and yet fitting. He draws it out, reveling in its syllables, imagining it in the accent of his youth. Le-git-i-mate.

He has cut the engine for the last part of his journey, gliding to a stop beneath a low-lying overpass. Not many people know about this small inlet off the wider waters of the Patapsco, south of the city and the Inner Harbor. Those who do probably think it's too shallow to be navigable. Good. That's why he chose it. But he has seen her here, once or twice. Which is okay, as long as she stays on the water, doesn't get out and poke around. He can't imagine why she would. But you never know.

Another day, another dollar. His father had said that, heading out every morning, and it was almost too literal in his case. Those were the years when the bay began to betray them: the bay and then the politicians, with their limits on this, their moratoriums on that. Starve this generation in order to feed the next, that seemed to be their plan. But who was going to harvest the oysters and catch the crabs if they let the watermen die out? Oh, they loved the watermen in the abstract, paid lip service to the history and the tradition, and they sure as hell loved the food when it came. Here in the city, they make a similar fuss over the Arabbers, the black men who sell fruits and vegetables from horse-drawn carts. But it's the horses they love, not the men. The people who do the dirty work aren't flesh and blood to those who rely on them, no more human than threshing machines or cotton gins. Folks seem to think the food appears on their tables by magic, and that it will keep appearing if the watermen could just get over being greedy.

He knows, better than most, how memories ripen to bursting over time, but everything really was bigger and better in his youth. Fried oysters big as your fist, bursting in your mouth, all brine and cornmeal. The steamed crabs were eight to ten inches across, monsters who could take a toe or a finger while alive. Then everything began to get smaller, smaller, smaller. The oysters, the crabs. His family. Even the island itself.

Yet his parents knew no other life and never wanted to. His father thought he was the luckiest man in the world because he spent his life outdoors, on the water. The bay rewarded his love by hastening his death by several years. What the sun didn't do, the water finally did, poisoning his blood. A simple cut became a death sentence when the dumb mainland doctor sewed it up, sealing the bacteria into his not-old man as neat as you please. Yet his father never once complained, even as the infection crept up his body, destroying it limb by limb. He had lived life on his own terms and taught his son to do the same. Do what you love and you'll love what you do. That was his father's mantra, his father's legacy, and he had taken it to heart.

But it hadn't escaped his notice that what you love might be the death of you.

He leaves the inlet, satisfied that all is well. He is in the Middle Branch now and his boat heads toward the Cherry Hill Marina, almost of its own volition. He does not risk this, not often. But he needs to see her today. He needs to see her with increasing frequency. It is hard now to remember a time when she was unknown to him, when she did not come to him in his dreams, promising him the one thing he wants. It frightens him to think of the coincidence that brought them together. What if he had not . . . ? What if she had not? He can no longer imagine a world without her.

He sees several eights on the water, a couple of fours, but no single scullers. He's too late, he thinks, and his heart, which seldom speeds up, lurches. The seagulls sound as if they are mocking him: *Too late, too late, too late.* The coxswains' exhortations seem meant for him as well. *Half slide. Full slide. Legs only. Full power.* The seagulls shriek back: *Too late, too late, too late.* The girlish voices rise, emphatic and shrill. *Full power. Full power. Full power.* The seagulls win the argument as the boats slide away, the nagging voices of the coxswains dying on the wind.

But no, she's the one who's late, the last rower to pass under the Hanover Street Bridge this morning. He knows her by her broad back, the brown braid that hangs straight as a second backbone. He cuts his engine and she gives him a chin-only nod, acknowledging his courtesy without looking at him, for that would disrupt her rhythm.

She is not pretty-pretty, and he has decided that's a good thing, although he once preferred a more delicate beauty. But a pretty-pretty face, or even a cute one, would have been a mistake on that body. Handsome is a word some might use, but he won't. Handsome is a word for men.

And there's nothing manly about her. The body — why, that belongs on the prow of a ship, in his opinion. It reminds him of Hera, in that cheesy movie with the skeletons, watching over Jason as he headed out to find the Golden Fleece. Stupid Jason: He used up Hera's three wishes so quickly, despite her warnings. Her long-lashed eyes closed, and she was lost to him forever. Jason deserved everything he got and more. Not that the movie told that part, oh no. But it had sent him to the myths on which it was based, just the way teacher had intended when she set up the rickety film projector and screened the movie as a treat on the last day of school. He had fallen in love with all the Greek myths, stories that seemed to have been written just for him. Aphrodite rising from the sea, only to be bestowed upon earnest hard-working Hephaestus, the one ugly god. Psyche and Eros, Pygmalion and Galatea. Epimetheus and Prometheus, racing to create the earth's inhabitants.

But the Golden Fleece remained his favorite, if only because it was his first. And the book was so much more thrilling than the movie. He was pleased to read of Medea's vengeance on faithless Jason, to watch Jason's new bride writhe in agony beneath the bewitched cloak that seared her flesh, to see Jason demeaned and demonized.

The only thing that bothered him was Medea's escape. It seemed an imperfect ending. She betrayed her father for a man, then killed her sons when the man betrayed her. Someone should have chased her dragon-drawn chariot across the sky and brought it crashing to the earth. Medea must die for the circle to be completed. Medea must die.

She has a tank top on today, he can see all his favorite parts, which are not the obvious parts, not at all. He likes those defined muscles at the top of her shoulders, those little dents that look as if someone's fingers lingered there the night before. He admires the long pouting collarbone, a shelf above a shelf. She has a beautiful forehead, as broad as a marquee, and a juicy bottom lip, overbit to begin with and sucked in beneath her top teeth this morning, a sign that she's concentrating.

He has never been quite sure of the color of her eyes, in part because they are as changeable as sky and water. Besides, it's hard for him to get close to her in public, harder still to look her in the eye when he does.

Here on the water, a baseball cap shadowing his face, binoculars concealing his eyes, this is as close as he dares to come.

For now.

# Chapter 1

It seemed like a good idea at the time.

Tess Monaghan was sitting outside a bar in the Baltimore suburbs. It was early spring, the mating season, and this bland but busy franchise was proof that birds do it, bees do it, even Baltimore County yuppies in golf pants and Top-Siders do it.

"Kind of a benign hangout for a child molester," Tess said to Whitney Talbot, her oldest friend, her college roomie, her literal partner in crime on a few occasions. "Although it is convenient to several area high schools, as well as Towson University and Goucher."

"*Possible* child molester," Whitney corrected from the driver's seat of the Suburban. Whitney's vehicles only seemed to get bigger over the years, no matter what the price of gas was doing. "We don't have proof that he knew how young Mercy was when this started. Besides, she's sixteen, Tess. You were having sex at sixteen."

"Yeah, with other sixteen-year-olds. But if he came after your cousin —"

"Second cousin, once removed."

"My guess is he's done it before. And will do

15

it again. Your family solved the Mercy problem. But how do we keep him from becoming some other family's problem? Not everyone can pack their daughters off to expensive boarding schools, you know."

"They can't?" But Whitney's raised eyebrow made it clear that she was mocking her family and its money.

The two friends stared morosely through the windshield, stumped by the stubborn deviancy of men. They had saved one girl from this pervert's clutches. But the world had such a large supply of girls, and an even larger supply of perverts. The least they could do was reduce the pervert population by one. But how? If Tess knew anything of compulsive behavior — and she knew quite a bit — it was that most people didn't stop, short of a cataclysmic intervention. A heart attack for a smoker, the end of a marriage for a drinker.

Their Internet buddy was in serious need of an intervention.

"You don't have to go in there," Whitney said.

"Yeah, I do."

"And then what?"

"You tell me. This was your plan."

"To tell you the truth, I didn't think it would get this far."

It had been six weeks since Whitney had first come to Tess with this little family drama, the saga of her cousin and what she had been doing on the Internet late at night. Correction: second cousin, once removed. The quality of Mercy was definitely strained, weakened by intermarriage and a few too many falls in the riding ring.

And perhaps Mercy would have been a trimester into the unplanned pregnancy she had been bucking for, if it weren't for a late-night hunger pang. Mercy was foraging for provisions in the kitchen when her computer-illiterate mother had entered her bedroom just in time to hear the sparkly thrush of music that accompanies an IM and seen this succinct question: "Are you wearing panties?" Within days, Mercy's hard drive had been dissected, revealing a voluminous correspondence between her and a man who claimed to be a twenty-five-year-old stockbroker. Mercy's parents had pulled the plug, literally and figuratively, on her burgeoning romance.

But by Whitney's calculation, that left one miscreant free to roam, continuing his panty census.

It had been Tess's idea to search for Music Loverr in his world. With the help of a computer-savvy friend, they created a dummy account for a mythical creature known as Varsity Grrl and began exploring the crevices of the Internet, looking for those places where borderline pedophiles were most likely to stalk their prey.

Whitney and Tess had both taken turns at the keyboard, but it was Tess who lured Music Loverr, now rechristened GoToGuy, into the open. She had finally found him in a chat room devoted to girls' lacrosse. They had retreated to a private room at his invitation — an invitation that followed her more or less truthful description of herself, down to and including her thirty-six-inch inseam. Then she had watched, in almost grudging admiration, as this virtual man began the long patient campaign necessary to seduce a high school girl. As she waited for his messages to pop up — he was a much slower typist than she — Tess thought of the movie *Bedazzled*, the original one, where Peter Cook, a most devilish devil, tells sad-sack Dudley Moore that a man can have any woman in the world if he'll just stay up listening to her until ten past four in the morning. Tess figured a teenage girl could be had by midnight.

Not that GoToGuy knew her pretend age, not at first. He had teased that out of her, Tess being evasive in what she hoped was a convincingly adolescent way. She made him wait a week before she admitted she was under twenty-one. Well, under eighteen, actually.

**Can we still be friends?** she had typed.

**Definitely,** he replied.

The courtship only intensified. They soon had a standing date to chat at 10 p.m. Tess would pour herself a brimming glass of red wine and sit down to her laptop with great reluctance, opening up the account created for just this purpose. Afterward, she showered or took a hot bath.

**Do you have a fake ID?** GoToGuy had IM'd her two nights ago.

Finally. He had been slow enough on the uptake, although not so slow that he had revealed anything about his true identity, which was what Tess really wanted.

**No. Do you know how I can get one?**

Sure enough, he did. Last night, informed that she had gone and obtained the fake ID, he had asked if she knew of this bar, which happened to be within walking distance of the Light Rail — in case she didn't drive or couldn't get the family car.

**And I can always drive you home,** he promised.

I bet you can, Tess had thought, her fingers hovering above the keys before she typed her assent. Her stomach lurched. She wondered if he had gotten this far with Mercy. The girl swore they had never met, but the tracking software was not perfect. E-mails could have been lost, along with some of the IM transcripts. Besides, she could have corresponded with him from school as well as from home, using a different account.

Tess had met Mercy only once, and it had been at least two years ago. But even in junior high, the girl had the kind of voluptuous body that adds years to a parent's life. She also had heavy-lidded green eyes that gave her a preternatural sophistication, and straight blond hair almost to her waist. She was juicy, no other word for it, even with all the nicks and scars left by a lifetime of field hockey. Did Music Loverr troll for young girls because he liked the innocence of high school girls or because he relied on their stupidity? Did he know how young his prey was or simply not care?

In Tess's day, such predators had the candor to wait in their cars near the high school bus stop. They showed their faces early, tipping their hands. It was harder to create the illusion of being a successful man if you had to approach from a busted-down Impala, eyes red with the pot you just smoked, spit dried in the corners of your mouth, little telltale flakes of desire.

Yeah, they really knew how to do pedophilia in my day, Tess had thought.

Varsity Grrl typed: **I'll meet you there at 8.**

GoToGuy: **I'll be at the bar. I'll have on a flowered tie.**

Go figure: There were three men in flower-patterned ties at the bar.

"Three flowered ties," Whitney said. "Only in Hunt Valley. These people give preppies a bad name."

"Well, Flower Tie Number One looks like he's leaving, and Flower Tie Number Two appears to be with that other guy. Ladies, meet our lucky bachelor, Flower Tie Number Three! He likes music, sailing, watching sunsets, and picking up underage girls on the Internet." Tess began to sing the Herb Alpert–esque theme to the old *Dating Game*, pounding out her own accompaniment on the dashboard.

"Will he be a dream," Whitney trilled, "or a dud?"

"This guy *aspires* to dud status. Look at him."

He was sitting sideways at the bar, watching the basketball game on the set mounted in the corner. His pink shirt ballooned a little on his narrow shoulders, while his disproportionately large ass ballooned over the stool.

"He drinks frozen margaritas," Whitney said. "Never trust a man who drinks frozen margaritas. He's probably already bribed the bartender to give you doubles of whatever you order. I'll bet you twenty dollars he recommends a piña colada or a daiquiri."

"Can I pass for seventeen?" Tess asked, leaning forward to study her face in the rearview mirror.

"You'll squeak by in that light, if only because he wants to believe you're seventeen," Whitney said, not unkindly, for her. "Besides when was the last time a man ever looked at your *face* upon first meeting?"

Tess glanced down. She was wearing a pale pink T-shirt and a flowery skirt, both borrowed from Whitney. It wasn't easy, being a thirty-one-year-old woman who was trying to pass for a seventeen-year-old girl who was trying to pass for twenty-one. She had unbraided her hair and let it fly loose around her face, a feeling she hated. But she hoped the hair would create a soft frame, offsetting the faint lines by her mouth and eyes. She also had on more makeup than she had ever worn in her life. Here, she hadn't had to fake a seventeen-year-old's ineptness.

GoToGuy — he had provided a first name, Steve, during that last exchange, although with seeming reluctance — stood up when she entered the bar.

"Are you — ?"

"I guess I am." She was nervous, which was good. Nervous was right. Nervous would work.

"What are you having to drink?"

"I don't know. A beer?"

He sized her up. "A strawberry margarita would go well with your outfit."

A strawberry margarita — that was even worse than a daiquiri. Plus, she had an instinctive dislike for men who ordered for their dates. Still, she nodded. The bartender swept his eyes over her and didn't ask for an ID. Damn him. But Whitney was right. Steve, primed to see a seventeen-year-old, saw a seventeen-year-old, even if no one else did.

"After all that trouble for a fake ID," he whispered wetly in her ear. His nonchalant supposed-to-be-suave chuckle sounded hollow and rehearsed, as if he were a little lost without his keyboard. "Want to go sit in a booth?"

"Sure, I guess."

They took their drinks and she led him,

without appearing to lead, to one of the booths along the windows, so Whitney would still have a good view of them over his shoulder.

"So, did that place work out for you?" he asked.

"What place?"

"The place I sent you to get a fake ID."

"Oh, yeah, that place. Yeah, it was great."

"Can I see it?"

She had not counted on this. "What?"

"Can I see the ID?"

"Sure, why not?" She pulled out her real Maryland driver's license, and he studied it in the dim light. The licenses were supposed to be impossible to counterfeit, with their double-photo images, but it had been a few years since they were introduced. Tess was counting on the local forgers to have caught up. She couldn't give him her private investigator's license.

"Wow, he just gets better and better. This looks like the real thing." Steve squinted. "Why does it say you're thirty-one?"

She took it back, blushing. "I screwed up the math. Added fourteen years instead of four."

"So, your real name's Theresa?"

She was so startled to hear the longer version of her name, the one no one ever used, that she almost said no.

"Yes, but I go by . . . Terry."

"On-line you sometimes called yourself Rose."

That had been Whitney's invention, Tess recalled, in the early days of the hunt. So he had been watching Varsity Grrl before he approached her, tracking her through sites devoted to sports and boy bands and the latest television shows.

"I'd like to be. Rose, I mean. It's a much prettier name than Theresa."

"You may be Rose, then."

"And you will be —"

"Steve. That's my real name."

"Don't I get to check your ID too?" She tried to be kittenish, the way she imagined a seventeen-year-old girl might be, although Tess had never been particularly coy, at that age or any other.

He laughed, but he didn't produce his ID. Too bad. That was all she wanted. If she could get his full name, her plan was to excuse herself to the bathroom and wait for Whitney, who would meet her there and take down the information. Whitney would then drive to a nearby restaurant and use her cell phone to call their computer source on standby, who would run him through every database in the state to see what they could get on him: his home address, his debts, his criminal record. Once they had his identity, there was no shortage of things they could do to him. Tess would then fake a headache, or a seventeen-year-old's forgivable cold feet, and disappear into the night. Her car was parked behind the bar, next to the Dumpster.

Steve folded his hands over hers.

"Terry, Terry, Terry," he began, in what he appeared to think was a dreamy, romantic tone.

Tess had to fight the instinct to yank her hands out from under his, which were moist and sweaty. "I thought I got to be Rose."

"Check. Rose. You're really beautiful, you know that? I had no idea. I mean, I thought, I hoped — you think you can tell what someone will look like on-line. But you have so many moods, it was almost as if you were two different people."

I *was,* Tess wanted to say. The Irish-Catholic German Jew you see before you and a blond WASP straight out of the pages of *Town & Country.* They had kept copies of their early forays, so they could be consistent. But they couldn't quite mimic each other's on-line voices. Whitney was a little clipped and brittle, a little too wary. Perhaps it wasn't an accident that Tess, with her breezy nonchalance about men, had been the one who had engaged him one-on-one.

"You are beautiful," he repeated, staring into her eyes with what he obviously intended to be a soulful look. If Tess had been seventeen, she might have experienced it as such. *You're beautiful.* It should be illegal for men to say that to women under twenty-five, maybe women under forty-five. She knew she wasn't beautiful. Attractive, yes. Striking, sure. Not beautiful, never beautiful.

But at seventeen, she had wanted to be, and

she would have been suckered by any man who told her she was.

At thirty-one, she found it easy to see through this man opposite her, to detect the little signs that he was not the big success he was pretending to be. His pink shirt had pilled at the underarms, advertising its cheapness. His watch was too big and he wore an aggressively tacky ring on his right hand. His features were even, but his eyes were too close together, his mouth an ugly shape. And his hair was styled in what would no doubt be the first of many attempts to disguise a receding hairline.

"You are so beautiful," he said again, as if it were a magic spell.

"I'm not —" She used her seeming embarrassment to pull her hands away and drop them in her lap. "I'm not beautiful."

"Of course you are. Beautiful inside and out. That's what makes you so special."

A waitress came by to offer them menus. Steve looked impatient at the interruption, but Tess was grateful. She ordered the most adolescent meal she could imagine: a cheeseburger heavy with trimmings, onion rings, and a strawberry milkshake. Steve frowned slightly when she asked for the onion rings, and she longed to taunt him. *See, this is what happens when you date children. They don't know not to order the onions.*

"Would you like another drink?"

"I'm not done with this one yet." Indeed, she

had taken only a sip. Tess could hold liquor, but she didn't want her senses dulled one bit tonight.

"It's happy hour, two-for-one, but only for a few more minutes." A cheap bastard too; that was always a nice quality in a man.

"No, really, I'm fine."

His hands fluttered to his waist, in a sudden reactive burst that Tess had learned to recognize as the Pavlovian response to a vibrating pager. Better than drooling, she supposed.

"My office," he said. "Shit. An emergency."

"An emergency at the investment firm?"

"The investment firm — yeah, exactly."

"But doesn't the stock market close at" — better not make it too specific; what teenager would know when the closing bell sounded — "at the end of the day?"

"Yes, but finance is a twenty-four-hour business. The . . . Indonesian markets are open now."

"Oh." *Bullshit, bullshit, bullshit.* "Well, I guess you better take it then."

"I guess I better."

The pay phones were at the rear of the restaurant, down a long corridor that led to the bathrooms. As soon as Tess saw her date's back disappear around the corner, she began rummaging through the leather jacket he had left hanging on the hook next to the booth. The night was cool, but not that cool. The jacket was clearly meant to impress. And it probably would have been impressive to anyone whose taste ran to suburban pimp. Tess found it sleazy and cheap, the alleged leather rubbery to the touch. She slipped her hands in the pockets, hoping he had left his wallet there. With one glance at his driver's license, she would have his real name, which was the key to knowing everything. If he carried a Social Security card, they could destroy him.

The side pockets came up empty, however, with not so much as a piece of lint, as if the jacket were brand-new. She shook it slightly, hearing a rattle somewhere within its folds, then patted it again. There must be an inside pocket. She slipped her fingers inside the concealed breast pocket and pulled out an amber-colored prescription bottle. Bingo! This would have his name and address.

But the bottle was blank. She looked inside at the pills, and suddenly she knew why Steve wanted her to drink faster, to take advantage of the two-for-one special.

The pills were round and white, bland as aspirin. But they had a line on one side and the letters ROCHE on the other, with the number 1 beneath them. They were Rohypnol, roofies, the date-rape drug. She tried to remember what she had read about them since they had become prevalent on college campuses. The victim could lose consciousness within twenty minutes and would have no memory of what happened the night before after passing out.

The drugs, legal in Mexico, could be purchased for as little as one to five dollars.

But what to do, how to proceed? The bottle looked full. Had he slipped one into her drink? No, she had watched the bartender make it and then carried it to the table herself. He had probably hoped she would excuse herself during the meal, at which point he would dose her drink. He had pushed that second margarita awfully hard, not unlike the wolf beckoning Red Riding Hood to come closer. The better to drug you and rape you, my dear.

Impulsively, Tess dropped one into his frozen margarita, then a second one for good measure.

"You got everything you need?" the waitress asked, arriving with the food. A college student, she was treating Tess deferentially. Everyone seemed aware of Tess's age. Everyone except Steve.

"Everything," Tess said.

"Problem solved," Steve announced, returning to the table a few minutes later. "I told them not to bother me again. Are we having fun yet?"

"I think so," Tess said, snapping an onion ring in half with her teeth. It didn't break cleanly, and she sucked the long translucent string of onion into her mouth with a loud lip-smacking flourish. Steve watched her, beaming goofily. It must be true love, because it was certainly too early for the drug to have taken hold.

"He's heavy," Whitney complained from her side. "For such a scrawny guy, I mean."

"I know," Tess said. They were like a team of oxen, trying to drag a rubbery, unpredictable yoke toward Whitney's little cottage, a guest house on the grounds of her parents' home. They had decided this afforded the privacy they needed, although they still weren't sure what they were going to do with their unexpected catch. It was like going surf fishing and coming up with a live manatee. Impressive, but possibly illegal and definitely problematic.

The pills had taken almost forty minutes to hit him, and Tess had begun to wonder if she had misidentified them. But when they took hold, it was swift and sudden. His speech began to slur, his eyelids to flutter with sleep.

"I don't know — maybe the tequila —"

"Let's pay the check and get out of here," Tess said, taking charge, no longer concerned with passing for seventeen. He had fumbled some bills and change out of his wallet and stumbled to his feet, grabbing for her hand in what was at once a gesture of intimacy and a desperate measure to stay upright.

"That's not even ten percent," she chided him.

"I tip twenty percent for food but not for booze. Booze is . . . jacked up, all profit for them. Besides, they . . . I think . . . they made me sick. I feel really woozy."

Tess threw a few more dollars on the table and began to drag Steve toward the parking lot, hoping the restaurant staff didn't notice how out of control his limbs were. No such luck. The host stopped them at the door.

"Certainly, he's not going to drive." Good, it was all about liability.

"No, I got the keys," Tess said. "I'll get him home."

She had planned to rifle his pants pockets and leave him in the parking lot, but now that the staff was on full alert, she dragged him to Whitney's Suburban and shoved him in the back.

"What the — ?" Whitney had asked, her features contorted with loathing for the fast-fading man in the backseat.

"I don't know," Tess said. "Just drive somewhere."

"My place," Whitney said, with her usual conviction.

And now he was lying on his back on a patch of Whitney's old pine floor, snoozing peacefully. He breathed through his mouth, like a little kid, but this did not inspire tenderness in the two women who stood over him.

Tess worked his wallet out of his back pocket, no mean feat, given how tight his pants were through the rear.

"Mickey Pechter," she said. "Baltimore County address. And here's an ID badge, a swipe card for one of those high-rises in

31

Towson. What do you want to bet he's not even a day trader, much less a stockbroker?"

She called the name, address, and birth date in to their computer liaison, Dorie Starnes, who had been standing by all evening — and charging them an hourly rate, she reminded them gleefully. But every check came up empty.

"Not even an overdue parking ticket," Dorie said. "This guy's a clean liver."

"Or lucky enough not to get caught," Tess said, hanging up the phone.

"Shit," Whitney said. "I assumed we'd find *something* on him."

"We've got his name and number," Tess said. "Isn't that enough? We'll pay a call on him when he's conscious, convince him to stop E-mailing little girls, and that's that."

"It's *not* enough," Whitney said. "We have to teach this guy a lesson, really throw a scare into him. He had those pills on him. If he hasn't raped someone, it's only a matter of time."

Steve — no, Mickey — sighed in his drug-induced sleep. His middle shirt button had come undone as they dragged him about, exposing a furry expanse of fish-white belly.

Whitney leaned over the man, prodding his chest with the toe of her loafer. "Hairy little devil, isn't he? I hate hairy men."

"Hairy body," Tess corrected. "Head's not going to be hairy for long. He'll be bald in three years, tops. So then maybe he won't be

32

able to hit on teenagers anymore. All we have to do is let nature take its course."

Whitney gave her a who-do-you-think-you're-kidding look, then announced, "I have an idea."

She went over to the old-fashioned planter's desk, one of the cast-off family heirlooms that her mother stored here. Digging through the drawers, she soon unearthed a plastic stencil sheet.

"What, we're going to make posters for the homecoming dance?" Tess asked.

"Wait, just wait." Whitney disappeared in the small bathroom off the hall and came back with a can of Nair so ancient that it was rusted at the bottom. "Truth in labeling. Let's tell the world what this guy really is."

She flipped him on his stomach and removed his shirt, grimacing when she saw the thicker mat of hair on his back. "Perfect." Carefully, she laid the stencil over his back, and filled one of the letters with foam. First a B, then an A, then a B again —

"Whitney, what are you doing?" Tess demanded.

"Spelling out Baby Raper on his back."

"That's ridiculous. After all, who's going to see his back? It's barely April."

"As a matter of fact, it's April Fool's Day and we have caught ourselves the number one fool." But when Whitney tried to change her design, the lines overlapped and she ended up taking all the hair from his back.

"Great," Tess said. "A salon would have charged him thirty bucks for that." She took the can from Whitney and applied it to the thinning hair on his scalp. No need for stencils here, she wanted to take all of it. She and Whitney rolled him on his back and did the front of his chest for good measure, using the stencil to spell out LOSER.

"The letters don't really stand out," Whitney said.

"We should have used a razor," Tess conceded.

"Or Nads. I really want to try Nads, every time I see that infomercial."

Tess unbuckled his pants and pulled them down to his ankles, applying what was left of the Nair to his thighs and calves. The aerosol had begun to rattle, close to empty. Here, the hair was paler and finer, more like a boy's. He wore black nylon briefs, unflatteringly tight.

"He thought he was going to get some tonight," Whitney said.

"That's pretty much guaranteed when you drug your dates," Tess said. "The problem is, they're usually not conscious by the time you unveil your lingerie."

It was after midnight when they left him, more or less denuded, in the parking lot of the restaurant, propped up against a blue Honda Accord. The restaurant was dark, having closed an hour ago. The Honda was the only car in the

34

parking lot besides Tess's Toyota, and his key fit the lock. Mickey Pechter still had on his briefs and socks, but Tess had thrown the rest of his clothes in a Dumpster behind a liquor store on York Road. She arranged his wallet, keys, and pager in a pile next to his head and draped his jacket over him.

At the last minute, she decided to keep the roofies, not wanting to return his weapon to him. She was unsure how difficult they were to procure, but why make anything easy for this predator?

"He looks awfully pink," she said.

"We're all pink," Whitney said. "White is a misnomer if you think about it. Just like black."

"But he's red-pink," Tess said. "He looks like he's been dipped in crab boil. Or like Humpty-Dumpty, after his fall."

Yes, that was it: Humpty-Dumpty. Tess wouldn't describe him as broken, but he was pathetic, curled up in his slumber, his pale body exposed to the night air, prickly with gooseflesh. She felt a wave of sympathy for him, belated, to be sure.

And then she remembered his plans for the evening and revulsion twisted her stomach, where a cheeseburger and onion rings sat on a few sips of strawberry margarita.

"Let's get out of here," she said, standing. Then, without really understanding what she was doing, or why, she turned back and gave him a sudden swift kick in the ribs.

If she had been wearing boots, he might have wakened at the impact, but the flat ballet-soft shoe she had worn to minimize her height didn't pack much of a punch. Still, it was hard enough to bruise his rib, to give him one last souvenir of their evening together.

Or so the Baltimore County cops told her the next day, when they took her into custody.

# Chapter 2

Baltimore County surrounds Baltimore City like a moat. Or a vise, depending on one's vantage point. The two broke up more than 150 years ago, heading their separate ways, and they're still fighting about who got the raw end of the deal. The city is broke, crime-ridden, and incapable of expanding. But the county is one of those no-*there*-there places. To city-born Tess, it might as well have been a foreign country.

Her trip through its legal system did little to change that perception.

"Hey, that's a thought," she said, sitting in the hallway of the county courthouse three weeks to the day after her date with Mickey Pechter. "Is it too late to petition for extradition?"

"I'm glad you can joke about this," said her lawyer and sometime employer, Tyner Gray. "I kept thinking at some point in the process — when they arrested you and kept you in county lockup overnight, when they fingerprinted you, when they charged you with felony assault — that you might start taking it seriously. But no, here you are, about to be sentenced, and you're still acting like it's one big hoot."

"It's not as if there's much suspense," Tess pointed out. "It's not even a sentence, really."

"Don't kid yourself. Probation before judgment simply means you won't have a record once you complete the terms of your probation."

"Now that's an interesting philosophical question: If a PBJ falls down in the forest and no one's there to hear it, does it make a sound?"

"Not funny, Tess."

"There are times in this life," she said, "when you can laugh or you can cry. I choose to laugh."

Tess had cried a little bit over the past three weeks, but always in secret. She never would have revealed such weakness to crusty old Tyner, or to anyone else for that matter. She had maintained a tough facade even in front of her boyfriend, Crow — not that he was fooled. Her lackluster appetite had betrayed her.

But now it was almost over, another bad memory to be condensed into one simple sentence for future biographers: "When I was thirty-one, I got into a little trouble with the law, but it was all a misunderstanding." The very term used for her plea, probation before judgment, PBJ, sounded innocuous, as if they were discussing peanut butter and jelly.

Tyner's mind must have been following a similar food track, for he suddenly said, "Time to make the doughnuts," did a neat three-point turn in his wheelchair, and rolled into the appointed courtroom.

Mickey Pechter sat in the first row, behind the prosecutor. It was the first time Tess had seen her "victim," as the legal system would have it, since that night in the parking lot. The hair on his head had grown back, duller but thicker. Perhaps she had found a cure for baldness. His skin looked normal to her, and she wondered if he had really suffered the severe allergic reaction he had claimed. Then again, he had wound up in the emergency room. She caught his eye and watched the emotions that played on his face: a reflexive fear, like a dog cowering before someone who had hurt him, a wisp of a smile, and, finally, a narrowed gaze of pure hatred.

It was all she could do not to mouth the word *rapist* at him.

Tyner tugged on her braid, reminding her to stand for the judge.

"All rise."

Judge Dennis Halsey was young for a judge and just missed being handsome. He had all his hair — why was she noticing men's hair more and more? — but there was a squareness about the head and body suggestive of a robot or Frankenstein's monster. Still, he was an up-and-comer, well respected. Short of a disastrous misstep, he would continue to rise ever higher in the state's judicial system, perhaps one day wearing the red robes of Maryland's highest court.

"Baltimore County circuit court is now in session."

And Halsey's career to date had been any-thing but disastrous. He had presided over the very date-rape trial that had provided Tess with her knowledge of roofies. The case had dozens of hot buttons — the defendant was white and upper class, his victims black, and everyone in-volved had blown blood alcohol levels well past the state's new legal standard of .08. Truth be told, they had blown past the old one of .10 as well.

Yet Judge Halsey had kept the defense at-torney in check, protecting the victims as much as possible, never letting it be forgotten who was on trial. Three juries had returned with three verdicts of rape in the first degree, and Halsey had sentenced the predatory premed to the harshest penalty possible.

So it should have been Tess's lucky day when her case ended up in his courtroom. Instead, it was just another fiasco, like everything else that had happened since that early spring night.

The first bit of bad luck was Mickey's allergic reaction to the chemicals in Nair.

"Oh, yeah," Tess had told Tyner, when Balti-more County police finally allowed him to see her. "You're supposed to do a scratch test with that stuff."

"A scratch test?"

"In the bend of your elbow. But no one ever does. Jesus, he broke out? What a wimp."

"He suffered burns, Tess. He had to be hos-pitalized."

And that was only the beginning of her mistakes. The second one had been showing Mickey Pechter her license. The police were at her door before noon the next day, with a search warrant for her weapon, described as "a chemical defoliant in a pressurized can and/or spray bottle."

They didn't find it, of course, but they did find the bottle of roofies. That would be mistake number three, keeping the roofies, which Pechter claimed were hers. After all, the drugs were in *his* system. Tyner had gotten the evidence excluded, pointing out that it was not reasonable to believe that a can of Nair would be in a woman's jacket pocket. Still, the roofies convinced the prosecutor, a sanctimonious preppie, that Mickey Pechter was a victim. The state's attorney and the detectives thought the drugs established her intent, that the assault had been planned in advance. *No, really,* she kept telling them, *I just wanted to find out his name. So I could do something really classy like — um — blackmail him!*

In Baltimore City, its courtrooms clogged with homicides and all the collateral damage of the nation's failed war on drugs, Tess's misadventure in vengeance would have been treated like the ill-conceived prank it was. But here the prosecutor was happy to take her on. Tess was charged with felony assault, and the prosecutor wanted to pile a rape charge on her as well, but the evidence wouldn't support it. Fortunately,

41

the case stayed below the media's radar, but only because all the men involved felt sorry for Mickey Pechter.

However, Judge Halsey was fascinated. "I am interested in the violence that flows between men and women," he had told Tyner and Tess at their first plea-bargain meeting. "It is a two-way street, despite what most people think. Physiologically, women are more likely to be victims, yes. But if they are strong enough — if they are, if you will, emancipated — will they turn on men, use violence as men have used it? Was your client really acting out of the need to protect teenage girls from an on-line stalker, or was something deeper provoked? There is so much anger, so much hostility, between men and women. I see it in my courtroom every day, and I find it unfathomable. The war between the sexes is far from over."

Tess would have been happy to tell him why she did what she did. But she had been slightly hamstrung by her impromptu decision, when the county cops first crossed her threshold, to say she acted alone. Not even Tyner knew Whitney had been present. Her muddled reasoning was that she was protecting Mercy, whose name she had never revealed, so she needed to protect Whitney as well. As a result, Judge Halsey looked down from the bench and saw some Superwoman, capable of drugging a man, dragging him through a parking lot, and then depilating his body and skull.

Yet Halsey wasn't so caught up in the socio-logical implications of the case that he couldn't notice inconsistencies in the evidence.

"The police find it odd that Mickey Pechter had so few abrasions," he had said at one point, when he and Tyner had discussed the terms of her PBJ in the judge's chambers.

"Abrasions?" Tess had echoed.

"Clearly, you had to drag him. But it seems more likely that you would have dragged him by his legs, not under his arms. Yet his shins are scraped as if someone had him by the armpits."

"What does Mr. Pechter say?"

"He says he doesn't remember anything."

"Hmmmm," Tess had murmured, but volunteered nothing more. Most liars are too emphatic, too definite. They talk too much. She knew this about liars because she had met more than her share. She knew this about liars because she was a good one when she needed to be.

In the end, her incomplete version had triumphed, more or less, because Mickey Pechter was such an unappetizing victim. He had crashed his computer's hard drive, thinking it would destroy the evidence. But Tyner had paid Tess's friend Dorie Starnes dearly to recover every incriminating message, every keystroke: the instructions on how to get a fake ID, the gentle pressure to come by public transportation so he might drive her home. Only the roofies and his intent were left to he-said/she-said

43

uncertainty. Suddenly, everyone — the cops, the prosecutor, Mickey Pechter himself — just wanted the case off the docket.

Everyone except Judge Halsey. "Vigilantism must not be condoned in a civilized society," he had told Tyner, when the lawyer petitioned the judge to drop the charges. "Whatever his intent, whatever your client's intent, the fact is she hurt him, and there must be an acknowledgment of this. A fine and some sort of community service, I think."

Tyner, who had convinced Tess they should avoid a trial at all costs, agreed. "As long as it's PBJ and her record is expunged in six months, I don't have a problem with that."

Six months, Tess thought, sitting in the courtroom. It was April 22 now, and the courthouse grounds were riotous with daffodils and tulips. The air was soft, and the breeze carried the wonderful greenish smell of fresh-mown lawns and just-spread mulch. In six months, the flower beds would be barren. It would be cool again, the days growing shorter, the rowing season drawing to an end. It seemed like a long time in some ways, but it was really the blink of an eye. Six months and all this would vanish, as if it never happened.

Her case was being called. Time for blind justice to hoist her scales.

Halsey placed his hands over the microphone in front of him. "The victim wants to enter an impact statement into the court record."

"But there's not going to be a record," Tyner said.

"Not once she fulfills the terms of her probation," the judge agreed. "But what's the harm in letting Mr. Pechter read his statement?"

During the weeks it had taken to reach this moment, Tess had been uncharacteristically well behaved. She had not contacted Pechter and told him what a worm he was for filing charges against someone he had planned to rape. She had not used her friends at the *Beacon-Light* to spin her own version of events, lest the publicity disrupt her plea bargain. She had sat still and nodded at the judge's ponderous exegesis on the violence between men and women. That was his phrase, always: "the violence between men and women." Halsey might be progressive as a judge, but he liked the sound of his voice as much as any man Tess had ever known. Still, she had listened, never contradicting and never daring to suggest that she knew a little bit more about such violence than this sheltered jurist.

Today, inches from the finish line, she snapped.

"He's *not* a victim," she said. "That's the harm in letting him enter an impact statement. It just punctuates this stupid, politically correct charade." Although she spoke in the raspy tone of a whisper, her voice carried to where Mickey Pechter sat, and he flinched at the very sound.

The judge's expression was inscrutable. He looked at Tess, then at Tyner, who shrugged

45

apologetically, and then over at Mickey Pechter, who was so focused on appearing angelic that Tess was surprised a cartoon halo didn't appear above his head.

"I think I'll allow Mr. Pechter to read his letter," he said. "It would not hurt you, Miss Monaghan, to be reminded that you did harm someone: You took the law into your own hands and put a man in the hospital."

Mickey unfolded a single sheet of lined notebook paper with sweaty, shaky hands and began to read.

"Since the vicious assault I received on the night of April first —"

Tess jerked her chin up at the word *vicious* but said nothing.

"— I have had trouble sleeping because of the injuries done to my skin. When I do sleep, I often have nightmares. My work has been affected as well. I estimate that I have lost money because I cannot work as much overtime as I used to. Respectfully submitted, Mickey R. Pechter."

He looked up expectantly.

"Is that all?" Judge Halsey asked.

"Do you want to know how much money?"

"How much overtime you've lost? No, I don't think that's necessary."

"Not just overtime," Mickey said, "but pain and suffering, too."

"It's part of the plea agreement that Miss Monaghan or her insurer will pay your medical expenses."

"Oh, she's arranged that already. But, you know, I figure this is where I get my pain and suffering."

The judge was mystified. Tess wasn't. Mickey Pechter thought a victim impact statement was akin to filing a civil suit. He wanted to be paid for being depilated. Even as she smiled at his clueless greed, she tried to remember if her umbrella insurance policy would cover such a nuisance claim. Or did it cover her only when she was working? Could she claim Mercy Talbot was a client? No, that would mean invoking the girl's name, the one thing the Talbot family didn't want.

Mickey said, "I talked it over with some friends, and we thought five hundred thousand — if it's not taxed as income — seven hundred and fifty thousand if it is. In other words, I think I should net five hundred thousand dollars."

"You are such a pathetic prick," Tess said softly. His head turned quickly at the sound of her voice, and she realized he was still scared of her. It was an interesting feeling. She liked it. "Instead of worrying so much about money, why don't you get treatment so you'll stay away from underage girls?"

"I never thought you were seventeen," he said. "Not once I saw you. A man would have to be pretty damn nearsighted to think that."

"Whether they're seventeen or seventy-one,

47

you can't get them into bed unless they're un-
conscious. Loser."

"Bitch."

"Asshole."

"Ball-buster."

"Like you have any to bust."

"Whore."

"Eunuch."

The bailiff was scrambling to his feet, as if he
expected a fight to break out, but the judge
simply raised his palm and the courtroom was
still.

"I am ready to pronounce sentence. As for
pain and suffering — if you think you have a
case, Mr. Pechter, then hire a lawyer and file
one in the proper court. However, I will remind
you that your lifestyle, your *character,* will be
open for full and complete examination in a
civil trial."

Mickey looked crestfallen. "Okay, so I'm not
going to get any money. But why is she getting
off without a real sentence? I know what probation before judgment is. In six months, it will
be as if this never happened. That's not right."

"I can assure you, Mr. Pechter, that in six
months Ms. Monaghan will be a changed
person. She will be rehabilitated — which is, in
case anyone has forgotten, one aim of the criminal justice system. Not just to punish but to
change."

Tess tried not to smirk. If Halsey thought she
would be a changed person after paying out

48

fines, medical bills, and donating time to a program for abused children, the agreed-upon community service, so be it. Given the chance, she knew she would do it again. Maybe not the kick, but the kick had never been the issue. But the Nair, the roofies — she figured she had taught Mickey Pechter an important lesson in empathy. Perhaps she should have insisted on a trial, just to see if he had any other victims who wanted to come forward.

Mickey returned to his seat and Tess stood to receive her sentence, her eyes downcast, her smile barely hidden. She had not let Crow come to court with her — as much as she craved his company, she didn't want him anywhere near this sordid episode — but they had made plans to go to lunch, to treat the day as a celebration. They were going to drive into the country, with their dogs in the back of the car, and find a place to let them run. Then they planned to find a tavern or restaurant with outdoor seating, where the dogs could accompany them to lunch. One of the lovely perks of self-employment was that you didn't have to squander the beautiful weekdays that had a habit of cropping up after weekends where it did nothing but rain.

Tess was so far into the future that the judge's voice was washing over her, his words stuck together like so much melted chocolate. Then an unexpected phrase popped out, forcing her to focus. "And of course Ms.

Monaghan also will be asked to complete a six-month counseling session in anger management, either in one-on-one treatment or a group therapy setting."

She knew better than to speak but she looked at Tyner, who shrugged, surprised as she was. The words meant nothing to Mickey Pechter, who looked distracted, as if he were mentally returning all the things he had planned to buy with his phantom $500,000. The harried assistant state's attorney already had another file open in front of him. Justice ground on.

"Miss Monaghan will meet monthly with a parole officer and present evidence that she has attended weekly sessions with a psychiatrist, psychologist, or clinical social worker. She may choose the professional of her choice, but the court stipulates that the sessions must be focused on anger management and the issues that arise from this condition."

Tess was excused, and the next case was called. Dazed, she left the courtroom with Tyner.

"Can he do that? Drop the community-service provision and make me go to therapy?"

"He just did. I guess he assumes it's no different from ordering a drunk driver to go to AA meetings. It's funny, though. He never once mentioned anything about counseling in all our meetings. I bet it occurred to him just now. I suppose I could have objected, but it will actually take up less of your time than volunteering. That was going to be three hours a week for a year."

"But why would the judge change the terms of our agreement at the last minute?"

Tyner, usually happy to criticize or rebuke her, was slow to answer.

"There was something in your face, Tess, when you looked at Mickey Pechter. Something dark. I hate to say it, but Judge Halsey may have a point."

# Chapter 3

"You drink how much?"

The court-ordered psychiatrist, Dr. Marshall Armistead, had been droning efficiently through a laundry list of medical history when an inattentive Tess tripped herself up by telling the truth. Tess was so bored, so detached, she couldn't remember what she had said to provoke this reaction. Two drinks, three drinks. Was that really so much? Should she claim she was French on her mother's side or backpedal?

Backpedal.

"I mean, not every night. But it's not unusual for me to have wine with dinner, maybe two glasses. And I like to go out with friends at least once a week, have a cocktail."

"Do you drink alone?"

"Sometimes."

"Do you drink to relax or to reward yourself?"

"I wouldn't describe it that way."

"Do you often feel hung over in the mornings?"

"Never." She tried not to sound too hostile, too defensive. "Look, I know this drill. I don't have a drinking problem."

"Okay, we'll move on. Drugs?"

"Only pot now."

One eyebrow seemed to twitch at "only." They were notable eyebrows, with an old man's wildness, although Dr. Armistead appeared to be relatively young, no more than forty. He was bald, but in the nonchalant manner of a man who had lost his hair young and never mourned it. He had a full mouth and a prominent nose. The eyes beneath the animated brows were deep-set, a changeable hazel not unlike her own. But beady, Tess decided.

"*Only* marijuana *now*," he echoed, picking apart her words. "So you've used other drugs?"

"I tried cocaine once. It made me speak very, very, very fast, and even I could tell I was inane. I don't need to speed up. I was too old for the rave-and-ecstasy fad by the time it got to Baltimore or I might have tried that, just out of curiosity. But really I'm essentially drug-free. One nice thing about being self-employed, though, is no one can make me pee into a cup."

"Essentially drug-free." He checked his notes. "You do drink quite a bit of coffee."

Tess sighed and rolled her eyes. "I know I don't have a caffeine problem, because if I go a day without coffee, I don't get headaches. And, really, I hardly smoke pot at all anymore. It's a hassle to get it, and I have to worry about the consequences."

"Consequences?"

"There's a risk, given what I do, in breaking

53

the law. As I get more successful, the risk is less worth taking."

"And yet . . . you committed a felony."

"I was charged with a felony. I pleaded to a misdemeanor."

He frowned at the piece of paper in front of him. "But the original charge was a felony."

"Charges don't mean a thing in our system. Innocent until proven guilty, remember?"

He went back to the standard questions, and Tess's attention wandered again, taking in her surroundings. She had expected grander surroundings at the famed Sheppard Pratt Hospital. After all, Zelda Fitzgerald had been treated here once. But the Jazz Age was over and the era of psychotropic drugs and HMOs was a bad fit for the once-elegant hospital. A certain genteel shabbiness was rampant inside the buildings, although the grounds were still lush. Here, for example, Dr. Armistead's window was propped open with a small piece of plywood, so the outside breezes could combat the dry overheated air pumped out by the old radiator. Tess was especially struck by the dowdy wing chair in which she sat. The arms were so worn they were nothing but silken strings.

The doctor caught her combing those strings with her fingers and made a quick note on his Palm Pilot. Was it considered hostile to fiddle with string? Angry? Anal? Like many people who wandered into a psychiatrist's office for the first time, Tess was worried she wouldn't be allowed to leave.

"Is there mental illness in your family?"

"No, not really." Her reply was automatic, and she immediately doubted its veracity. Really, insanity was the only explanation for some of them. But there was no *diagnosed* mental illness in her family, so she was telling the truth. Besides, the doctor was barreling ahead. There was no chance to revise or revisit her answers.

*How did she sleep?* Fine, most nights. *Most nights?* Well, everyone had a bad night now and then, right? *Did her bad nights usually follow drinking?*

"I told you I drink almost every night," she pointed out.

*After heavy nights of drinking, then?* That wasn't the pattern.

"So, there is a pattern?"

"No, that's not what I meant. It's just — I have bad dreams, sometimes. They come with the territory, the kind of work I do. I've seen more than my share of . . . disturbing things. But it's not as if I'm a police officer, or a paramedic —"

"Or a doctor," he said, gently making the case for his own profession. "Doctors see a lot of death too."

"Not the kind of death I've seen, not unless they're in the emergency room. And it's not just death, anyway. The death is the least of it.

55

I've seen what people will do to one another to get what they want, rationalizing all the while that it's fair — or even moral."

"Which is what you did, is it not?"

His voice remained gentle, nonjudgmental. She knew he was testing her, asking her to evaluate her behavior in the context of what she had just said, to hold it up to the light of her own logic and see if there were any holes in it.

Still, the question pissed her off.

"I tried to stop a pedophile from picking up little girls on the Internet."

"Not a pedophile, as I understand it, not by clinical definition. He may have been stalking underage girls, but he wasn't interested in little-girl girls, was he? Otherwise he wouldn't have sought to meet you in a bar."

"Okay, underage girls. Whom he apparently plied with roofies, which have no purpose except for date rape."

"Yes, I saw the reference to that in the file the judge sent me. But do we know if he's ever used those drugs?"

"He had them. It was only a matter of time."

"So you took the law into your own hands."

"I had heard about him from an underage girl I knew. She was safe, but I had to protect other girls who might run into him. To do that, I needed to figure out who he was."

"Do you feel that way a lot? That you have to protect others?"

"Not particularly."

"Have you ever used violence to protect — your word — anyone?"

Tess shook her head. She was proud of the fact that she relied on her wits more than her Smith & Wesson. She seldom fired her gun outside a range.

"Really? Judge Halsey sent me a note that I should ask you about the time you tried to beat a boy, down in Pigtown. It apparently came up in the prosecutor's presentencing investigation."

"I beat a boy in Pigtown — ?" It was hard not to finish with the lyric "just to watch him die," but she didn't figure Dr. Armistead, with his wallful of degrees, for a Johnny Cash fan. The memory kicked in a beat later. The doctor's bland encapsulation had taken the incident so far from its context that she hadn't recognized her own past. "It wasn't quite the way you make it sound. The 'boy' was a killer, barely human. He had used a young girl without any thought to the consequences. I snapped."

"So you *do* have trouble controlling your emotions?"

"No, no, not at all. It was a most unusual circumstance."

"But there was this boy and now there's Mr. Pechter. And in both cases the trigger seemed to be the man's manipulation of a younger, more inexperienced girl."

"Twice isn't a pattern."

"Is twice all there is?"

Tess glanced at one of the several clocks in the room. They were all small and subtle, placed throughout the study as if they were nothing more than part of the decor. But wherever one looked, there was a clock, and they were all ruthlessly synchronized. She thought there should be a huge digital readout, showing the seconds counting down and the dollars going up, like that national debt clock that used to tour the nation. An hour with Dr. Armistead cost $150, of which her insurance would pay $100. That was a good deal, according to Tyner, who had used his contacts to find the doctor after almost every other therapist in town had claimed to be too busy or not a part of her insurance plan.

"I think our hour is up," she told the doctor.

"The intake interview usually takes a little longer. As my secretary told you when you made the appointment."

"Oh." She went back to combing the strings on the chair's arms.

"How's your appetite?" He was reading from the form again.

"Lusty."

He smiled. Good, he had a sense of humor at least.

"Sexual desire?"

"Um — well, I'm hetero. I told you I had a boyfriend."

"I'm asking if you've noticed any changes in

your sex drive as of late, whether it's increased or decreased."

She had to think about this. Crow was only twenty-five, six years younger than she, and his need for sex was so regular that she seldom pondered her own level of desire. She ate at mealtime, she had sex at bedtime.

"No change. Actually, my relationship is one of the best things in my life."

He looked up as if he had never heard a more startling revelation. Talk of good relationships must be suspect here, or rare. It was probably more common for people sitting in this wing chair to confide they were diaper-wearing shoplifters with a fetish for rutabagas.

"Good, good for you. Do you exercise regularly?"

"Almost obsessively."

Another verbal minefield. He paused, his pen poised over the sheet clamped to his clipboard. "What makes you say that?"

"I was joking. I *am* pretty intense about my exercise regimen — it's the reason I can afford to eat as much as I do, and I love to eat. I row in the warm-weather months, like now, and also run and lift weights. Rowing is great exercise, but it's also very meditative. I get a little crazy in the winter, when I can't get on the water."

Crazy, she had just described herself as crazy. The word seemed to hover over her in a balloon, like an exclamation from some comic strip character. But Dr. Armistead didn't seem to notice. He was double-checking his list, what he had checked off, what he hadn't, trying to decide if she was naughty or nice.

"That seems to cover it. Now Theresa —"

"Tess, please." Mickey Pechter had called her Theresa too.

"Tess. It's clear you don't want to be here. Even if I didn't know your counseling was court-ordered, I could tell by your body language, your avoidance of eye contact, that you have no desire to enter therapy. Well, I'm going to let you in on a little secret. No one wants to be here. Many of my patients are here conditionally — because of substance abuse or arrangements they've made with their employers. Those who seek me out are unhappier still, almost desperate in their pain. I'm a doctor. No one likes to go to the doctor."

"Or the dentist," Tess said. "The dentist is even worse, for some reason."

"All you have to do is show up every week for the next six months, and you'll have fulfilled the court's mandate. You can come in every week, on whatever day and time works best for you, and tell me you feel fine, and we can talk about the weather or the Orioles. I'll make a mark on your card and you can take it to your probation officer, and everyone will be happy. Except you."

"I *am* happy."

"At times, perhaps. Certainly you have every reason to be. You're an attractive woman with

60

what appears to be a successful business. You're in a relationship that sounds healthy and nurturing in every way. I think you drink more than you should, but you don't seem to abuse alcohol or any other substances. So how do we reconcile that woman with the woman who decided to remove a man's body hair and then, just for good measure, kicked him as hard as she could?"

"How can they know *I* kicked him?" Tess caught herself, horrified by what she had almost said. She had been about to point out that it could have been Whitney. She had stopped short of perjuring herself, but Judge Halsey would not be pleased if he learned she had withheld information. Less than one hour in therapy, and she was ready to give up a secret she had kept from everyone, even Crow.

"He had a bruised rib. It's on the hospital report." He looked at her keenly. "Is that what you meant? Why are you so surprised?"

"I just didn't think a bruised rib showed, you know? But this is confidential, right? You can't tell anyone what I say here?"

"Absolutely. Nothing you say here will be repeated to anyone, not even Judge Halsey." He waited to see if she had anything else to say. She didn't, but she was relieved to have the ground rules made explicit.

"Look, are we done yet? I know you said this could take longer than usual, but I told a friend I would meet her at the Casino Shop at noon. She wants to take me to lunch to make up for . . ." Tess's voice trailed off. It wasn't that she was, once again, about to implicate Whitney. No, Tess had been on the verge of saying *to make up for me having to go through this crap,* and she didn't want to appear that hostile.

"The Casino Shop?" It was a thrift shop housed in the hospital's old recreation hall, run by the ladies' auxiliary. "Does she volunteer there?"

"She shops there, if you can believe it. She's decided that she's really into her heritage, but her heritage happens to be white-bread WASP. So she buys martini shakers, and those old mixing glasses that have drink recipes on the sides. In fact, she's begun drinking sidecars and Manhattans. If anyone ought to be here, it should be her. She's clearly nuts."

And the Nair had been her idea, after all. Everyone thought Tess was the bad influence. If only they knew.

"I'll keep that in mind. But for now, Tess, for the next six months, it's you and me. Let's make it worthwhile."

"The problem is, I don't have a problem."

"Perhaps you're right. But why don't you open yourself to the possibility that our sessions can be beneficial — if not in the way the judge intended, then in some other ways instead. That won't hurt, will it?"

She wanted to clutch her middle and stagger

around the room, gasping "It hoits, it hoits," like one of the Jets in *West Side Story*, taunting Officer Krupke. Instead, she shook Dr. Armistead's hand and told him she would see him next week.

"I'll even try to remember my dreams," she promised.

"I would be curious to hear about the bad ones, but it's not required. We do more than dreams in psychotherapy."

"Yeah, but my dreams may be all we have. What can I tell you, Doctor? Despite what the judge thinks, I'm just not that angry."

The eyebrows shot up, twin caterpillars caught by a sudden gust of wind. He could not have looked more skeptical.

# Chapter 4

"What do you think about this?" Whitney opened a grocery bag and pulled out a lamp with a crude wooden base and a yellowed parchment shade that showed mallards in flight.

"It looks like someone's shop project," Tess said, grateful for the Corner Stable's reliable gloom. "And not even a high school shop project, but middle school shop, or from the arts and craft class at a camp for children with no motor skills."

"I know it's kitschy, but I thought it was good kitsch, not bad kitsch." Whitney never sounded more WASPish than when she attempted a word like *kitsch*, which wasn't Yiddish but should be. Still, her mere proximity to the item did give it a certain cachet. With her sharp-featured face and chin-length bob of butter-yellow hair, Whitney had an aristocratic air that was virtually contagious. The Corner Stable looked better because she was sitting in it, and the lamp was almost tolerable as long as she was holding it. Almost.

The problem was, Whitney couldn't hold it all the time. Not unless she wanted to become the Statue of Liberty of Greenspring Valley, raising her mallard ducks to the skies, a beacon welcoming the waves of nouveau riche that continued to wash up on her shores.

"Trust me, it's bad kitsch. If I look at it much longer, I'll have nightmares. Which would at least give me something to talk about to *Herr Doktor* next week."

"That's right, your shrink. Are you cured yet? Or does he think you're a hopeless case?"

"Actually, he seems pretty optimistic. But then, he hasn't known me that long."

Their meat arrived — a chopped barbecue sandwich for Tess, a well-done hamburger for Whitney. They had both been feeling particularly carnivorous today, and the Corner Stable was a good place to indulge such urges. Besides, Tess had thought it would be easier to drive north and away from the hospital than to fight the traffic toward downtown. She hadn't realized that the suburbs were now more congested than the city, their modest streets carrying far more traffic than any planner had ever imagined. It had taken them almost forty minutes to creep five miles to this junky strip of fast food places and liquor stores near the state fairgrounds.

"You know, I would have taken you to McCafferty's," Whitney said, slicing off a bit of her burger to make sure no pink showed inside. Her taste buds had been destroyed by her mother's indifferent cooking, and the various meat scares of recent years had made her only more determined to eat her beef shoe-leather brown. "My treat. Not that I don't like a burger as much as the next girl, but I wanted to buy you a filet mignon."

"I can't stand to see what you do to a twenty-eight-dollar steak," Tess said. "Besides, I keep telling you — you don't owe me anything. Leaving you out of this mess was the best thing I ever did. Good Lord, if they had known there were two of us, that judge probably would have insisted we go to trial. And given Mickey Pechter's avarice, your family's deep pockets would have been enticing."

"Still, maybe you should have gone through with a trial," Whitney said. "It would have been a great opportunity to really humiliate that guy."

"Yeah, it sounds good in theory. But when you're faced with two choices — pleading to a misdemeanor that will disappear in six months or risking the vagaries of a jury trial — you realize just how dicey principle is. And how expensive. Tyner wasn't working for free. I owe him a lot of work now."

"Work. Yes, work. That's really why I wanted to take you to lunch today." When Whitney was full of herself, which was often, the blueness of the veins at her temple, throat, and jaw seemed to become more pronounced.

"What's up?"

"I've got a job for you. A great job."

"Whitney — no pity stuff, okay? Let me re-peat: *You don't owe me.*"

"This has nothing to do with our little escapade. In fact, it wasn't even my idea to hire you. Someone else on the board asked me to tap you for this job."

"Someone on the board? What board? Your family's foundation thingie?" After several restless years in which she had effortlessly succeeded at anything she tried, Whitney had decided there was no shame in running her family's charity. She liked giving away money. Moreover, she liked it when the city's best and brightest came to her and begged for money.

"I guess it's more a coalition or a consortium than a board. Nothing formal. But several local nonprofits that are interested in women's issues have been brainstorming about ways to reduce the number of domestic-violence homicides in the state."

"I know how," Tess said. "Nothing could be simpler."

"Really?"

"Every time a man is so brokenhearted that he decides to go out and kill his girlfriend and then kill himself?"

"Yes?" Whitney leaned forward, her food forgotten.

"Just convince him to do the suicide part first."

"Honestly, Tess, this is serious. We want to show a significant decrease in the number of domestic homicides statewide."

"I can't imagine it's a very big number to

begin with," Tess said. "Not as a percentage of the whole."

"Exactly," Whitney said. "Which is why there's no political will to attack the problem. Yet it's perhaps the most preventable category of homicide, if you think about it."

"Maybe. So take it to the legislature."

"We were oh-for-four there during the General Assembly session that just ended. We couldn't get one bill out of committee. The chairman of Judiciary put them all in a drawer and wouldn't even take a vote on them. It didn't help our cause that the creep who killed all those people and took his girlfriend's family hostage had been treated right by the system. The lawmakers basically threw up their hands and said they couldn't come up with preventive measures for crazy people."

"Please," Tess said. "Those of us with mental health problems prefer to be known as *reality-challenged.*"

"Very funny. Anyway, next year we have to go back with better information, more persuasive arguments."

"Where do I fit in?"

"One of our members believes the rural police departments and the state police, which don't handle a lot of homicides, may have bungled some domestic cases. We have files on five open murder cases from all around the state. We need someone to reexamine them, review the police work —"

"Review police work? On old cases? Jesus, Whitney, that's impossible."

"They're not that old, six years at the most. The most recent was last December. We're not asking you to solve these cases, Tess. We just want to know what the police did and if the victims' significant others ever went on to hurt anyone else. If we can find even one case where sloppy, inexperienced police work left some creep at large, we can lobby for funding and training for small-town cops. C'mon, Tess. How often do you collect your hourly fee and do some good at the same time?"

Tess smiled ruefully. Whitney should know she wanted nothing more. The private detective's life was a sleazy one at times. Even a PI like herself, who turned down divorce work, seldom felt altruistic. The thing is, she distrusted those who cloaked themselves in their own goodness. There was nothing more dangerous than people convinced of their own good intentions.

"We'll pay your top rate and kick in a per diem when you're out of town. The board won't breathe down your back — a monthly report, maybe a face-to-face briefing after you've done some preliminary scouting."

"And no press," Tess said.

"What?"

"No media. I don't want any of these eager do-gooder organizations sending out a press release, announcing their crusade. The local cops are going to be hostile enough when an investigator shows up and starts asking questions. We need to be discreet. How many people are on the board?"

Whitney ticked them off on her fingers. "Someone from Safehouse, of course. My family's foundation. Baltimore's Kids and New Solutions. The William Tree Foundation —"

Tess stopped her. "The William Tree Foundation? The one run by Luisa J. O'Neal?"

"Nominally. She's not active anymore. Her health deteriorated after her husband left her."

"Good," Tess said, biting into her chopped beef sandwich so hard that it sent a little shot of pain through an upper molar. Her dentist said she ground her teeth at night, but she couldn't bring herself to be fitted for a mouth guard.

"I know you hate her," Whitney said, her eyes steady on Tess's face, "but you've never told me why."

"Hate her? How could I hate Luisa O'Neal, Baltimore's benefactor, planter of trees, creator of parks, builder of grand public spaces. Like everyone else in town, I owe her everything — including my career."

"I'd forgotten. Your first case, as it were. That lawyer who got killed worked for Seamon O'Neal. But the O'Neals didn't have anything to do with his death."

"No, they didn't." Another death, yes, but

not his. "Whatever happened to Seamon? I haven't seen the O'Neals in the society pages for a while."

And she looked for them, Tess realized. Every Sunday.

"He ran off to North Carolina with a paralegal. Died of a heart attack six weeks later."

"On top of her?"

"No, that would have been tacky. On the golf course. It was probably the nicest thing he ever did for Luisa. Stopped all the messy wrangling about money, which was only fair, as the money was hers anyway. Still, it took something out of her. She had a stroke, ended up in Roland Park Place. My mom went to see her recently — they used to play in the same tennis foursome."

"I remember." That relationship had kept Tess from telling Whitney about the things Luisa had done. "She's not active, you said. So she won't be there when I meet with the board?"

"No, she's not involved at all. Just her money. I doubt if she even knows what the Tree Foundation does. From what my mother said, she's lying in bed, waiting to die and refusing to talk to anyone. She wants to be with Seamon."

"She wants to be with the man who routinely humiliated her throughout their marriage, spending her family's money on a never-ending parade of paralegal tarts?"

"He dated a few associates, don't forget. Anyway, she loved him. Why do you think she put up with him?"

"I don't know. Perhaps your consortium should put some money toward solving that age-old problem. Why do people stay with people who treat them that way?"

"Why do women stay with men, you mean."

"Men stay with women, too, when they shouldn't. As Judge Halsey would be the first to remind you, the violence between men and women is a current flowing in both directions."

Lunch finished, they stepped out in the bright day, eyes blinking after the dimness of the Corner Stable. In the instant it took for her eyes to adjust, an image came to Tess, an image she thought she had buried long ago.

She saw a man in flight, his body hurled through the sky, the malevolent shape of an old Marathon cab disappearing into the thick morning fog. It was her nightmare, the bad dream that disrupted her sleep every now and then. Was it her hour with Dr. Armistead that had dredged it up or the talk of Luisa O'Neal?

"Whitney — about my fee. How much does each group kick in? Do you divide it evenly among yourselves or is it prorated according to how much capital each group has?"

"Prorated," Whitney said. "My family's foundation will pay a third. It's not based on means but on each organization's commitment to domestic violence. Baltimore's Kids is kicking in only a tiny amount, for example, because it's not really what they're about."

"The William Tree Foundation, in particular. What percentage of my fee will they pay?"

"No more than ten percent. They're more about building stuff than doing stuff. If they can't put a plaque on it, proclaiming their philanthropy, they're not much interested. I'm surprised they want to be part of this at all."

Ten percent. Tess figured she could live with that. She would tithe that amount to some good cause, a belated apology to the man in the sky, whose death was still officially an unsolved hit-and-run. She needed to mark his memory in some way, to remind people that he had existed. She couldn't afford to erect a plaque, but she could do something. She could do this.

After all, with Seamon O'Neal dead, and Luisa O'Neal on her way, a day would soon come when only Tess knew how her old boyfriend Jonathan Ross had come to be murdered while she watched.

He has another job, this one all the way down toward Virginia Beach. Most people would take 95, but, as much as he drives, he is never comfortable on the interstates. He crosses the Bay Bridge, takes 13 South. It's about as close to home as he ever gets these days.

When people ask what he does, he says different things, depending on his mood. "Biomedical waste disposal," for example. Or "Sales. Marine accessories." His answers are designed and delivered to assure no follow-up. Still, he's sometimes disappointed by his success. People are so incurious. They don't really look, don't really hear. People on the mainland think of everything as infinite — food, water, fuel. Other people.

The island had fewer than two hundred residents, which made it the smallest of all the inhabited islands in the bay: smaller than Smith, smaller than Tangier. His parents had gone to grade school there, but by the time he came along, the one-room schoolhouse only went to sixth grade. The older kids had been ferried back and forth to school by boat. By high school, most of his friends went to stay with relatives on the mainland, but he didn't have any people off the island. The students on the mainland were nice enough, but they couldn't be friends, not really. Not when you had to catch that boat every afternoon. No friends, no after-school activities. He had wanted to go out for a team. "Are we all supposed to wait for you, then?" the skipper had asked. He thought the others might be able to go to the library, read, and do their homework. But the little ones needed supervision and the big ones didn't want to wait.

This is my whole world, he would say to himself, sitting on the boat as it made its way across the bay. I will never know anyone else. If I marry, she is on this boat right now. It scared him, to think he had such a small group of people from which to find his true love. The island had five surnames, give or take. It would be like marrying family, he supposed, but that's what royalty did. He thought of the poem he was always having to memorize, each and every teacher thinking it was so clever, having the island boy learn the poem in which island was a metaphor. *If a clod be washed away by the sea/Europe is the less.* His first year in the mainland school, someone had laughed when he had recited those lines. He couldn't know for sure, but it was a mean laugh, cutting. They were laughing because he was a clod, because they wouldn't miss him if he were washed away, not one bit.

Then, in junior high, a new girl showed up. He knew, the minute he saw her, he knew. It was as every song, every poem, every story had prophesied: She was the one. Better yet, she knew. She liked him until she loved him. She loved him until — no, she loved him still. She had never stopped loving him, even if she had left him. He believed that with all his heart. From seventh grade on, there was no one in his world but her. He was never unhappy or impatient if she was there. Separated from her — she took French while he took Spanish, went to the mainland for singing lessons on the weekends — he was miserable.

It didn't escape his notice that her family, such as it was, was shunned on the island. Not in an obvious way, for the Coopers and the Winslips, the Pettys and the Seeleys, even the Goodwins, were not obvious people. Living at once so close and far apart, on top of each other and yet isolated from the rest of the world, they had developed a great economy of expression. A word, a look, told you all you needed to know.

But she and her father were newcomers. They did not realize, not at first, how unwelcome they were. Unwelcome generally, because everything new was suspect. And unwelcome specifically, because the father was said to be up to something. He was studying them, that's what people said. He meant to write about them some day. Not like that fella who had written about Smith Island but in a different way — made up yet not made up. The names would be different but not much else was. It was going to be *Days of Our Lives*, but on the island.

One of the Winslips, Aggie, cleaned his house every other week, and she had seen some of the papers in the trash. They weren't nice, the things he wrote. He treated them like animals in a zoo. He talked about who went to church and who tippled and who poached, and although he didn't use the right names, it was easy for anyone from the island to know who was who. But mostly it was the tone, as reported by Aggie Winslip. "Sneery," she said. "Not nice." He used a lot of curse words, too.

Still, this revelation didn't affect him and Becca. The island was generous enough to allow her to be more than her father's daughter. "She's like that duck who thought he was a cat," his mother said once, harking back to a bit of island lore about the store cat who was found in the yard one day with four new kittens and a baby duck pressed against her. It was only later that he realized his mother thought Becca silly for not knowing she was a duck.

The island left them alone, as much as they could leave anyone alone. For the first time in his life he envied mainland kids, with their absent parents and abundance of roads to cruise.

You could do things in a car you couldn't do in a boat. He and Becca had nowhere to go, and hardly any time to go there. And they had both wanted to go, she as much as he, maybe more. She was urgent for it, and he realized she had done it before, but that just made her longing for him sweeter. She wasn't settling. She knew what was what, and she still wanted him. "Again," she would say, when they finally found a place. "Again." It was as if she was saving it up, so she would have enough to hold her until the next time. "Again."

One afternoon, they took his boat out to a small piece of land, too small to appear on any map. Certainly, no one had ever lived there — no person, no bird, maybe not even mosquitoes. They did it again and again and again, until he was sore and they were out of protection. Still, she wanted more, and he never said no to her.

He has reached the outskirts of Virginia Beach. He checks his directions beneath the dome light, realizes he missed his turn a few miles up. The job is in a bad neighborhood. His jobs were almost always in bad neighborhoods, or at least ended up there. If people knew — but they didn't, not unless something went wrong. That's why he got as much work as he did. So no one would discover the secrets hidden in plain sight. He made things disappear. He could make anything, anyone, disappear.

# Chapter 5

Five files, five dead women. No — one was a man, it turned out. How shrewdly egalitarian of the board members to throw in this case as a sop to the mostly male General Assembly. How happy Judge Halsey would be to see a male vic among the females. See, we know men can be affected by domestic violence too; women can be aggressors. Now give us some money, you assholes.

It was the day after Tess's lunch with Whitney, who had wasted no time in providing these files. In fact, she had them in the backseat of her Suburban. She knew Tess that well and knew herself better: As recent events had proven, she could talk Tess into almost anything. Tess sat on the floor of her office, spreading the files around her, trying to figure out the most logical and efficient way to proceed. I'm not procrastinating, she told herself, I'm thinking. There really was a difference.

Her office had a quiet shabbiness that was conducive to deep thoughts. Or maybe it was the not-quite-vanquished fumes from its past lives, which included a stint as the Butchers Hill dry cleaners. Since she had bought a house in North Baltimore a year ago, this East Baltimore location no longer made much sense, but the rent was low, the paint was fresh, and it was convenient to several major bus lines. The customers of Keyes Investigations Inc., as it was known on its tax forms, tended to travel by bus. Besides, it amused her to think about how the Monaghan-Weinstein family had come full circle in just one century. She was back in the very neighborhood that both families had escaped before World War II.

Tess looked at the slender manila folders fanned out in front of her, labeled by name, dated by death. She could proceed chronologically, moving backward through the cases, saving the worst for last. The oldest case, which went back almost six years, would have the fewest living witnesses. Or, more accurately, the fewest sentient witnesses. Once she got beyond family members, she knew sources would be hard to find and their memories would be unreliable. People moved, people forgot. People didn't really care about other people, once the short-term pleasures of gossip were past. Even in small towns. Especially in small towns.

Or Tess could start at the beginning and work forward, make her mistakes — and she was resigned to making mistakes, they were part of the process — on the cases that were least likely to yield results. That held even less appeal.

She wished she had real case files, not just

these sad little folders of newspaper clippings and crude computer printouts, assembled by what was clearly an amateur researcher. Ah, well, these boards had to rely on volunteers. Tess had been spoiled in recent years, getting contraband copies of files through her source in Baltimore PD. She could go to the state medical examiner's office, where all five cases would have been autopsied, and get those reports. But cause of death was not an issue here. The point was to make sure that each case had been investigated properly, that these homicides did not remain open because of raging incompetence or a police department's myopia about domestic violence.

Three of the victims, all young women in their twenties, were gunshot victims — two in the chest, one in the head. The fourth woman, whose DOB placed her age at forty-eight at the time of her death, had died in a suspicious fire. The man had been struck by a car while jogging, but it wasn't clear if the case was a hit-and-run or merely an accident. Funny, she had the most information on him, because he was a prominent doctor on the faculty at Johns Hopkins, and his death had prompted lengthy obituaries in the *Beacon-Light* and the Washington papers. Even *The New York Times* had taken note of his passing.

But the women had died quietly, or as quietly as victims of violence ever die. They had generated a few stories in their hometown papers and the kind of obituaries that funeral homes pay for, one line at a time. Among these death notices, the only detail that caught Tess's eye was from the older woman's, who had not a single survivor listed to her credit, not even the generic "host of friends and relatives." The funeral home had asked that donations be sent to the Chesapeake Bay Trust in lieu of flowers. The youngest victim, and the most recent, didn't even have an obit. All Tess had for her was a typewritten piece of paper providing her name, address, date of birth, and the cause of death. She was the one who had been shot in the head.

Tess scribbled town names on the five thin folders and placed them around her, as if she were Baltimore and the bare wooden floor of her office was Maryland. The state was much wider than it was tall. It was typical of her luck that the cases, once arranged, made a ragged line from west to east.

The oldest case was 60 miles to the west, on the outskirts of Frederick; that was gunshot victim number one, Tiffani Gunts. A little less farther west was the arson, in Sharpsburg, a town on the Potomac River. Hazel Ligetti. Then came the young woman with the skimpiest file, in the far northwestern reaches of Baltimore County, near Prettyboy Reservoir. Julie Carter. That case had happened just this year, but Tess didn't recall it. She supposed she should be shocked that a local woman could get shot to death and not make the newspaper, but she was inured by now to the *Beacon-Light*'s failings.

The line shot up abruptly from there, a long diagonal, almost all the way to Delaware and the headwaters of the bay. This woman had died in a town where a singular lack of imagination must have overcome its founders, for it was known merely as North East. The victim's parents had suffered no such lack; they had named their daughter Lucy Carmengia Fancher. Impossible to tell from the short newspaper articles about her death whether it was Car*men*jia or a mangling of the old VW convertible, Karmann Ghia.

Finally, there was the male doctor, Michael Shaw, killed on Route 100, an east-west highway between Baltimore and Annapolis. It was the nearest case by far, and the most recent, only five months old. It also was the least interesting.

One thing was clear: The board was going to owe her dearly for mileage. No matter how she plotted her course across the state, her old Toyota would rack up a lot of miles.

"So what do you think, Esskay?"

Tess often consulted her greyhound as if the dog were a Magic 8-Ball of sorts. Esskay raised her head, miffed at being disturbed, snorted, and dropped her head with a heavy thunk that give the impression that it might be hollow. Tess interpreted this look as "Outlook unclear."

"What about you, Miata?" The other dog in her life, as accidental an acquisition as the first, was a terrifyingly well-behaved Doberman. Left alone with a roast on the table, Miata would not dream of leaving the blanket that was her bed. Now she cocked her head, ready to do whatever Tess instructed, even if it meant she had to give up licking the stuffed toy lamb, a replica of Shari Lewis's Lamb Chop, she dragged with her everywhere.

But, as always, the Doberman took no initiative. Miata was a born follower, a beta dog, maybe even an omega dog.

"Road trip," Tess declared. Being the boss had its privileges, even if her only subordinates were two canines, indifferent to her brilliant decision-making. She would head west, wrap up Frederick and Sharpsburg over two days, spending a night. It wasn't that far — each was an easy day trip, no more than an hour's drive — but she saw no reason to travel the same roads twice. Esskay could go, but Miata would have to stay home with Crow. The backseat of the Toyota simply could not accommodate 160 pounds of dog, not when 70 pounds of it — Esskay — insisted on complete horizontal domination.

Frederick is where the soft dark shape of the Appalachians first appears on the horizon, where the road opens up and hints at the vastness of the country beyond. Tess had never liked this expansive view. In her mind, Frederick was nothing more than the hometown of Barbara Fritchie, the little old lady who allegedly stood up to Stonewall Jackson, flying the U.S. flag as Confederate troops marched north toward Gettysburg. The highway into town had been lined once with reminders to visit Barbara Fritchie's candy shop and Barbara Fritchie's souvenir shop and Barbara Fritchie's café. The signs were gone now, but John Greenleaf Whittier's lines were burned into Tess's memory. She wondered if the poem was still taught.

*"Shoot, if you must, this old gray head,/But spare your country's flag,"* she said.

Had she really said that? Probably not, Tess decided. At any rate, the township that Fritchie had so vigorously preserved for the Union was a sprawling exurb now. People were willing to drive more than an hour to jobs in Baltimore and D.C., in order to have a little more house and a little more land for a little less money. Talk about a deal with the devil.

Tiffani Gunts had lived outside Frederick, in a warren of new town houses not far from the Monocacy River. Tiffani Gunts had died there too. Six years ago, shot by an apparent intruder. Frederick had a decent daily newspaper, so Tess had been able to find out a little more about the young woman, only twenty-two when she died. A student at the local community college, she worked part-time at a convenience store. She was living with her fiancé, Eric Shivers, and her three-year-old daughter from a previous relationship. Shivers had been out of town on a business trip when someone broke into the town house. Tiffani must have surprised the thief, for he shot her to death in the kitchen.

Eric Shivers didn't turn up in any of the telephone databases that Tess searched, but the Guntses were easy to find. There were only two listed in the Frederick phone book, Tiffani's parents and an older brother and his wife. The senior Guntses lived in an older part of Frederick. Not the nice-old part, which had dark red-brick houses and broad front porches that dated back to the Barbara Fritchie era. Wallace and Betty Gunts lived in the sad-old part, a neighborhood of tired-looking ranch houses. Forty years ago, this area must have held the promise of better times, but that promise had been broken long ago. *Worn down* was the phrase that occurred to Tess as she turned down their street — for the neighborhood, for the house, and for the Gunts family too, once she met them. The quartet — Mr. and Mrs. Gunts Sr., Mr. and Mrs. Gunts Jr. — had pale, dull skin and flat eyes. They looked as if they had been rubbed so hard by life they didn't have any pores left.

The Guntses took her to the family room, an extension built off the back of the house. The beige wall-to-wall carpet crunched beneath

Tess's feet, and there was a curious fist-size hole in the drywall, as if someone had punched it one day, but the room was otherwise neat and clean. Wally Jr. was the apparent spokesman. His father was almost catatonic in his stony silence. The two women kept their eyes fixed on the sliding glass door to the back-yard, where three children played in the not-quite-warm April air. One of those must be Tiffani's child, but Tess wasn't sure if she lived here or with her aunt and uncle.

"I'm sorry to ask you to dredge up un-pleasant memories," Tess said, "but there is a possibility it could do some good."

She had seldom made this claim before in her work, at least not honestly.

"We were glad you called," Wally Jr. said. "We never felt like the sheriff's office did all they could. They were nice enough, but every time we asked about this thing or that thing, they'd tell us we watched too much television. The investigator did tell us he was going to give the case a special kind of number, see if it matched similar cases in other states."

"A VICAP number?"

Wally clearly didn't know, but he wanted to be helpful. "That sounds right."

"But they didn't find anything."

"Not that they ever told us. Fact is, all I know they did for certain was call pawnshops, looking for Tiffani's engagement ring, or the microwave and the blender. Eric was so organized, he even had the warranties on the electric stuff, so they could have ID'd it if it turned up. But like I kept telling 'em, the guy's not going to pawn anything here in Frederick. You'd think they were scared to make a long-distance call."

Tess decided to play devil's advocate. "Investigators are usually pretty determined to solve homicides."

"Yeah, I guess so. But it was kind of like they thought they did solve it, just because they had a *theory*. They were sure some guys came up I-270 from Washington and decided to break into the town houses because they were new then, and not all were occupied. A brand-new refrigerator and stove had been stolen from one of the empty units two weeks earlier. The lock was jimmied in the same way. But nothing big was stolen from Tiffani's place. Because Tiffani was — Tiffani was —"

Wally Jr.'s face reddened as he tried to suppress the tears that brimmed in his dull brown eyes. His mother and his wife didn't bother to fight them, they just sat with tears coursing down their flat, pale faces. Only the father remained impassive. Six years, Tess thought. Does this kind of pain ever end? Would it be different if their daughter's killer had been caught and convicted?

"I know what happened." Shot to death in the kitchen, as her child slept upstairs. "Guy used a pry on the lock, and it gave way pretty easy."

"The bottom lock, yeah. I don't know why Tiffani didn't have the dead bolt on, Eric being on the road and all. She wasn't as timid as she once was, but she still wouldn't have gone downstairs if she thought a burglar was in the house."

"What would she have done?"

"She'd have grabbed the portable phone and locked herself in the baby's room. She was a smart girl. She would have done the smart thing. I'm telling you, it doesn't make sense."

"Is there any possibility it wasn't an intruder? Do you think the investigation should have focused on a different scenario, or someone else in Tiffani's life, such as her daughter's father?"

Wally looked puzzled. "No, I think they're probably right about what happened, but I don't understand why they can't find the guy. When they really want to solve a crime, they always do. Ever notice that? If you kill a rich person, they get you. Cops come to your house and take footprints and tire tracks and use that weird stuff that makes even tiny traces of blood shine. I know. I watch the Discovery Channel. But some lowlife shoots a twenty-two-year-old woman who never hurt anyone, whose life was just getting good after being bad for so long. . . ." Wally Jr.'s voice thinned out, taking on a telltale nasal quality. He was trying so hard not to break down.

"Why had Tiffani's life been bad?"

"Oh." Wally Jr. exchanged looks with the two women. "The usual. Ran with a bad crowd in high school, got pregnant, had to drop out. Bum boyfriend."

"Eric Shivers?"

"Oh, not Eric." Wally's wife, a Katherine who went by Kat, spoke for the first time. "Eric was great. Eric was the best thing that ever happened to her. No, the boyfriend before, Troy Plunkett. Older guy. He was mean, just rotten. Got Tiffani pregnant, said it wasn't his, fought the support for two years. Then the DNA come back, and it said Darby *was* his. He still didn't pay. Said he didn't have any money."

Tiffani Gunts. Darby Plunkett. It occurred to Tess that the more people fought their hard, unglamorous surnames, the more they called attention to them.

"Did the sheriff's department consider Darby's father a possible suspect?"

Wally Jr. took back the role of spokesman. "They asked us questions, same as you. Troy is an SOB. But he had actually calmed down some when he heard Tiffani was going to get married. He thought it meant he wouldn't have to pay support."

Tess knew something about child support laws. Tracking deadbeat dads and searching their assets was one of her sidelines. "Did he find out he was wrong?"

"Yeah, Tiffani told him a week or two before —" He stopped, not wanting to define the date. "It wouldn't have mattered. He didn't pay it when she was on her own, he didn't pay it when she moved in with Eric, he doesn't pay to this day, and he's all that little girl has in the world. He gets a job, we get a garnishment order, he quits and finds some cash job that doesn't show up on the books."

"Who's raising Darby?"

"We are." It was the first time Tess had heard the voice of Betty Gunts, who had merely nodded when they were introduced. "I take care of Kat's two while she works, so it makes sense for Darby to stay here with me. She's a good girl."

"Which one is she?" Tess asked, looking out the sliding glass doors.

"You can't talk to her," Wally Jr. said, swift as a cat. "She was only three, she never saw or heard anything. She was still sleeping the next morning, when a guy from the town house two doors up from Eric and Tiffani's saw the back door standing open."

"She slept through a gunshot?"

"They think the guy used a silencer."

"A man who was stealing appliances from town houses he assumed were empty used a silencer?"

Wally Jr. shrugged. Discovery Channel or no, the detail didn't seem odd to him.

"And Eric Shivers? What happened to him?"

The brother looked at his parents, as if he now needed permission to speak.

"Oh, that was sad," Kat murmured. "Just so sad."

"Eric was really good to Tiffani," Wally said. "We all liked him a lot. He convinced her to go back to school part-time, study to be something. They were going to get married after she graduated. He paid all the bills, he was nice as he could be. And he was like a father to Darby. But he wasn't blood. When Tiffani died, Darby had to be with family. If my parents hadn't taken her, Troy Plunkett might have petitioned to get her, and we couldn't have that. Eric understood. But it was hard on him. He lost Tiffani *and* Darby."

"He got awful thin," Mrs. Gunts said. "And he tried to keep seeing the girl, to stay connected to her, but I think that made it worse. She looks just like her mother."

There was a photograph of Tiffani Gunts, one of those blue-background school portraits, on the far wall of the family room. Tiffani had masses of dark hair, dark eyes, and tiny features. It all added up to a baby-deer delicacy that was almost as good as pretty. Her smile was shy and tentative, but she didn't look defeated, beaten down by life. Then again, she was young in the photograph, a mere teenager.

And she had the advantage of not having to live with the pain of her own murder.

Tess glanced at the three children in the backyard. All three had dark hair and dark eyes. She guessed Darby was the middle one, but only because the other girl looked too young, more like five, and the tallest was a boy. The resemblance didn't seem as striking to her, but then Tiffani had not been her daughter, her sister.

"What happened to Eric?"

The subject of Eric Shivers was one the sister-in-law seemed to relish. "He moved south. Georgia?"

"North Carolina," Mrs. Gunts said. "He sent us Christmas cards. For a while."

"He was good-looking," Kat said, glancing at her husband. "Better-looking than Troy, I mean. I was happy for Tiffani."

"And where was Eric the night that Tiffani was killed?"

Wally Jr. answered. "On the road, in Spartina, Virginia. He traveled all the time. He was a salesman, sold supplies to those mall camera shops. Police called him and asked him to come back and identify — to identify —"

Tess tried to distract him from his own memories. "Was it generally known that Tiffani was home alone a lot?"

Wally's eyes seemed to brighten. "Do you think — ?"

"I'm not *thinking* anything," Tess said carefully. Back in Baltimore, this assignment had seemed theoretical and bloodless, more public policy than detective work. She had not anticipated how difficult it would be for the families to relive these memories. "But I am curious about Troy Plunkett."

Wallace Gunts Sr. spoke at last. He had a

voice like a rusty gate. "He's mean enough to kill. He's just not smart enough to get away with it."

"Is Troy Plunkett still around?"

But Wallace Sr. was done. He reminded Tess of that famous flower in England, the one that bloomed for only a day and gave off a noxious stink when it did.

"Yeah," Wally Jr. said. "He goes away for periods of time, but he always comes back. People like the Plunketts don't go very far. His family's strewn up and down the Old Thurmont Highway like so much garbage. You'll find Troy there, or drinking at the No-Name Tavern."

"The No-Name?"

"That's what we call it. Because it's got no name. It's just a place on the highway, with no name and no sign. You go up a little ways, past the John Deere store, and then it's there on your left."

Tess waited to see if more precise directions would be offered, but the Guntses appeared to feel this should be clear enough. She said good-bye to each in turn. Everyone's handshake was limp and damp, except for Gunts Sr., who squeezed her hand almost too hard and looked as if he blamed her for his daughter's death. They were nice people. Tess wanted to like them more than she did. If their daughter had died differently — from a preventable illness, in an act of terrorism — they might have been filled with a sense of purpose. But the murder

94

betrayed a certain lower-middle-class tackiness. Nice people just didn't die this way.

But the Guntses were so passive, so bewildered and overmatched by life in general. Had they always been this way? Tess didn't know, and she didn't care. She just wanted to get away from them, and away from the wispy, unknowing smile on Tiffani's face.

# Chapter 6

The Old Thurmont Highway was not easy to find, but Troy Plunkett was. Tess overshot the unmarked road at least twice and drove so far out of her way that she almost hit Camp David. It turned out there was a Thurmont Highway, an Old Thurmont Highway, and this narrow stretch of falling-apart farmhouses, which might have been called the Older-Still Thurmont Highway. Tess didn't see any signs of life in the littered yards, most of which were posted with NO TRESPASSING signs. She did see the name Plunkett lettered on several of the old mailboxes, however, and at the end of the road she discovered the No-Name. A concrete rectangle on the edge of a cornfield, it looked like a good place to sit out a nuclear war.

Tess ordered a beer, a Rolling Rock, which was served with a smeary glass and a skeptical look.

"Most women order light beer," the bartender said.

"When it comes to light beer, I've always wondered: What's the point?"

The line had charmed many a bartender back in Baltimore. But this was not Baltimore.

96

The bartender made a point of turning his back to Tess and pretending great interest in the television on a shelf behind the bar. A baseball game was on. It looked odd, perhaps because it was in black and white. No, the players had big sideburns and builds that were at once stockier but less sinewy than today's pumped-up professional athletes. It was a rebroadcast of some game from the seventies, on that ESPN classics station. Now that was the definition of pathetic to Tess's mind: sitting in a bar on a spring afternoon, watching a baseball game that was decided three decades ago.

Besides, it was the World Series with Pittsburgh, the 1979 one the Orioles lost. Traitors.

She glanced around the compact room. Little space was wasted here. It was a serious place, a place for drinking, watching television, shooting pool. It was not a place where a stranger, male or female, could announce, "So, anyone here know Troy Plunkett?"

Eavesdropping, another much underrated tool, also yielded little. The men here barely used nouns at all, it seemed, just grunted monosyllabic adjectives at one another.

"That's good," said a man at a nearby table.

"Yeah," his buddy said.

"I mean *real* good."

"Real good."

"Yeah."

"Yeah."

They could be talking about their beer, the

Orioles, the weather, or Fermat's Last Theorem, Tess thought.

She was getting ready to try and engage the hostile bartender when the door swung open and everyone in the bar recoiled a little, vampires catching a dose of sunlight. A man's backlit silhouette, slightly bowlegged, crossed the threshold. Real Good Man number one lifted his hand perhaps an inch from the table. Even the gestures were laconic here.

"Troy," he said.

And Tess was reminded, as she so often was, that it's smarter to be lucky than it's lucky to be smart.

"Yeah," Troy said.

He took a seat at the bar two stools down from Tess and gave her a curious look. Not a predatory one, just a glance of mild surprise, the way an alcoholic might regard the pink elephant on its second or third appearance in his living room.

"Troy Plunkett?" she asked, adopting the local custom of verblessness.

He looked at her as if the pink elephant had tentatively brandished a small knife — and he was trying to remember where he had stowed something larger and meaner.

"Humph," was all he said.

"I'm a private investigator out of Baltimore."

He hunched his shoulders and bent forward over his beer, as if he hoped she would be gone the next time he looked up. She wasn't.

"So?" He fit a lot of menace into that one small word.

Troy Plunkett was a small man, with the bristling belligerence peculiar to runts. He wore cowboy boots beneath tight grimy jeans, and the heels were hooked on the lowest rung of the chrome stool. If there had been no rung, his legs would have swung free, several inches above the floor. His exposed skin was dark, a farmer's tan that appeared to be almost a stain at this point in his life, which Tess judged to be about thirty to thirty-five years under way. She had assumed he was Tiffani's high school classmate, but Tiffani would be twenty-eight if she were alive now. Cleaned up, trying to charm, he probably had a modest way with some women. Unworldly women. Young women.

But he was not clean now, and he was not trying to charm.

"I'd like to ask you a few questions."

"No," he said.

"Just a few."

"Ask all you want. I'm not answering."

"I'll pay you twenty dollars for your time."

He sized her up.

"Forty."

His appraisal had fallen short of the mark. Tess would have been willing to go to sixty. She pulled two twenty-dollar bills out of her wallet, crisp, sticky ones fresh from a Frederick ATM, and put them on the bar. Not quite between them, a little closer to her than they were to

99

him, and pinned down by her right elbow.

"Six years ago, a woman was killed."

Troy's face was blank.

"A woman named Tiffani Gunts. The local authorities think she was killed by an intruder, but they never made an arrest."

He couldn't even be bothered to shrug both shoulders, just popped the left one up.

"Understand this: I don't care who did it. But I care about how the police went about their job. Get me? I'm not a cop or an officer of the court. I'm a private investigator who's trying to figure out if local law enforcement agencies know what they're doing."

He either didn't believe her or didn't want to believe her. He stared ahead, so she was looking at his profile. It wasn't a bad profile. Tess could see how a woman could be lonely enough, or desperate enough, to ignore the dozens of warning signs that Troy Plunkett gave off.

"You get me? I'm just examining the police work in the case."

"Like internal affairs, or something."

"Right."

"I had an alibi," he said, as if it were a piece of information he had to dig for. "Yeah, that's it."

"So you were interviewed?"

"First thing, you bet."

"Cops can be real assholes when they're trying to close a case."

A corner of his lip curled. He wasn't buying her fake sympathy.

"I've been interrogated myself," she added.

"For what? Shoplifting lipstick?"

"I saw a murder once."

This interested him. It interested most people. Sometimes, even Tess found it intriguing. Then she remembered what it had been like, and all she wanted to do was forget it.

"Just saw it?" Although it sounded more like *sore* or *sour* in his mouth.

"Right. So the only way you can one-up me in this conversation is to have actually committed one."

She managed to get the tone right, so this came off more as a flirtatious dare than an accusation. He turned to face her.

"Well, sorry, I never did. And if the sheriff's department doesn't know anything else about Tiffani's death, they know that much. I had an alibi."

"So you said. What was it?"

"I was in bed with some old gal." He grinned. "And when I sleep with a woman, there's not much sleeping and no forgetting I was there."

Tess furrowed her brow, pretending confusion. "What do you mean?"

"I leave 'em sore," he said.

"You mean you hit them?"

"No." He was angry that her obtuseness was

forcing him to explain his offhand sexual boast. "I mean, I can do it all night long."

"Oh." Then, falsely contrite, "I didn't mean to suggest you've ever hit a woman."

He nodded curtly, accepting her apology in a he-man's wounded fashion.

"Except — you have, haven't you?"

"Have what?"

"Hit women. Hit Tiffani, at least. My guess is the reason the cops came to talk to you is that there was a string of district court arrests from your relationship with her."

It was literally a guess. Tess hadn't thought to check the local court records. After all, the Gunts family hadn't mentioned abuse. But it was an explanation that would make some jagged pieces fit — the father's anger, the sense that everyone else in the family was in some form of denial.

"Every charge was dropped," he said.

"They often were, before the law changed and state's attorneys pursued cases even when the women decided they didn't want to go forward."

"Yeah, women say shit and people believe them. They say you hit them, and how are you going to prove you didn't? They bump their leg on the kitchen counter and wear shorts the next day, and all of a sudden you're the worst guy in the world."

"Or they say they had your baby and blood tests bear them out."

"Blood tests." He tossed back the rest of his beer and a fresh one materialized. The bartender was hovering close — protective of Troy, his regular customer. "I don't believe 'em. I bet one day we're gonna find out it's all bullshit, this DNA, just some crap the government made up to stick it to regular guys. I mean, how you gonna argue with it, you know? You'd have to be a scientist or something. And it's never a hundred percent. Nothing is ever a hundred percent."

"Did the cops know about the arrests, the blood test? Did they press you on this stuff?"

Her prey retreated at such direct questions. Plunkett was back in profile, staring at the television.

"I'm sorry. I know this isn't something you want to talk about. But you're making money, remember?" She indicated the two twenties, still beneath her elbow. "I need to know. Did they really treat you like a suspect, or was it enough for them that you and your lady friend agreed on your whereabouts?"

"They didn't bother me much. Because I didn't do it."

"Did they bring you in more than once? Administer a polygraph?"

"They talked to me at my house, and they poked around in all the Plunkett houses. When they didn't see any new appliances, they knew I didn't do it. You know how far I'd have to go to sell some brand-new refrigerator without someone knowing who I was? Pretty far. Besides, that's not my gig. You checked my records, right?"

Tess nodded, taking her lie to the next level.

"Okay, then. So you didn't see no burglary charges. I don't steal."

"No, you just hit women and refuse to pay child support."

He turned back to her. His eyes had the heavy-lidded, sleepy look that some call bedroom eyes. But there was nothing sensual in this look.

"Let me explain something to you. A man has to assert himself in this world. I've hit other men, standing up for myself. If I had a child — and I don't happen to believe I do — and he talked smart to me, I might hit him. Women are always talking about equal treatment. Well, that's what I give them. They get above themselves, I bring them back down. The only thing that keeps me from teaching you a lesson, right now, is that Joe doesn't let anyone fight in his place, and I respect his rules. So maybe you ought to leave before I take it in my head to follow you out of here."

"When you hit a woman, she knows she's been hit," Tess said, mocking his earlier boast.

"I don't do things halfway."

"What was her name?"

"You already said it: Tiffani. Tiffani Gunts. Dumb Gunts. Her brother was in my little brother's class over at the high school. You're

104

such a smart lady, I bet you can guess what they called Wally Gunts when he was a kid."

Tess could. "I didn't mean Tiffani. I meant the woman you were with, your alibi."

"Shit, I don't remember. It was five years ago."

"Six."

"That just makes it one year harder. Can you imagine how many women I've been with in the past six years?"

"I don't know. How many women in Frederick County have IQs under a hundred?"

The question slid by him. "Whoever she was, she was just someone to spend a night with. Which is all Tiffani was to me. That's what bugs me about women. You're trying to have a good time, nothing more. They tell you they're all fixed, you don't have to wear no rubber. Then she shows up with a baby she knew you never wanted, trying to play house. That's not for me."

Tess, having seen the Plunkett estate, couldn't disagree.

"What do you do? I mean, for a living."

"Whatever I can. There's a lot of work off the books, if you know where to find it." For the first time, he looked panic-stricken. "Hey, if you're from the IRS —"

"I'm not. I told you the truth. I'm a private investigator. I'm second-guessing the police, not you."

"Well, I hate to give them credit, but our

dumb-ass sheriff did his job as far as I was concerned. They would've loved for me to do it, tried to hang it on me every which way. But I didn't, and they couldn't."

Tess slid the money down to him. "Consider this a gift. I don't want you to feel you have to report it on a 1099 at year's end."

Her conversation with Troy Plunkett would end up being the day's most productive. As Tess had feared, the investigators who had handled the Gunts murder had moved on. Not up, just on. One was now a traveling salesman for a home security outfit, the other had gone back to school to become a pharmacist.

"A pharmacist?"

"He heard there was a shortage," said the sheriff, who was new in the job, as of the last election. He even looked new, very spick-and-span, with a shiny well-scrubbed face and glossy white hair. "What's your interest in this old homicide? Did some information come to light? It's an open case. If a civilian knows something, we'd expect you to cooperate."

"It's a routine matter. Almost like an accounting thing."

"Life insurance, something like that."

"Yeah," Tess said. "Something like that."

"Well, I can't open the file to you — it's an open case, you know. Homicides stay open forever. But it's the kind of thing that's not gonna get solved until the man who did it gets taken in on some other charge, decides to confess. Could be years. Could be never. That's how it works sometimes. Public doesn't like to hear it, but we're human. There's only so much we can do."

"Can you at least tell me if her former boyfriend was questioned, the one who fathered her child?"

He looked at the file. "Troy Plunkett? Oh, most certainly. Troy's well known in our offices."

"What about the fiancé, Eric Shivers?"

"Appears so. Two deputies drove down to Spartina that morning, where he was staying in a motel. One of the deputies had to drive his vehicle back. Boy just fell apart. He was a mess. I've heard that part of the reason they looked so hard at the old boyfriend is because they didn't want the new one to go after Plunkett. They had to convince him it wasn't anyone he knew. Between us, they looked at her father and her brother, her co-workers from the Sheetz store. Whatever these boys were, they weren't sloppy and they weren't lazy."

"What about the crime scene? Investigators who don't have a lot of experience with homicide can disrupt crucial evidence."

The sheriff drew himself up. "Look, miss, I didn't care for the gentleman who had this job before me. That's why I ran against him. But we're not a bunch of dumb hicks out here. We know how to do our jobs. Sometimes a person's just in the wrong place at the wrong time. If your insurance company wants to fight a claim, that's between you and your conscience. But don't drag us into it."

It wasn't what Whitney's board wanted to hear, Tess realized, but she wasn't being paid to bring home what they wanted. That's why being a private investigator was better than being a reporter. The bosses couldn't fault you when reality didn't match the story they envisioned in their heads.

Tess had decided to spend the night closer to where she would begin her next day, in Sharpsburg. There was an overdone inn on the West Virginia side of the Potomac with wonderful German food. The only problem was that it didn't allow dogs, which meant she would need the cover of darkness to smuggle Esskay into her room. To kill a little time on her way out of Frederick, she stopped at the development of town houses where Tiffani Gunts had died and called Crow on her cell phone.

"How's it going?"

"Not great," she said. "But it seldom does at the beginning. I'm sitting outside the place where the first woman was killed."

"What does it look like?"

"Seedy. Sad."

"Would you feel that way if you didn't know someone had been murdered there?"

If she didn't already love Crow, such a question would have clinched the deal.

"It looks like a place that had big plans for itself, you know? Plans based on dreams that didn't materialize. It has such a pretty location — it backs up to the Monocacy River — but the town houses have fallen on hard times."

Studying the complex in the fading light, Tess decided the very touches that had been designed to give the town houses an upscale look — the wall sconces, the ceramic address tiles — were its downfall. Most of the sconces hung crookedly by their wires, and the tiles had faded until the numbers were barely legible. There were other telltale signs of neglect and carelessness. Deck furniture was cracked and dirty from sitting out all winter, the Dumpsters were overflowing, and some windows had newspaper for shades.

"Maybe the murder changed everything," Crow suggested. "People sometimes shun a place if they know a homicide has been committed there."

"It's really off the beaten path," Tess said. "One of those places that sprang up like mushrooms when the economy seemed invincible."

"What goes up must go down."

She knew Crow was talking about the stock market and the dot-com bust, but the observation applied to Tiffani as well. She had been on her way up — new job, new man, new house, new life — and someone had brought her down. Just one of those things, the Frederick sheriff said. In the wrong place at the wrong time.

Yet the wrong place had been her own kitchen, the wrong time had been the middle of the night. "If that's wrong," Tess said out loud, "then no one's ever safe."

"What?"

"Nothing. Just stay on the phone with me until I cross the Potomac, okay?"

"Okay."

# Chapter 7

Sharpsburg was pretty in a bed-and-breakfast kind of way: red-brick houses that glowed in the morning sun, large shade trees, window boxes full of pansies and petunias.

But the unsolved homicide of Hazel Ligetti had taken place in less gracious precincts, away from the main streets that tourists saw. Her neighborhood was plain, verging on desperate, block after block of boxy wood-frame houses. Rentals, by the looks of the yards, which were shaved closer than a new marine's skull.

Except for the lot where Hazel Ligetti's house had stood. Two years after the fire, nature had taken back this patch of land. Ailanthus trees staked their claim at the edges of the property, while the foundations were wrapped in furry thorns of wild roses, like the brambles that surrounded Sleeping Beauty's castle. Tess picked her way through the weeds, gathering burrs with every step.

She knew, from the newspaper accounts she had found on-line, that no accelerant had been found, just evidence of an ordinary small campfire built inside a storage shed a few yards from the house. The shed was gone too, of course. Tess paced it off, trying to figure out where the blaze had started. It had been March, an unseasonably bitter night. The supposition was that a passing vagrant, or maybe some teenage boys, had built a bonfire. The winds had been high and the flames needed little encouragement to race toward the house. The neighbor who called the fire department seemed almost awed by the fireball next door, according to the 911 transcript. On paper, the caller's words seemed flat and thoughtful, punctuated by the occasional "Golly!" and "There it goes!"

The caller could afford to be blasé. He had lived upwind and across the street. No sparks on his roof, Tess thought.

Hazel Ligetti died from smoke inhalation, probably in her sleep. It was arson because the fire had been set by a trespasser. It was a homicide because someone had died, but that did not make it a murder, an act of intent: Problem Number One.

Problem Number Two: Tess could not make this case fit any domestic paradigm. Hazel Ligetti, according to her landlord, had lived alone and died alone. She had no spouse, no partner. No boyfriend, no girlfriend, no friends. The lack of survivors in her obituary had not been an oversight.

"She wasn't what you would call . . . an attractive woman," the landlord, Herb Proctor, said later that morning, settling behind his desk with a sigh and taking a long pull on a Big Gulp. "Walleyed. Fat. Hair so thin it was like she was going bald in spots."

Tess wished she could recite back a list of Proctor's notable features. Paunchy. Pitted skin. Toupee so bad you might as well glue Astroturf to your head and paint it brown.

Instead, she asked, "Could the fire have been an intentional one, made to look like a stupid accident? I've seen the other houses on the street. It doesn't take a genius to realize how easy they'd burn. They're little more than kindling."

Proctor rolled his eyes and patted his hair cautiously, as if any movement might disrupt the alignment of his fake hair with the fringe of real hair at his neck.

"No one ever did figure that out. My money's on some kid playing with matches. He panicked and ran."

"A kid would have a hard time keeping a secret like that."

"Well, it had to be an accident. Believe me, the insurance investigators were all over it. It was awful, what they put me through. You'd think I'd set the fire. As if I'd kill a woman to collect fifty thousand bucks. You saw the lot; it wasn't even worth my while to rebuild. And Hazel Ligetti was like a good municipal bond fund, paying off a little every month. A dream tenant. Now, some properties you wish you could burn down because of what the renters do to them. But Hazel was neat as a pin. When you're a landlord, there's no downside to a woman who doesn't entertain, doesn't smoke, and has good hearing."

"Good hearing?"

"Doesn't play the television or radio loud, so you don't have any neighbor complaints. Why, Hazel didn't even have a cat, the way so many of these single women do."

"Where did she work?"

"For the state. She was a secretary at the Department of Health and Mental Hygiene up in Hagerstown. *Administrative assistant* is what she called herself. Why do you think that is?"

"Because everyone wants to sound important," Tess said, fingering the embossed business card that read HERBERT L. PROCTOR, CEO, HALCION PROPERTIES INC. She wondered if he had meant to name his company after the prescription drug, or if he was simply a poor speller. "Did anyone claim her body or make arrangements for the funeral?"

"I did." Tess felt a stab of guilt for her harsh thoughts about Proctor. "She had a little life insurance policy, and I do mean *little*. I had to dip into my own pocket to make up the difference." Tess no longer felt guilty.

"Where she's buried?"

"Local cemetery."

"Is there a marker?"

"A little one, very plain." Tess frowned, and Proctor rushed to defend his cheapness. "That's the way they do it, that's their custom. Plain boxes, plain stones."

"They?"

"Jews."

"Hazel *Ligetti* was Jewish? Was it her husband's name?"

"No. I told you, she was never married. I assumed she was Eye-talian myself, and I asked her one time if she was a good cook. She explained to me that the name was Hungarian, but it was supposed to be spelled slightly different — L-E-G-E-T-E, pronounced Le-*get*. Immigration changed the *e* to an *i*."

"And changed a Jew into an Italian."

"Well, who could complain about that? It's not much of an improvement, but it's definitely a step up."

"Umph," Tess said. It was a noise she had learned to make when she didn't know what to say. Tess's mother's maiden name was Weinstein, and Tess's own middle name was Esther, from the queen of the Jews — not the one in the Bible, but her grandmother's sister, the oldest and most imperious female in a family of imperious females. "That Essie," Gramma Weinstein always said, "thought she was the queen of the Jews." But with the surname of Monaghan and her summer crop of freckles coming in, Tess looked like the good Irish Catholic girl she never was.

"Could you tell me where the local cemetery is?"

"Why?"

"Someone ought to say kaddish," she said.

"Is that like gesundheit?"

"Sort of."

It wasn't much of a trick to find Hazel Ligetti's grave in the small cemetery at the edge of town. The stone was plain, as Proctor had said, with only Hazel's name, the forty-eight-year span that was her birth and her death, a Star of David, and a few lines in Hebrew, which Tess had never learned to read.

But there was one unexpected touch: a few small stones left on the marker's rim.

Someone else knew Hazel was Jewish, Tess thought. *Someone who knows this custom.*

It took a beat for another thought to occur: *Someone knew Hazel. Someone has visited her.*

But how could that be? She had no family, and Proctor said no friend had come forward when she died. But someone *had* visited this grave, someone who was not fooled by the Italian-sounding name.

Then again, the stone had a Star of David, some lines of Hebrew. Perhaps a visitor to a nearby marker, a more popular one, had felt sorry for lonely Hazel. Tess found a pebble and added it to the others. She felt a strange tickle at the back of her neck, that feeling sometimes described as someone walking across your grave. Tess had never understood that description. Dead, one felt nothing. She could jump up and down on this spot right now, and Hazel Ligetti would never know.

★ ★ ★

On the way back to Baltimore, Tess stopped at Antietam. It was her favorite of the various Civil War battlefields she had visited, and she had visited many. It seemed to have been her fate to take up with men who were obsessed with the Civil War. Crow was so avid he had threatened to get involved with local reenactors, but his hours weren't compatible with marching around in a gray suit. (Crow, a romantic with a twisted family tree with branches in Virginia, would choose the South, of course. Most reenactors did.) Jonathan Ross had been more bookish, content with the oeuvre of Foote and Catton and the Shaaras. When they played Botticelli, he had used obscure-to-Tess Civil War officers to stump her.

Then again, perhaps all men were obsessed with the Civil War, or war in general. Why was that? She supposed a certain boyish interest in things with engines led, inevitably, to tanks and aircraft carriers and fighter planes. But why did they know all the generals' names and all those battles? Tess found war baffling. Even war movies baffled her, with the sole exception of *The Great Escape*. Getting out, running away — that was an impulse she could understand. Face-to-face combat all day long, until the cornfields ran red, was unfathomable.

How did men do it? Tess asked herself, not for the first time. How did they talk themselves into thinking it made sense to march toward

117

gunfire for some larger, greater cause? Even if she believed in a cause — and it seemed to her a good idea to keep the United States united and to abolish slavery — she couldn't imagine sacrificing herself for one. She didn't want to die.

Damn. She wished she hadn't let her thoughts go there. This was the trap she had sidestepped in the graveyard. A door in her brain opened up and took her over the threshold into the abyss of infinity. She was going to die one day, she was going to cease to exist. How could that be? She wanted to believe in higher powers, in reincarnation, in anything that held the promise that she wouldn't simply cease to be. But she didn't think it worked that way. You had to be a believer first, and only then did you get the reward of afterlife, or second life, or perpetual life through reincarnation. You couldn't bargain or barge your way into immortality, like some desperate man fleeing the *Titanic*, holding a child in his arms. You had to believe in something first. The only thing Tess honestly believed was that she was scared of dying.

She drove back to Baltimore as fast as she could, racing the sun, telling herself that her only concern was getting back to the city before its early rush hour began.

# Chapter 8

"You're going to die, Tess."

It was Monday and she was back in Dr. Armistead's office, sulkily pulling on the wing chair's fringe. It had seemed to her that her Antietam epiphany was just the sort of story one brought to therapy, but Dr. Armistead did not seem impressed or even interested. It was as if she had shown up for a dinner party and the host had frowned at the label on her proffered bottle of wine.

"Well, I don't know what else to tell you. I thought it was the most interesting moment of my week."

"Really? What about your encounter with that man in the bar?"

"Troy Plunkett? There was nothing particularly interesting about that. It's what I do. I talk to people. Sometimes I have to pay them."

She had told him about her work only to provide some context for her Antietam moment, although she was confused about the crosscurrents of confidentiality here. Was it breaching confidentiality if she spoke of the matter in a setting where all was presumed confidential?

119

"I think it's quite interesting. You'll excuse me for playing armchair psychiatrist" — he smiled at his joke, so she did too, out of politeness — "but I couldn't help noticing the similarities between that encounter and the one that brought you here."

"Similarities? I talked to a guy in a bar. He didn't make a pass at me, and I didn't attempt to remove his body hair."

"You went to that bar on a mission, with an agenda you masked to some extent. After all, if you honestly believed this man had killed his girlfriend all those years ago, I suppose you would go to the police and tell them what you discovered, not attempt to interview him on your own."

"Well, yeah, of course. But that's not how my job works. I don't *solve* cases, not on purpose. I look into things, I make reports. Sometimes I come at it sideways, sometimes I don't. It's a judgment call. After all, I was straight up with the landlord, the guy in Sharpsburg."

"I suppose that's something we share."

He had lost her.

"The public misperception of what we do, and the role of the mass media in perpetuating stereotypes."

"Sure," Tess said. *For one thing, you talk more than I do.* But she liked that. She had worried it would be up to her to fill the hour, which was part of the reason she had stored up the Antietam story and told it in such detail. But if it was going to be all back-and-forth like this, more a conversation than an interrogation, she could probably ride out the six months. Tess had been a reporter for a few years, which had taught her how to draw people out. And she had been a woman all her life, so she knew men were always happy to talk about themselves.

"Come to think of it, the mass media has done much worse by my *old* job."

"Your old job?"

She kept thinking he was omniscient, that he knew everything about her life to date.

"I was a reporter before I became a licensed investigator, back at the old *Star*. But when it folded, the *Beacon-Light* didn't hire me, and I had to change careers. At the ripe old age of twenty-seven."

"Did that bother you?"

"Of course it did." Tess tried to keep her words light, but she was surprised at how much the memory of that rejection still rankled: the token interview with the editor in charge of recruitment, a bulldog-ugly woman who wouldn't even deign to touch Tess's résumé. She felt the blood rush to her face, her cheeks burn.

"Why?"

"It was the only job I ever wanted. It took me two years to find a new career for myself, and that was mainly luck. Now I see it was for the best. I'm a much better investigator than I was a reporter. I still go out, ask questions, collect facts. But I'm no longer obligated to cram them

121

into the limited templates of newspaper journalism. I'm much happier now."

He didn't speak right away, letting the last sentence sit there, naked and conspicuous, shivering in its exposure.

"That seems a good thing to have learned," he said at last.

"What?"

"A devastating rejection is often the only path to a better life. Endings can be beginnings."

"If you don't figure out that life lesson by the age of thirty-one, you shouldn't be free to walk the streets without a keeper."

He seemed mildly offended to have his insight dismissed so cavalierly. But he was a pro, he kept going.

"I'm not so sure. After all, there must be a reason why that Robert Frost poem, 'The Road Not Taken,' resonates with so many of us. When he stops in the woods on that snowy evening, he's not a child. He's a grown man, and it's not clear if he's happy with the choice he made, simply that the choice mattered. He takes the less-traveled road. And, according to the poem's end, it changes his life."

"But he doesn't say if it's for better or worse, just that it made all the difference."

"I've always assumed it was positive."

Tess shrugged. She wasn't so sure. Frost should have written a sequel to clarify. "You've conflated two poems, by the way."

"Excuse me?"

"You said he stopped in the woods on a snowy evening, but that's the title of another Frost poem. You know, Whose house is this, blah, blah, blah. Frost is a great poet, of course, but he's a bit Norman Rockwellian, don't you think? So *good* for you, so American, so beloved it sticks a bit in the throat, like oatmeal. I prefer Auden or Yeats."

"Do you have a favorite poem?"

"Yes — but it's as much of a chestnut as 'The Road Not Taken,' if I'm going to be truthful."

"That's the one rule here," the doctor said, his manner grave. "You must be truthful. Lying to me is like going to a doctor and telling him the pain in your knee is really in your neck. It won't help and it could hurt. So what is this . . . chestnut?"

" 'To His Coy Mistress.' " Dr. Armistead betrayed no recognition. "Andrew Marvell. The one about the guy who is trying to persuade a woman that life is too short for a prolonged courtship and they have to go for it right now." Which was not exactly how she had worded it in her college term papers, but it was succinct.

"I'm not sure I know it."

"You must. It's one of those things they don't let you get out of school without learning.

*"Thus though we cannot make our sun stand still, yet we will make him run. The grave's a fine and private place, but none, I think, do there embrace."*

"A morbid image."

"That line always makes me think about a song we sang as kids. 'Did you ever think when a hearse goes by, that one of these days you're going to die?' There's some line about the worms playing pinochle in your snout. Now *there's* an image."

Dr. Armistead laughed, which pleased her in some way she didn't fully understand. "I must say you have a broad frame of references. From the Civil War to Andrew Marvell to pinochle-playing worms. But we're back where we started."

"Which is?"

"In the grave, which is a fine and private place. Like it or not, Tess, you are going to die. Everyone does."

"So far. But I hear they're working on some solutions to that problem over at Johns Hopkins."

Was it a coincidence that the old nightmare returned that night? Tess thought not. She opened the French doors off her bedroom and crept out onto the deck. In her perpetually-under-renovation bungalow, this deck was one of the few finished spaces. Damn Dr. Armistead and all his talk of death. Damn her, for hanging out in graveyards and battlefields, thinking about death. Jonathan Ross had been buried more than two years ago, and it had been a year since she had this nightmare, the one in which she watched him die again and again.

The April night was cool, and she wore nothing but a thin cotton robe, but it felt good, clearing her head. She leaned on the railing, looked out into the darkness that was Stony Run Park. There was light at the edges of the view — streetlamps from the major streets to the north and the south. But here, with the neighbors' houses dark, it was inky black and quiet.

Jonathan had not been her boyfriend, not by the time he was killed. They were something much less and something much more. They had been each other's first post-college relationship, which had allowed them to mistake one another for adults. They became each other's benchmarks, former lovers who gauged their progress through life by the other's achievements. Jonathan had been far ahead of her when he died, a rising star at the newspaper. He was killed for a secret he had not yet uncovered, a secret that fell to Tess to divine and keep. Tess, without a newspaper in which to publish her suspicions, had not been important enough to kill.

Or so Luisa O'Neal had told her at the time.

Was Jonathan's death the catalyst that had changed her life? Tess could never decide. She had been a failure when he died, essentially jobless and loveless. Now she owned her own business and her own house — a house where the world's best boyfriend was now sleeping. Her adventure with Mickey Pechter had put all those things at risk. She pulled the robe tighter around her shoulders.

"If you could see me now," she whispered to the night sky. "I'm doing really good."

Then she thought of her case, how she must report to the board before the end of the week and how little she had to tell them, how far she was from developing any information that would help them lobby for new funds.

"Well, pretty good," she amended.

Tess could not leave bed for more than five minutes before Crow awoke as well. He said the temperature dropped when she slipped away, but she thought the real story was that the greyhound sneaked into her spot, and Esskay's horrible fishy breath would rouse the soundest sleeper.

"You haven't had insomnia for a long, long time," he said, coming out on the porch. He was bare-chested, nothing but baggy sweats hanging on his long lean frame. She knew that men like Crow often fattened up in middle age, but it was impossible to imagine an extra pound on him. Impossible to imagine him in middle age.

"I had a bad dream."

"The usual?"

Crow knew all about Jonathan Ross, but he begrudged her no memory, which was more than she could say for herself. For a young man inclined toward monogamy, Crow had been awfully generous with his charms before they hooked up.

Still, she didn't want to tell him the truth, for fear he would want to talk about it. And talking about it was only going to make the nightmare recur.

"No, no," she lied. "One of the flailing dreams."

"Who was the target this time?"

The first lie had seemed acceptable, compounding it with a second did not. So she tried to get back on honest territory by remembering the last flailing dream she had had.

"My parents. Of course. It's almost always my parents."

"Never me?"

"Never."

"Would you tell me if it was?"

"Probably not."

They laughed, Tess out of relief that she had come full circle, out of a lie and into the full truth. She had never had one of her flailing dreams with Crow. And if she did, she probably wouldn't tell him. Those dreams were as disturbing, in some ways more disturbing, as the reruns of Jonathan's death. In them, she windmilled her arms helplessly, crying hysterically, trying to get someone to listen to her. But her blows were puny, weak, ineffectual. And the object of her assault walked away, unimpressed. Clearly, it would make great material for Dr.

Armistead. Clearly, she wasn't going to talk about it with him.

"Hey," she said, intent on changing the subject. "Did we make love tonight?"

"You can't remember? Well, there's a boost for my self-esteem."

"My head is kind of fuzzed. Too much work, too much analysis."

"I was at the club late, and you were asleep by the time I got home."

"Right." He was responsible for booking the musical acts that played at her father's bar on Franklintown Road. This did not make their schedules very compatible, but Tess considered this a good thing. They were less likely to take each other for granted. And if they ever did, he had a scar on his abdomen to remind them how foolhardy that could be. She had almost lost him, too. She was a regular black widow, come to think of it.

"So let's," she said.

"Okay." He stood up to go inside.

"No." She took off her robe and spread it on the deck like a blanket. "Here."

He looked at once surprised and amused. Crow was usually the one who pushed for innovation, while Tess was inclined toward a series of greatest hits.

"The neighbors might hear us," he pointed out.

"Only if you do it right."

He leaves when they start making love. He doesn't need to see that or even hear it. Which isn't to say he's jealous. Quite the opposite. He feels sorry for her, sad that she has settled. Her boyfriend is just that, a boy. He knows, once he claims her, they will enjoy a closeness she has never experienced with anyone. Their lives are already intertwined, even if she doesn't realize it. And she, better than most, respects destiny. She will welcome him, embrace him, be grateful for him. She understands so much — trajectories, physics, probabilities. What she doesn't understand, he will teach her. Tides, toxins, the number of places that remain uncharted and unmapped in a world ruled by measurement.

No, he leaves because he has to go to work. Luckily, this job will take him down to Anne Arundel County, and he can go see his mother when he's done.

The Western Shore was a compromise. She wanted someplace closer to home, which was totally impractical. They kept the house on the island, leaving it vacant, and he set her up here, near the Severn River. She complained about the lack of a view. She said he had promised her a water view, which he never did. She said he had told her she would get free premium cable, and that the stove would be gas, not electric. He doesn't know where she gets these ideas.

Lately, however, she doesn't complain at all, and he finds he misses her querulous laments. She is shrinking, becoming fearful and small. She isn't even fifty-five, but she looks much older than her neighbors here. Then again, they had cushier lives. She hasn't made friends, which is probably a good thing, but it makes him sad and angry for her. She's a lovely woman, his mother, but her background makes her shy. She's probably right to be shy around these snobs. Real rich people — and he knows something about real rich people now, has realized in hindsight how rich Becca's father was — are much nicer than these folks, who made middle class by the skin of their teeth. Real rich people don't worry about losing what they have.

His mother doesn't have to worry about money, at least. He has made sure of that. But she worries anyway. She, who was so brave and calm, is anxious about everything.

She is sleeping when he lets himself into the house and enters her bedroom. Her hair is thinner but still brown. Does that mean his own hair will never turn white? He smooths it back from her forehead, says her name. Ma. Ma. Wake up, Ma. Ma. Ma.

She wakes with panicky eyes. "Who — what?"

"It's me, Ma."

"Oh." She squints at him, as if to make sure. "What time is it?"

"Not quite seven. I had a job down this way."

"Did it pay well?"

"They always do."

"Don't be afraid to ask for more."

"I'm not."

"I mean, just because you're in business for yourself, doesn't mean you don't feel inflation too. And with gas going sky-high —"

"I do better than most, Ma. You don't have to worry."

"I saw something on the news last night."

He sighs, knowing it could be something on the news last night, or a week ago, or a month ago. It's possible it was never on the news at all.

"They found bones, in this forest. And they could tell who it was. A woman went out to buy milk on New Year's Eve ten years ago and never came home. And all they had was bones, but they know she was shot and dumped there. Because there's a nick, see, on one of the bones. It's amazing, the things they can do."

"Yes," he says, wanting to be agreeable.

"No secret ever stays kept. Everything comes up. Nothing stays buried or lost, the way you might think."

"Some things do."

"But even in your work, you've said, sometimes —"

"Sometimes. But that's usually someone else's fault. Not mine. Other folks get greedy, or careless. They think they don't need me, they try to do it themselves, they don't take precautions, they don't realize when a place is tapped out. Those are the ones who get caught, Ma."

Her brows knit. She struggles to a sitting position. She won't travel much farther today. From sitting here to sitting in her little living room. She is willing her body into atrophy. What does it matter if the stove is gas or electric? She lives off prepared food and microwaved dinners. Horrible things, microwaves. He'd never choose to live with one.

He admires his mother in a way that her doctors can't, or won't. Animals know when death is coming for them. Why shouldn't his mother? But he can never decide if this new fear is for the past, and what lies there, or for the lack of a future. Does she look forward to death because she thinks it will put an end to these fears? She was so strong when he needed her, so capable. He owes her everything. That's what the doctor could never understand. She's a good person, sweet and kind. She gave him life twice. How boring it was, how banal, to be quizzed about her. She was not the problem. She was the solution.

He fixes her breakfast, cereal made hot with boiling water, a sliced banana on top. She has all her teeth but she prefers soft, mushy food. When will he have to feed her a spoonful at a time? Five years, ten years, twenty years, thirty? And then what happens? How can he spare her the final indignities of life? He makes her a cup of Sanka. Hideous stuff. He wonders if she's ever read the label. Then he gives her some Hydrox cookies, which she will dip into the Sanka until they too are soft.

Her doctors have told her to watch her fat intake. She has a fierce sweet tooth, and if she can't bake five-layer cakes anymore, she wants to have her Hydrox. Hydrox, not Oreos, never Oreos. And Hydrox are getting hard to find. He has to go on the Internet, buy them from some Texas company that tracks down disappearing foodstuffs. He rather likes the woman he deals with, so peppy and full of enthusiasm for her job. There are so many needs to be filled in this world, so many people, like her and him, filling them. The Endangered Snack Act, he thinks, that's what the country really needs. Something to protect Hydrox and Hostess Snowballs and Charleston Chews.

She holds the cookie down in the Sanka, dunking it until it almost falls apart, then pops it in her mouth. He turns on the television, the program with the silly morning men, the ones who make people sing "Manic Monday" at the start of every week. A small trail of brown saliva dribbles from the corner of her mouth, and he dabs it for her. More and more, she has trouble swallowing, although the doctors say there's no reason she should. She has perpetual heartburn.

"Everything comes up," she says absently, her eyes on the screen. He's not sure if she's talking about her food or the past. "Everything comes up."

"I know, Ma. I know."

# Chapter 9

Tess sailed out into Tuesday morning, optimistic about life in general and hopeful about her work in particular. It was the kind of fresh spring day that made everyone but T.S. Eliot feel hopeful. She just felt in her bones that today's homicide, the one with the skimpiest file, was likely to yield the greatest dividends.

That feeling vanished when a dead woman opened the door to her home and invited Tess in for tea.

The brick Cape Cod in far northwest Baltimore County was absurdly small, but so was its tenant. The woman behind the storm door was not even five feet tall. The doll in this dollhouse had long dark hair, wide blue eyes, and pink-white cheeks. She looked delicate and fragile, the type of woman who inspired solicitous feelings in men and women alike.

But she was undeniably, indisputably alive, so Tess first assumed she must be a relative or friend of the deceased.

"I'm looking for someone who might know something about Julie Carter," Tess had begun.

"I can't imagine anyone who could know more than I do," she said, projecting her voice so it could be heard through the door's acrylic covering. The voice was unexpected, dry as beef jerky. It sounded Western to Tess, not in its accent so much as in its smoky, sun-baked timbre, which was suggestive of mesas and cactus and turquoise jewelry. "But I don't much care for someone asking questions about me."

"About *you?*"

"Well, I'm Julie Carter. Seems to me you should know that, if you're going around and looking into me, asking questions about me. What are you?"

Not who, but what, Tess noted. That choice told her quite a bit about Julie Carter's life, the kind of person who was apt to show up on her doorstep.

"It was my information . . . my under-standing —" There did not seem to be any polite or effective way to tell someone she was included on a list of homicide victims. "I'm a private investigator, looking into some old cases. I was told you were . . . dead. Clearly, there's been a mistake."

"Oh, I don't know. Some days I feel like I'm dead." She folded her arms and leaned against the doorjamb. The house sat off by itself, as if it might have been a farm before this part of the county was developed. "You come up from Baltimore?"

"Yeah."

"It's farther than you think, isn't it? From Baltimore, I mean."

"A bit, yes." Tess was confused. She had gotten the bum's rush in considerably less awkward situations. But Julie Carter appeared to be prolonging their encounter, enjoying it.

"Yeah, I thought it was a real find, this place. Cheap, and it doesn't look that far from I-83. And it isn't, as the crow flies, but I'm not a crow. It takes at least an hour if you want to get to Baltimore, have a little fun." She smiled broadly. "Which I do. Look, you wanna come in, have a cup of coffee?"

Why not. "Why not?"

"Cool." She clapped her hands, the way a little girl might show delight, and unlatched the door. "Except it has to be tea. I just remembered I don't have any coffee. That's another thing about living out here in the sticks. It's not like you can run out and grab something at the corner store. There is no corner store. There is no corner. 'Course, I guess someone who works at a grocery store ought to always have groceries, right? But when my shift finally ends, all I want to do is get out. So I never have any food in the house. Is that ironic or what?"

Literal-minded Tess was tempted to say no, this was not irony, merely absentmindedness. But she sensed something needy beneath Julie Carter's cheerful banter. She must be lonely, a young single woman plopped down in the middle of these middle-class families.

"Tea is always nice."

"So, someone thinks I'm dead," Julie said, putting a kettle on to boil and bringing out a basket of teabags, no two alike. "I get 'em at restaurants. You oughta see my mustard collection. And ketchup. I've got a lot of ketchup. How did I die?"

"You didn't, obviously."

"I know. It's probably some other Julie Carter. I get that all the time."

"Probably. But I did have this address. In fact, your name and address were all I had."

"So, was I murdered?"

Tess was so taken with Julie's foghorn voice that she wasn't really listening to the words, just the tobacco-cured vowel sounds. Julie was a heavy smoker. Being inside the house was like crawling into a pack of Marlboros.

*"Well?"*

"Well, what?"

"Was I murdered?"

"Your name was on a list of open homicides. Murder is a legal term." She sounded priggish, but her tone didn't seem to bother Julie Carter.

"Gunshot? Knife? Poison?" The teakettle sang, a muted whistle, and her hostess shook a basket of sweeteners at Tess, hundreds of white and blue and pink packets.

"I don't have that information. There's no information to have. You're alive."

"I once thought about being a private investigator. But I think I'm going to open my own flower shop instead." She laughed as if this were uproarious. "Who am I kidding? If I don't get my ass in gear, I'm never gonna accomplish anything."

"I don't know," Tess said, assuming she was expected to object. "You have a nice house here." It was neat and well-kept, even if the white walls had yellowed from cigarette smoke.

"A rental. I wouldn't be here at all if it weren't for this guy I once dated. He convinced me to move out here, then dumped my ass. The stories I could tell you. I sure can pick 'em."

It occurred to Tess that the error that had sent her to Julie Carter's door might at least be rooted in fact.

"Bad boyfriends?"

"Nothing but."

"Have you ever been . . . stalked?" Somehow, this seemed more acceptable than asking a stranger if she had been hit or assaulted. "Had to take out a restraining order?"

"Most of the men I get involved with can't be restrained. That's the problem. It's gotten to the point where, when I start dating a guy, I feel like saying, 'Look, why don't you just sleep with one of my friends now and get it over with?' Honest. I figure if he did it in the beginning, he'd get it out of his system and I wouldn't feel cheated on."

"Oh." That kind of restraint.

"They're different, aren't they?"

"Who?"

"*Men.* What else are we talking about? Although, I gotta say, when I find a good one, I get bored. The good ones can be so boring. Like the guy who wanted me to move up here. He paid the rent and all, so I thought, Why not? But he was so dull, never wanted to do anything, and got mad when my friends came by. He said I had to choose, them or him. Then he left, so I didn't have to choose after all. What are you going to do? Go with boring and faithful, or exciting and jerky?" She fixed her eyes on Tess, as if she were some oracle.

"I think that changes, depending on where you are in your life."

"No, I mean what do *you* do? You look like fun, you've got a hot job. You married? Or are you still running free?"

"I — why, neither. My boyfriend's great." Crow was great. Saying it out loud reminded her just how great he was, how lucky she was. "He's warm and funny and spontaneous, loyal as a dog."

"No such thing," Julie said. Her incongruously deep voice gave her words an unearned authority.

"How old are you anyway?"

"Twenty-two."

"You're awfully young. You can't have had that many boyfriends."

"I've had enough. All ages, too, all the way up to thirty."

"Thirty. Wow."

Julie didn't catch the sarcasm. "And that was when I was seventeen. But I don't like old men. They're boring. How old is your boyfriend?"

Tess did the math. "Twenty-five."

"Oh, a *younger* man." Julie Carter's certitude on this fact stung a little. Tess liked to think she could pass for twenty-five, at least. "Well, maybe that's the way to go. After thirty, I mean. But I like a guy who has spending money. Is that too much to ask? A nice guy, good sex, a little money so we can go out on the weekends, not count pennies. Last guy I went out with got mad when I ordered a third rum and Coke. You know what he said? He said, 'You're already drunk enough to screw me.' I said, 'You know what, honey? I'll never be that drunk.' Walked out of that bar and hitchhiked home. But that's another story."

"Yes," Tess agreed, feeling a little dazed by all these words, all this information.

"A lot has happened to me. I mean — *a lot*. But I'm alive and never been anything but. In fact, I've never had stitches, even though I almost cut my toe off once." She propped her bare foot on the table and grabbed her second toe, as if beginning a game of Little Piggy. The second toe was considerably longer than the big one. The foot was absurdly small, even for someone as tiny as Julie Carter, plump and white as a baby's.

"See that?"

"See what?"

"My scar. I was walking in the surf at Ocean City after graduation — you know, we all drove down, got a motel room: six girls, six blow-dryers, blew the fuses every night — and I felt this little tug, like a fish nipped me. I said to my friend, 'I'm going up to my towel, there's fish in this water.' Then I saw my toe, hanging by, like, a thread, and I started to scream. There was a boy on the beach, said he was premed at Maryland, he wrapped his T-shirt around my foot. They took me to the clinic on Fifty-third Street, but they didn't know what to do. But there was no — what did he call it? — no topical skin loss. The doctor in Salisbury just patted it back in place and I was fine. I was on crutches a whole week. You want to talk about a good way to meet boys, walk around on crutches."

"It looks . . . good." The story seemed confusing to Tess, implausible even. The thick skin at the base of the toe didn't look like any scar she had ever seen. But the story also had made her queasy, and she didn't want to ask questions lest Julie Carter provide more information.

"So, I've never had stitches, never been in a hospital at all. Except when I was born, I guess. I've never even had a near-death experience. That's when your life passes before your eyes, right? I hope when I do, it's not just me stacking cans at Mars. What a bummer that would be."

Julie was rocking in her seat now, beating her hands on the kitchen table, ignoring her tea. She sniffed once, twice. The tip of her nose was pink as a rabbit's. Tess finally put it together then: Julie's need to get to Baltimore on a regular basis, the rapid-fire speech, the eyes that were all iris. It might be speed, it might be cocaine or even crack. But it was something that juiced you up, not down.

And now Julie was moving in to close the deal, as sure of her mark as any Fuller Brush guy, any tin man.

"Look," she said. "I know I just met you, but you seem so nice. Not stuck up. There's been this terrible computer mix-up at work. The checks are, like, frozen inside the computer because the bank's computer crashed and we're not going to get paid for another two days, after they make a wire transfer or something like that. Could you lend me a little money so I could get some food for the house? I'm good for it, you know. But I live check to check, and when the check is late I'm hosed."

The easy thing would have been to hand over a twenty. The futile thing would have been to lecture, or even call attention to the bullshit. Tess chose to play Julie's game, Julie's way, piling lie on top of lie.

"Gosh, I wish I could. I don't have any cash on me, or even my ATM card. I'm overdrawn myself. Got a little out of control, playing the Delaware slots last month. And the people I'm working for, they haven't paid me a dime yet. I have to wait until the end of the month to see dollar one."

Julie sniffed once, twice. "I guess that makes sense. Because whoever told you I'm dead doesn't know their shit, do they? That is some weird-ass job you've got, going to people's doors and telling them they're dead."

Tess thought so too.

# Chapter 10

"Be calm, be polite, play the game."

Whitney's advice, hissed in a whisper in the corridor of her family's foundation offices, was undeniably good. Still, it infuriated Tess, who felt she had earned the right to her snit.

"Play the game? I'm sorry, I didn't realize this was just a game. I thought I was working for a group of people who were sincerely interested in making a difference in the world."

"Poor choice of words." Whitney was maddening when she was reasonable. "One doesn't go charging into a meeting with people who are paying you — paying you quite well, by the way — and accuse them of being incompetents. There were bound to be a few glitches along the way."

"*Glitches?* I was told Julie Carter was dead and she pops up alive. Hazel Ligetti died in a fire that appears to have been set accidentally by someone who didn't even know her. The investigators in Frederick may not have been brilliant, but they were competent. These cases are worthless."

"Let us worry about how to lobby the General Assembly," Whitney said. "For now, make nice with the board. You work for the entire group, remember?"

Tess did. She took a deep breath and smoothed back a tendril of hair that had snaked from her widow's peak, just like the little girl with the curl. She would be good, she would be very, very good.

They were the last to arrive, a Whitney power play: Summon everyone to your office, then make them wait. Tess watched with barely concealed amusement — and impatience — as the other members of Whitney's consortium unpacked the lunches they had brought to their "brown bag" meeting. Lunch told so much about a person. Even how one carried a lunch indicated a lot. Only one person here, for example, had a literal brown bag, and it happened to be the group's lone male member, Neal Ames. He pulled a bologna sandwich on white bread, an apple, and a bag of Utz pretzels from the soft crinkled sack, which had obviously been recycled several times. Earnest and idealistic, if not particularly imaginative, Tess decided.

Now the woman in the middle of the table, Miriam Greenhouse, the executive director of the city's best-known women's shelter, had brought a fashionable-looking salad, a chocolate cream cheese muffin, and a Diet Mountain Dew: caffeine junkie, much too busy to pack her own lunch. The two other women, still in their twenties, had Diet Cokes, Greek salads, and low-calorie yogurt, which Tess found mildly depressing. Regular yogurt should be abstemious enough. Finally, there was Whitney, who wasn't eating at all. Probably another power play on her part.

Tess unwrapped her own lunch and tried to decode what message she was sending: turkey sub with lettuce, tomato, and extra hots, a bag of Utz crab chips, and a real Coca-Cola. She didn't know what those gathered around the table saw, but she knew who she was: a diet-averse, shellfish-allergic hometown girl who had never tasted crab seasoning until Utz had the brilliant idea of putting it on potato chips.

"So bring us up to date," said Miriam Green-house, the woman from the shelter, taking the lead. She was the kind of woman to whom others automatically deferred — confident, calm, with a hint of an edge that allowed her to stay confident and calm, because no one wanted to find out what would happen if she was pushed. "What kind of lapses have you discovered so far? What warning signs were ignored, what clear signs of danger were missed in these women's cases?"

Tess, who had just bitten into her sandwich, had to work her way to the end of the mouthful, holding a finger aloft as she chewed for what seemed like a lifetime.

"Sort of the opposite," she said, after swallowing. It had the feel of an anticlimax.

"You've made no progress? But Whitney said

you've already submitted expenses for your trip to Frederick and Washington counties."

"I submit my expenses weekly. It is possible to rack up quite a bit of mileage without —" She paused, not sure of what she wanted to say, how she wanted to phrase it. She had come in loaded for bear. How had she ended up on the defensive?

The man, Neal Ames, rushed into the pause. "That wasn't a cheap meal you had in West Virginia. Nor was it a cheap motel. Couldn't you have stayed in lodgings more reasonable than the Bavarian Inn?"

No one had second-guessed Tess's expenses since her newspaper days, when the accounting department flagged any tip above 15 percent. "I could have avoided a hotel altogether, driving back and forth over two days. But that would have doubled my time on the road — which is billed hourly — and resulted in extra mileage of almost seventy-five dollars. So I think, given that information, I was entitled to stay where I wished and eat what I wanted."

But his attack had emboldened the others.

"What about this line item, forty dollars for Troy Plunkett?" asked the one Tess thought of as Strawberry Yogurt, because she not only had pale pink yogurt in front of her, she had on a pale pink blouse and a gingham plaid headband with the same shade of pink in it. "Did you get a receipt?"

"I paid Plunkett to speak to me. It's not uncommon in my business."

Now Banana Yogurt, who had not color-coordinated her outfit to her lunch but did have hair just a shade darker than her Dannon, stared at Tess with round eyes. "You pay people to talk to you? Isn't that unethical?"

"Not in my business, no. It's a consideration of their time. I pay people what I think their time — and information — is worth."

"And did you get forty dollars' worth out of Mr. Plunkett?" This was Ames, who seemed awfully pleased with himself for having opened up this line of inquiry.

"Yes, I did. But I got the biggest bang for my buck just by driving out to northwest Baltimore County, near Prettyboy Reservoir, where I met one of our 'victims' face-to-face. Julie Carter is alive, ladies and gentleman. A fact that, coupled with the dead ends on the other two cases, makes me wonder if this board has its collective head up its collective ass. How did you come up with these names, anyway, throw darts at a dartboard? Just plug HOMICIDE and MARYLAND into a search engine and see what kicked out?"

Whitney raised an eyebrow at Tess, and Whitney was capable of encapsulating a world of meaning in that small gesture. The problem was, Tess couldn't decode this facial semaphore. Was she overstepping, forgetting whom she worked for in this situation? She had intended to play nice but had lost her resolve when they began poring over her expenses. The Yogurt Twins looked shocked, while Neal Ames was tapping his pen on the table's edge as if he wished he could bounce something off her skull.

But Miriam Greenhouse, the ostensible leader, looked amused.

"Our selection was random, I admit. We thought that was purer, if you will. We picked open homicides outside Maryland's incorporated cities and the bigger counties. Neal, you compiled the list, right?"

"Actually, it was a volunteer for the Tree Foundation." Ah, Tess had forgotten he was Luisa O'Neal's representative on the board. Well, she had disliked him from the start, so she came by her revulsion honestly. "An *unpaid* volunteer," he added.

"As opposed to the paid variety?" But Tess's nitpick sailed over the lawyer's head as he deflected blame to his poor anonymous volunteer — and then cloaked himself in righteous virtue over the fact that anyone would try to blame a poor anonymous volunteer.

"Well, at least two of them have been in the ballpark so far. The Tiffani Gunts case is ripe to reopen, right? The new sheriff says the old one was incompetent."

"Yes, but the ex-boyfriend is not a suspect, so it's not a domestic. Look, I met the guy. Whatever he is, he's not some criminal mastermind

150

who staged a robbery to kill his girlfriend because they were fighting over child support. He has more ingenious ways of avoiding his obligations."

"How's that?" Miriam asked, eyes narrowed. Financial support was an important component of the shelter's work. If Safehouse's staff couldn't get estranged husbands to pay battered women child support — or have the man evicted from the house — the women's odds of escaping were greatly reduced.

"He told me he takes cash jobs, off the books. You can't get blood from a turnip, and you can't get money from a man who doesn't seem to have any. Can't attach his income tax refund when he has no reportable income. Can't take his car or his house when he doesn't have either one of those."

"We can get his license suspended," Banana Yogurt said.

"A guy like Troy Plunkett will drive without one. Look, you can't even threaten to reduce his visitation, because he doesn't want any. The guy's snake-mean. Tiffani's family just gave up after a while."

"Still" — Miriam looked thoughtful — "the case fits our purposes. He beat her when they were together. She ended up dead."

"She was shot," Tess said, "in a robbery. How are you going to obscure that piece of information?"

"Let us worry about how we present our

case. Just bring back reports on the next two homicides. If those prove as futile as the first three, we'll find more for you to examine. We're pursuing a worthwhile goal. The facts will fit. We'll make them fit."

Something in Miriam's argument didn't sit right with Tess. Lord knows, she was against domestic violence. Who wasn't? But she believed in other things, too. Being truthful, for example, and not bending the truth toward any ideological end or purpose.

"You know, I did a little reading after I signed on with this board," she began. Everyone looked surprised. The private detective can read. Whitney's eyebrow was jumping so violently it looked like a facial tic. "And I found an interesting article, based on Justice Department statistics. The number of homicides that are classified as domestic violence haven't gone down, not significantly, in twenty years."

"So?" Miriam said. "Doesn't that prove our point? This is a preventable crime, yet the numbers are not going down."

"It would prove your point if nothing had been done in the last twenty years. But a lot has been done. Shelters have been built, laws changed. Yet for all this effort, the number of women killed by their partners has held remarkably steady. Why?"

Miriam's good-humored tolerance of Tess had vanished. "Because we need more laws, more funding. I am tired of reading newspaper stories about men who kill women because they love them too much. That's not love."

She actually pounded the table as she spoke, and her husky voice grew shrill. Tess had a quick insight into the consortium's political problems. If Miriam spoke this way to legislators, she'd never get what she wanted.

"Agreed," Tess said. "I've always said when a brokenhearted man contemplates murder-suicide, he should do the suicide part first. We really are on the same side here. So let me ask you again: How did you get these names?"

Everyone stared at her blankly. That is, the women stared blankly, while Neal Ames gave the impression of someone trying to fake blankness.

"Did the people on this list seek help from you, or from any of your sister organizations, before they died? Is that how you got their names?"

A long silence, broken by Miriam Greenhouse. "Such things are confidential."

"But you would know," Tess pointed out. "You would have access."

"The names were chosen at random," Neal Ames said, "from on-line resources — newspaper databases, things like that."

"So you said before. By an *unpaid* volunteer. But how does a volunteer end up including Julie Carter on the list? Right name, right age, right address, just no fatal bullet wound to the head. How does that mistake get made?"

"Some people are fallible, Miss Monaghan," Ames said, his voice nasal with sarcasm. "You, for example, miscalculated your mileage. The going IRS rate is thirty-two and a half cents per mile."

"Where did you get these names?" Tess repeated. "I can always ask the volunteer directly if you don't know."

"No, you may not," Ames snapped. "You'd only harangue and harass her, and no one deserves that for the simple sin of trying to be helpful. May I remind you there are two more cases on your list? Why don't you concentrate on those — do the work you're actually paid for doing? You may yet find out something useful. I'm just sorry there's no luxury hotel for you to visit up in Cecil County."

Miriam Greenhouse shot Tess a look that was at once sympathetic but cautionary: *He's an asshole,* her face seemed to say, *but please don't pick this fight.*

"I'll let you know what I find out," she said, crumpling up the white waxy bag from the carry-out sub shop. "And I'll try to get my mileage right next time."

Two years ago, a little more actually, Tess had written a letter to herself and mailed it to her Aunt Kitty.

Tess being Tess, the envelope had carried this slightly melodramatic notation: *To be opened only in the event of my death.*

154

Kitty being Kitty, she had never opened it or even thought to inquire about it. Nor did she seem particularly curious when Tess stopped by the bookstore after her lunch and asked to check the safe, to see if her letter was still there. Kitty was preoccupied, getting a tutorial from Crow on her own computer system.

"Inventory," Kitty said absently, running her fingers through her hair until the red curls stood up in strange little shapes all over her head. But Kitty made even bad hair days look good, just as she gave shape and elegance to the baggy, vaguely ethnic outfits she favored. "It's gotten harder since Tyner computerized the system, although he swears it will be easier once I get used to it. By the way, he said to ask if you were fulfilling the terms of your probation."

"To the letter."

Kitty was too distracted to catch the surly tone in Tess's voice, but Crow wasn't. Tess refused to meet his questioning gaze. It unnerved her, sometimes, how attuned he was to her every nuance.

"Combination still the same?"

"Sure, sure," Kitty said. "Now, why is this computer saying I have two hundred and forty copies of *Valley of the Dolls?* That can't be right."

Kitty's bookstore was in an old drugstore, her living quarters above. Tess took the envelope from the safe and used the elevator, put in just for Tyner, to go to the second-floor kitchen and dining room. She found a beer in the refrigerator and helped herself. Then she helped herself to a wedge of Roquefort, several crackers, and some grapes. The envelope sat on the table, propped against the vintage salt-and-pepper shakers, slender and innocent. She didn't need to break the seal. She remembered its contents all too well.

The letter told the story of how Luisa O'Neal had made a deal with the devil, or the closest thing to the devil to ever roam the state of Maryland: Tucker Fauquier, a notorious serial killer. O'Neal, working through intermediaries, had persuaded Fauquier to add one more body to his résumé, that of a child killed by her own son. Fauquier had twelve bodies on his ledger and was already facing the death penalty. What was another corpse between friends? Especially when the friend was promising expert legal help and a financial stipend to Tucker's mother back in western Maryland. Luisa O'Neal had then placed her troubled son in a maximum security psychiatric hospital, where she had promised Tess he would stay until he died. In Luisa O'Neal's mind, this had been a form of justice.

And perhaps Tess could have seen her point of view if Jonathan Ross hadn't been killed when he came too close to figuring it all out.

"Hey."

Crow's voice so startled her that she jumped, banging her knee on the underside of the table.

156

"Shit, Crow. Don't sneak up on me like that."

"Sneak up on you? If you didn't hear the elevator whining up and down, you're in another world." He took a seat next to her. "So, the letter. Still here, after all this time."

"Yes."

"What brought this on?"

"Luisa's foundation is one of the groups underwriting my review of these unsolved homicides."

"You told me. But I thought Luisa was essentially non compos mentis since her stroke. You're not working for her, you're working for her money. And it's a good cause."

"Maybe."

"Maybe it's a good cause?"

"Maybe it's incidental that the Tree Foundation is involved. Luisa and Whitney's mom were tennis partners once upon a time. That's how things work in Baltimore: tennis partners team up on philanthropic missions, members of the Maryland Club hire each other's sons."

"College roommates," Crow said gently, "throw gigs each other's way."

"Point taken. I am a Baltimorean, first and foremost. Still, it creeps me out. Whitney said it was *her* idea to hire me, but I don't know. The Tree Foundation has always been more into building things than doing things. As Whitney said, if the O'Neals couldn't hang a plaque on it, they didn't see the point. None of this makes sense."

"Maybe Luisa is shopping for a little redemption before she dies. One good deed for the road."

"Luisa reserved all her good deeds for her family."

Crow massaged the muscles in her neck. Until he touched her, she hadn't even realized how tight she was. Too many miles in the old Toyota, too much time in meetings.

"Put it away, Tess. Literally and figuratively."

Reluctantly, she picked up the envelope and stood up, ready to walk it back to the safe. Perhaps it was her imagination, but it felt warm to the touch, not unlike a feverish forehead — or an infected limb.

# Chapter 11

North East was what it said it was, a compass point to the north and east of Baltimore. But it wasn't much else.

Tess caught herself. She was being unfair to this little town at the head of the Chesapeake. It had a sleepy down-to-earth charm, despite the weekend homes and the proliferation of those baffling gift shops found in tourist spots. North East was a real town, a place where people lived and worked year-round. Water was a source of work and leisure here: The marinas outside of town were filled with sailboats and small yachts from as far away as Philadelphia and New Jersey. But it wasn't as built up as some beach resorts.

Tess realized she was cranky because Cecil County was so much farther than she had remembered and she had hoped to finish today. This was her last stop. She was torn between wanting to have something — anything — to tell her clients and yearning to be done with the whole mess. She felt as if she had been on the hillbilly tour of Maryland. So many sad, tired houses. So many sad, tired lives — except for Dr. Shaw, of course. But even his death had spooked her a little.

She had started the day with the doctor, driving south from Baltimore to the stretch of highway where Michael Shaw had been killed while jogging. It turned out he lived on Gibson Island, the ultimate gated community. It was a literal island, a private patch of land with a gatehouse where the guard was vigilant about keeping the uninvited away.

Using Michael Shaw's name to try and gain entrance only made him more skeptical.

"He hasn't lived here for some time," the guard said. Tess noticed he didn't say that Shaw was dead. He was cagey, this guarded guard.

"I know. But I wonder if his family —"

"Doesn't have any family."

"Doesn't have any family living here." But her voice had scaled up in spite of itself, and the guard caught the uncertainty.

"You didn't know him, did you?"

"No, but —"

"Well," the guard said. "It's too late now."

The Anne Arundel County cops were more welcoming, at least, if not more helpful. They provided copies of the reports filed when Shaw was killed, late last year, and sent the investigating officer out to speak to her. Detective Earl Mutter — who defied his last name by speaking in clear, ringing tones — appeared downright cheerful about how little he knew about the Incident, as he insisted on calling the fatal hit-and-run.

Mutter explained that Shaw was a serious runner training for the Marine Corps marathon in Washington. He had been hit in a blinding rainstorm and his body was thrown clear of the highway into a ditch, where he remained for hours. The accident was classified as a hit-and-run, but Mutter believed the driver never realized someone had been struck and killed.

"Rain was so heavy that day you could barely see your hand in front of your face," Detective Mutter told Tess. "There was no sign of anyone losing control of his vehicle, no swerve marks, no tracks in the mud along the highway. My guess is the doc was hugging the road pretty close and was thrown so far that the driver wouldn't have seen his body even if he stopped and looked around. Driver probably came up over a rise and — *whomp*."

"They say that's the way the world will end," Tess said. "Not with a bang but a *whomp*."

"Huh?" Mutter asked.

"Never mind."

Actually, she understood Detective Mutter's willingness to take the driver's side. She thought about the times a human form had suddenly emerged from the darkness when she was driving — careless pedestrians trying to cross busy highways, cyclists riding toward the traffic instead of with it. She had wondered why people weren't hit more often, given their stupidity. She glanced over the report that the department had provided her.

"It says here he was wearing a bright orange reflective vest."

"It does?" Mutter turned the report back around so he could read it. "Yeah — but it was morning. Driver has to have his lights on in order for the vest to have something to reflect."

"I thought state law said you had to have your lights on if you have your windshield wipers on. In rain that heavy, you'd be using your wipers, right?"

"You don't have to tell me what the law is. But people out here in the country are different, you know? A little more independent in their thinking than you city folk."

Tess found this rationalization hilarious. There were a few rural pockets between Baltimore and Annapolis, but the area had long ago run together, like a batch of failed cookies spreading over the pan. Anne Arundel County was nothing more than a big suburb. Besides, independent thinking had never been one of its hallmarks.

"Still, technically it's a homicide, right? So the case stays open."

"Sure. And we did everything we do with a hit-and-run. We took it to the media, in case anyone saw anything — or in case the driver could be persuaded to come forward after the fact. We checked with body repair shops in the area, to see if anyone brought a car in, claiming they had hit a deer or something like that."

"Did you look into the doctor's personal life?"

"What do you mean?"

"Was he married, did he have a girlfriend, did anyone come into money because he died?"

"There was a guy who kept calling himself the doctor's *partner*, but I don't think they were in business together." The detective didn't bother to hide his smirk. "I guess the doctor considered himself married, even if the state didn't. But the doctor forgot that death doesn't always make an appointment. There was no will, so everything bounced into orphan's court. It's still there, I think. I mean, it was five months ago that he died."

Tess looked at her notes. According to his obituary, Dr. Michael Shaw had been a psychiatrist at Johns Hopkins Hospital, where he had been involved in several groundbreaking studies, including one on chemical castration. He also had worked at Clifton T. Perkins, Maryland's prison hospital for the criminally insane.

"But you looked at the partner, right? You checked his alibi, ran records checks, made sure there was no ongoing strife in the relationship."

"That guy? Jesus, if you met him, you'd know he couldn't pull off something like that. Not even if he hired someone to do it. He was a mess. Said they had a fight right before it happened —"

Tess looked up from her notes.

Mutter shook his head. "About running in the rain. He told him not to do it. And then he felt bad, because that was the last conversation they ever had. I never understand why people feel so bad about those things. I mean, if your life really passes before your eyes, then you remember the happy stuff too, right?"

"I don't know," Tess said. "I imagine a lot of people die grumpy. I know I will. So what happened to the partner?"

"Moved away. To California, I think, some place he has family. A lawyer is trying to untangle the estate. The doctor had money, but not as much as you'd think. Most of his net worth was in the house. They sold it and put the profits in escrow. You got a will?"

The question startled her. "I'm only thirty-one."

"I'm thirty-eight. Had one drawn up when my first kid was born, when I was twenty-five. It's inconsiderate, not looking after your affairs. Think of it that way."

"I guess I don't want to think of it at all."

"Exactly," Mutter said, waggling a finger in her face. "That's what the doctor did. Which is why his partner had to move back to California without a cent."

Back on the highway, heading toward Baltimore and then beyond on I-95, Tess wondered who else on her list had forgotten to make a will. Tiffani Gunts had nothing, but she did have a daughter. Did she have a life insurance

164

policy, a trust? Whatever Hazel Ligetti owned had probably gone to the state, to become one of those mysterious unclaimed accounts advertised by the comptroller's office. Julie Carter was alive and, if she kept going down the reckless path she appeared to be set on, wasn't likely to leave much behind for her heirs. Four down, one to go.

Lucy Fancher, you are the last remaining hope of my hopeless amateurs. If I can't find a domestic angle to your death, it's a shutout.

Still, she should have thought to ask about wills, Tess admonished herself, pulling off in Perryville when she saw a Dairy Queen sign beckoning to her. Here she was, grading local cops on their ability to investigate homicides and she had neglected a basic check.

By day's end, she'd regret not making another basic check. But at least she had considered, however fleetingly, pulling the autopsy reports for her victims.

It just hadn't occurred to Tess that someone who died of a gunshot wound might have been discovered in pieces.

# Chapter 12

It was late afternoon by the time Tess found the cottage where Lucy C. Fancher had lived. It wasn't much, but it was all Tess had. Perhaps Lucy had felt the same way. As best as Tess could determine, there were no other Fanchers in the area — not on the voter registration rolls or in the local courthouse files, either as defendants or plaintiffs. The only Fancher listed was Lucy, and the only public record of her existence was a speeding ticket. She was named in a warrant for not paying the fine, the interest on which had been compounding steadily since her death.

*Going 50 in a 40 mph zone. Conditions: Dry and clear.* Tess checked the date on the ticket. October 29, three and a half years ago. Two nights before Lucy Fancher died.

She looked at the articles from the local paper, the *Elkton Democrat.* The accounts of Fancher's murder seemed incomplete to Tess, but she chalked that up to the inexperience of the local reporter. Margo Duncan probably hadn't written many homicide stories. Still, all the more reason for the paper to go hog-wild with the story, instead of running these strangely prissy mishmashes that raised far more questions than they answered. The first article said only that state police were investigating the apparent homicide of Lucy C. Fancher. A follow-up, which appeared two days later, spoke of a "break" in the case and said Cecil County officers were now working with the state police and the Maryland Transportation Authority's law enforcement agents. The second article noted that the cause of death, pending an autopsy, was a gunshot wound to the chest. But Margo Duncan provided no information about the break or why these three disparate agencies had joined forces.

And that was that. A year after Lucy Fancher's death, the paper ran the obligatory anniversary story about her unsolved homicide, "which rocked the bucolic community of North East." Lucy had been a student at Cecil County Community College and worked part-time for a small real estate firm. She seemed to have no friends, or no friends the newspaper could find, and the officers involved in the case issued terse no-comments. Clearly, something was being withheld — details the paper wasn't reporting or wouldn't report. A sexual assault? Evidence that only the killer could know? Tess supposed she could drop by the paper and ask to speak to Margo Duncan, but it was unlikely that the reporter was still there. Three years was an eternity at a small-town newspaper.

So she looked for Lucy Fancher's last-known

address instead, getting lost in a series of meandering roads that dead-ended at the river.

The house sat off by itself, in a grove of trees. It was nothing special, a dull rectangle with rust-red asbestos shingles for siding, and it appeared to have been vacant for some time. A generic For Sale sign, peppered with dirt and water stains, listed to one side at the driveway's edge. Tess got out and walked around the small house, largely for something to do. The house may have been plain, but the view from the rear was extraordinary, all water and sky. The trees, a mix of sweet gums and evergreens, formed a natural screen from the houses on either side. No water access, but it was probably only a matter of time before Fancher's landlord sold the place. Expensive new houses were sprouting up all over these narrow lanes. The lot must be worth a fortune.

"You interested?"

The voice, hoarse and rusty, made Tess jump. She turned to find a man in his forties with a weatherbeaten face beneath an old Caterpillar gimme cap. Grimy and unkempt, he looked like a drifter, but she could hear an engine running on the other side of the house. North East must be a small enough place for people to stop at the sight of a strange car.

"Excuse me?"

"You interested in buying the place?" The shadows were so deep here, under the trees, that it was hard to see much of his face.

"Owner will give you a good deal on it. It's been empty for a while."

"Since —" She stopped to think about how to phrase it, how much she should reveal. "Since when?"

The man scratched his chin. "Four years? Three? Around that. I live just up the road."

"It's a great location. I'm surprised someone hasn't snatched it up."

"Owner got greedy, I think. People had a lot of money when he put it on the market. Then they didn't, and he wanted to sell, bad. Now, every time he gets a contract it falls through. People talk."

"What do you mean?"

"Something happened here."

His country terseness was wearying, and Tess decided to speed things up.

"The girl who lived here" — she figured *girl* would be the local parlance for a woman of twenty-three — "she was killed, right?"

He nodded.

"Did you know her?"

"Just to say hello." He raised his hand to demonstrate, throwing his left arm up as if waving from a car.

"Did she have a boyfriend?"

"A fellow lived with her. I guess that made him a boyfriend."

"Did you know his name?"

"No, I knew him just —" The left arm saluted again. "They didn't live here that long, before . . . He looked nice, though. He kept his van real clean and tended to the yard when he was here. It wasn't so overgrown then."

A clean van and a neat yard. Tess guessed those clues to a man's character were as reliable as anything else glimpsed from a distance.

"What happened to him?"

"No one knows." The man leaned forward, lowered his voice. "People said he . . . kind of lost it. Not right away, funny enough. He was okay with the first, but not with the second."

He looked at her expectantly, as if he wanted her to fill in the next part.

"Second what? Was someone else killed?"

"Because . . . because" — he looked offended — "don't you know? I mean, can't you imagine?"

"I know his girlfriend was shot and they never solved the case."

The neighbor scratched his chin. "I'd forgotten that the newspaper didn't tell it. But everyone knows."

Tess shook her head. "I don't."

"It was October thirty-first, Halloween?"

She nodded, confirming that October thirty-first was Halloween.

"That was the first part."

"The first part?"

"They found Lucy Fancher's head in the middle of the Route 40 bridge, about two a.m. Just sitting on the median strip, almost exactly at the county line between Cecil and Harford.

Her head and her driver's license, in case anyone couldn't make the ID with just the head."

Suddenly, everything was too sharp: the deep itchy smell of the evergreens, the bay-tinged breeze, the blue eyes of her cheerful informant.

"That wasn't the worst, of course."

Of course.

"Two nights later, the body shows up, here on the back steps. It's waterlogged, like it's been submerged somewhere. People say the person who done it had found a jack-o'-lantern, left over from Halloween, and propped it on her neck for a joke. Yes, she was shot, and that was the cause of death. But it always seemed the point was to get at her boyfriend, to taunt him in some way."

Tess was beginning to see how those elliptical newspaper stories fit together. If Fancher's head had been found on the bridge, a cop who worked for the Maryland Transportation Authority was probably first on the scene. But it was only when the body was found that they could determine the cause of death — the so-called break in the case. Which meant the head had been removed postmortem. The bit about the jack-o'-lantern was the kind of thing cops would withhold, even if the whole town was alive with gossip about the case.

"Was she —"

"Raped?" It was creepy how quickly he filled in her unvoiced thought. "They never said."

171

"What happened to the boyfriend?"

The man had scratched his chin until he opened up a small cut, but he kept scratching, smearing blood. "I don't know. He moved away. Some said he went crazy. Who'd blame him?"

"Did she have an ex-boyfriend around, or an ex-husband?"

"Don't know. Only knew her by sight, as I said, and the only man I ever saw around here was her boyfriend. They looked like a nice young couple, with everything in the world to live for. I sometimes wonder if that was the point."

"The point?"

"Of what that crazy man did. Because he'd have to be crazy, wouldn't he? And he'd have to be a man — just to carry her back here, I mean. Couldn't have been easy, the body waterlogged as it was. Not easy to cut off a person's head, come to think of it, even after they're dead. You'd need proper tools. But I always thought the person who done it hated him more than her, you know?"

"Someone killed Lucy Fancher to get at her boyfriend?"

"I'm not saying he knew them. I'm saying he mighta saw 'em. In town, or at the diner up on Route 40. They looked happy together. There are some men who would begrudge another man the love of a pretty woman. You ever play checkers when you were a kid?"

172

"What?" The conversation became more sur-real at every turn.

"I used to go to a friend's house, after school, play checkers. His little brother wanted to play, but it's a one-on-one game, and there's no way to make it three-person. Besides, he didn't know how to play for beans. So we told him to go away. Well, he — he —" The gabby neighbor was suddenly at a loss for words. When he spoke again, his voice was lower, as if he feared being overheard. "He whipped it out and sprayed that board like a dog marking his terri-tory. If he wasn't going to play checkers, no one was going to play checkers."

"This theory of yours — is it part of the local gossip, too, or just based on your observations about human nature?"

She had tried to sound respectful, but the man drew himself up, affronted.

"It's good as anything they ever come up with. Better than anything ol' Carl Dewitt came up with, and I didn't go crazy in the process, did I?"

"Who's Carl Dewitt?" Tess asked. But he was already walking away, leaving her alone in the backyard. Tess glanced at the concrete back steps, trying to imagine how the scene had looked on a grayer, colder day, when the sun set so much earlier. From a distance, in the dark, the body had probably looked like a straw man, some child's tasteless joke. Close up? Close up, that discovery could be enough to drive a man crazy. She wondered if Carl Dewitt was Lucy Fancher's boyfriend, the one whose happiness another man might have begrudged.

And she knew it would be a long time before Lucy Fancher's landlord ever sold this property.

After almost five years at the *Elkton Democrat*, Margo Duncan almost quivered with ambition. When she heard that a private investigator from Baltimore wanted to talk to someone about the Fancher case, she crossed the small newsroom in three bounds, chattering before she reached Tess's side.

"That was *my* story," she said. "The editors totally screwed it up. They kept saying, *You can't have decapitations in a family newspaper!* Why? It's the news, it's a fact. It's not like I dwelt on the details. Do you know how hard it is to sever a human head?"

Tess nodded, fearful this young woman would tell her if she didn't.

"So it's her, right? I mean, they have the head and her driver's license. But I'm not allowed to say they have just a head. They change it to 'North East woman has been found dead on the toll bridge, an apparent victim of foul play,' blah, blah, blah. As if it could be a suicide! And then, when her body shows up, propped up on the back steps —"

"With a jack-o'-lantern. Or so I've been told."

"Well, how do you write that when they don't let you say in the first place that all they had was a head? Besides, the cops were saying I couldn't include the jack-o'-lantern part because it's something only the killer knows, and my bosses took their side. So small-town. I looked like an idiot. I think the publisher was just thinking about real estate values. That area was going up then. Visions of property taxes danced in his head."

Margo's rat-a-tat rhythms seemed to have been modeled, in equal parts, on Rosalind Russell in *His Girl Friday* and the little chicken hawk who dogged Foghorn Leghorn through so many Saturday-morning cartoons. Tess felt weary. It had been a long day and she was at least sixty miles from home. She yearned for her bed, her boyfriend, and her dogs, in more or less that order.

She took Margo by the elbow. "Isn't there a break room around here?"

There was, there always was. No newspaper could publish without a row of vending machines somewhere in the building, filled with salty snacks and sodas and scalded coffee that missed the paper cups three out of five times. Margo Duncan chose a box of Mike & Ikes and began tossing them back as if they were tranquilizers and she was the main character in a sex-and-shopping novel.

"Want one?" She rattled the box at Tess.

"No, thanks."

"No fat. I'm not saying they're good for you, or even low in calories, but it's pure sugar. You burn it off."

Margo clearly did. Although she was of medium height and build, she had the jangly nerves of a toy poodle.

"I used to be a reporter," Tess said. "Down in Baltimore."

"At the *Beacon-Light*? Can you get me an interview?"

"I worked for the competition before it went under." The frown on Margo Duncan's face indicated she had forgotten Baltimore was once a two-newspaper town. "But you can use my name to get your foot in the door. The editors know me."

They also hated her, but let Margo discover this on her own.

"Why are you interested in the Fancher case? Is there a story in it for me?"

A typical reporter's question. "No, it's pretty boring stuff. I'm just looking at open homicide cases, chosen at random. It's an exercise in statistical analysis."

That shut her interest down. In fact, Margo became positively sullen. She slumped in her seat, fishing the green Mike & Ikes from the box.

"I'm curious to know if there's anything else that didn't make the paper — besides the head thing, I mean."

"Does that suck or what? They said it didn't pass the breakfast test. Postmortem, I kept telling them, postmortem."

"I imagine it's hard to remove someone's head *before* death," Tess said.

"Which isn't to say it hasn't been done. Let me tell you, I've read all the books, all the life stories: Bundy, Dahmer, and lesser-known ones like Maryland's own Metheney. People do some seriously sick shit."

But books were the only place where Margo had encountered the seriously sick. She was no more than twenty-seven, and she was a young twenty-seven, with a face so clear and untroubled that Tess knew she had seen very little of the world. Margo Duncan was all talk.

"In your opinion," she began, and Margo sat up a little straighter, delighted someone wanted her opinion, "in your opinion, how'd the local cops handle the case?"

"The local guys were cool. The state cop was a little jerky, but it turned out he had never caught a case like that either. Carl Dewitt was the king of *no comment*. Like he had anything to say anyway."

It was the second time Tess had heard that name in as many hours. "Carl Dewitt was an investigator?"

"Carl Dewitt was the Toll Facilities cop who found the head and was, you'll pardon the expression, like a dog with a bone. He couldn't let go of the case. To his detriment. The state police finally wrestled it away from him, after he had to take a leave for knee surgery." She stopped to think, using her index finger to work a piece of candy out of her teeth. "Or maybe it was back surgery. Something bad enough to get him disability, I remember that much."

"Did they have suspects? Was it one of those cases where they just couldn't make the case?"

Margo shook her head. "They didn't have anything."

"Did they look at the boyfriend?"

"Sure. Alan Palmer was down the shore in Saint Michaels, camping out before a big estate sale."

"Camping out?"

"Palmer was sort of like a go-between for decorators and high-end antique dealers in Baltimore, Wilmington — even Philadelphia. I think they call them pickers, something like that."

"Scouts," Tess said.

"Really?" Margo wrinkled her nose. "Anyway, he shopped the auctions and antique sales with their wish lists. A huge estate sale, the whole contents of the house of some one-hit wonder of a writer, was scheduled for eight a.m. October thirtieth. Palmer went down October twenty-ninth. They were going to start handing out numbers at five a.m., and he wanted to be in the first batch of people let in. He planned to sleep in his truck."

"So the cops go down to Saint Michaels and find him shopping an estate sale?"

Margo nodded.

"How did he take it?"

"Better than you think, actually. At least, he was okay for Part One. Maybe he was still in shock, I don't know. But he got through identifying her head. It was when the body showed up that . . . I think someone came to town and took him away, kind of quiet-like. Later, the cops told me he was hospitalized, in a rehab facility somewhere out of state."

"Drugs?"

"No, it's physical rehab. He broke his neck in a car accident. Might be DWI, I dunno. Who could blame him?"

"Had Lucy been married before? Did she have an ex, or even family members that the police suspected?"

"There's an ex-boyfriend, a super-scary guy. His arms are so tattooed he looks like he's always wearing sleeves. But they never charged him. Best I can tell, the cops have given up."

"The state police just gave up?"

"The case is still open. Homicides never —"

"Close, I know. Still, it doesn't seem like the kind of case cops give up on."

"They think it was a drifter, someone passing through. So it's not as if it's a public safety risk for the county. And it's not as if it's happened again. But my theory is the other investigators look at Dewitt and figure they don't want to end up like that." Margo looked thoughtful, which in her case meant she managed to still her twitching limbs and features for about five seconds. "The Fancher case is like one of those mummy's tombs, you know? There's a curse on everyone who had anything to do with it.

Dewitt screws up his knee — or his back, whichever — the boyfriend cracks up his car. I wonder if I'm next."

She hugged herself, delighted by her ghoulish theory. Margo was probably trying to calculate if there was a marketable first-person narrative in all this tragedy. After all, what was the use of proximity to a great case if it didn't further your career?

"What was the ex-boyfriend's name?"

"Bonner. Bonner Flood."

"Sounds like someone out of a Faulkner novel."

"He wishes. He's a creep, but a petty one. As I said, the police never charged him. He works in one of the marinas, when he can hold a job."

Tess got up to go, then remembered she had one more thing she wanted to ask. "Did you ever get to interview Alan Palmer?"

"No, but he was the best thing that ever happened to Lucy, apparently. She was working some minimum-wage job, didn't even have her GED, when he came along. Hey, I have a question for you. What do you think of Margo A. Duncan?"

It was always a bad sign, someone speaking of herself in the third person.

"I think . . . you've been a great help," Tess ventured.

"No, I mean the name. I think my byline might be holding me back. I want something more *New York Times*-ian. My middle name is

Alice, which doesn't really work that well, but M.A. Duncan sounds like I've got a master's in doughnuts. Or I could go with M. Alice Duncan."

Tess didn't have the heart to point out that this would simply turn Margo into Malice. "Sounds great," she said, edging toward the door. "I'm sure it will make all the difference."

# Chapter 13

The man with the tattooed arms ended his day with a cheeseburger and a beer, which he all but inhaled, so that a gob of the head stuck to his nose. It was a long pointy nose, like a hound's. That nose would turn out to be the only sharp thing about Bonner Flood.

When he put down his glass and saw Tess, holding out her card, he sighed. "I don't wanna," he said.

"What do you mean?"

"Whatever it is you want, I don't wanna talk about it. I'm off, okay? This is my time, my dinner."

"I'll buy you dinner."

"I don't wanna."

"And give you some cash for your time."

"I don't wanna," repeated this modern-day Bartleby. "Come back tomorrow."

"I don't wanna," Tess said, taking the seat opposite him in the booth. It had not been too hard to find out that Bonner Flood took his evening meal in this diner on Route 40, an authentic one with hand-lettered signs advertising the specials and not a speck of self-conscious charm. The Riverview Diner might be a find, but it could just as well be a dump, staying in business by cultivating a clientele that cared more about prices than food. A waitress shuffled over and, looking much put-upon, took down Tess's order of a Coke, a cheeseburger with everything, and french fries with gravy.

"Lucy Fancher," Tess began.

"Tell Carl Dewitt to go fuck himself."

"Excuse me?"

"My lawyer said he's gotta stop doing this shit to me. If the cops want me, they can jack me up official-like. But they gotta let me live my life in peace."

Dewitt again. It seemed impossible to have a conversation about Lucy Fancher without having one about the former Toll Facilities cop as well.

"I don't know the man," Tess said. "And he probably doesn't want to know me, given that I'm here to examine his work. I'm looking into how some cops do their job."

"Yeah?" That brought his nose out of his beer mug. "I can tell you how. Like it's Nazi Germany, that's how they do their job around here. Like a man's got no rights at all. Dewitt won't stop, and he's not even a cop anymore. Not that he was ever a real cop."

"He hounded you, then?"

"I almost filed police brutality charges against him."

"He hit you?"

"Well, he was dogging me. He talked to me

over and over and over again. He knew I didn't do it, from the first. He said as much. But for some reason he just likes to hear me tell the story. I took a polygraph. Passed it, too. But a week didn't go by that I didn't see Carl Dewitt staring at me. Down at the marina, in the bar up the street, here. Like a little freckled ghost, following me around." Then, as an after-thought, "I *hate* freckles."

Flood finished the rest of his beer with one deep inhale and wiped the back of his mouth with his arm. The tattoos had once been dis-crete designs. But there were so many crowded together, and the lines had faded over time until his arms looked more discolored than anything else. The right was blue-purple, like a bruise, the left more reddish, as if he had been badly burned.

Tess sipped the beer the waitress had brought in lieu of her Coca-Cola. Bad sign. She drank so Bonner Flood might feel more companion-able. Now that was something to tell Dr. Armistead: She had to drink for her job some-times, even when she didn't want to. What would he make of that?

"I'm Tess Monaghan," she said in her best voice, a sweet, serious tone she knew men liked.

"Bonner Flood," he said. "But you seem to know that."

"Tell me about Lucy."

"I thought you weren't here to hound me."

184

"Not about her death. About *her*, her life. What was she like?"

"She was okay. We were together two–three years, off and on."

Tess had done her homework at the district court this time. She knew the "off" times Flood alluded to usually came on drunken weekends when he threw Lucy around the living room. By Monday morning, he was sober and she was forgiving.

"You break up with her, or did she break up with you?"

"Neither. I ended up in jail for six months."

"Assault?"

"Uh-uh, more serious. Poaching." There was not a wisp of a smile on Flood's face. "I had to do a little county time while waiting trial, and then I got time served. I come out, Lucy's got this new guy. And I'm glad, you know, I'm just glad for her. Plus, it makes her somebody else's problem. I don't have to hear any more about how I should be doing this or doing that. You see, Lucy wasn't any better'n me — but she wanted to be."

"Where was she from? I couldn't find any other Fanchers in these parts."

"Virginia? North Carolina? Somewhere south of here, I know that much."

"And you weren't mad when you got out of jail and found out she had a new guy?" The cheeseburger arrived, but plain, without the "everything." It barely had cheese. The french fries had

come in gravy, as requested, but they were ice-
cold on the inside and the gravy appeared to
have been salvaged from Jiffy Lube.

"Wasn't her fault. Truth be told, when I went
to jail, she couldn't make the rent on her own.
She had to find a new man. A girl like Lucy,
that's how she lives. Waiting tables, working at
the Royal Farm, she's not gonna make enough
to cover her expenses. I took Lucy away from
someone, someone took her away from me. She
was like Tarzan."

"Tarzan?"

"She went from tree to tree, and she always
knew where the next vine was."

"Was she pretty?"

Flood stared at the ceiling, as if this question
were of cosmic significance. "Not when I knew
her. She had a figure — she was one of those
tiny girls with big breasts, you know?"

"No," Tess said.

"You've got —" Flood began.

"I'm not tiny," Tess said, stifling what Flood
obviously believed to be a compliment. "You
said Lucy wasn't pretty 'when I knew her.'
Something change?"

"Uh-huh. I saw her at Happy Harry's, about
a month before she died. Her hair was cut different, really short, which I don't much care
for. Turns out she had a pretty little face under
all that hair. She'd gotten her teeth bleached
and fixed — she'd had a big space between the
front two and a snaggle tooth with a gold

186

crown. I didn't much care for what she was wearing. Like I said, she had a good figure, and she had taken to hiding it away, like it was a secret. I tried to talk to her a little, but she didn't have time for me. Said she was running late, on her way home from her community college class."

"Sounds pretty rude," Tess said.

"It was more than rude. It pissed me off. I knew Lucy Fancher. She wasn't better'n me."

"Maybe she was."

"What? No one's better'n anyone else. Not in America."

"You believe that bullshit? Whoever you are, there's someone better than you and usually someone worse. Someone nicer, with better manners and more money."

"Having more money doesn't make you superior."

"Then why do we call it *better off?* Look, I'm not saying it's right. I'm just saying it *is*. When you were bouncing Lucy off the walls every Saturday night —"

"Not *every* Saturday night," Flood objected, a sudden stickler for accuracy.

"— you were on the same footing. You went to jail, Lucy started moving up in the world. Did you want her back?"

"No. I had a girl by then. I don't have a problem getting women."

Flood was probably telling the truth, a sad commentary on her gender. Tess found herself thinking about the boyfriend who had cheated on her. Actually, there were more than one, and Jonathan Ross had been a member of the club. But right now she was thinking about a particularly smarmy guy back in college, a guy who seemed to think his dick was like the root of a plant: If he didn't get it damp on a regular basis, it was at risk of drying up and falling off. The last time she had caught him cheating — and it was to her everlasting shame that there was a *last* time, as opposed to a one-and-only time — the last time she caught him, he had explained that the woman in question was his old girlfriend. Apparently ex-girlfriends were like territories on which he held lifetime mineral rights.

"I'm not saying you wanted Lucy back," Tess said. "But maybe once? For old times' sake?"

"I called her the next day, told her how nice it was to see her, asked if we could have a drink some time. She liked that. She said it was *civilized*, having a drink with her old boyfriend. She said her fiancé — that was her word, fiancé — was out of town on business, and she'd meet me for a drink. I remember she ordered a white wine spritzer. Very fancy, she was, all full of herself."

"How'd the evening end up?"

"The way it usually did with me and her." Bonner Flood was smirking, proud of himself. "Lucy with her legs in the air, asking for more."

Tess studied the man. It was unfathomable to

her that he could be sexually desirable to anyone, under any circumstances. There weren't enough white wine spritzers in all of Cecil County.

"You know," she said, "Oliver Twist didn't ask for more because the gruel was good."

"Huh?"

"If Lucy was always asking for more, maybe it was because she never got enough."

Flood reached his blue-purple right arm toward the soiled creases of his blue-jeaned crotch. "You wanna see what I got in here? You wanna see?"

"God, no."

"All right, then," he said, as if he had won some debate. Tess didn't have many flashes of intuition, and she didn't trust many of the ones she did have. But she knew, in that instant, that Bonner Flood had *not* reconnected with his old flame. She saw Lucy — or Lucy as she imagined her, for she had never seen so much as a photograph of the girl — arrayed in her version of business attire, primly shaking Flood's hand outside the bar. Lucy had turned Flood down.

Which would explain why the ex-cop, Dewitt, had been dogging him all this time. It wasn't a bad motive, not that motives counted for anything. And Flood worked in a marina. He could keep a body in water for a couple of days.

"You didn't sleep with her. Not that night."

"I did." Moral outrage, as if lying about

sleeping with another man's girlfriend was worse than doing it.

"I don't believe you."

"Look, I'd take it back if I could. Believe me, I'd take it back. If I knew that some crazy cop was going to dog me until the end of my life, asking me over and over again about the last time I saw her, what she said, how she looked, if she mentioned anything unusual."

"Carl Dewitt."

"Carl Dewitt," he said wearily.

Tess gave up. She gave up on her cheeseburger, which tasted like compressed cardboard. She gave up on her fries. She gave up on her beer, which was flattish and briny, as if it had been mixed with river water. She gave up on Bonner Flood. Whatever had happened here, the police had not been lax or indifferent. She threw some money on a table, enough to cover both their meals, and stalked out. Job over. What a waste of time and mileage.

She hated to admit it to herself, but she was disappointed. Despite her cynical protestations, she had wanted this job to be what Whitney had promised. She wanted to work for the good guys. She wanted — did she dare say this out loud? — to be a force for good. Part of the solution. She wasn't so sure the state's laws needed to be changed and revised, but she knew Maryland's mind-set did. Miriam Greenhouse was right: Every time a man killed a woman, it was reported as another love story gone bad, especially if the man then finished himself off. Where was the love in this?

A light rain had started to fall. April was a petulant month in these parts. Tess sat in her car, anxious to get home, too weary to turn the key in the ignition. From here, the diner looked charming and cozy. Talk about a trompe l'oeil. A young couple sat in one of the front booths, leaning toward each other, laughing at some shared joke, the kind of laugh that was almost like a kiss, only better. The young man reached out and touched her face. It made Tess ache, and she had someone at home.

*There are some men who would begrudge another man the love of a pretty woman.* That had been the lunatic neighbor's theory. By the light of day, it had seemed ridiculous. People killed for a lot of reasons, but rootless envy was not on that list to Tess's knowledge. Besides, if you yearned to be part of a happy couple, wouldn't you kill the man and make a play for the woman? No, it made no sense.

Still, something was bugging her. She dug through the folders in the passenger seat and found Tiffani Gunts, the grainy reproduction of her high school graduation photo. Lots of dark hair, tiny face. Lucy Fancher's physical particulars were the same, before the haircut. The life was even more similar. Abusive ex-boyfriend, followed by a new life, full of promise, a new place to live, a fiancé. Then a sudden violent force rips through the happy

191

household with the power and rage of a natural disaster, a hurricane coming to shore at the spot it is least expected. The woman is dead, the man is destroyed.

The storm moves on, implacable, searching for another place to come aground.

Tess went back into the diner, found the phone book, and tore the page she wanted from its residential listings. Dome light on, map propped on her steering wheel, she drove haphazardly through the streets of North East, running into the same dead ends and cul-de-sacs that had plagued her throughout the afternoon. North East nights were darker than Baltimore ones. Even with a full moon, it was like swimming through black water. Tess began to fear she would end up in a ditch or miss the curve on one of these back roads and slam into a tree.

But eventually she found the house she wanted, a white bungalow with a front porch and only a sliver of land between it and the water. There was a dock, the silhouette of a sailboat visible in the moonlight. The house was dark except for the throbbing blue-white glow of a television set, the light pulsing through lace curtains.

The man who opened the door had gingery hair, sad blue eyes, and so many freckles crowded onto his round, placid face that he gave the impression of being striped, like a red tabby cat.

"My name is Tess Monaghan. I'm a private investigator from Baltimore, and I think there may be a new angle on the Lucy Fancher case."

"About time," said Carl Dewitt.

# Chapter 14

"I saved everything," Carl Dewitt said. "Copies of everything, I mean. I didn't take away anything official, not even my own notes. But I xeroxed everything I could find."

He was digging through a cardboard box, looking at various papers, frowning at them, clearly in search of something in particular. The box was sitting in the middle of his small living room as if he had, in fact, been waiting for Tess's knock. Or anyone's knock. Judging by the faint circles on the top, he had been using it as a makeshift coffee table, setting glasses on the box as he sat in his Barca-lounger and watched the enormous flat-screen television that dominated one wall.

When he came upon photographs, he would thrust them at Tess and continue his methodical search. She wished he wouldn't. The only thing more unsettling than photographs of Lucy Fancher's head were photographs of Lucy Fancher's body. But Carl didn't seem to notice. He hummed tunelessly as he sifted through papers. He didn't seem the least bit perturbed that a stranger had shown up on his doorstep in the dark, babbling about the possibility that the

Fancher homicide could be related to one in Frederick several years earlier. If Tess had to describe his mood, she would say he was happy, almost excited.

"Did you know Lucy Fancher before —" Tess stopped, groping for the right words.

He lifted his eyes from the box. "Before I found her head on the bridge?"

"Yes."

"North East isn't that small. Sometimes I think I might have seen her once or twice in town. But that's wishful thinking."

"Wishful thinking?"

"Wouldn't you rather know someone as a whole living, breathing person instead of just a head?" His voice was mild, no different from someone expressing a preference for chocolate over broccoli. He had found whatever he wanted and settled back into the Barcalounger, the only piece of furniture in the small living room that seemed to fit him — literally. Its contours had molded to his body over the years so it was almost like a tailored suit. The rest of the decor tended toward flowers and doilies and chintz.

"Now see, this always bothered me," he said, flapping a large cardboard rectangle at Tess. "They kept a calendar. The days that her boyfriend were gone were crossed off — see?"

He handed Tess a calendar from a local insurance company, the months noted by not-very-good photographs of the Chesapeake Bay. Shot through a gauzy sentimental fog, the photos managed to render the bay generic and uninteresting. Beneath a harvest scene, the last three days of October had been circled.

"You said you took *copies* of everything. But this is the real thing. Shouldn't it be logged in with the rest of the stuff?"

Carl blushed, which made him appear to be the same red-orange shade from the open neck of his shirt to the top of his scalp. "It's something I found later, and nobody else seemed to care, so I just kept it. Otherwise it was just going to be packed away, with all the other stuff in the house. But I thought it might be significant."

"How?"

"Like I said, it shows the dates her boyfriend was away." He flipped through, showing her where days were circled.

"It doesn't say what these days were," Tess pointed out. "They're just circles."

"Yeah, but we know he was away those three days in October. So I worked backward from that. Someone else could've figured it out, too."

"You think someone saw this ahead of time? That the killer had this information?"

"Yeah, maybe. Only the calendar wasn't out in the open, like it would be in most houses. I found it in a kitchen drawer, one of those drawers where people keep their junk."

"So if it's not where someone can see it, how can someone know when the boyfriend — what was his name?"

"Alan Palmer."

"How can they know when he's going to be away?"

"I figured whoever killed Lucy hid the calendar, so no one would make the connection. But if it was on the refrigerator — and there's a mark, up on top, as if it had been held in place by a magnet — it would have been in plain view."

Tess held the calendar closer to a small table lamp. She couldn't help noticing it had a rose-colored shade that was fringed in maroon. There was a faint rust-colored line, the kind a metal clip might leave behind.

"Anyway, let's say you're a plumber or a cable television installer. You come and go through people's houses all the time, you see things, you take notice of things. You realize there's a pretty young woman whose boyfriend travels a lot. You realize the calendar is the key to when he's gone. Maybe she even tells you that's what the circles are for, or you're making an appointment and she says, 'No, not then, because Alan is away at the end of the month.' But if you take it off the refrigerator and put it in a drawer, nobody else makes the connection."

"So did Lucy have anyone do work on the house in the year before she was killed?"

Carl's shoulders slumped. "Not that I could find. But that doesn't mean she didn't use somebody. There are a lot of fellas around here who work off the books, you know? Who do stuff on a cash-only basis."

197

Tess was following her own thoughts, down a different track. "If the same man killed Tiffani Gunts and Lucy Fancher, how did he come to meet them, to fixate on them? You couldn't meet such women by sheer accident. There's a connection we haven't figured out yet. And why are the deaths so different?"

"You said the girl in Frederick died of a gunshot wound," Carl pointed out. "So did Lucy."

"Yes, but Tiffani's body was — well, intact. Lucy's head was cut off postmortem, and the killer kept the body for a couple of days. That's a pretty big change in just eighteen months."

"Serial killers do change their methods, contrary to popular belief. And they don't leave little notes for the cops, egging them on, inviting them to come and find them."

"Who said anything about a serial killer? We're talking about two homicides, and we haven't proved they're connected. It's just a wild hunch on my part."

"A serial killer doesn't have to kill dozens and dozens of people," Carl said. "Law enforcement guidelines used to say it has to be three or more, but others say two is plenty. Maybe we're seeing this guy early in his career."

"Please don't use that word to talk about homicide, okay? Killing is not a *career*, unless you're a hit man."

Carl leaned forward in his chair, which took some effort, for he fit so well into its deep-set grooves that its slick surface stuck to his skin. He almost had to peel himself away, which made a rude sucking sound wherever chair met flesh.

"You came to my door, remember? You're the one who made this link. Don't be afraid of your own intuition. I stopped being a cop almost three years ago. But I never stopped hoping for a break in this case."

"This isn't what I was hired to find. Quite the opposite. I'm looking for evidence that law-enforcement types who don't handle a lot of homicides make basic mistakes —" She broke off, realizing a second too late how rude she must sound. *I'm here because you and your ilk are supposed to be bozos.* But Carl just nodded, signaling her to continue. "My clients care about domestic violence, not the random acts of some psychopath. This has nothing to do with what I've been asked to investigate."

"I dunno." Carl's face glowed in the lamplight. His head was very round, and the orange cast of his hair and complexion made Tess think of a jack-o'-lantern — which unfortunately made her think of Lucy Fancher. The photos that Carl had plucked from his cardboard box were still sitting in plain view, on a dainty table covered with a lacy antimacassar. She nudged them away with her elbow.

"These are crimes against women, after all," Carl continued. "You said you thought it was all about jealousy, that someone had set out to destroy two people and their happiness. Do you know where that other girl's boyfriend ended up?"

Tess shook her head. "Out of state, according to her family. He was heartbroken because he couldn't have custody of his girlfriend's daughter. It was easier for him, apparently, just to cut off contact."

"Well, as you know, Alan Palmer is stuck in a hospital, living on a ventilator. The hospital social worker called me when he was transferred, said he'd probably live out his days there."

"The reporter at the local paper seemed to be hinting he had a breakdown."

"The reporter at the local paper," Carl said, "doesn't know shit. She thinks everyone's always having a breakdown because she's constantly on the verge of one."

Having met Margo Duncan, Tess could see his point.

"Anyway, let's say you're right. Let's say this killer wants to hurt the guy as much as he wants to kill the girl. Maybe more. So that's why he had to ratchet it up, raise the stakes. He didn't manage to destroy the first guy, but he sure as hell ruined Alan Palmer. I'm not sure the guy even took a drink before this happened. Two women dead, two men shattered. That's a kind of domestic violence, isn't it?"

"You keep saying *he*. Is that just generic sexism? Or do you assume a serial killer — assuming this is a serial killer — has to be a man?"

"More bunk," Carl said, waving his hand in front of his face as if to dispel a bad odor. "There are plenty of women serial killers. But I just figure this is a man. It's the kind of jealousy a man would feel, you know? I hate to say it about my own kind, but when you see a guy with a good-looking woman, you're kinda like, 'Hey, how did he get that?' And then, 'Where can I get me one?' Alan Palmer was a nice enough guy, but ordinary. If someone saw him with a pretty girl, they'd want to know how he did it. What about your guy?"

For a moment, Tess thought he was talking about Crow. Even when she understood the question, she wasn't entirely comfortable with this your guy/my guy rhetoric. It made it sound as if they were in a rotisserie baseball league, swapping stats about starting pitchers.

"I don't know what Eric Shivers looked like. But Tiffani was pretty enough, almost like a changeling. It was hard to imagine how such a tiny, elfin girl emerged from that sour, doughy family."

"And what did your guy do?"

"Salesman — in camera supplies, I think. Or maybe it was film. Something to do with photography."

"Hmmmm." Carl stroked his chin. "Hard to see how someone hooks up professionally with these two, one being in camera supplies, the other an antique scout. Where was he the night she died?"

"Spartina, Virginia. It's a college town in the Shenandoah Valley."

"Out of town. Just like Alan."

"Yeah."

Carl stood, with some difficulty. It wasn't just that his chair held him tight. One of his knees, the left one, seemed to give him some trouble. He wobbled a little, but he didn't lose his balance.

"Let's go." He was remarkably pleased with himself.

"Go where? It's nine o'clock. The only place I'm going tonight is back to Baltimore. This has been the creepiest day I've spent in a long time, and I just want to sleep in my own bed, with my dogs. And my boyfriend."

Carl looked disappointed. "I didn't really mean — didn't you get it? 'Let's go.' "

"To Spartina? Right now? It's almost nine o'clock."

"No, you don't get it. 'Let's go.' It's the key line of *The Wild Bunch*. William Holden says, 'Let's go,' and there's, like. . . ." His voice trailed off at the incomprehension in her face. "You'll have to see it sometime. It's only the greatest movie ever made. I've got it on DVD and wide-screen VHS. The scorpion in the opening shot looks six feet long!"

He gestured to the bookcases that flanked his large television. There were some books there, but there were far more DVDs and videocassettes.

"So you don't want to go anywhere? You're just doing movie dialogue?"

"No, I think we should go to Spartina. Your guy went there a lot, isn't that what you said?"

"At least once a month, according to his almost in-laws."

"And Alan had to go down the shore on a regular basis, to hit the auctions. Okay, picture this. There's a bartender, works in some nowhere place. Guy pulls his girl's picture out when he's had a few beers. She's pretty. She's wonderful. He's going to marry her. Can't stand being away from her so much. Or maybe he shows her photograph to another traveling salesman type, a guy who can't get a girl, doesn't have anyone back home."

"Sounds a little crazy."

She caught a flash of ire in Carl Dewitt's face, a stereotypical redhead's temper.

"It's not *crazy*. Maybe far-fetched, but I'm just talking out loud, trying to think this through. You came to *my* door, remember? Well, now you're here, so listen to me.

"I know everything about how Lucy Fancher died. I know everything about Lucy Fancher. I know her birth date and her perfume — lily of the valley. I know she wore a color she called periwinkle, although it looked like just plain lavender to everybody else. I know she had put a hundred dollars down on a wedding dress and veil on Labor Day weekend. It was going to be a Christmas wedding. I know what the weather was like the night she died — cold, for October, and damp. I know the tides for that day and that the moon was new. Her nearest neighbor watched the ten o'clock news before he went to bed, the next-nearest neighbor gave out Butterfingers and Baby Ruths to the trick-or-treaters."

"I —"

But Carl was too wound up to hear her, to hear anything. "You think the hot-shit state trooper who was in charge of the case knows even half of what I know? One-fourth? One-tenth? I don't know if there's any link between her and this girl who died out in Frederick. But if there is, I'll be the one to see. No one else can help you, assuming you want any help. Assuming you really understand what you've found here."

The photographs of Lucy Fancher were still in view. They were poorly lit, the kind of black-and-white crime-scene photos that Tess rushed past whenever she steeled herself to read text-books on investigative techniques. Death was so undignified. That was its real power. People looked stupid when they were dead.

"If you come down to Baltimore tomorrow, we can drive to Spartina together. It will be a long day, but with two of us driving it shouldn't be so bad."

Carl nodded at the photos. "She got to you, didn't she?"

Tess started to shake her head no but ended up agreeing.

"She gets to everyone, eventually."

He awakens by the side of the road and for one panicky moment cannot remember where he is. Can barely remember who he is. But slowly he gets his bearings. There is his old patchwork pillow beneath his cheek, which he imagines still carries the scent of his boyhood home, although the cover has been washed many, many times. Not a week goes by that he doesn't stop at a Laundromat and watch the faded gingham pieces turn somersaults through the porthole of a coin-operated dryer.

He is in the back of the van, parked somewhere off Route 5 in southern Maryland. The rear of the van is windowless, but light is playing at the edges of the windshield, sneaking in. It had been late when he finished last night, and he was bone-tired. It's hard work, what he does, physically demanding. The people who hire him don't always get that. They understand the mess, the need for care and discretion, but they don't realize how strong you have to be, how much manual labor is involved. Exhausted, incapable of driving the rest of the way home, he had pulled into a parking lot near the Amish flea market and slept his usual dreamless sleep. He is here, the time is now, he is whole, all is well.

He had a real scare in Saint Mary's City last night. He thought he saw a woman he once knew, peering hard into his face. Luckily, he doesn't have the beard and his hair is back to its normal shade, but someone who had been close to him might see the resemblance. Then again, people don't see what they don't expect to see, and no one ever expects to see him. Still, the incident served to remind him of all the places that are lost to him.

That's why he's trying to get everything under control. He was not meant to live like this. He wants to put down roots, stay put. He wants what everyone wants, and there's no crime in that.

He rolls up his sleeping bag, places the pillow in its usual spot, on the passenger seat of the van, and sets off north, the rising sun almost painful in the perfection of its shape, the flatness of its color. This is not the sun he grew up with. This is an angry sun, querulous and irritable, appearing on the horizon with great reluctance, then shooting up into the sky as if it wants to get the day done. He asked his mother once if she noticed how many colors she lost upon moving here, how the more subtle shades and variations had been drained from the sky and the water, even the trees and the land. She just looked at him as she often did — fond but uncomprehending, utterly baffled. Love does not guarantee understanding.

Today, as he glances at the sun off to the right, watches it ascend in the sky and change from plain red to dull yellow, he realizes they are in the same boat, him and the sun. They are in exile, unhappy and hollow. The earth still revolves around the sun, but the world tends to forget that fact, even as the sun's rays reach through the thinning atmosphere, quietly claiming more victims.

Ah, but he has a plan to fix his life. The sun will have to save itself.

# Chapter 15

Carl Dewitt was given to unnervingly long and deep silences. Such a capacity for quiet could be construed as a sign of strength and power — when the person squinting at the horizon was Clint Eastwood or Dewitt's beloved William Holden.

But in Carl's case, his inability to make conversation on the long drive to Virginia simply made Tess aware of his crippling shyness. Unless the subject was Lucy Fancher, he was incapable of warming to any topic. Sometimes, even he became so unnerved by the silence between them that he punctuated it by reading the highway signs out loud.

"BEST BISCUITS AROUND," he said, as they turned south, not far from Hagerstown. Then, a few miles later: "FLYING J TRUCK STOP. CLEAN RESTROOMS, SHOWERS. CRACKER BARREL. VISIT OUR GIFT SHOP."

His readings, however, were not endorsements. Carl was appalled when Tess asked where he wanted to stop for breakfast. "I brought along a box of Chix 'n' Stix," he said, pulling out a brand of chicken-flavored crackers that Tess thought had ceased to exist years ago. She declined, and they compromised on a drive-through just outside Martinsburg, West Virginia. Tess had liked the bacon biscuit, soaked with grease, more than she cared to admit.

Back in the car, Carl also seemed to find the radio barely tolerable, grunting when Tess punched the buttons to keep the NPR newscast coming in as they passed through one public radio station's universe after another.

"That's news?" he asked at one point, after a report on the funding crisis of an Italian opera company.

"Sure, it's news. You have to think of the broadcast as an entire newspaper. A story like that would be in the arts section."

Another grunt.

"Let me guess. You read sports, the front page, and nothing else."

"I glance at the front page. I don't follow sports anymore."

"Anymore?"

"I don't know. Seems pretty trivial. I liked the Philadelphia teams when I was younger, but only because that station came in clearer than the Baltimore one. But, as the Bible says, I've put away childish things."

"Are you religious?"

"Not particularly. I just remember that verse from when my parents dragged me to church."

"Which was —"

"Methodist."

"No, I mean where did you grow up?"

"Right in North East, in the house where I live now. I've lived my whole life in Cecil County except for college."

"Which was —"

"University of Delaware." He allowed himself a small smile. "The Fighting Blue Hens. I didn't finish."

There was something almost compulsive in that last tacked-on sentence, as if he didn't want to be caught embroidering his résumé in any way.

"Why not?"

"My mom got sick. So I came home and took the job with the state. When I found out I would be stationed at the bridge, right outside my hometown, I thought it was the luckiest day in my life. And I guess it was. . . ."

He did not finish the thought. But Tess thought she understood. The murder of Lucy Fancher had cut through this man's life, separating him from the person he once was as surely as her killer had separated Lucy's head from her body. She wondered if Carl had daydreamed, in the boredom of his old job, about doing something more exciting than helping stranded motorists or chasing down people who didn't pay their tolls. It would have been natural for a young man to yearn in such a fashion.

More natural still to regret those yearnings in the wake of what had happened.

"And your mom?"

"Died. Going on eight years this summer. Time flies."

"So it does. We're almost to Spartina."

Spartina was on the long stretch of interstate that cut through the Blue Ridge Mountains in Virginia, near the Shenandoah River. A college town, home to one of the state colleges, it looked like any other small city on an interstate. Lots of fast-food restaurants and one mall, which had leached the life from downtown, now a place of empty shops and small diners that closed by early afternoon. Only the landscape and the syrupy-thick southern accents reminded Tess that she had traveled quite a way from Baltimore.

Their first stop was the small motel, an old-fashioned motor court, where Eric Shivers had spent his last untroubled night on this earth. Spartina had several chain motels, but Eric had been a regular at this family-owned place off the beaten path, a U-shaped arrangement of whitewashed stucco, with planters of geraniums outside the office entrance. The place lacked the amenities that most business travelers considered crucial — a twenty-four-hour restaurant, voice mail, and rooms wired for laptops — but it was homey and restful, the Shenandoah visible from the trampled side yard, where rusty spikes stood waiting for a game of horseshoes.

"Eric Shivers?" The man behind the counter was jolly-looking, with a round flushed face.

Bald, he had allowed his remaining fringe of hair to grow wild and woolly, so he looked a little clownish, but in a good way. "Oh, Lord, I haven't thought of that poor boy for years."

"You remember him, then?" Tess took the lead automatically, although she and Carl had not discussed this beforehand.

"Surely. I think I'd remember Eric even if it weren't for that awful thing that happened. I still remember those police officers calling here, then coming down from Maryland to break the news. He couldn't drive, one of them had to take his van back up there. Oh, he was broken up." The old man shook his head, lost in the memory. "He came here regular-like, at least once a month for six months, when he was on business. I suppose he'd still be coming, if it weren't for what happened."

"And what did he do exactly?"

"Salesman?" But the manager-owner's voice scaled up, unsure. "He paid calls on customers, but I was never clear — something about chemicals?"

"Photographic supplies, perhaps?"

"That was it." He looked relieved. "Something to do with chemicals for photographs."

"So did he go to camera shops or local photography studios?"

"I don't rightly know."

"Did he have a regular client he always visited?"

"Oh, Lord, I don't know. I just checked him

in, didn't quiz him much. He'd usually get down here in the evening, so he could be up and out early the next day, making his rounds, stay one more night, then head out the next day. So I guess he had a lot of customers in the area, but I never knew who they were. I was grateful for his business. We're more of a seasonal operation, though we do get the overflow on the big school weekends. Eric was a small-town boy."

Even as Tess and the manager spoke, Carl had slid the local yellow pages from the desk, opened it to CAMERA SUPPLIES, and jotted down every store listed. He then found a listing for PHOTOGRAPHY STUDIOS and did the same.

"So what happened to Eric?" the manager asked. "He go home?"

"I'm not sure. His in-laws" — it seemed only polite to refer to the Guntses this way — "said he went back home, somewhere in the South."

"The South? This is the South. Maryland's north."

"It's all below the Mason-Dixon line," Tess said. "But I meant his original home."

"Oh. I just assumed he always lived in Maryland. Now where did I get that idea? Boy, I haven't thought of him in years. We had some real nice chats that winter, we sure did."

"About what?"

"He told me all about his plans, even asked one time what kind of diamond I thought girls like best. 'Big ones,' I said, meaning it as a joke. But he took everything so seriously. His eyes got all big and dark and he said, 'Not my girl, Mr. Schell. If I gave her a piece of chicken wire she'd wear it as if it were the Hope diamond. She loves *me*, not the things I give her.' Oh, he was a literal boy in his way. You couldn't tease him for anything."

"The Hope diamond?" Carl spoke up for the first time since he had grunted his name. "Isn't that the one that's cursed?"

Mr. Schell looked perplexed. "I thought it was the big old diamond that Richard Burton gave Elizabeth Taylor. But I could be wrong. Memory's not what it was."

By day's end, Tess and Carl had canvassed almost every camera supply store and photography studio in the greater Spartina area. It seemed to Tess that they had questioned almost every person in Spartina who owned a camera, even those disposable ones.

"Modern society is too damn mobile," she grumbled.

"What do you mean?"

"In the six years since Eric Shivers last visited this town, the jobs at these stores and studios have turned over four–five times."

"Not the managers," Carl pointed out. "Besides, what did you expect? The person we're looking for moved on, most likely. You heard the man back at the motel. Eric Shivers couldn't help bragging on his girlfriend. So some twisted minimum-wage slave takes it into his head to go up to Frederick and kill her. Then he moves on."

"So how does he meet Alan Palmer if he's working in a camera store?"

"I don't know. Maybe he's shooting studio portraits in Kmart. Lucy had one of those done about two weeks before she died. Maybe he's selling hot dogs at Orange Julius."

"Then why are we here?" Tess was getting angry at herself. She hated errors of momentum, mistakes born of rushing forward without taking time to think. It was the one thing she tried never to do. "What can we possibly find if we're looking for someone who's no longer in Spartina?"

"Something. Anything. Look, we turned Cecil County upside down looking for answers to Lucy's death. And, best you could tell, the Frederick sheriff's department did a pretty thorough job up there. So this is all we've got."

"No, *this* is all we've got," Tess said, pulling up outside an old dust-filmed photography studio in a business center that had fallen on hard times. The smiling graduation photographs in the windows of Ashe's Studio Portraits & Fine Photography were clearly fifteen or twenty years old. Caps and gowns didn't change that much over time, but hairstyles did, and makeup. It had been a decade or so since such full bushy brows had been considered fashionable for women, since lips had gleamed through so many layers of iridescent gloss.

Yet the man inside the studio was not as old as Tess expected. Mid-forties, perhaps, tall and thin with the posture of an al dente noodle, he would have been a college student himself when the window displays were put up. He looked surprised to see any one enter his store — and not happily so.

"You lost? Need directions back to the interstate?"

"No," Tess said, "we're investigators —"

"From the state? I'll have to see some identification."

"I'm a Baltimore-based private investigator," she said, pulling out her billfold and showing her ID.

"And him?" The man jerked his head toward Carl.

"He works with me. Maryland requires an apprenticeship." The lie jumped out on its own, catching Tess off guard, as her lies often did, and irking Carl. She saw him frown, unhappy at the word, mouthing it to himself: *apprentice*. But the man's assumption that they were "from the state" had jarred some instinct. This was someone who worried about trouble crossing his threshold. A particular kind of trouble, brought by a particular brand of authorities. State investigators.

"Are you Ashe?"

"Son of. What does Maryland want with me?"

"We're looking for people who used to do business with Eric Shivers, a Maryland man who worked this area as a salesman."

"Yeah?"

"Yeah as in 'Yeah, I knew him,' or 'Yeah, go on'?"

Ashe had one of those faces that revealed its flaws gradually. His skin tone was splotchy and uneven, his nose a pointy little beak, his chin nonexistent. And his yellow-brown eyes bulged slightly, with so much milky white showing at the edges they made Tess think of deviled eggs gone bad.

"Both," he said at last. "Although my dad was still alive then, so he was the one Eric dealt with."

"I'm sorry to hear your father passed away," Tess said. "Has it been long?"

"A few years back," the man said, scratching his nonexistent chin. "Five, I think. And don't be sorry. He was old."

"What did Eric sell?" This was Carl, his voice too hard, too rushed. It was a traffic-stop voice, not the more consciously casual tones a skilled investigator used.

But the question, despite its argumentative edge, seemed to catch the man off guard. "What — I mean, you were the ones who came in here saying he was in photographic supplies, not me."

"No, we didn't say, actually." Carl stepped forward, getting as close as he could to Ashe

217

Jr., given the dusty counter between them. "We said he was a salesman. What did he sell?"

"Paper." But it was a question in spite of itself.

"I don't think so."

"Well, I don't know. Okay? I don't know. I know Eric called on my father, but I never took much interest. I'm just sitting on this place until the market recovers and I can get a fair price for the property, put it into something a little more dynamic, you know? I'm not a photographer, and if I'm going to run a business, it's going to be something a little exciting, with potential for real growth. This isn't what I wanted to do with my life."

"Yeah?" Carl leaned forward, so he was nose to nose with the weedy, feckless man. "Well, join the club, buddy. Join the club."

# Chapter 16

"Did anything about that strike you as unusual?"

Carl stopped in his tracks on the sidewalk outside the photography studio. "Wait, I know that line. It's from a movie. Don't tell me. I can see the guy who said it, all serious and stone-faced. He's a really famous actor."

"No, I mean —"

"I said, don't tell me. I'll get it in a second. God, I'm so close. *48 Hours*? No, no, that's not it. One of the *Godfathers*?"

"Carl —" Tess was not inclined to touch people she did not know well, but she grabbed Carl Dewitt's left arm and swung him around. "I'm not playing movie trivia. I am not asking a rhetorical question. Let me repeat: *Did anything about that strike you as unusual?*"

"Yes," he muttered, yanking his arm from her and rubbing it, as if she had left a stain on his sleeve. "You called me your apprentice, which is one step above flunky. Why'd you do that?"

Tess got into her car, waited for Carl to do the same, then started the engine and began to drive, although she had no destination in mind. They weren't done with Spartina, she was sure of that much.

"The guy was clearly paranoid about state authorities. It was his first question: 'Are you from the state?' I wanted him to feel safe with us, at ease. I told an expedient lie. I wasn't trying to demean you. You've got no ID. What were you going to show the guy, your Blockbuster Video card?"

Carl folded his arms across his chest and thought about this. After several quiet minutes, he nodded, satisfied. "Just so it's not what you really think."

"He said five years."

"What?"

"He said his father died five years ago 'I think.' "

"Five years, four years, six years." Carl shrugged. "Not everybody is exact about dates."

"When did your mother die?"

"Eight years ago February."

Tess didn't bother to say anything, just let him listen to the precision of his own words.

"If his dad died around the time Eric was here, it would be sharper in his mind. The two things would be connected."

Tess nodded. "I think so, yes."

"So why would he lie about it?"

"Because he doesn't want us to associate him with Eric. And, by extension, Tiffani. The guy back at the motel couldn't have been chattier about Eric, and Eric apparently was pretty chatty his ownself. That Ashe guy lied to us. People usually lie for a reason."

"So let's go back, jack 'im up."

Tess winced a little at the slang, picked up, no doubt, from a movie or a television show.

"We're not cops, remember? We can't drag Ashe to an interrogation room and keep him there for hours, playing mind games. My intuition about people is pretty good, but it doesn't give us any legal standing."

"So what do we do?"

"I know of only one place to go when I'm stumped."

The Spartina Public Library was plain, with an emphasis on best-sellers, but it had the Internet connections Tess needed. Using the wireless modem that Dorie had installed for her at an astronomical price, Tess booted up her laptop and began searching the on-line archives of the *Spartina Messenger*, while Carl flipped through the bound paper versions. Like most newspapers, the *Messenger* had an on-line database, but it charged for retrieval of articles more than thirty days old.

"So what are you going to do?" Carl asked, distracted momentarily by a page of movie ads.

"Hey, that's what per diem expenses are for." Tess signed up for the archive service and began downloading the articles that popped up, beginning with an obituary on Ashe's father.

"Look at the date."

Carl leaned over her shoulder. "Son of a bitch. It's *seven* years ago."

"So he wasn't doing any business with anyone six years ago." Other Ashes came up, but not the ones Tess wanted. She noticed the Spartina paper had a police log, where petty crimes were listed by address. She tried the address of the photography shop. She found a dozen listings over the past ten years, but they were the kind of petty property crimes one would expect in a depressed business area: smashed shop windows, car break-ins. And the addresses were not precise, so it was impossible to tell if the crimes had affected Ashe's Studio Portraits or its downtrodden neighbors. She narrowed the search to the months before and after Tiffani Gunts's murder. Here she found three calls to the fire department for "suspicious odors," which was mildly interesting but didn't explain why Ashe Jr. had lied to them about knowing Eric Shivers.

A subdued voice on the PA system reminded them that the library closed at 5 p.m. on Friday nights. Tess checked her watch and quickly plugged Ashe's name into the form for the local telephone directory. The number popped up, along with a link offering to map the way. Modern life was almost too easy.

"Let's go," she said to Carl, then winced, lest this prompt another cinematic reverie on his part. But his mind was elsewhere.

"I thought you said there was no reason to go back and talk to Ashe if we didn't know anything."

"Yeah, I know what I said. But people get squirrelly, sometimes, when you show up at their houses. They don't realize how much of their lives" — she patted the computer — "are inside these babies. It's one thing to drop by a man's business, another to go to his home un-invited. Total power play."

"You showed up on my doorstep, and it didn't bother me at all."

Tess didn't have the heart to tell Carl Dewitt that this was only evidence of how odd he was.

Ashe lived in a raw new development sur-rounded by shiny fields of mud. A sign at the main entrance promised LUXURY HOMES STARTING IN THE $200s, which seemed a lot to pay for the shoddy skeletons under construc-tion here. It was as if the first two little pigs went into the building business, Tess thought, and let their brother come along at the end and slap brick veneers on these palaces of sticks and straw.

Ashe's house was the only completed one on his cul-de-sac. Two cars were parked in the driveway, a midsize Japanese car and the inevitable SUV. A child's Big Wheel had been left behind the SUV, and Tess knew it was destined to be crushed beneath the SUV's wheels one morning.

A tired-looking blonde still in her day-job clothes answered the door. A television was blaring in the background, and a child appeared to be trying to outscream it. The presumptive Mrs. Ashe looked at once apprehensive and hopeful. The corners of her mouth lifted, as if she had not quite outgrown the fantasy that Publishers Clearing House would show up on her doorstep. But her eyes drooped with the knowledge that all news was bad news.

"Henry's in the family room," she said.

This suited Tess. Family rooms were now customarily built alongside the kitchen, creating vast cavernous spaces that offered no privacy. Ashe would have to talk to them in full view of his wife — or risk her suspicions by asking them to go somewhere else. Tess didn't know what secrets Ashe kept from his wife, but it was a good bet that he had at least a few going.

"What are you doing here?" he asked, lifting his eyes from the television set. It was tuned to one of the financial networks, a summary of the day's stock market gyrations flowing across the bottom.

"Your father died seven years ago," Tess said.

"You don't have to tell me when my father died."

"I think I do. Because when we stopped by your studio, you said he was the one who dealt with Eric Shivers. Well, Eric last visited here six years ago."

Ashe turned his gaze back to the television, which was just a way of not making eye contact. "Gee, pardon me. I'm sorry that in the confusion of settling my dad's estate and getting married and having a child I forgot when I met with some guy named Eric Shivers. I guess I'm just a bad, bad guy."

Ashe was in a stuffed chair, his feet propped up on an ottoman. Carl walked over and kicked Ashe's legs from their perch.

"Hey!" Ashe's yelp made his wife turn from the kitchen, where she had been pretending not to listen while she tended something on the stove. Tess stepped forward, angling her body so she was between the two men. She hated this kind of macho posturing. It was so unproductive and so phony. Just more movie shit.

"You didn't forget *when* you met with him," she said. "You forgot that you met with him at all. That's why we came back. We're curious about why you'd lie about such a little thing. Unless it's real important to you to distance yourself from Eric Shivers for some reason."

"Look, I don't know what Eric Shivers has stepped in, but I haven't seen him for years. We did a little business together. That's all. He told me he would follow the regs, and I believed him. Did his price seem too good to be true? Yes. Could I afford someone else? No."

Tess was confused. "Follow the regs?"

"When my dad died, the only thing I inherited was a photography studio. An old-fashioned, run-down, behind-the-times photography studio that wasn't worth as much as the land it's sitting on."

"So?"

"So I paid Eric to clean it up, get rid of all the crap on the premises. There were gallons of chemicals and fixes, things I had no use for, things so old even people backward enough to be using them wouldn't want to buy them. Eric said he would do it right, and I'd never have to worry about *this*."

"This?"

"Investigators up my ass, trying to bust me for improper disposal of chemical waste. He promised."

"So the last time you saw him six years ago —"

"He came to pick up his last payment."

"In cash?"

"In cash." Ashe shrugged. "He was a bargain. And he did what he said he would do. He cleaned the place out so I could put it on the market. Too bad the market went south. But if I ever do get a contract on it, I won't have to sweat the inspection."

"Except for the lead paint and the asbestos in the insulation," his wife said matter-of-factly from the kitchen, as if she wanted to remind Ashe that she was there, within earshot, and she knew some of his secrets, if not all of them.

Carl frowned. "Doesn't the law say you have to make full disclosure? Won't you have to tell a prospective buyer that you once stored all sorts of chemicals and shit on the site?"

"What are you, anyway, real estate cops? It's a photography studio. If a buyer wants an environmental inspection, he can fuckin' well pay for it."

Tess took the lead back. Carl was too prone to tangents. "The last time you saw Eric — do you remember the day?"

"It was March, and winter was still hanging around. That's the best I can do. Sorry." His tone indicated he was anything but.

"Did he ever talk about his personal life?"

"We were in business. I never asked about his life and he never asked about mine. Do you show your baby pictures to the garbageman?"

Could be a lie, Tess thought. Ashe had shown himself to be a liar, and he might be the jealous, vindictive man they sought. But his very posture spoke of an endemic laziness. It was hard to imagine him mustering the energy to kill someone for any reason.

"And all he did was come by for his money. How much?"

"I dunno. Couldn't have been more than three hundred dollars, because I got it from an ATM."

"You said you don't remember the date," Carl put in. "What about the time?"

"Night, after dark. I was the only one left on the street."

Carl glanced at Tess, and she nodded. Eric had checked in at the motel at midday and gone on his "rounds." He had returned by evening, and the van had been parked there the rest of the night, according to the observant manager. The Maryland state troopers came for Eric the next morning and roused him from sleep to tell him that his fiancée, and his life, had been shot through the heart. One trooper drove Eric's van home because he was too upset to drive himself.

"What was he driving?" she asked.

"Driving? I don't know. What does it matter? There was nothing left to haul."

"Tell us again."

"Tell you what?"

"What time did he get there? What time did he leave?"

Slumped in his chair, his chinless face receding into his neck, Ashe looked like a turtle half in his shell. "I don't know. It was six years ago. It was dark, it was late. How much more do you need to know?"

"We need to know," Tess said, "if there's a car rental place within walking distance of the motor court, the one near the river."

"A car rental by that dump? Jesus Christ, I doubt —"

"But there is, Henry," his wife interrupted. "You probably never noticed, but there's one of those combination gas station and convenience stores with a car rental franchise in it. If you want to rent a car after six p.m., it's pretty much the only place in town. Remember when you cracked up the Explorer and we had to get a rental for a whole month, while it was in the shop? I called around and —"

"Yeah, yeah, yeah," Ashe said. "So there's a car rental. So what?"

Tess already had a pen out and was turning over the map she had used to find Ashe's home. "Could you give us directions? Real explicit ones. Because we're strangers here, and it's getting dark."

"A convenience store with a car rental and a car wash and video rentals," Carl said. "What's next? How many more things are they going to put under one roof?"

"Everything," Tess said absently. "I'm surprised the big hospital companies haven't started buying up those corporate funeral home chains and started advertising 'birth-to-earth' service."

"That's from —"

"*West Side Story*. I know. But I bet I know something about that movie that you don't."

"What?" Clearly, Carl didn't think this was possible.

"In the stage version of *West Side Story*, the character said they would be friends 'from sperm to worm.' But you couldn't say that onscreen, not in the sixties."

"Really?"

"Really. No sperm, not in the sixties. I don't even think they could say womb to tomb."

"And now every other word on HBO is fuck this or fuck that. But you don't really need that hard-core language. In *The Wild Bunch* —"

But they were in the store now, so Tess was spared any more discussion of William Holden and the opening shot of the scorpion.

The manager at this multidimensional convenience store was a veteran — he had been there for a staggering three years, "two years longer than anyone else on staff," he told them proudly. Which was an impressive feat, no doubt, but of no help to Tess and Carl.

"Unless —" Tess said, drumming her fingers on the change mat.

"Unless what?" Bright-eyed and eager to please, he was one of those rarities, a young man in the service industry who wanted to provide service. "How can I help you?"

"We're screenwriters." The lie just popped out, a by-product of their *West Side Story* conversation. "And we try to be as accurate as possible. We're working on a thriller for —"

"A director we dare not name." Carl jumped in, sensing that Tess was about to falter. "But trust me. It's someone you know."

"Are you going to film here in Spartina?" The manager's eyes were wide.

Carl held a finger to his lips and smiled conspiratorially.

"Well, gosh, what do you need to know?"

"Do you keep records of your car rentals? If you had someone's name going back, say, six years, could you find him in the system?"

"Maybe with a date —"

"How about —" Carl had taken complete charge, and Tess let him go, impressed by his skills. In day-to-day life, he was an odd little fellow. But when he snapped into cop mode, he could be effective, as long as he stopped short of kicking people's legs off their ottomans. "How about March nineteenth, six years ago. And use the name — oh, Eric Shivers."

"That's kind of an odd name."

"It's the name of our major character," Carl said, winking at him. "Know about clearances? We can't use the name if it turns out there really is an Eric Shivers renting cars in Spartina."

The starstruck manager pounded the keyboard with those one-note clicks peculiar to car rental clerks and ticket agents, but found nothing. "You're in luck. No Eric Shivers, not even a Shivers in all this time. I told you it was an odd name."

"So you can search by name?" Tess asked.

"Yeah, most of the time. We put people in the computer so we can call up their stats, remember any preferences they have. Company pretends it's a service, because it cuts a few seconds off the time it takes to do the paperwork. But just between us, I think they sell the information to direct-mail firms."

"What about by date? Could you print out every car rented from here on that particular date?"

"I'm pretty sure I *can't* do that." More clicks. "No, we changed computer systems since then, and we never reconciled the records. Maybe back at corporate."

"Oh." Tess leaned against a rack of chips,

disappointed. They had seemed to be on to something. What, she wasn't sure. The fact that Eric Shivers had left his van at the motor court all evening, and taken a different vehicle to see Ashe, had seemed fraught with significance, the way jagged pieces of information often do. But he might have taken a cab. Or the motor court manager could be mistaken. What would have prevented Eric from going out for half an hour and coming back, with no one noticing?

As for the fact that he had fudged the nature of his work here in Spartina — well, he probably was in photography supplies and saw an opportunity to pick up some extra cash from Ashe. For all they knew, he had recycled some of the chemicals he had transported. She picked up a package of potato chips, studying the label as if the calories and the list of ingredients could dissuade her from wanting them. Talk about chemicals. Maltodextrin, dextrose, wheat starch, partially hydrogenated vegetable oil —

"Palm oil," she said.

"Bad stuff," Carl said. "Do they have anything with canola oil?"

"I mean" — her mind was playing a word association game, one that seemed improbable and stupid — "palm oil. Palmer."

"You think — ?" His eyes widened.

"Try Alan Palmer," Tess told the manager.

"Is that another character?"

"Just do it."

"Okay. But, man, I can't believe you guys do all this research and the movies turn out as silly as they do." *Click, click, click. Click, click, click.* It seemed to take forever.

"Well, what do you know? Alan Palmer did rent a car that day. And he was from Maryland too, same as y'all."

"You need a valid driver's license to rent a car, right?"

"Oh, yes, indeedy. Driver's license and credit card, a real one, not a debit."

It was all Tess could do to find her voice, thank the young man, leave the store, and make it back to her car. It felt as if the small parking lot was a mile wide. Carl followed, just as dazed. They did not get in the Toyota but just leaned against it, looking up at the night sky. They were far enough out in the country so the sky was riotous with stars.

"What's happening here?" Carl asked at last. "Did Eric and Alan Palmer know each other? Was it some *Strangers on a Train* scenario? You kill mine and I'll kill yours?"

"No," Tess said, surprised by her own certainty. "Alan Palmer hadn't met Lucy Fancher by the time Tiffani Gunts died. They wouldn't meet for another year, remember? Their relationship began the spring of the following year."

"Then it makes no sense."

"There's one way it makes sense." Her mouth was dry, and she had to lick her lips to get the next sentence out. "Eric Shivers and Alan Palmer are the same person."

"No way. That's not possible. You heard the guy. Alan Palmer had a driver's license and a credit card. How can he have those things if he's really Eric Shivers?"

"Such things can be faked," Tess said, thinking of the forger to whom Mickey Pechter had referred her just a few weeks ago. "Don't you get it? By the time Tiffani Gunts died, Eric Shivers had already made the preparations to disappear, already had his next identity picked out. Alan Palmer could have done the same thing — had his new identity ready to go, rented a car, leaving his van where it would be seen, where his whereabouts would be presumed."

"Alan Palmer is in a hospital in Connecticut."

"Oh, I'm sure someone named Alan Palmer is in a hospital in Connecticut. And I bet he has a broken neck from a car accident. But did you check to see when he was admitted, or did you just take the word of that caseworker who called you?"

Carl looked down at the ground. "Didn't seem like something a person would lie about. He was in the hospital. Never occurred to me to ask when he got there, because I thought I knew."

"Eric is probably a real person, too. He's just not the Eric Shivers who courted and wooed Tiffani Gunts."

"Do you know what you're saying?"

"The same man killed Tiffani Gunts and Lucy Fancher. And he's still out there somewhere, probably in a new relationship. He's found another dark-haired girl, a girl with a history of bad relationships, and he's changing her life for the better. He's getting her teeth fixed, helping her establish credit, urging her to go back to school and find a better job. Her friends and family love him, swear he's the best thing that ever happened to her. They're happy, they're in love, and they're going to get married."

"You think —"

"I think this guy is the perfect boyfriend — up until the day he kills you."

# Chapter 17

The Maryland State Police are strangely invisible to the people they protect. An average citizen, asked to explain what this branch of law enforcement does, would know only that they give out speeding tickets along the major highways. Those who read newspapers might recall that an undercover state trooper is almost always involved when a Marylander attempts to arrange a contract hit on a loved one. Troopers receive the most attention when they get killed in the line of duty.

Otherwise, no one seems quite sure what they do or why they exist. Not Tess, at least. But Carl had worked with troopers on the Fancher case and, presumably, knew what they did.

"I wish we didn't have to depend on these guys," Carl muttered, as he and Tess waited ten, twenty, thirty minutes past the scheduled meeting time. "Couldn't we have gone straight to the FBI?"

"You know better than I that the FBI has no jurisdiction. Our guy may have rented a car in Virginia, but as far as we know he's killed only within the boundaries of Maryland. Besides, the state police seemed awfully keen when I called."

"If they're so interested," Carl said, "why are they making us wait?"

"To remind us that they're more important than we are," Tess said complacently. "Or to convince themselves of their own importance."

"Trust me, they never doubt their own importance. They're dicks. I hated working with them up in Cecil County."

"They were in charge of the Lucy Fancher case, right?"

"Yes, and they were dicks. Know-it-all dicks. They'll cut us out of this investigation in a heartbeat. Treat us like ordinary citizens."

"We *are* ordinary citizens," Tess pointed out. "But follow my lead in there, and we'll be able to keep our hand in."

Another five minutes elapsed before a secretary ushered them into a conference room where three uniformed men waited. In their stiff khaki uniforms, their broad-brimmed hats on the table in front of them, they gave the impression of wearing mirrored sunglasses, although they were not — their eyes were simply that flat and expressionless. No one offered an apology for making them wait, although the youngest of the three nodded at Carl.

"Carl," he said.

"Corporal Gregg." He nodded back.

"*Craig.* And I've made sergeant since we last met."

"That's right, you assisted on the Fancher case for a while, Mr. Dewitt," said the middle of the three men. His nameplate identified him as Lieutenant Green. "Sergeant Craig briefed us on that situation. All water under the bridge, you'll pardon the expression."

Tess tried not to make a face at the ill-advised pun.

"Now we've looked at the two cases you believe are linked and already contacted VICAP," Lieutenant Green continued. "No obvious connections have jumped out, but we have forty open homicides of adult women over the last five years — including another decapitation, although an arrest was made in that case. And in that case the body was found before the head."

He looked quite pleased with himself for knowing this chronology was relevant. The oldest of the trio, Major Shields, rewarded him with a smile. This appeared to make Sergeant Craig, a boyish blond, eager for his share of approval.

"We're also looking at domestics that were resolved as murder-suicides."

"*Resolved?*" Tess echoed.

Major Shields caught her tone. "Resolved in the sense that they're not ongoing cases. But we have to be open to the possibility that this killer — assuming you're right about there being just one — has stopped killing because he's already dead. Or he's in another state. In which case, there's not a lot we can do but put the word out and hope someone else is checking VICAP."

"He wouldn't kill himself," Carl said. Tess wasn't so sure, but she didn't want the state police to see them as less than a united front, so she put a cautionary hand on the side of Carl's leg, beneath the table where it couldn't be seen. He let it rest there for a moment, then shook it off.

"No," the major agreed. "Not if you're right about his pattern. But it's hard to deduce a pattern from just two. Sam here has been down to Quantico and trained as a profiler." He nodded toward the lieutenant. "These things are not as cut-and-dried as you might think."

Again, Tess tried not to make a face. She had a friend in Baltimore City homicide who had gone to Quantico on a consultation once, for two seemingly random homicides that had happened in two of the city's posher neighborhoods. It was a red ball squared, to use cop parlance, but the trip to Quantico had been more public relations than police work. The profiler had looked at the files and said, "Both these crimes occurred at night. So now we know your killer is nocturnal." That turned out to be the only useful information derived from the session. The homicides were unrelated, after all, and the two independent perps who were ultimately arrested proved capable of committing crimes at any time of the day or night.

"What about closed cases?" She tried to sound deferential, noncombative. There was a bad feel to the room, the sense of some un-resolved grudge between Carl and Sergeant Craig.

"Closed cases?" Lieutenant Green looked baffled. "Closed cases are closed."

"But what if the person who committed these crimes is in prison for another crime?"

"Well, of course. We're always open to that possibility."

"Or what if one of your resolved cases was re-solved incorrectly? What if the wrong man was convicted for a crime, allowing this killer to continue?"

"That's" — the major searched for a word — "an *interesting* notion. We'll consider that too. We do appreciate your help, your cooperation. This case may turn out to be quite important."

The troopers were giving them the bum's rush, just as Carl had feared. Tess could sense his anger building, but she knew they needed to be tactful, almost servile, to get what they wanted. Like beta dogs, they had to roll on their backs and offer up their stomachs to the alpha dogs. This was a hard lesson for men, but it came naturally to most women.

"We called the state police because we want to help. We'd like to work *with* you."

Major Shields smiled at her. "The state po-lice doesn't work with civilians."

"Of course." She paused for a beat, and the troopers smiled, full of the warm feeling that comes from getting one's way effortlessly.

"Only this extremely sensitive information grew out of *our* investigation. I'm still under contract. My work hasn't ended. You could even say I *own* this information. Me and my clients."

The troopers were no longer smiling.

"You are free to continue whatever it is you do," the major said, "where it does not overlap or interfere with official police work."

It was a bluff. Tess shook her head, calling him on it.

"My clients are well-connected people. They're not used to being pushed aside or controlled in any fashion. They already know what I've uncovered. And so far they haven't gone to the media or made a stink. Nor will they — as long as I'm involved. If I tell them you've shut me out, they'll be all over television, screaming cover-up."

"Cover-up?"

"My clients will press any advantage they have to get more funding for domestic violence prevention. They could make a lot of hay over the Fancher case, how you let the boyfriend slip away. Especially if it turns out he killed again."

"Alan Palmer would have fooled anyone," Sergeant Craig sputtered. "He was an upstanding citizen. Everyone who knew Lucy Fancher approved of him. He's in a hospital, for Christ's sake."

"Someone named Alan Palmer is in a hospital," Tess said. "But he was there before the

241

Alan Palmer you knew left North East."

"Well, the guy we knew had a pretty good alibi. As far as I'm concerned, he still has an alibi. Just because —"

The major silenced him with a look, then said, with impressive menace, "Don't threaten us, Miss Monaghan."

"These aren't threats, just facts. My clients feel a certain proprietary interest in what I've uncovered. The best way to assure them they're not being cut out is to let me — and Carl — work with you."

"You are not a public safety officer and Carl is no longer one. What could you possibly do?"

"Small tasks, even scut work. Field interviews you don't have time for. We can answer phones, take tips, pass out leaflets with Alan Palmer's driver's license photo. By the way, does it match Eric Shivers's?"

The troopers' quick glances among themselves told Tess they had not yet checked. She saw Lieutenant Green make a quick note on his pad.

"Carl and I could even look into the two men's lives, try to see if they overlap in any way."

"They don't —" Sergeant Craig began, only to get another cautionary look from the major, the kind that can make words shrivel on the tongue. Either Major Shields was thinking about her request, or he didn't want the young trooper to reveal anything the state police had learned.

"If we allow you to work with us, even in the most tangential way," the major said, "it must be understood that everything we do is confidential. No leaks to the press. If this man has remained in Maryland, he believes he has escaped detection. His sense of security is one of the few advantages we have."

"Also, it would appear he has long dormancy periods," put in the lieutenant.

*Duh,* Tess yearned to say, but Shields and Craig beamed at him for this insight. Perhaps she should let the profiler strut his stuff.

"Tell us what else you've been able to figure out by looking at the case files."

"This killer seems particularly methodical."

*Double duh.*

"Assuming it is one killer. That's by no means certain."

"What *is* certain?" Tess asked, as if she had not assembled half the facts of the case to date. "Have you put together a timeline for the case?"

"Tiffani Gunts was killed in April six years ago. About two months before she died, 'Alan Palmer' renewed his license at the DMV in Mondawmin, in Baltimore City."

"Renewed?"

The lieutenant shrugged. "Maryland licenses come up for renewal every five years. The real Alan Palmer had a motorcycle accident when he was twenty-six, about eighteen months before the license was renewed. But being comatose doesn't invalidate your driver's license. It remains in the system."

"Even if you don't keep up your insurance?"

"Loss of insurance flags the registration, not the license. As far as the DMV computers were concerned, Alan Palmer was entitled to drive, brain dead or no, even if he hadn't renewed his license when it expired. He was still in the twelve-month grace period. Whoever took over his identity must have known this somehow and arranged to get other documents that allowed him to renew the license — a Social Security card, a certified birth certificate."

"What address was on Alan Palmer's driver's license? The most recent one, I mean." Tess cupped her chin in her hand and leaned forward as if mesmerized.

"We did check that." Lieutenant Green granted her a smile. He was warming to her. Men usually warmed to women who listened to them in this fashion. "It looked like a real street address, but it turned out to be a box in one of those Mail Boxes chains in Baltimore. He used the street address and made the box number look like an apartment number. A month before he came in for the renewal, he filed a change of address, so the paperwork went to that box."

"Still, they have a photo of the real Alan Palmer in front of him. And he wouldn't match."

The lieutenant rubbed his chin. "Yeah, but

he's a young guy, and young people can change a lot over a six-year period. Plus he was a lot skinnier. The original Alan Palmer weighed two thirty-five; this one put his weight at one seventy-five. If the eye color, hair color, and height were close enough and the age wasn't too far off, he could fake it."

"And he went to Mondawmin," Sergeant Craig said. "Those are some surly —"

He caught himself, but Tess's head snapped up. This remark she couldn't let pass. "Go ahead, Sergeant. Feel free to finish the racial slur. Or is it the gender of the DMV workers that gets under your skin?"

"I'm not a racist." Then, a beat later. "Or a sexist."

"Let's chalk that up as a moot point. The fact is, you're probably right."

Carl, Major Shields, and Lieutenant Green looked at Tess in horror.

"No, I mean the pseudo–Alan Palmer probably chose Mondawmin because the government work force in the city tends to be exclusively African American. And you know what? We *do* all look alike to them."

"Who's the racist now?" Sergeant Craig asked.

"I have a friend, Jackie Weir, who has a three-year-old toddler. The other day she saw Julia Roberts on television and began pointing at her, yelling, 'Tesser! Tesser! Tesser!' All because she was wearing her hair in a braid."

The troopers saw her point with unflattering speed. Sergeant Craig even sneered a little and repeated the actress's name to himself, then shook his head in disbelief.

"You're so much bigger —" he muttered.

Tess decided she didn't need to let him finish that sentence.

"Look, he's a clever guy, whoever did this. He can't control everything, but he plays the percentages. By using a living person who was incapacitated, he got himself a whole new life. There was little risk he would be caught as long as Alan Palmer's in a vegetative state — and as long as he didn't do anything to attract attention to himself. He's like a parasite who's just passing through. You don't notice the tick that jumps off you after sucking up only a little blood."

The major and the lieutenant nodded. Tess may not have won all of them over, but she now had a quorum.

"You're on the money," Major Shields said. "Identity theft is usually committed to rip other people off: open a charge account, get some stuff, move on. Alan Palmer had exactly one charge account, with a relatively small line of credit, and he paid the bills promptly. I'm not sure why he bothered to get a credit card at all."

"He needed to rent a car," Tess said. "To do that, you need a driver's license and a credit card. Tell me this: Does Alan Palmer still have any open accounts?"

"He closed out the credit card a little over two years ago," Lieutenant Green said.

Sergeant Craig leaned forward, eager to assert himself. "Which turns out to be a month after I got a call from a woman who said she was a caseworker with the state and wanted us to know he was in a hospital out of state."

"She called me too," Carl said. Tess poked his leg under the table again.

"Did you call the hospital to check?"

"Of course." Sergeant Craig had the good grace to look sheepish. "I confirmed the Social Security number and DOB but let it go. I didn't think to ask when he was admitted."

"You didn't find it odd, getting a call from some unidentified woman?"

"No, because Alan had been calling every month, asking if I knew anything. In fact, he was becoming a pest. The only thing I thought was, That is one unlucky guy."

"Follow-up questions," Major Shields said. "You have to remember to ask those simple questions, the ones that seem so dull and obvious. That's where you find the inconsistencies."

"It was a woman who called me too," Carl said.

Everyone in the room looked at him, wondering why he was stuck on this point.

"Indicates an accomplice," he said.

Score one for Carl, Tess thought. But it didn't fit with what she thought she knew about this man. He was a loner, peripatetic, moving from town to town, woman to woman.

"Or a new girlfriend," she suggested. "Another sweet dark-haired girl who wouldn't ask too many questions if her new perfect-in-every-way boyfriend asked her to make such a call. Maybe he told her it was a prank, that the sergeant and Carl were old friends he wanted to fool."

They sat in glum silence at the idea that the man was with a new girlfriend. Or would be, until the pattern kicked in. Why did he kill, why did he move on, what set him off?

"What about his other identity, Eric Shivers?" Tess asked. "Is that his real name, or did he steal that too?"

"Eric Shivers died fifteen years ago, at the age of seventeen," Major Shields said. "But, sure enough, he had a valid Maryland driver's license ten years after he died. It expired about a year after Tiffani Gunts did. Still in the system, but no one renewed it. Issued originally on the Eastern Shore."

"How did Eric die?" Tess asked.

"Massive asthma attack, apparently. It was in a hospital over in Salisbury, although his family lived in Crisfield."

"Hospitals." Carl's voice was too loud, almost a bark. "That's one link between Eric and Alan: a place where someone with access to records can get Social Security numbers. You've got to look at hospitals."

The major's voice was not unkind. "We're

checking into that. We also searched registration records, but neither Eric Shivers nor Alan Palmer had a car in his name, not in this state."

"Yet he drives," Tess said. "More evidence of an accomplice — or yet another identity, a fixed one that he returns to in between. . . ."

"Dormancy periods." Lieutenant Green supplied the term again, but Tess no longer felt the urge to mock him. Clearly, there *were* dormancy periods, long ones.

"You gotta give him credit," Carl said. "His organizational skills are formidable. Most people can't get through the DMV with the right documents. Here our guy is, zipping through with phonies."

"I don't know," Tess said, thinking of Mickey Pechter. "There's a booming business in fake IDs out there. Even nerds from Towson know how to get them. What bothers me is the degree of planning, the care he takes. Yet he had no financial incentive to kill these women. They were dirt-poor, they had nothing to give, and they weren't in a position to take anything from him. They weren't even common-law wives under Maryland statute. He could have walked away without a care in the world."

"Maybe he has a fear of commitment," Sergeant Craig offered. It wasn't meant as a joke, Tess realized, which only made it worse.

"You know what I think? He's always planning. He knows when he starts dating a girl that this day will come. Yet his grief appears authentic. You never doubted Alan Palmer's emotions, right?"

Her question was for Carl, not Craig. She didn't think the sergeant was the best judge of human emotion. Of course, Carl was only marginally better.

He thought for a moment, shook his head.

"No, I never did. Which bothers me to this day. He was devastated. Now I may not have a lot of experience in homicide" — his eyes shot around the table, daring the troopers to note he had assisted on exactly one such investigation — "but I don't get this: How did he manufacture grief for a woman he killed? A woman he butchered?"

"Postmortem," Tess said. "Both women died from gunshot wounds to the chest."

"The guns —" Major Shields began, a note of hope in his voice.

"No match," Lieutenant Green said glumly.

"He sawed off Lucy's head so his breakdown would be more credible." Tess realized she had begun speaking in Carl's definitive fashion — no "I think" or "what if." She was creeping inside the killer's skin, although not in the fashion of a profiler. She felt the way she did when she had crushes in junior high school, the kind where you slowly assembled a dossier on the object of your affections. You learned his class schedule, watched what he ate in the cafeteria, figured out who his friends were — all so you could time an accidental meeting at the water fountain, impress him with your wit and flipping hair.

Major Shields looked skeptical. "He shoots a woman, then cuts off her head and keeps her body with him a couple of days. In water. Someone that sick can't pass for normal."

"But he did, didn't he? He does."

Tess had spoken as quietly and softly as possible, not wanting to sound as if she were contradicting the major. Because she wasn't. He was right and yet he was wrong. The man they sought was capable of passing for normal. But only for a while. Then something happened and he had to escape. So why did the women have to die? Was it a foregone conclusion in his mind that he would kill them, or was he trying to have a normal life and failing?

"There's a girl out there," Tess said. "She has dark hair and light eyes. She's petite, and if she's not quite beautiful, she will be once he gets hold of her — fixes her teeth, convinces her to get a great new haircut. She works at a convenience store, as Tiffani did, and Lucy. Right now, in fact, this girl could be leaning forward on her elbows, laughing at the charming stranger who has started coming into the store regularly. If I could do anything, I would like to save this girl's life."

"You did," Major Shields said, "just by picking up the phone and calling us. Now let us do what we do."

Tess shook her head. "I can't let it go. I just can't. There have to be things that Carl and I can do, no matter how small."

"Hell," Sergeant Craig said, "you're both as crazy as he is."

Carl almost came to his feet on that, but Tess saw it coming and hooked her hand in the back of his waistband, jerking him back to the chair. Major Shields narrowed his eyes thoughtfully, as if that gesture told him something he needed to know.

"Okay," he said. "You can come in every day, work from an office here. I'll try to find ways to keep you involved and informed. But the ground rules are this: You tell us everything you know as soon as you know it. You don't talk to anyone without clearing it through me. If I wake up and see even one detail of this in the local paper, your ass is out on Reisterstown Road. Can you live with that?"

Tess looked at Carl. He nodded a little grudgingly, as if he thought they could do better. Or perhaps he believed *she* was holding him back. But he had given his assent, so she reached her hand across the table and shook Major Shields's hand, as her father had taught her to do — firmly, surely.

Sergeant Craig looked disgruntled, but Lieutenant Green reached over and shook Tess's hand as well.

"You'll bring the woman's perspective to things," he said. "That could be helpful."

"Well," Tess said, "there's a first time for everything."

# Chapter 18

Their first task was predictably small: Take a photograph of "Alan Palmer" to the private mail franchise where he had kept a box. The store was on Guilford Avenue, a stone's throw from the city jail and state prison complex.

A stone's throw was not necessarily a figure of speech in this neighborhood. Broken windshield glass crunched beneath their feet as they crossed the street, which was so pitted that the bones of Baltimore's long-vanished trolley system peeked through in parts. Carl glanced around, unnerved.

"People *live* here?"

"It's not so bad," Tess said. "Walk two blocks west and you'll be in some of the prettiest real estate in all of Baltimore."

"And walk two blocks east and you'll be dead."

"Oh, not even. In fact, the neighborhood around the prison is probably safer than some, if only because cops are always coming and going. Now, go another mile east beyond there, and you'll be in some serious trouble."

The mail store was small to begin with, and the owner's decision to stack empty boxes in ramshackle towers made it feel more cramped. Tess and Carl threaded their way through this cardboard maze and approached the counter, where a cheerful young man was listening to his Walkman and eating a sandwich, letting the crumbs fall into a box he was packing. He had a round face that was some unknowable stew of ethnic identities: almond-shaped green eyes that were flecked with amber, pale brown cheeks with a scattering of dark freckles. If Tess had to guess, she'd put him at part Japanese, part African American, with maybe a little Irish blood like her own.

Whatever his ethnic heritage, he was one hundred percent happy. Joyful even. He was perhaps the giddiest person Tess had ever seen on the business end of a cash register.

"Hel-lo," he practically sang at their approach.

Tess showed him the photograph of Alan Palmer. This had been taken from the driver's license photo, enlarged on the computer, and then printed out, so the quality was good. But in the photo, Alan Palmer had a full beard, a telling detail. Carl didn't remember the man having a beard at all; it was just another part of his plan, a way to confuse those who noticed he didn't quite resemble what was supposed to be his younger self. The beard obscured his face shape, which both Carl and Sergeant Craig remembered as a simple oval. They didn't know if Eric Shivers had been bearded when his driver's license had been renewed; he had done that before the state went to the digital imaging system, and there was no copy to be found. But Tess would bet anything that he had, that he began to grow a beard whenever he planned to take on a new identity, shaving it once his transformation was complete.

Why, maybe he even let his new girlfriend cajole him into losing the beard.

"How long have you worked here?" Tess asked the man.

"Too long." He sighed, but there was no pain in it. He was an actor, a clown.

"We're working with the state police." Funny, the truth sounded like a bigger lie than any she had told. "We want to know if this man is one of your customers."

"Our customers," the young man said, his tone still lilting with his innate joy of life, "receive a guarantee of confidentiality, just like the U.S. mail. Mail is private. Mail is *sacred.*"

Tess supposed that if one ended up working in a shipping-and-mail outlet, it helped to see the job as part of a higher calling.

"We don't want to read his mail, we just want to know if he's still a customer. We know he was using this address five years ago."

"Five years ago? That's a lifetime here." But he removed the plastic headphones from his ears and studied the photo. Steel drum music, tinny but infectious, came bouncing out of his headset. "Maybe, maybe not. He's definitely not someone who comes in now.

You wouldn't forget that face, would you?"

"You wouldn't?" To Tess, their quarry was disturbingly normal. Not handsome, but not unattractive. Medium height, medium build. It would be too easy for him to move through life without drawing attention to himself.

"Man, he looks like the Unabomber." He tapped the bushy beard in the photo, the only similarity that Tess could see between Alan Palmer and Ted Kaczynski. "Does he blow stuff up?"

"Only people's lives," Carl said.

They had other photos, just no places to distribute them. Major Shields had said they could drive back to Spartina, if they were so inclined, and check with Ashe to see if Alan Palmer's driver's license matched the man Ashe had known as Eric Shivers. But Tess was already certain of the answer — after all, Spartina was where they had found this link. She'd much rather go back and see what the Gunts family remembered. Of course, the state police had deemed that interview much too important for Tess and Carl to handle, or even observe.

"Eric Shivers," she said. "Think he had a family?"

"Almost everyone does."

"He was from Crisfield, right? Or around there."

"Yeah, so — no."

"No, what?"

"We're not supposed to be doing that."

"We're not supposed to be trying to talk to hospital personnel, or looking for a connection between the place where Eric died and the place where Alan Palmer was treated in-state. We're not supposed to talk to anyone directly connected to the victims. But what about Eric Shivers's family?"

"What about them?"

"They could tell us about Eric. The hospital is one possibility, but it's not the only possibility. Maybe it will turn out that he and Alan Palmer went to the same . . . band camp."

"Band camp? What, this all began over some chance meeting with a tuba? You're throwing too wide a net. You have to be focused in police work, methodical."

They were back out on Guilford Avenue. Tess glanced up at the expressway that loomed over the street. How easy it would be to go up there, get out of town, head east instead of west.

"Look, we have two choices. We can drive back to Spartina, retrace our steps, and talk to the same guy we talked to last week. Or we could go back into that mailbox store, pay to fax the photo to Ashe in Virginia, and head to the Eastern Shore to learn something new."

"They told us not to do that."

Tess was becoming impatient. She couldn't help thinking how quickly Crow or Whitney would warm to such a plan. How had she ended up being saddled with this strange stick-in-the-mud, this know-it-all?

"They told us we couldn't interview people they had earmarked. But clearly they can't get angry if we develop a few new leads. If we don't learn anything, they'll never know we were in Crisfield. If we do, they'll be thankful."

"Thankful enough to ignore the fact that you disobeyed the prime directives?"

"The prime directives?"

"From *RoboCop*," Carl said. "Serve the Public Trust. Protect the Innocent. Uphold the Law."

"Look, I can handle the state police," Tess said, surprised at how confident she felt, how cocky. "The fact is, we still have my trump card. If they cut us loose from this, I can go to the press."

"You told me you hated the press."

"But *they* don't know that."

Carl chewed the inside of his cheek, puzzled. His mind didn't work on a lot of levels, Tess realized. If you threw him a football, he'd run straight toward the goal. If you dealt him a bad hand in poker, he'd fold. He wasn't dumb, far from it, but he had a directness about him that could be a handicap.

She'd have to remember that — and control for it.

# Chapter 19

Tess always forgot how far Crisfield was, how deep Maryland dipped down on the other side of the bay. Starting out, she assumed it was closer than Ocean City and the Delaware beach towns, which took a solid three hours to reach on a summer weekend. But Crisfield was just as far.

She also had forgotten the feeling that this was where the world ended. The main drag of Crisfield essentially dead-ended into the bay, which opened up before them, as vast as any ocean here, so it seemed all water and sky. The result was almost unbearably bright on a spring day. Tess felt naked and exposed.

"The current address for the Shiverses is on Princess Anne Court," Carl said. "Take a left here."

"You want to stop and get lunch first? It's almost one o'clock."

"No. Besides, when we called from the road, we said we'd be there by one-thirty."

"Well, it's not one-thirty."

"I don't do lunch."

Carl Dewitt didn't eat conventional meals at all, as Tess was learning. He went the entire day on Diet Mountain Dew and then ate one huge helping of protein and grease at night — not unlike a boa constrictor. But she conceded, in part because Crisfield had few restaurants for the crab-averse. There was a Dairy Queen back on 50. She'd hold out for that.

Still, she could have the last word. "You know, you'll end up gaining weight, living that way."

"How do you figure? It's not more than two thousand calories, and I don't take in empty calories like alcohol." He gave her a pointed, superior look. Carl found the consumption of alcohol decadent and had almost passed out from shock when Tess ordered a beer with a midday meal. "I burn at least two thousand calories every day. Besides, I don't want to be a little stick, like that boyfriend of yours."

Crow had come out of the house in his pajama bottoms just that morning to wish her well on her various errands. Tess had thought he looked admirably lean, not unlike the greyhound by his side. The morning, Baltimore, Crow — it suddenly seemed very far away.

"Well, first of all, it's horrible, what you're doing to your digestion. I have a theory — my own, I'll grant you, not a dietitian's — that your body can absorb only so many calories at a single sitting and any extra is more readily converted to fat. Your body's not a cash register. It doesn't reconcile accounts at day's end, decide whether you finished up in the red or the black, and adjust your weight accordingly."

"But if you're in deficit when you sit down to eat, it's like being an empty gas tank. It's better than what you do, filling yourself every three hours, every time your dipstick drops a level."

"You're mixing your automotive metaphors."

Carl snorted. "I forget. You seem like a normal person most of the time, but you're one of those overeducated types. What did you study at college? Let me guess, one of those weird things that no one really knows what it is. Ethnography? Symbiotics?"

She started to correct him, only to catch his wisp of a satiric smile. "The fact that you know enough to make a joke about semiotics tells me you're not as ignorant as you'd like people to believe."

"Man, I grew up in Cecil County and joined the Toll Facilities Po-leece when I was twenty, a college dropout. I'm just a dumb hick. Couldn't you tell that by the way those fellas treated me over at Pikesville?"

"I can tell you like to play that part. But it occurs to me that there were some books in your house, and they weren't *Reader's Digest* Condensed Versions. You read some, don't you? I mean, when you're not memorizing movie dialogue."

He was sheepish now, caught. "I do like history, especially the Civil War."

Tess sighed and made a mental note not to teach Dewitt how to play Botticelli, no matter how many long drives they had to spend in each other's company.

The woman who opened the door at the Shivers house could have been anywhere between twenty-five and forty-five. Lines fanned out from the corners of her eyes, while her sad mouth seemed to be encased in double sets of parentheses. The price you pay for all this light, Tess thought.

"Mrs. Shivers?" Carl asked. Tess noticed that his voice had shifted in some indefinable way. He was playing his Upper Shore card for all it was worth. Not that a Crisfielder would have much affection for someone from Cecil County, but it was preferable to Baltimore.

"Hallie Langley. I am — I was — I am Eric's sister." She stopped, still puzzling over tenses after all these years.

"I thought your parents were going to be here."

"Maybe it sounds funny to you, but my parents still don't like to talk about Eric's death. It was so sudden, so unexpected, and he — well, he was their favorite. I'm not saying they slighted me. They didn't. But he was their first child and their only boy, and they never got over it."

Once Tess might have been surprised by such a candid, easy confession, especially from a hard-shell Eastern Shore native. But she had learned people were often anxious to tell their secrets, if only someone would ask. Strangers made the best confidantes. Hallie Langley led them into the shadowy living room, a place that did not appear to have changed much over the past two decades.

"Eric was born in the hospital over in Salisbury?" This was Carl. Tess had agreed he could take the lead here.

"Born there and died there. But we always lived here."

"Now I'm not clear how he died. The hospital records say it was an allergy attack, but there was no autopsy."

"I guess people would call it a freak accident. It was the big bull and oyster roast, you know the one?"

Tess did. It had been an obligatory stop for the state's politicians as far back as she could remember.

"So, you know, it's safe as houses. My parents took us over there and gave us money, told us to do what we wanted to do. Eric was four years older'n me. He sure didn't want to be with his little sister."

"Yeah, well," Carl said. "Boys."

That moment of inarticulate empathy hit Hallie like a drug. She began talking in a rush.

"He ditched me to be with some boys in his class. And some girls. They wanted to meet girls. I made a fuss, but he gave me some money and said he'd hook up with me at five o'clock near the front gate. He gave me plenty of money, but I was mad at him. I hoped my parents would beat him to the gate, so I could tell what he'd done. Then five o'clock came and he didn't come and he didn't come —" Her hard, tanned face went slack, and Tess could almost see the little girl she had been, standing forlornly by the front gate, time stretching out the way it does when someone makes you wait. As the minutes go by, impatience turns to anger. Anger slides into fear, then back to anger again.

Unless the person never shows up.

"My parents got there and started asking, 'Where's Eric?' By then, I didn't want to tell them he had ditched me, I knew he'd get in trouble, only not too much trouble, because they did favor him. In fact, I always thought my mother blamed me a little for letting Eric buy me off. She always has a way of figuring out how things are my fault. Anyway, we found him in a grove of trees, outside the fairgrounds proper."

"Was he dead?" Tess winced at the bluntness of Carl's question, but it didn't seem to bother Hallie.

"Probably. The paramedics came and took him to the hospital, working on him all the while. But, even as a little girl, I thought it was just for our benefit."

"Still," Carl said, "to die from an asthma attack."

"Wasn't asthma, exactly, it was shellfish. He

was bad allergic, real bad. It was almost a kind of joke, someone growing up around here allergic to shellfish. We used to say Eric could die if the wind cut the wrong way. Well, all it took was for a little crabmeat to get into a hamburger, and that's what happened. Someone was broiling burgers and crab cakes on the same grill."

"I'm allergic to shellfish too," Tess said. "But if you have a reaction, there's usually time to get a shot. And if you're really allergic, you can carry an EpiPen, right?"

"Yeah, *now.* But he didn't have an EpiPen and he didn't get help fast enough."

"Was he alone?" Carl's question was a good one, open-ended but shrewd. Tess shot him an approving look.

"They said he must have been."

"*They* said. But what do you think?"

Hallie Langley pressed her lips in a hard line, determined not to cry. Tess realized that suffering, as much as the sun, had set the woman's features into these premature creases.

"No. No, I don't. Someone had to be with him. Whoever it was must have panicked. They had" — she lowered her voice, as if this were still a secret, all these years later — "they had been smoking dope and drinking beer. I saw the cans, saw the cigarette where it had fallen. My daddy put that butt in his pocket, but I never forgot it."

"Did you see who he went off with that day?"

"I saw him with his friends from high school. But his buddies told everyone he went off with some girl. She swore up and down that she didn't, and one of her friends swore by her, saying they were together most of the afternoon. So maybe everyone was there, or no one was there. I don't know."

Carl leaned forward. He was close enough to touch Hallie Langley or take her hands in his. He was smart enough not to.

"What do you think, Ms. Langley?"

"Miss Shivers."

"I thought —"

"I left my husband six weeks ago. So I guess I'm turning back into Miss Shivers." She frowned, thinking something through. "Langley's a better name, isn't it?"

"It's a pretty name, Langley. It suits you. But Shivers is a good name too, and it's your family name."

"With no one to carry it on. Not since Eric died." Hallie shook her head, as if to clear her mind of some memory. "I'm sorry. To answer your question — no, I don't think he was alone. I think he did go off with that girl, Becca. Becca Harrison. His friends would've known what to do if Eric had an attack, because they grew up with him."

"Wasn't she from here too?"

"She went to the high school, but she was one of the Notting Island kids." Hallie smiled. "We called them Not-heads back then. Stupid thing, but it made them so angry. Why do kids say such stupid things to each other?"

"I thought I knew the bay, but I don't know Notting Island."

"Most people don't."

"Virginia or Maryland side?"

"Well, we like to say it depends on which way the tide is going," Hallie said. "But, officially, it's Maryland. Past Smith. Really, it's like a piece of Smith that fell off."

Tess couldn't hold back any longer. "Is her family still there?"

Carl gave Tess a look, as if she were headed off on a tangent. But it seemed crucial to her. A boy had died under mysterious circumstances, only to have his name and Social Security number appropriated by a man who had reason to need a fake identity. Who would know better that his identity was available than someone who had witnessed his death? Becca Harrison might have clearer memories of the day.

"I wouldn't know. It's been fifteen years. I don't even remember much about her. Becca Harrison. Not *Rebecca*, mind you. Becca. If you called her Rebecca, she'd get all high and mighty and say, 'Rebecca was in the Bible. I'm Becca.' As if it would shame her, somehow, to be in the Bible."

"Perhaps," Carl said, "this Becca would not say, as Rebekah did, 'I will go.' Remember when Abraham's servant goes to fetch a wife for Isaac?"

Hallie nodded. Tess, who always confused Rebekah and Isaac with Jacob and Rachel, was clearly out of her league, biblically.

"No, this girl never said, 'I will go' to anyone in her life."

"So what are the odds she's still there?"

"Slim to none. She was one of those people who was on her way to leaving from the moment she arrived. But those who are there should remember her, and someone might know where she's gone. For what it's worth, but I don't think it's worth much."

"Why not?" Tess insisted. Carl frowned at her, a reminder that she was breaking their own ground rules. But Tess was not used to keeping quiet.

"She's just one of those people who never admitted to doing anything wrong. Held herself like she was so perfect. Look, my family knows no one meant to hurt Eric. People panic when things go wrong. It was an accident. All you ask is that people own up to what they did. You can't forgive them until they do."

"And you can't move on until you forgive." That was Carl, his voice so low he might have been speaking to himself.

"How do you get to — I'm sorry, I've forgotten the name of the island already."

"Notting," Hallie said. "It's the westernmost of the inhabited islands, the one beyond Smith. When you've gone as far as you can go and there's nowhere else — that's Notting Island."

"How does one get there?"

Hallie smiled for the first time. "Boat is the preferred way. Unless you're a real strong swimmer."

# Chapter 20

"There is no boat to Notting Island," said the craggy-faced man sitting on his boat along one of Crisfield's docks, eating a late lunch and washing it down with something in a paper sack. Tess realized she had been watching people eat all day, but had not eaten anything herself since her 7 a.m. bagel.

"Then how do people get there?" Carl asked.

"I mean there's no ferry, no regular-like boat. You want to go there, you have to charter something."

"There's a boat to Smith Island," Tess said. "Notting's just a little beyond that."

"Yes, ma'am, there is. Because people got reason to visit Smith Island. It has an inn and that whatchamacallit, the visitor center. Notting's got nothing like that. Notting's got *nothing*. In fact, some say —"

"Yes, we know what some say," Tess said. They had been traversing Crisfield's docks for almost forty-five minutes, and they had heard the old yarn about Notting's name at least four times.

But they had yet to find a way over.

"Well," the semi-ancient mariner said, peeved

to have his story rebuffed, "the fact is, no one goes to Notting but those what live there, and they have their own boats. There's the school boat —"

"Then put us on that," Carl said.

"It's not mine to put anyone on. Besides, the school boat would put you there after four, with no way to get back, and you'd be stuck there all night. There's no place to stay, no motels or the like." He gave Tess a once-over. "You don't look like you'd be inclined to sleep on the ground, getting bit by bugs. No, best thing to do is charter something in the morning, like you was going fishing or sightseeing. Then you can come and go as you want."

"Isn't there anyone who will charter a boat now?"

"Those who got boats to rent don't have 'em this late in the day, not on a day this pretty. Fishing is for early risers."

"I've been around boats all my life," Carl said. "If you'd let me use your boat, or even rent it —"

"I'm not Hertz," he said, after a quick sip from his bag. "I'm not even Avis. I don't try harder."

The man laughed a beat late, as if caught off guard by his own wit. His face was a topographical wonder, creased with lines, the nose and forehead rising out of the folds like mountain ranges. His thick white hair had a texture closer to fur. He looked as if he lived under the dock, crawled out during the daylight hours for the sun, and then retreated into the shadowy damp at nightfall.

"Did we tell you we were working with the state police?" Carl asked.

The semi-ancient mariner spat in reply.

But Tess was sliding crisp twenties from her billfold, counting them covertly, because people are more apt to notice the actions one tries to hide, just the way ears perk up at a whisper. She had ten in all. Something clicked in the man's eyes when she peeled the fifth bill off the roll. She handed them over, along with her ID.

"So you know we have to come back."

"You'll bring her in by dark? I'd like to go home for supper tonight."

"Guaranteed."

Not quite convinced, he gave Carl a measuring look. "You really know boats?"

"Yes, sir. I grew up in Cecil County, have my own sailboat. I've sailed the upper waters of the bay, as well as the Susquehanna."

"Well," the man said, "I guess that almost counts as growing up on water."

The bare-bones powerboat wasn't much for speed, yet Crisfield faded behind them almost too quickly. It seemed to Tess a long time before land came into view, and that was Smith Island, nine miles out. They kept going, Carl consulting the bay chart he had thought to buy, until a smaller, more compact land form came into view.

"Notting Island," he said.

"Some say it was meant to be Nothing Island."

"Yeah," he said, catching their benefactor's odd accent just right. "That they do."

"But others say Knot Island."

"That they do."

Tess began laughing, and Carl allowed himself a smile. In their search for transportation to the island, they had not only been forced to hear the story of its curious name over and over, they had heard the legends about its would-be names. One version had that it was once Knot Island, for it was a lumpy fist of a place when first charted, tight as a good knot. Others said it began as Nothing Island and cited as their proof a line from Father Andrew White's diary, kept on that first voyage to Maryland, when the *Ark* and the *Dove* had sailed into the bay. He wrote about seeing "an island so small it might as well be nothing" not long before arriving at Point Lookout on the Western Shore.

For such a tiny island, it had more than its share of lore. The men along the Crisfield docks had told them that Notting Island almost disappeared in the early twentieth century. Literally. The bay began to beat at it from all sides, eroding its shores. Other islands in the bay, such as Shank, had been pummeled in this fashion, becoming uninhabitable. Notting had seemed bound for a similar destiny. Then a huge storm came up, and when it was over the bay had somehow reversed itself and decided to spare Notting. Or so the old men said.

They also said Notting was cursed, haunted by the ghost of a young waterman killed in a drunken brawl, the only homicide recorded on any of the bay islands in the last fifty years. He had been accused of poaching, which was to an island community what horse-stealing was to the Old West. Falsely accused, it turned out, for the poaching continued after he was dead. He was said to haunt the island to this day, stealing other young men like himself.

"Do you believe in ghosts?" Tess asked Carl as he guided the boat into the narrow channel that led to the main dock in Tyndall Point, the larger of the two towns on the island. She was learning that such impersonal questions were the best way to draw him out. He had come a little bit out of his shell, over the time they had spent together, but he was still quick to retreat.

"Lord, no. And definitely not this ghost. It's just a story and it does what stories do."

"Which is — ?"

"Stories make the truth less painful. Young people leave these islands because there's no more work, no way to making a living. I bet not even two hundred people live on this island now. The bay may have spared Notting, but the twenty-first century won. It's dying. It's easier to blame that on some nonexistent ghost than to face up to the reality that a way of life is passing."

Not even two hundred. Tess tried to fix that number in her mind, to find some context for it. Her high school graduating class had almost twelve hundred students. Camden Yards held forty-five thousand fans. Two hundred was tiny.

Then again, how many people did she have in her life proper? Even with her large family and her almost promiscuous attitude toward friendship, there could not be fifty people on the planet who truly mattered to her. And she had carved that fifty out of a metropolitan area of almost two million. If you started with two hundred, would you have more close friends or fewer?

Tyndall Point was forlornly picturesque, with white clapboard houses scattered along crooked streets. The focal point was clearly the weathered general store, a dingier white, with two sets of gas pumps — one on the dock and one on land — although it was hard to see where cars could go on the island. Then again, there must be some use for cars, because a field of rusting auto carcasses and abandoned appliances sat not a hundred yards from the store.

"Let's hope," Carl said, "that we walk into that store and find some old busybody who has been keeping track of anyone and everyone since time began. Because this is not a place where a stranger wants to go knocking on doors."

The girl behind the counter was younger, at

least in years, than Tess. But there was a curious wisdom in her young face, a cool indifference that would have been at home on Baltimore's toughest drug corner. Smooth was the word that came to Tess's mind — the girl had shiny hair that had been pulled back in a ponytail that deserved to be called silken, creamy skin, blue eyes so dark they were opaque. And her manner was slick as marble. Polite but hard, with nothing to grasp.

"We're trying to find someone who lives here," Carl said, leaning on the counter. Tess found herself wishing he were just a little better looking, or a lot more charming. "I suspect if they're here, you know them."

"I wouldn't claim that," the girl said.

"This girl — she'd be a woman now — I'm not even sure she's here anymore. But she was a teenager here, maybe fifteen years ago."

"More likely my mother would have known her," the girl said. She did not, Tess noticed, offer to find her mother.

"Her name was Becca," Tess put in. She did not mind Carl's new deferential manner, but she wondered why he had not identified himself, flashed his badge, and said he worked for the state police. Most people want to cooperate with the police. Not in West Baltimore, perhaps, but certainly the law would be welcome here.

"Becca," the girl repeated, with no show of recognition. "Not Rebecca?"

"No, just Becca."

"Hmmm. You don't recall a last name?"

"Harrison," Carl said.

"That's not one of the five families."

"Five families."

"The year-round residents. There are only five surnames in Tyndall Point, give or take an odd cousin or a newcomer. She must have been summer people. But they tend to come for one season and not come back. Can't say as I blame 'em. I sure wouldn't choose to live here."

She was projecting her words, speaking for someone else's benefit. But for whom? The store was empty as far as Tess could tell.

"So Becca doesn't ring a bell?"

"Huh?" The girl had drifted off, bored with them.

"Harrison," a voice pronounced from behind a floor-length pair of oilcloth curtains that hung in a doorway behind the counter. A woman came out, and Tess felt as if she were staring at one of those cruel computer-generated projections of how a face ages. For here was the smooth girl in thirty years' time, dried and gnarled. The shiny brown hair would turn gray and wiry, the complexion would mottle. But it was the hands that caught Tess's eyes. They were huge, with ropy tendons and long thick fingers so big they appeared permanently splayed.

"The Harrisons lived here some years back. This one was in diapers then, if she was born at all." Mother gave daughter a hard look. "For all the sense she has, maybe she should be in diapers now. What has it been, twenty years?"

"Closer to fifteen," Carl said.

"Twenty, seventeen, fifteen, ten. The fact is, it seems like it was forever ago, and it seems like it was just yesterday. That's how you know you're getting old, when it all blends together."

Old? The woman couldn't have been more than forty-five.

"So you knew this girl, Becca Harrison?"

"I wouldn't say I *knew* her." Tess understood that "knew" was not a word to be used lightly here. "We were aware of them, of course. And the father, he was said to be someone. Come to think of it, he was the one who said it. I never heard of him before, and no one heard from him after, so I don't know how famous he could have been."

"Famous for what?"

"He wrote for magazines. Or so he said. I never saw his name in nary a one." She gestured at the dusty racks in front of her cash register, where she had copies of *TV Guide*, *People*, and *Sports Illustrated*. "He said he was going to write a book about the island, but that never came along neither."

"Do you remember his name?"

"He went by Harry Harrison. I suppose there may have been parents foolish enough to call their boy such a thing, but I hope he had a real name too. I just never heard it."

Tess's fingers itched to take notes, but she

had learned that nothing made people dry up faster than seeing their words scratched onto a pad. She was trying to train herself to listen hard enough so she didn't need to write things down. But it was tricky. Her memory wasn't as good as she wanted to believe it was.

"How long has it been since he lived here?"

"Like I said, he wanted to write a book about Notting, a made-up story. So he moved on, found some other place to write about, I guess."

"And Becca went with him?"

"Well, I swagger a man's children should go where he goes, don't you?"

*I swagger.* The unexpected localism was so charming, so unexpected, that Tess almost missed the woman's neat evasiveness. She hadn't said yes, she hadn't said no, and her expression was cat-sly.

"Is there anyone here who knew Becca well, who counted her as a friend? Or her father, for that matter?"

"The Harrisons kept to themselves. The father claimed to like it that way. Said he had a clearer vision of what he was seeing here. We liked it that way too. He was . . . a *frivolous* man."

"How do you mean? Did he drink, act silly?"

"Ah, you won't catch me making judgments about those who drink. Drink is legal here, in Tyndall Point." She nodded toward the refrigerated cases, three in all. Behind two were the greens, golds, and browns of domestic beers, while the third held a few essentials, such as eggs and cheese and milk. "Just beer, no hard stuff. The store over to Harkness, now, they don't carry anything."

"What made Harry Harrison frivolous?" Carl asked.

"Why, he didn't do a lick of work that anyone could see. People work hard here. His idea of working was to wander around asking improper questions. Now, we're used to being studied. College students, reporter people, those folks who care more about the marsh grasses than they do about human beings —"

"Environmentalists?"

"So they call themselves. Anyway, we know something about people who are making a study. But Harry Harrison, he was just interested in himself and how Notting affected him. He couldn't see the way he affected Notting."

The old woman looked thoughtful, as if she had said something she had long felt but never found the words for until today.

"But Becca — is there anyone here who would remember Becca or would still be in touch with her?" Tess pressed. As interesting as it was to contemplate the hapless Harrison, wandering around the island in his solipsistic state, it was his daughter they needed.

"Oh, I doubt it. As I said, they kept to themselves. Now" — the woman leaned forward and pressed her hands on the counter, until they looked like a griffin's talons — "now, I suppose you'll be wanting to buy something."

Tess understood they were expected to repay the woman for the time they had taken, although it appeared that time was an abundant commodity on Notting Island. She picked up a bag of Oreos. The woman raised one eyebrow. Tess added a few cans of beans, a Slim Jim. The eyebrow stayed up and didn't budge until Tess had amassed about $40 worth of groceries she didn't need. Really, this woman could beat Whitney in an eyebrow Olympics.

"Do you think they were telling the truth?" she asked Carl as they headed back for Crisfield, racing the setting sun. It had been a clear day, but a few clouds had drifted onto the western horizon, creating a spectacular sunset. The world was turning purple and rose, and Tess was drinking a beer, part of the toll back in the general store. She wondered if the woman always charged six dollars for a six-pack of Old Milwaukee.

They had not relied on the old woman's testimony that no one in Tyndall Point would remember Becca Harrison, much less know her whereabouts. Old woman — funny, how Tess kept thinking of her that way. They probably weren't much more than fifteen years apart in age, and Tess did not plan to be old at forty-five. But the woman in the store had been like some withered sage in a myth, full of obscure portents and warnings.

And, like the heroes in a typical myth, they had ignored her hints. They had knocked on almost every door in Tyndall Point. Some were answered, but most were not. The few residents they found were female, and some looked to be in their early thirties, but not a single one recognized Becca Harrison's name. Reminded of her father's stay on the island, they allowed they might have known her, but no one had kept in touch with her. One said she thought Becca meant to be an actress, another said Becca planned to be a singer.

"Never did hear of her again, though," this last woman said. "So I guess she wasn't quite so good as she thought." Tess wondered if this flash of malice lurked below the surface of every Notting Islander who remembered the Harrison family. Certainly, neither the father nor the daughter was missed.

"Why does Becca matter?" she asked now. Crisfield was coming into view and they could see the semi-ancient mariner waiting for them, his white beard and hair blowing in the breeze.

"You were the one who wanted to go on that wild goose chase, not me."

"Bear with me. I'm thinking out loud. Eric Shivers died. Someone may have watched him die. Certainly, whoever took his identity knew it was there for the taking. Knew he had a license in the system, knew the real Eric Shivers had no use for it."

"Are you thinking Becca is our killer? What,

she got a sex change over at Johns Hopkins, got herself turned into a man, prosthesis and all, then began killing the women she dated? And you think *I* watch too many movies."

"No, I'm going a different way. The man you knew as Alan Palmer — he had a female accomplice. A woman called, remember? Called you and Sergeant Craig, said she was a caseworker with the state. Maybe the man who took Eric Shivers's identity had help too. Maybe there were two people who saw Eric die, and they protected each other. As vague as everyone on Notting was, they did confirm the fact that Becca left the island more than fifteen years ago, not long after Eric Shivers died. Perhaps her father sent her away to protect her."

"A middle-class guy like that? If he knew, he'd make his daughter stand up and take responsibility for what she had done."

"You'd like to think so," Tess said. In her experience, upstanding citizens could be enormously flexible about the law when it was applied to them. That had been Luisa O'Neal's fatal flaw.

"Look, when you were a Toll Facilities cop, did you ever have to chase down drivers who didn't pay the toll, just busted on through?"

Carl stiffened noticeably. "There was much more to my job than that."

"I'm sure there was. But I'm asking, Weren't there people who didn't throw the quarter in the basket?"

"You know, one person who ran that toll ended up killing a cop. A stupid kid driving a stolen bakery truck, all the way from New York City. It wasn't a joke, what I did. It mattered."

"I know, I know. But there's a point to where I'm trying to go here. Weren't there people — fine upstanding people in nice cars — who blew through the toll?"

"Yeah, sure. On occasion."

"And didn't they always, *always*, have a reason for why they did something wrong? Hadn't they decided the rules didn't apply to them?"

Carl got the point, smiled.

"Rationalization," Tess said. "That's what really separates humans from the rest of the animal kingdom. It's the opposite of Darwinism. Animals do what they have to do to survive, but it's all instinct. Humans do what they want to do, then work backward, trying to make a case for why it was essential to their survival."

"So does Eric-Alan have a reason for what he does?"

"I bet he believes he's justified on some level."

"Maybe. Or maybe he's a monster." The sun had dropped below the horizon with astonishing speed, and Carl's features were not as visible in the murky light. "Some people are just born evil."

"You don't believe in ghosts, but you do believe in monsters?"

"I believe in evil, yes."

"I'm not so sure. It's not like there's evil in one's DNA. Something has to form your character."

"But now you're doing what you just accused other people of doing — rationalizing. *My mommy did this, my daddy did that, and I'm all mixed up.* I've got no patience with people like that. I don't have much use for psychiatry in general."

"Well, me either, but — *shit.*"

"Am I coming in too fast?"

"No. I just remembered I had an appointment today with my own shrink. It totally slipped my mind. And what do you want to bet that the fact I forgot is only going to be used as proof of my hostility toward the whole process?"

Did she really think he wouldn't know she had been there? His mother kept in touch with her old friends. It was only a matter of hours before one of them happened to ring up and say — casually, almost as an afterthought — that some strangers had come around, asking about Becca Harrison. Which set her off, and now she was on his phone, almost in a panic.

"Don't worry, Ma. It wouldn't matter why they came or what they asked. You know no one there would confide in strangers about anything."

"But they spoke of her by name —"

"And they think she's someone they can find."

This gave his mother pause. Even on the buzzy, unreliable line of his cell phone, he could tell she was turning this thought over, sifting through it the way a gardener might spade a patch of earth. She had such a good mind. He liked to think he had inherited this quality from her, this ability to analyze a problem. Then again, he often wondered if her tendency to examine things so thoroughly

had come from years of picking crabs, separating out the meat from the waste in those
small bodies. In which case, the trait could not
be inherited. But it could be learned, through
careful study.

Natural selection — the words came back
to him from seventh grade social studies,
swimming through the years, as fresh and
sacrilegious as they had been the day he first
learned them. He had come home from
school, eager to tell his mother about how
evolution really worked, how the giraffe had
not grown a long neck, but that the long neck
had come to be favored and the short-
necked giraffes died out.

"Don't talk that trash in front of your father,"
she had warned.

But his father, when he came home that
evening, had said it made sense. "If these
crabs get any smarter," he said, "they'll be on
the skiffs and I'll be burrowing in the mud,
trying to keep them from catchin' me. What's
the point in being married to the best picker
on the island if I can't bring her enough crabs
to pick?"

She wasn't the best. That was a devoted
husband's hyperbole. But she was good. A
woman like his mother, who had picked for a
living, could do things to a crab that no casual
tourist feaster could ever do. Her personal
best was fifteen pounds in an hour. But it
wasn't her speed that made her exceptional, it

was her thoroughness. There was nothing left on a crab when his mother got through with it.

Technically, what his mother and all the island women did was illegal. The crab meat they picked was not inspected by the state's health inspectors. They all knew what it was like to have a carton seized, to see a day's work taken away. How they hated those unhealthy-looking workers from the health department, those prissy, pinch-faced spoilers.

For the men, the enemy was the Natural Resources police, who enforced the always-changing rules on crabbing and fishing. Growing up on the island was not unlike living in a colony or some close-held territory. They had a hard-earned skepticism of all authority except God. So even if anyone there had ever questioned the not-quite-told story of Becca's flight, all those years ago, they would never speak of it to outsiders.

But they hadn't questioned it. And they did not speak of it, even among themselves, because they would not want to hurt his mother, presumed to be in denial ever since the day his boat was found, drifting on its own, near Shank Island. Suicide was such a shameful thing. Of course, almost as shameful was the possibility that an island boy like himself had drowned by accident, had made a miscalculation when the storm came up. Confronted with those two possibilities, people chose simply not to speak of what had happened to Audrey's boy. After all, she had just lost her husband to bad blood and now she had no boy. She had carried this falsehood fifteen years now, constant and unswerving. It was only lately that she seemed to worry so much.

She began again. "June Petty said —"

"June Petty. Never has a woman been so aptly named."

"June said there was two of them. She thought they might be DNR, but they never showed no badge or said exactly why they wanted to find Becca."

He knew, but he could not tell his mother. There were only so many secrets she could be expected to keep. She did not know how Eric Shivers had come magically back to life, much less why. She knew he used an array of fake names but assumed those were for his business. His mother had no problem with what he did for a living. A person whose ancestral home was almost swallowed by the bay tends to have more respect for nature, but also less. Everything the earth produces must be allocated and reallocated. Survival of the fittest.

"Did June say what they looked like?" he asked, as if he did not know. His mother would not expect him to know.

"The man was orangey, like a Cheshire cat, and speckled as an egg. The woman was tall, with a braid. June said she just missed being pretty."

"June Petty," he said, with more heat than he intended, "thinks everyone just misses being pretty, except herself and her daughters. I wonder if she's looked in the mirror lately. She was a hag when God was a boy."

"She was the best-looking woman on the island in her prime."

"Which is quite an achievement when you consider that the island had maybe — oh, three hundred and fifty people in June's heyday."

"What's got into you, son? It's not like you to be so sharp."

"Nothing." He backs away from the anger. "I'm sorry, Ma. It just bothers me that June ran to the phone, eager to tell you all this. She likes . . . pitying you, always has. First when Dad got sick, and then after I —" He doesn't need to finish the thought. "Are you sure you weren't the prettiest girl on the island and June Petty's just trying to get you back after all these years?"

His mother laughs, the sweetest sound he has heard all week. Just then, the telltale buzz of a bad cell begins. He is losing her. He says good-bye hurriedly, hating the feel of being cut off. Whatever happens, he never forgets to tell his mother "Good-bye" and "I love you."

He slips the phone into the well beneath the radio and drives on. It's raining today, and the temperature is barely in the fifties. The past few days had been sunny and almost hot, close to eighty. A typical spring in these parts. He knows a moment of envy and resentment: She has been to the island, a place denied to him now for fifteen years. He doesn't even dare to go to Crisfield or Princess Anne. Those who would seek to punish him will never be able to equal the pain of this exile from the place he loves above all others.

The end of April in Harkness. The hackberry trees would be coming into their own just now, and the marsh grass would be that soft shade of green he has never found on the mainland. It is too early for the snowball bushes to bloom, but they would be well on their way. Most of all, there would be the excitement that slowly builds when the rush is imminent as the blue crab mating season gets under way and the jimmy starts to court the sook, holding her to him for hours and hours. Beautiful swimmers indeed.

He wonders if her city-bred eyes and nose could begin to absorb the teeming bounty that was around her in those few hours. He could teach her. He could show her.

He has so much to teach her.

# Chapter 21

"I charge for missed appointments. I thought I made that clear at our first meeting. You must cancel twenty-four hours in advance, or you will be billed in full."

"But in the case of an emergency —" Tess protested.

"I do not consider driving to the Eastern Shore at the last minute to be an emergency."

"Sorry," she said, sullen as a child, reduced once again to pulling on the strings of the old wing chair. "I'm just trying to track down a serial killer, so I came in on Wednesday instead of Tuesday. God forbid that should make me a day late for this court-ordered charade."

She had been more authentically contrite when their session started. But Dr. Armistead had been maddeningly indifferent to her explanation, which struck her as much more interesting than most of the mundane utterances made in therapy. Carl had a point: It was all my-mother-this, my-father-that. Yet Dr. Armistead had been downright incurious about her work. All he wanted to know was why she had not thought to call, how she could have forgotten her appointment.

At times he had seemed more like an aggrieved suitor than a doctor.

"We all think our work is important, Tess," he began now.

"Yes, only I'm *right*. My work is important, okay? This man has killed at least two women and stolen two identities. He could have three–four victims by now. He could be in another relationship, weeks, even days away from killing a new woman."

Armistead had a habit of clasping his hands and holding two index fingers to his lips, where he tapped them softly. *A tell,* Tess thought, but what was he telling?

"Let's talk about you and impulse control, Tess."

"Impulse control? I don't think I have a problem with that."

"I didn't say you did. I'm not here to say you have this or that problem. But can you identify any patterns in your behavior when it comes to impulsive action? Do you think you are more prone, or less prone, to following every novel idea that pops into your head?"

"No. No, I don't." But her own body language made her realize what a brat she was being. She had slumped in the chair until her chin was on her chest and her legs were stretched out in an adolescent's defiant posture. Sheepishly, she straightened up and made eye contact with the doctor. Although eye contact was a bit of misnomer, for she was always distracted by those bristling eyebrows, so much more compelling than the small deep-set eyes beneath them.

"I think I have a lot of self-control," she said, but her voice was more tentative.

"How about the night you attacked Mickey Pechter?"

"I didn't *attack* him."

"Excuse my use of the term, then. But can you see any way in which your actions were impulsive, that things escalated from what I'll call emotional momentum. Is it fair to say you got carried away?"

"Carried away by what?"

"I don't know. You tell me. I might describe it as . . . a sense of righteousness, perhaps. A certitude that your actions were justified."

*"But they were."*

"Perhaps. The question of whether you did the right thing doesn't interest me as much as whether you have a tendency to think you're always doing the right thing."

He was accusing her of being like the people she had described to Carl, the ones who thought they could always justify their own actions. But she wasn't one of them. Was she?

"I'm trying to catch a killer."

Dr. Armistead's index fingers tapped faster on his lips. "I thought the state police were in charge of the investigation and you were merely assisting them."

"Yes, but —"

"Tess." She did not like to hear her name on his lips, although she couldn't say why. It sounded presumptive, as if he thought he knew her, and this was only the third time they had spoken. He did not know her, could not know her, not after three sessions, not after thirty.

"Tess, I'm trying to get you to think about your own actions. I'm not saying you are right or wrong. But you need to look at your behavior as part of a larger whole, that's all. It could be helpful to you."

She did not agree but it seemed easier to placate, to pretend. "I know."

"Now, how do you feel when you think about this serial killer?"

"I *feel* that there are two people who ask people how they *feel* — psychiatrists and television reporters."

"What are you inferring?"

"Nothing." It amused Tess that even an educated person would confuse *infer* with *imply*. Then again, she had heard smart people, people she actually liked, misuse *hopefully* and *comprise*. It drove her mad. Now there was a thought: A serial killer motivated by poor grammar. She imagined Eric Shivers/Alan Palmer whiling away his days in domestic bliss, only to have Tiffani or Lucy come in and say *between you and I*.

She smiled at her own folly, then remembered these were real women, real victims, and regretted her black humor. A coping device, one used by reporters and cops alike. She often thought Jonathan would have a lot of funny things to say about his own death.

"Do you have any idea," Dr. Armistead asked, "how much happens in your face in the span of a few seconds?"

"No." She always imagined she had a poker face, but perhaps that was only when she was playing poker.

"If your feelings — sorry I keep returning to that topic, but it is what I do — if your feelings were any clearer, you'd be a danger to yourself."

"I guess I'll have to work on it."

"I wish you wouldn't." He smiled, as if he had won a point, although Tess wasn't sure of the game they were playing. Continual one-upmanship? "I'll waive the fee for the missed appointment this one time, given that you re-scheduled so promptly. But don't let it happen again. If it's a true emergency — and we'll have to reach a mutual understanding about what constitutes an emergency — we'll work it out."

"What about the terms of my probation? Do I get reported to Judge Halsey if I miss a session?"

"Not this time. But if it were to become a pattern —" Dr. Armistead did not need to finish this congenial threat. He wrote the time and date of their next appointment on a small card and handed it to her. "I'll also have my secretary leave a message on your voice mail the day before, just to nudge your memory."

"Why not? The dentist does."

"And, as I keep trying to convince you, I'm a doctor like any other."

His voice was soft, persuasive. If she didn't have to look at him, Tess thought, she might like him better. It was such a nice voice, deep and rumbly. *A doctor like any other.* Yeah, sure. Frankly, she'd rather have leeches applied to her body.

"Can you tell what I'm thinking?" she demanded of Carl, when she arrived at the state police barracks twenty minutes later.

The question seemed to make him irritable. "I barely know you. If I'm doing something that bugs you, just say it right out. I can't stand the way women hint about stuff."

"No, I mean in general. Does the expression on my face betray what's going on in my head?"

"That's a lot to put on any face. I'm not sure that a mouth and one set of eyes could convey everything that goes on in there." He tapped his own ginger thatch of hair. "For example — I never saw that question coming, and I have no idea why you asked it."

"Good. Now, what happened while I was gone? Any calls come in?"

"None that mattered." Carl looked around, as if he expected someone was eavesdropping. "Close the door."

The state police had given Tess and Carl a makeshift office in a corridor that was en route to, but rather distant from, where the real investigation was under way. Tess thought it might be a mark of respect. Carl was convinced it was a way of keeping tabs on them.

One theory, Tess decided, didn't rule out the other. She glanced into the corridor and, seeing no one, shut the door.

"Officially," Carl said, "I've been manning the tip line. Major Shields seems a little suspicious about our whereabouts yesterday. And when I told him you had a doctor's appointment this morning, he thought I was kidding."

"Why? Did you say what kind of doctor's appointment?"

"You ashamed of being in anger management?" Carl looked genuinely curious.

"No, but — it's *private*."

"Well, I told him you were at the podiatrist. Sounds like psychiatrist, you know. Head doctor, foot doctor — how would a dumb country boy know the difference?"

Tess gave him a crooked grateful grin. "So did the tip line yield anything?"

"Mainly crackpots. But what do you expect when you put up fake MISSING PERSON signs in convenience stores?"

"You expect — hope, pray — that someone's going to see Alan Palmer's photo and say, 'Hey, I know that guy and he's definitely not missing.' "

The state police had thought the plan through, in Tess's opinion. Palmer's family, which had been questioned at length about their son's associates, had been told not to worry when the signs went up. The idea was to tease out a local woman who may have had a near-miss with the man. And if the man himself saw it? The poster was designed to appear as if it had been made and distributed by one of Lucy Fancher's nonexistent relatives, for it intimated that they had information about her estate that would be relevant to Alan Palmer. The call even had a fake Cecil County prefix, which was set up to ring in this office.

"What about Becca Harrison?"

"I can't find a trace of anyone with that name. But women get married, change their names. Women are hard to find."

"And her father?"

"A Harold 'Harry' Harrison with an appropriate date of birth died thirteen years ago, according to the Social Security database. Last known address was upstate New York. If he ever did write a book, I can't find it, not on Amazon."

"My guess is that Harry Harrison's work, assuming it ever existed, is long out of print."

"What about the high school yearbook? Did that yield anything?"

They looked at the copy of the *Crisfield Courier*, the usual slender volume, bound in green, a gold seal stamped on its front. They had found it in the Crisfield library. It was a noncirculating reference book, but it had been easy enough to pilfer it. Tess planned to FedEx it back, with an anonymous note of apology and enough cash to buy a few new novels.

"It's too easy for people to disappear these days," Tess said. "We think we have all these tools, but if you really want to vanish it can be done."

"Well, Becca did it in the good old days. Turns out Harry Harrison did file a missing persons report with Talbot County, which patrols Notting Island."

"You tease! Where'd you get *that?*"

Carl patted the side of the old IBM clone they had been given. "There's more software on here than you know. You just have to know how to use it. And I do. It was April, around fifteen years ago."

"A few months after Eric Shivers died."

"Yep. Her father told police he thought she might have gone swimming."

"Swimming in April?"

Carl nodded. "I know. Pretty cold in the bay that time of year. Besides, it's hard for the bay not to let go of a body. Eventually."

"So, Becca disappears two months shy of her high school graduation — and, coincidentally, a few months after Eric Shivers dies. Her father files a missing persons report, but people on Notting Island think she's gone off to become a singer or an actress. Her dad moves away not long after. Is he heartbroken or covering up? Does he think his daughter drowned or ran away? We can't ask him, and we already tried to ask everyone we could find on Notting Island."

Tess sometimes liked to sit very still when thinking. Carl, on the other hand, rocked in his chair, teetering wildly until she was tempted to kick the legs out from under him. Maybe she did have a problem with impulse control. Instead, she got up and opened the door. Closed doors invited suspicion.

"You think they got anything new, after talking to the Guntses and the Palmers?" Carl jerked his chin toward the open door, indicating the world of official police just beyond their threshold.

"Possibly."

"You think they'll tell us when they do?"

"Probably not." Tess grinned. "They made it clear this is not a two-way street. We're tenant farmers. We owe them our yield, but they don't share anything with us."

As if to prove her point, Sergeant Craig rushed by, eyes averted, as if he was worried they would try to engage him.

Carl rubbed his knee. "Weather's going to change."

"You feel the weather changing in your bum knee?"

He shrugged, as if it baffled him too.

"Look, I'm hungry. Want to blow this pop stand and get some lunch?"

"You know I only eat at the end of the day."

"Yeah — I know that's idiotic. Come on, let's

go eat something, see if it jars anything loose in our brains. I can't stand sitting in this room anymore, pretending to work."

"Seafood?" he asked hopefully. Great, Carl had finally consented to eat a midday meal, only to choose her least favorite thing on the planet.

"If you're willing to drive a ways."

"Sure." Then as an afterthought, almost suspicious. "Why?"

"I'm not a big seafood fan, but I like the setting at Jimmy Cantler's, especially this time of year. Let's go there."

"You don't like seafood, but you like to sit next to water when you eat?"

"Yeah. Do you think that makes me crazy?"

"I don't know. Ask your doctor. He's the one who's getting the big bucks to figure you out."

They were a few miles north of the turnoff to Annapolis when Carl said, "Someone's following us."

"What —"

"Don't look," he said, catching Tess's neck with his right hand before she could turn her head. "Car's been on us since we left Pikesville. It didn't seem too weird at first — a lot of folks head into the city down Reisterstown Road. But he's following us."

"He?" Tess asked.

"I think it's a he. With the glare on the windshield, all I can be sure of is that there's only one person in the car."

Tess flipped open the mirror on the visor above her seat, as if to check the makeup she wasn't wearing. Carl was right — it was impossible to see anything except a shape. The shoulders and the suggestion of a baseball cap indicated it was a man, but that's all she could say for sure.

They were in Carl's car, a not-old, not-young Saturn. Gradually, he pushed it to seventy, then eighty, and finally ninety mph. Interstate 97 was sometimes called Maryland's autobahn, for its smooth, easy curves seduced drivers into higher-than-legal speeds. But the Saturn was almost vibrating as its odometer needle climbed. It felt as if Carl could lose control at any minute. Tess knew the road, knew there was a big curve coming, where 97 turned east and the straightaway led down an old state highway.

"Carl —" she began.

He didn't seem to hear her. He drove as if all the other cars on the road were stationary objects, and his only goal was to move between them. He slid in the far left lane, pushing the speed higher still.

"He still with us?" Carl said.

"He —"

"Don't look," he hissed.

Carl's Saturn went faster still. Tess looped her hand in the handle above the door and braced the other hand against the dash. They were coming to the turnoff, where the road split and the highway had a long tapering curve that required even the best drivers to slow down. Carl showed no signs of doing this. He seemed to be counting to himself, grimly.

"Almost, almost, almost — *now*." With one quick, precise turn of the wheel, he sailed back into the right lane, edging in front of an eighteen-wheeler and taking the straightaway, while a dark blue car — Tess was not sure of the make or model, it was just another foreign sedan, a Toyota or a Nissan — continued down the highway. Carl, belatedly prudent, had taken his foot off the accelerator and was letting his car slow down gradually.

"Do we need to double back to 97, or can you get there from here?" he asked, as if nothing had happened.

"Jesus, Carl, what kind of boneheaded move was that? If someone's following you, just lead him along, take him to the fucking police station. But don't try to drive a Saturn like you're the king of fuckin' NASCAR."

He stiffened, hurt. "If I were alone, I might have risked a confrontation with the guy. But I thought it was better, with you in the car, to lose him."

"Hey, no fake chivalry bullshit, okay? I'm licensed to carry a gun. I'm good at taking care of myself. My boyfriend doesn't pull this kind of macho shit on me. Where do *you* get off?"

"Well, maybe he should."

"What are you saying?"

"I'm saying —" He paused for a breath, and whatever adrenaline kick he had derived from the little chase was beginning to ebb. "I'm not saying anything. I know you can take care of yourself. But that guy was definitely following us."

"I never doubted that part," Tess said. Although, come to think of it, maybe she did. Carl Dewitt was about as paranoid as anyone she had ever met. "I just didn't like the way you handled it."

He was slowing, looking for a place to turn around. "You made your point. Do you have to make it in that tone of voice?"

"What tone?"

"That superior I'm-the-boss tone. I'm a pro too, you know. I deserve to be treated like one."

She started to point out that he was not, that he was the most amateurish of amateurs. He wasn't making a nickel off this case, while she was able to bill her time to her consortium of nonprofits. But the thought brought her up short. Why *was* Carl doing this? What was in it for him?

Instead, she asked, "How do you support yourself, since you stopped working for the state?"

"My knee."

"Your knee supports you?"

"I fell at work, in the parking lot. I probably was headed that way anyway, but the fall meant I had to have replacement surgery. I'll live long enough to need at least one more, maybe two. The rehab was hard, and I ended up screwing up my back as well, needing disk surgery. By then, I'd been out six months. I retired at age thirty-five on full disability."

"Some folks probably envy you that."

"Yeah, well, in the land of the no-knee men, I guess the one-knee man is king."

Tess laughed. "That's pretty good. Is it yours, or is that another movie line?"

"I don't know." Carl was driving with an old man's deliberateness now, as if to make up for scaring her. "Maybe. It should be, don't you think?"

# Chapter 22

Tess had taken to sleeping with the case files of Tiffani Gunts and Lucy Fancher, although not intentionally. She crawled into bed each night, intent on reading and rereading the complete files to which she finally had access, only to nod off with the light on. She had done this every night since the trip to Notting Island, and she did it again on this balmy Friday night. The next thing she knew, Crow was kissing her awake, gathering up the photocopies spread around her and placing them in a neat stack on her bedside table.

"How — was —" She groped for the word, her mind blank — "work?"

"It was okay. We brought in the Iguanas for a late Cinco de Mayo celebration. We couldn't get them for the real thing."

"Very cool," she said on a yawn. She adored the Iguanas.

"Yeah, but all these frat boys kept screaming *Happy Independence Day.*"

"So?"

"It's not."

"Well, it's Mexican Independence Day, Crow. Their independence counts too."

"It's not anyone's independence day." He stacked her papers, clearing a space for himself, turned out the light, and slid into bed next to her. She liked the warm, smoky smell he brought to bed after a night at work. It made her feel as if she had been out clubbing and dancing.

"Huh?"

"Cinco de Mayo," he said, reaching around her and finding her breasts, as if she might have misplaced them during the day, as if he needed them to anchor himself at night. "It commemorates a naval battle against the French, near Puebla. Mexican Independence Day is September sixteenth — *diez y seis.*"

"I love you for knowing that," Tess said.

"Then show me."

She did.

Sex, usually the perfect sleeping pill, served only to make Tess more wakeful. There was too much stimulation in her life these days, she thought, staring at the ceiling, where shadows flowed like water. She had been having trouble sleeping for a while now. She tried to pin the beginning of her insomnia down. Since she had taken the case? No. Since she had met Carl Dewitt? No.

Since she had kicked Mickey Pechter in the ribs? Maybe. Or maybe a few weeks later, when Dr. Armistead had started nosing about in her head.

She thought Crow was sleeping, but he suddenly turned and placed his hand on her abdomen, her least favorite body part. No matter how strong she got, or how lean, this was always soft and round, untamable. He liked it, though.

"Have you ever been pregnant?" he asked.

"God, no. What a strange question."

"Not so strange. It happens. Even to people like us, who are careful. Yet in all the time we've been together, you've never been late by even a day."

"How do you know? Do you keep track of my cycle?"

"Not exactly. But I've just observed that there's a five-day period each month when you become so unpredictable, so volcanic in your emotions, that it's a given what will follow. After all, if a woman's *pre*-menstrual, she's definitely going to be menstrual."

She bumped him with her shoulder. "I'm not that bad."

"You're horrible. Even the dogs have figured it out. I can't swear to it, but I think Esskay has scratched out a calendar in the backyard, where she crosses off the days."

"Why are you thinking about this stuff anyway?"

He was behind her, so she couldn't see his face, but his voice sounded sheepish. "I sometimes think I should be able to tell when you're ovulating, but I guess that's just a fantasy."

"I'd imagine so," Tess said. "Unless that's a thermometer between your legs."

"*What?*"

"It's a method of testing fertility."

"Oh, yeah. I knew that."

"Of course. You know everything, Mr. Cinco de Mayo."

They laughed and luxuriated in the pure sensation of a laugh rippling through two naked bodies at once.

But the laugh died so abruptly in Tess's throat it sounded as if she had inhaled a piece of food and choked on it.

"What?" Crow asked.

"The files. Grab my files." She didn't give him a chance to do what she asked; she turned on the reading light next to the bed and found them first.

"I never thought to ask for a catalog of items taken from Tiffani's house after she was killed. I don't know if the Frederick cops found anything there, although they must have photographs of the scene. But Carl made a list. He showed me a calendar, one with markings that indicated when Alan Palmer was on the road — or so we thought. Every month, two to three days would be circled. He found it in a drawer and assumed the killer had put it there, to throw him off. Which made sense when we thought an outsider might have killed Lucy. But Alan wouldn't have bothered to hide it. Not if the calendar was part of his alibi, right?"

"So who put it in the drawer?"

"Lucy. She was keeping track of her cycle, trying to figure out when she was fertile. Which is old-fashioned and incredibly unreliable, but some people might still do it that way."

Tess had found the place in the file where Carl had inventoried the things he took from the rental house. Yes, there was the calendar, with a description of the markings that appeared over the last three months of Lucy Fancher's life. They had assumed these notations showed Alan's travel days, when he had chosen the time of Lucy's death.

But Lucy's body had, in effect, chosen those days. From the moment she began keeping this record, probably at her beloved's request, Lucy had begun her own countdown to the day she would die.

"Women do that?" Carl asked, blushing redder than Tess had ever seen him.

"Some do, I guess. It's not mandatory. They don't hand you a calendar when you turn thirteen and say, 'Hey, get cracking.'"

"Jesus, Tess." Carl dropped his head so low in embarrassment that his nose was almost touching the place mat at the Suburban House. Tess had convinced him to leave the barracks for lunch a second time in a week, a great triumph. Getting him to this Jewish deli was an even bigger coup. Carl seemed mildly alarmed by everything here, from the mock-tough wait-

311

resses to the Yiddish witticisms on the paper place mats. And he hadn't even seen the pots of schmaltz.

"Actually, from what I know of friends who have been seized by the desire to reproduce, it's not a very good method. I'm surprised they were using it. I'm surprised they were using anything."

Carl lifted his head warily. "What do you mean?"

"This was a pretty newly minted relationship."

"So? Not everyone waits ten thousand years to have a baby."

Was he making some veiled reference to her and Crow? Tess let it pass. "Yes, but even if they had decided to conceive a child, they wouldn't have needed a calendar."

"I don't follow you."

"Carl, I'm trying to be respectful of your apparent delicacy when it comes to such matters, but when you're young and allegedly in love, you don't need to keep a calendar of the best time to try to conceive a child."

"Why not?"

Tess's voice was louder than she intended. "Because, Jesus Christ, Carl, when you're in a new relationship you have sex all the time."

That got everyone's attention, especially the waitress who was standing over them, waiting to take their order.

"Y'all want anything?" asked the woman, a

312

tall, solidly built black woman. "I mean, from the menu."

Carl meekly ordered a roast beef sandwich, adding a bowl of matzoh-ball soup when Tess promised him it was really just chicken soup with a bonus. She asked for the kreplach and kishkas with gravy.

"I don't think you can make generalizations about people's sex lives," Carl said, barreling through the sentence as if he just wanted the topic to go away. "And in the case of a serial killer, you have to recognize that he derives a great deal of sexual satisfaction from his crimes. The man we're looking for may not be able to function normally. He may not be able to function at all."

"Did you ask any of Lucy's friends about her sex life?"

Carl's face was now redder than his hair.

"Not straight on, the way you would. But I gave them open-ended opportunities to discuss the relationship. You know the rest — everyone said he was perfect. She never confided the least bit of doubt about him, except to wonder how she had gotten so lucky."

"Look — your theories and mine don't necessarily contradict one another. Lucy was keeping a record of her fertile days. Let's say that our killer does have a difficult time" — Tess tried to think of an expression that wouldn't make Carl dive under the table from sheer embarrassment — "meeting expectations in this one sphere of the relationship. Maybe he turns this into a strength. He could tell the women — I don't know, that he doesn't want to have sex just to have sex, he wants to make a baby with them."

"Or that he's born again," Carl said, "and he wants them to wait until they get married. I knew a guy like that at headquarters."

Tess nodded. It took time, but she and Carl eventually got in sync. "Think how romantic that would seem to young women like Tiffani and Lucy. Young as they were, they probably had their fill of bad, indifferent sex. Maybe he even chose" — she groped again for another delicate turn of phrase — "to please them in alternative ways."

"Alternative — oh, you mean — ?" Carl looked around the restaurant, as if convinced that the tables of elderly customers were hanging on their every word. But most were simply scooping up chicken fat and diving into belly lox without a care in the world.

"Right. What if — bear with me here — what if he is a she?"

"How can that be?"

"Ever read *Yentl the Yeshiva Boy*?" As Carl's roast beef sandwich on whole wheat with mayo arrived, Tess realized he didn't have even a passing familiarity with Isaac Bashevis Singer. Besides, film was Carl's preferred reference point. "Or that movie *Boys Don't Cry*, about the teenage girl who pretended to be a boy?"

Carl shook his head. "Not my kind of movie. But I saw the documentary, which came first. Besides, she was found out. She didn't keep her secret for long."

"Okay, but what about the real-life case of Billy Tipton? He passed as a man through five marriages. No one knew he was born Dorothy Tipton until the day he died."

"That's not possible."

"It is. It was. Billy bound his chest, saying he needed the support because he'd broken his ribs in a car accident. I won't go into the details of how he did what he did — I'm afraid you'll pass out from that level of technical detail — but if you get curious, there's a very good book about his life. The point is, it's doable. It's been done."

A thought was nagging Tess, buzzing around her like a gnat. She waited for it to settle, to sit still long enough so she might snatch it up and examine it. But it faded away as quickly as it arrived.

"Can they make a woman into a man?" Carl asked, and it was as if a child had asked a single penetrating question, cutting through to what is profound and essential in the world. Tess sat, a spoonful of kreplach halfway to her mouth. *Can they make a woman into a man?*

"I'm not sure. Certainly, the task is more formidable than making a man into a woman. But —"

She let the idea sit there, not quite yet exposed, even on a Saturday, waiting to see if it would wither as it was exposed to air and light. No, it was still there.

"If Becca Harrison became a man, one way or another, she wouldn't exist anymore. It's natural that she would take the name of Eric Shivers, the boy whose death she witnessed —"

"Maybe caused," Carl put in.

"Still, there's no connection to Alan Palmer. Not that we know of. We could throw her name at the state police, but then we'd have to explain how we came to have it."

They sat in silence, chewing. Carl was the first to get to the end of a long mouthful.

"You know, if you're a woman passing as a man, there's one thing you can't fake."

"What?"

"You know." He made a baffling hand gesture.

"An erection? Honestly, Carl, have you ever heard of dildos? Or even the concept of a rolled-up sock filled with birdseed?"

"That's not what I meant."

"What then?"

He made another indecipherable gesture.

"I'm sorry, I guess I don't speak 'Toll Facilities cop,' because that doesn't mean a thing to me."

"Semen!" Carl sputtered, earning the undivided attention of every blue-haired diner in Suburban House. "Sperm! You can't make a baby without those things, so what's the point of keeping all these careful records if you're not?"

"I don't know," Tess admitted. She still felt the presence of that damn gnat, hovering close to her ear, still determined not to tell her what it knew. "Maybe none of this matters at all. Do you think we should go to Frederick?"

Carl knew she meant visiting the Gunts family. "That's specifically against the rules."

"Right. So you'd rather sit in the office all day, even on a Saturday, waiting for phone calls that never come, rereading case files we've practically memorized, in the hopes that the state police might at least tell us when they've arrested our guy, let us come to the press conference and stand on the dais?"

Carl thought for a moment. "Let's go."

"*The Wild Bunch*," Tess said. "William Holden, Ernest Borgnine."

"You finally watched?"

"Last night. It's no *Once Upon a Time in the West*, but it's pretty good."

"You know that movie too?"

"Yeah, but I prefer *Once Upon a Time in America*." Tess fell back in her chair, faked a dying croak. "Noodles, I . . . *slipped*."

Carl smiled as if she had just presented him with a wonderful gift.

# Chapter 23

Things had changed in Frederick — things that couldn't be explained by the passage of less than three weeks. Had it really been so long ago? Had it really been so recently? Tess was beginning to feel like the old crone on Notting Island. One thing was clear: The Gunts family no longer considered her an ally, a friend. Of course, they had been stiff and taciturn the first time, but she detected a new coolness to their closed-in ways. Or maybe it was simply that they had been caught without their usual spokesman, the brother, who was on the road. His chatty wife, Kat, was at work as well. It was just the mother and father today, and neither seemed eager to speak.

"The state police have already been here," the father said.

"Yes," Tess said. "I thought you'd be pleased."

"Pleased you think that sweet boy did this?" This was Mrs. Gunts, but the father grunted something that sounded like assent.

Carl tried, deploying his small-town charm. "There's a strong chain of circumstantial evidence linking him to the murder I investigated on the upper shore —"

"We know all about that — that . . . nasty thing. But Tiffani was shot in her kitchen by a burglar. Not some crazy who took off her head and kept her body and —" The mother shook her head. Clearly, she considered Tiffani's death more dignified than Lucy Fancher's.

"I can understand how distressing all this is," Tess said. "You've been so sure, for so long, that she was killed by an intruder. It's hard to readjust your thinking. But I just have a few questions."

"I don't think," the father said, "that we have any answers. We made that clear to the state police."

The front door opened, and a burst of noise, cheerful and high-pitched, swept into the gloomy house. The grandchildren had arrived home from school. Now that Tess had met Troy Plunkett, she could see the striking resemblance in the one girl's face. There was no denying this child, as they said on the streets of West Baltimore, although Plunkett had tried. It was too bad that Tiffani's sweet but indefinite features had been vanquished by Plunkett's tougher genes. If the girl didn't catch a break in adolescence, she was going to end up with her father's all-over feral look.

The children paid no heed to the four grown-ups gathered in the family room, just ran past to the kitchen, opening cabinets, grabbing things from the refrigerator.

"One each," Mrs. Gunts called out. "You can have any treat you want, but just one each."

"Does a soda count as one?"

"Yes. But milk and juice don't."

There was some grumbling about this, but the children accepted the edict and began the difficult selection process.

"May I —" Tess gestured toward Tiffani's daughter.

*"No."* Mr. Gunts's raised voice lashed like a whip. Tess flinched, wondering what it was like to grow up with the threat of that sound. But she wasn't his daughter. He had no say over her.

"One question. A simple one, not about the crime but about something her mother may have told her in the weeks before she died."

"She was barely four then. She wouldn't remember anything."

"I imagine if your mother dies when you're small," Tess said, "the memories that might be lost in a different life only become stronger."

"You're going to ask something about Eric," Mrs. Gunts fretted. "Something nasty."

"No, I'm not even going to mention his name. Or Tiffani's death. But please, let me speak to her for five minutes."

They were clearly torn. Why were they so reluctant to know the truth about what had happened to their daughter?

"Please," she said. "Five minutes, and we're gone."

The little girl — Darby, Tess had forgotten the name — seemed unfazed by the idea that some strange woman wanted to talk to her.

"One minute," she said. "I'm going to have a Ho-Ho." With great concentration and delicacy, she unwrapped the cake and then slipped her free hand into Tess's and led her to the backyard. Tiffani had probably offered her hand with the same ease.

"Do you remember your mother?" she asked, when they were seated on the back steps.

"Oh, yes. She was pretty. Maw-maw says I look just like her."

"You do," Tess lied.

"She . . . told me stories. At night. She said I could have a puppy one day. But we needed a yard." The girl looked around. "Now I have a yard, but I still don't have a puppy. People are allergic."

"Did she ever say you might have a brother or a sister?"

"Instead of a dog?" She wrinkled her nose, as if she considered this a less-than-fair deal.

"No, just maybe. One day."

Darby wore a tight pink T-shirt and jeans with zippers at the ankles. Her dark hair had been swept up to one side of her head and fashioned into a fluffy ponytail. For such a little girl, she had a preening self-confidence. Tess found herself hoping she could hold on to this sense of herself.

"She asked me once if I would like one."

"Really?"

"On my birthday. I had a party, and I got a

lot of presents. Uncle Eric gave me a dollhouse. I still have it."

"And your mommy said —"

"She said I might have a baby sister or brother before my next birthday. She asked if I would like that. I said I'd rather have a puppy."

"When's your birthday, Darby?"

She announced it with the pride that children always reserve for that most important date: "March seventeenth, which is Saint Patrick's Day."

It was also, Tess knew, just a few days before Tiffani Gunts had died. She would have asked Darby a few more questions, but Mrs. Gunts came out on the back porch, a kitchen timer in her hand. She had taken the request for five minutes with Darby as literally as possible.

"Will you bring me a puppy the next time you come?" the little girl asked. Her grandparents said nothing, but their anger was so strong it almost came off them in fumes.

They hate me, Tess realized. They would kill this messenger if they could. Because of her, they would have to reinvent the coping mechanisms they had built over the years, revising the stories they had told themselves. The myth of Tiffani was that she was a young woman on the verge of her greatest happiness when a stranger came and took that from her. They did not want to accept this new version because it made the last months of Tiffani's life a bitter lie. They did not want to admit that her happiness was an illusion. They wanted her to have that brief golden time she had been denied.

But wasn't the illusion real? If Tiffani believed in her love, then it was true. At least, it was true up to the moment she flicked on the light in her kitchen and stood face-to-face with her perfect boyfriend, the man who had given her everything. And the man who, with one shot to the chest, took it all away.

"It's something," Carl allowed, on the drive back to Baltimore.

"I think it's more than something. I just don't understand —" Her voice trailed off. Carl wasn't listening to her, not really. He was tracking something in the rearview mirror, craning his neck at a slight angle.

"What?" she asked.

"I can't swear to it, but I think he's back there again."

"Same car?"

"Yeah. Dark sedan. Foreign."

"Don't try to lose him this time," Tess said, laying a hand on Carl's arm.

"Why?"

"Let's see what this is about. Maybe the state police are following us. Or maybe —"

"You think?"

"Anything is possible."

Carl was in the left lane, moving at a steady clip, slightly above the 65 mph speed limit. He passed another car, but in an unhurried fashion, and then edged into the right lane, only to pick up speed. It was bad driving, but it was a good way to gauge if someone was trying to keep tabs.

"He's hanging in," Carl said, "but hanging back."

"Take the next exit," Tess said, "but signal this time. Give him a chance."

Carl did, leaving the highway at a spot that was neither suburban nor rural. The dark sedan followed. Again, the glare made it impossible to see much more than a silhouette at the wheel, and it was too far back to see the front tag. But the car appeared to be a Nissan Sentra.

There was a traffic circle just south of the road leading from the exit. Carl whipped around it so fast that he was almost able to lap the Nissan as it entered. But it handled better on the curves than Carl's Saturn, and it sped ahead.

"A little faster," Tess said, "and maybe we'll be able to see his license plate."

"What do you think I'm trying to do?" He pushed the car harder, but the Nissan picked up speed too, slipping around the curve, its license plate obscured. Carl pushed the accelerator to the floor and Tess became aware of other cars waiting at the yield signs that led into the circle, scared to merge. She thought the Saturn and the Nissan might end up melting into butter, like the tigers that ran around and around the tree in the old folktale.

But at the next turn, the Nissan shot to the south just as they were overtaking it. Carl couldn't react quickly enough, so he had to make another full turn around the circle. By the time he had completed the revolution, the sedan was a speck in the distance.

"State cops?" Tess asked.

"I don't think so."

"Eric-Alan, keeping a watch on the Guntses' house, waiting to see if anyone goes there? Or keeping a watch on us?"

"No," Carl said. "He couldn't risk that. I know what he looks like, remember? A beard, losing or gaining weight — I spent enough time talking to him to remember him. He can't afford to get too close to me or to Sergeant Craig."

"Still —"

"Still nothing. He burns his bridges, this one. He doesn't go back. He's done with everything — the place, the women. He wouldn't go back on a bet."

They had returned to the highway and were heading toward Baltimore. The roadside views were familiar to Tess now, and she found solace in that familiarity.

"Carl —"

"Yeah?"

"You talk sometimes as if you're in his head."

"I'm not," he said sharply. "And I don't want to be. I've just made a commonsense determination about what he would do, based on what he's done. He never came back to North East, not even once."

"He might have —"

"No, I'd have known. People would have gossiped, that stupid newspaper reporter would have called me. I'm not inside him. I'm outside looking at him, the way you'd look at an animal in a zoo."

"Except he's not behind bars."

"No," Carl said. "He'll never be."

"Don't be defeatist."

He gave her a quick, level look. "Don't be naive."

"What are you saying?"

"When we catch this guy, don't be surprised if he has to be taken by force. He's likely to be violent."

"You're *hoping* he'll be violent."

"Whatever. We'll have to protect ourselves."

"We? You and I? Or the state police?"

"Just don't be surprised."

"You're saying they'll kill him if they can justify it. Just like that guy in Baltimore County, who they said was going for his gun, only it turned out to be a cell phone."

"You ever been a member of a SWAT team? You ever gone into a house in the middle of the night to confront a person you know has killed five people and is determined to keep going until he gets what he wants? That's what that guy in Baltimore County did. Don't be so quick to make judgments."

"I'm not. But this guy, our guy —" The plural possessive gave her pause and she lost her train of thought for a moment. "This man, whoever he is, has to be taken alive. How else will we know the entirety of what he's done? We think he's killed at least two women. What if there are more?"

"They can work backward. They won't need his confession to figure out everything he's done. It's not like he buries his bodies. He leaves them out in the open."

"Anyway, it's a moot point. We're not going to be there when this comes down. They're not going to let us get that close."

"Maybe it's not in their control. Maybe even as we work the edges of the case, we're making significant discoveries."

"Significant? A few minutes ago, you seemed to think the trip to Frederick was a waste of time."

"It was — until someone tried to follow us. Someone wants to know what we're doing and where we're going."

"I still think it's the state cops," Tess said.

"We should be so lucky."

# Chapter 24

Back at state police headquarters, something was up. Tess sensed it, the way one senses a coming thunderstorm. The air seemed to hum and everyone was moving a little faster, as if trying to get things done before the skies opened up. She could see the change, too, in the quick sidelong glances from Sergeant Craig, Lieutenant Green, and Major Shields as they barreled up and down the corridor.

But, most telling, Major Shields was suddenly very keen for them to stay in the office and wait for the phone to ring. Which it seldom did. Tess began to feel as if they were caught in a loop not unlike that traffic circle off Interstate 70, chasing their own tails. Nothing is more tedious than make-work, and Tess wondered if the state police had decided to bore her and Carl into giving up or dropping out.

The stalemate continued for three days: Tuesday, Wednesday, Thursday. On the third straight day of doing nothing, Tess got out a sketchbook and began making lists.

"What are you doing?" Carl demanded over his shoulder. He had been tapping disconsolately on the computer, playing with search engines, reading out-of-town newspapers to see if there were unsolved homicides in other states.

"Brainstorming. Reorganizing what we know, looking for links."

"That's pointless."

"You got a better idea?"

He turned away from the computer and watched as Tess began sketching, jotting down everything she knew about Tiffani and Lucy, looking for any other similarities they might have missed.

"Pretty. Small, fine-featured. Bad ex-boyfriends. Both worked in convenience stores."

"Good place to meet women when you're new in town." Like a sulky child who claimed he didn't want to play a game, Carl couldn't resist once the pieces came out and he saw his playmate having fun.

"But it helps if they have bad ex-boyfriends," Tess said. "And you can't know that just by looking at some woman who's selling you a Slim Jim."

"Well, there's a similarity you've overlooked. These girls were bubbly, according to those who knew them. Unguarded. They probably told their life story to anyone they waited on more than twice. And look." He pointed to another item on Tess's list. "They worked overnight shifts. Imagine a guy coming in, regular-like, buying a few things. How many visits would it take before he asked, 'So a pretty girl like you has to have a boyfriend.' And she'd tell him all her troubles, like he was a big brother. He didn't come on strong, remember? With Lucy, he got her to rent the house and only moved in later."

"Which also has the advantage of keeping his fake name off the lease and the utility bills."

"Right. Hey, let's graph this."

"Graph it?"

"On a map, like."

"It won't be much of a graph, just a straight point from Frederick to North East."

"I don't know. What if you add" — he took an old framed map of the state of Maryland from the wall and marked the two hometowns with silver thumbtacks — "the places where he spent the night before." He added a thumbtack to Saint Michaels and placed one in the lower left-hand corner, about where Spartina, Virginia, would be.

"I'm not seeing a pattern emerge here," Tess said.

"Wait." Carl removed dental floss from his pocket.

"You carry dental floss?"

"My dad had gum disease. You'd floss after every meal too, if you saw your old man coming home from the dentist in a wife-beating mood."

"Interesting turn of phrase," Tess said primly.

"I don't use it as a figure of speech."

His back was to her, and Tess needed a

minute to deconstruct what he had said. "Oh — hey, I mean, I'm sorry. I'm really sorry."

"It wasn't your fault."

"You know what I mean."

"It wasn't so bad. I got my growth early. By the time I was thirteen I could take him. And I did. He moved out and on." He was fixing the dental floss along the points he charted. One mint-green line from Frederick to North East, two small lines dangling down to the places their killer had used to set up his alibis. "It still doesn't look like much, does it?"

Tess studied the map. Again, she had that sensation of a gnat in her ear, a buzzing memory she could not capture.

"Try this," she said. She removed the strings that attached the two cities to their satellites, then held out her hand for the dental floss, breaking off another piece. "Now look."

She balanced the map in her lap, stringing a line from the speck that was Notting Island to Frederick and adding another one between the island and North East. The resulting triangle was almost a perfect isosceles. Its sharpest angle formed where the dental floss intersected Notting.

"What's the point?" Carl asked. "We don't know that Notting Island has anything to do with this."

"But there's a similarity," Tess said. "Water."

"What?"

"Water. Water, water everywhere. Wherever

he lived, he could see water. From Tiffani's town house, which backed up to the Monocacy, to Lucy's house in the trees, also with its river view. And there's no point on Notting Island that you can't see the bay."

"That doesn't eliminate a lot of the earth's surface, Tess."

"But it eliminates entire towns in Maryland. We're not talking about someone who just *likes* water. We're talking about someone who wants it within his sight as much as possible. I've been to Tiffani's house — you could see the river from the back deck. I stood in Lucy's yard — you could see the river glinting through the trees."

"Water?"

It was Major Shields who asked the question, leaning against the doorjamb with a too-deliberate casualness. Tess tilted the map toward her, so he couldn't see how they had defaced it with thumbtacks and dental floss.

"You got a lead?" the major prodded.

"No," Tess said, with her best girly smile.

"Not really." Carl was playing the country boy. Tess glanced over at his Huckleberry Finn visage, all freckles and sunburn, and thought about the confidence he had just shared. He must have been an exceptionally patient and deliberate little boy, waiting all those years to be big enough to beat the crap out of his father. You had to be strong to be that patient.

You had to be a little scary, too.

"Well, we've got one," the major drawled.

"Yeah?"

"Down in Saint Mary's City. Want to come?"

Tess and Carl looked at each other. It was as if he was trying to shake his head no without moving it at all. She, too, sensed a trap. But she couldn't see how they could say no to any opportunity. Could they have found him?

"Sure," she began, even as Carl said, "No."

"No? I thought you'd be glad to be included in the investigation, Carl. Why don't you want to go to Saint Mary's City?"

"Well, we're pretty busy here."

The major walked around the table and looked at their map. "Why, this looks very . . . interesting. But it will wait, won't it? Saint Mary's City is a long way, and I want to get down and back before rush hour, if possible. Besides, this gal doesn't have all day. She has to go to work at three p.m., she says."

"What gal?" Tess asked.

"Just a gal who says she knows something. Might be a wasted trip, for all we know. But I got a good feeling about this and thought you should be there. After all, you brought this to us. We owe you."

Tess looked at Carl and tried, as casually as possible, to point to Saint Mary's on the map: water. Saint Mary's City was also on the water. Carl nodded, but he didn't look happy. Later, thinking back, Tess would recognize the expression. It was the face of a man who was cornered.

Saint Mary's City was where Maryland had begun, with the arrival of two ships, the *Ark* and the *Dove*. It had been years since Tess had ventured this far south along the bay's Western Shore, and the usual desecrations had sprung up in this once-lovely country: the drive-through burger joints, the fast-oil-change places, the strip malls that looked as if they had been built overnight.

"Where are we going?" she asked the major, who had insisted they ride with him, not follow in Carl's car, as Carl had suggested. "I know you said Saint Mary's City, but where exactly?"

"Just outside of town."

"And this woman — what does she know?"

"She may have seen our guy. That's a pretty significant break."

"Recently?"

"No. Been almost two years ago. But she's pretty sure she saw him."

"You forget." She leaned forward, so her head was even with Major Shields, who sat in the passenger seat while Sergeant Craig drove. "Carl has seen him too. He interviewed him. So what's the big deal?"

"Oh, I think this could be a very big deal," Major Shields said. "Don't you, Carl?"

Why did he keep addressing Carl, who was slumped in the backseat, arms folded across his chest? The major had never struck her as sexist before, but he was suddenly acting as if Tess didn't even exist.

"Why?" she persisted. "Why would it be significant?"

The major took so long to respond that she wondered if he had heard her at all. Men, in her experience, often retreated so far into their own worlds that some voices — women's voices in particular, it occurred to her now — reached them as if on a delay. Even Crow, whom Whitney had once dubbed the perfect postmodern boyfriend, could become absent-minded and dreamy, until she had to tug on his sleeve and bring him back to earth.

For some reason, this made her think about Dr. Armistead. As much as he irritated her, he always listened. He wasn't always good on the nuances, but he at least heard every word. Maybe that's what it took to get a man to listen to every word you said: $150 an hour.

Even as Tess reached a hand toward Major Shields's shoulder to jolt him into response, she was thinking again about the man they sought. *He listened.* Oh, how he listened. From the moment he arrived in a woman's life, he was the most attentive and solicitous of men. He listened because he was gathering information, preparing for the day he would betray the trust of these young, naive women. Because he was the perfect man, the perfect boyfriend. He listened because he was less likely to betray his own complicated history if he didn't talk about himself.

"It's up ahead and down to the left," the major said. He turned his head to face them, seemingly unfazed by the fact that Tess was so close to him, hovering near his ear.

"Let's go," he said as Sergeant Craig rolled to a stop and put the patrol car in park.

"What, are you a *Wild Bunch* fan, too?"

"Never saw it."

"You should," Carl said. Tess realized it was the first time he had spoken since they had merged onto the Baltimore beltway two hours earlier. "It's only one of the best movies ever made."

"But it's all the usual outlaw shit, right?" Major Shields's easygoing drawl had taken on a new hard edge. "I don't get those movies where the good guys are obsessed with the bad guys, as if they're locked in some sort of immortal relationship. When you're an officer of the law, you lock up the bad guys and move on. It's not personal. It's not about individual glory or vendettas. It's a job, and you conduct yourself like a professional."

His eyes flicked at Carl, quick as the blue-yellow flame from a cigarette lighter, and moved away.

"In fact, let me show you how it's done."

# Chapter 25

The apartment complex was newish, a place with mild aspirations to class that began with the name — Dove's Landing — and ended at the front door. Once inside, the common areas were extremely common. Tess noticed that the carpet was dingy and a smell of ammonia lingered in the air.

"She's in 301," Major Shields said, beginning the climb to the top floor. Carl fell back. Tess glanced over her shoulder to see if his knee was troubling him, but he was simply moving with extraordinary care, as if he had no desire to reach the top.

The woman who answered the door to 301 wore an orange smock with a name tag, MARY ANN. Petite, with a face at once fine and coarse, foxlike. Much of it was hidden, however, by an extraordinary mane of dark curly hair styled in the feathery blown-dry wings of the late 1970s. The girl could not have been alive when this haircut was first popular, Tess thought. Tess herself had been barely alive, a grade-schooler who had yearned for such big hair, if only because her mother kept hers barbershop short.

"Miss Melcher?" Major Shields asked.

"Uh-huh," she said, showing them in. The apartment was neat but not quite clean. The carpet crunched beneath their feet. The framed posters, which ran to large-eyed kitty cats, were dusty and streaked. A cat was clearly on the premises as well, for Tess picked up the telltale odor of a litter pan that needed to be emptied.

Their hostess settled in a small rocker, while Major Shields and Sergeant Craig took the sofa, an overstuffed monstrosity of white cotton, its side shredded by the phantom cat. Tess took the only other chair in the room, while Carl was left standing.

"The cheese stands alone, huh?" said Major Shields, sliding over and patting a spot next to him on the sofa. "Have a sit, buddy."

"That's okay," Carl said, pulling a chair in from the dining alcove and setting it up at the edge of their circle, as close to the door as possible.

Mary Ann looked nervous. Her hands were tightly clasped in her lap, her head seemed to wobble a bit on her neck. Maybe it was the weight of all that hair, Tess thought. Then she did a mental double take.

*That hair. That smock.* Mary Ann Melcher was the living prototype of the killer's victims. Were they going to save someone's life? Had they actually arrived in the nick of time, like the cavalry in some old Western?

Major Shields said, "Mary Ann, I'd like you

to tell these folks what you told me yesterday, when you called our tip line."

She glanced nervously at Carl, then back at the major, who nodded his encouragement.

"I work at the Wawa? Going on three years?" She kept looking over at the major, as if he knew her life story better than she did. "About two years ago, a gentleman started stopping by there regular. He would buy a fountain soda and he would mix the Cherry Coke with the Diet Coke. He said it was the best combination — sweet, but not as many calories, and it tasted like the sodas you got at a real fountain? The other girls figured out he liked me before I did."

"What was his name, Miss Melcher?"

"Charlie. Charlie Chisholm. Like the trail, he'd say, but I didn't know what he was talking about. Later, he explained. Something about the West and cows. I don't know."

"Did you and Charlie" — the major had a delicacy, almost a tenderness, in the way he addressed the young woman — "did you have a relationship?"

"Not at first. He took a real interest in me. I was having problems with my roommate —"

"What kind of problems?" This was Carl, and his voice was as sharp as the major's had been soft. Something sullen crept into Mary Ann's face, as if she had heard this tone too many times in her life, had known a few too many bossy bosses.

"She was a little wild. Ran around with jerks. Which was her private business, but I had to put up with 'em too, and they weren't my boyfriends. Although some wanted to be. If she only knew —"

"Miss Melcher." The major's prodding tone continued soft. "About Charlie Chisholm."

She tossed her head. Tess wanted to tell her the effect wasn't as coquettish as she thought.

"He helped me get this place. Lent me money so I would have enough for the deposit, showed me how to get credit. All you have to do is get a little gas card and pay on it regular, he says, and bit by bit you can get everything you need. He also told me I should enroll at the community college, start taking courses so I could do something other than retail." She smiled at the memory. "He called my job *retail*. Or *the service industry*. I liked that."

Tess was confused. "You liked working in retail?"

"I liked the fact that he give it a name, didn't look down on me. He said it was hard, doing what I did. He said I had all sorts of talents, if only I'd use them."

Without warning, the girl broke down and began to cry. She was all of twenty-one, Tess figured, and still quite young in many ways, despite being on her own.

Major Shields was the kind of man who carried a handkerchief. He took this out and handed it to Mary Ann. "What happened to Charlie?"

"He came home one night and told me he wanted to take me to a fancy supper. We went to the Outback Steakhouse up in Waldorf. Come dessert, he took my hand, and I thought this was when I was going to get a ring, in a little velvet box. I thought he was going to propose."

Tess would have thought so too. But perhaps the fact that he didn't was the difference between being alive and ending up like Tiffani Gunts and Lucy Fancher.

Major Shields continued to push her gently, as if he didn't know the rest of the story. But he had talked to Mary Ann on the phone, Tess remembered. He knew where this was leading. "He didn't? What did he do?"

"He told me he was sick. He said he had been sick for a very long time, but he thought he could cure himself with . . ." — she groped for the words — "alternative therapies. He said he now realized he wasn't going to get well and he didn't want to be a burden on anyone. So he was going to go away."

"Go away?" Major Shields prompted. "Are those the very words he used — go away?"

Mary Ann nodded. "Yeah, I think so. I begged him not to. I told him I would stand by him, take care of him. But he said he was going to go home, let his family care for him. Which was the first I even knew he had family. I asked if he would come back for me if he got well, and he said he would. We didn't have dessert, of course. We drove home, back here."

"Did he make love to you that night?" The men looked at Tess, appalled at her tactlessness. But she knew it was important to ask.

"Yes. Yes, he did."

"Normally?"

Mary Ann lifted her chin. "I'm not sure what you mean by normally, but it was normal as far as I'm concerned." Then, wistful: "He was the best at that. Very considerate, if you know what I mean."

Tess did. The men in the room thought they did.

"Did you use birth control?"

*"Miss Monaghan!"* Major Shields had gone beyond appalled to shocked.

"I don't have to. I had a baby when I was seventeen and something went wrong. They had to give me an emergency hysterectomy."

"What happened to the baby?"

"My mama's got her. Simma's better off down there, because they live out in the country a little ways, in a good school district, and my mama doesn't have to work like I do."

"Did Charlie —" but Major Shields had decided that Tess had asked enough questions. He cut her off with a look, as stern a look as anyone had ever given her, and Tess had been on the receiving end of some pretty harsh looks in her time. He then transformed himself with almost disturbing speed back into the gentle, friendly inquisitor.

"Tell us what happened next, Miss Melcher."

"Two days later, I leave for work, and Charlie's here. When I get home at midnight, he's gone and there's a note, saying, 'I had to go. Please don't hate me. This is the only way to say good-bye.' I'm sad, but I think he's gone to his family, wherever they are. I never knew. But a week goes by and the police come around. Seems they've found Charlie's car and his boat trailer, the one he had for his boat, at Point Lookout. It's been there for a week, since just before a big storm come up on the bay. He filled out a float plan — they found it in the little box. He said he was going all the way out to sea to go fishing. Then, at the bottom, he wrote, *And I'm never coming back.*"

"Did they find the boat?"

"Just p-p-pieces." She began sobbing. "It was all a lie. Charlie didn't have any family to go to. He decided to kill himself rather than die slowly, using up all his savings. Turns out he transferred ten thousand dollars into my account the night before he left. It must have been all the money he had in the world."

It also, Tess knew, was the largest gift you could make to another person without having to pay a gift tax. "What did you do with it?"

"Paid off some bills. Bought a new car. My old one was on its last legs. Know something odd? Turns out that Charlie's car was in my name. When they found his van at Point Lookout, it was registered to me. So the title

343

was clear, and I was able to sell that too."

Major Shields turned to Tess and Carl. "We talked to the local police and the DNR police. Charlie Chisholm is missing and presumed dead."

"Presumed," Carl said. "Yeah, I'm sure he's counting on just that. Presumption."

"It's been two years," Major Shields said. "Two years, and we don't have another open homicide in all of Maryland that resembles the first two. He never faked his death before. Why would he? He just takes another identity and moves on, knowing the real so-and-so — Eric Shivers, Alan Palmer — will seal off the trail. The real Charlie Chisholm, in fact, is in Veterans Hospital in Baltimore. Been there on and off since the Persian Gulf War. Same date of birth as the others, same general description."

"Another hospital," Carl said. "Another chronic patient who's not going to get in the way of anyone who wants to appropriate his identity. It's not like there's any shortage of hospitals in the state of Maryland. And there's a large supply of men born thirty-two years ago."

Major Shields stood up. "I know, I know. You have a thousand arguments for why this guy is still alive. That's why you didn't even bother to pass along Miss Melcher's name and number when she called you on the tip line last week. If she hadn't called back, we still might not know about this. We'd be spinning our wheels and wasting our time and money, all because you think you know this guy better than the rest of us."

"I do," Carl said. "I met him. I talked to him. He wouldn't commit suicide."

"And maybe he didn't. But the boat was found, remember? Dashed to pieces in the storm. He let this girl live, for whatever reason. Maybe he began to experience genuine remorse, I don't know. I don't care. All I know is that he seems to be dead for all intents and purposes, and the cases are closed."

"You can't close a case when you don't even know his real name," Carl protested. "He's not Eric Shivers. He's not Alan Palmer. He's not Charlie Chisholm. He's alive out there, somewhere." Then to Mary Ann, his voice cracking with an odd hysteria that Tess had never heard before, "Do you have a photograph? Maybe it's not even the same guy. It could be a totally different guy?"

Mary Ann, still crying, shook her head. "He didn't like to have his photo taken."

Major Shields turned to Tess. "Did he tell you about the call?"

She shook her head numbly, remembering Carl slumped at the computer the day she returned from Dr. Armistead's office. *Any calls come in? None that mattered.*

"Carl —" Major Shields's voice was almost as gentle as it had been with Mary Ann. "I know you want to face this guy one more time.

I know you wish you could confront him, settle all these scores. That's part of your sickness."

Carl stood, heading to the door, as if he planned to walk back to Baltimore. "I don't have a sickness."

"Post-traumatic stress disorder is a legitimate illness. Cops get it. Paramedics. You see horrible stuff, it can affect you. But it doesn't give you the right to skew an investigation the way you did. You lied to us. We only knew about Mary Ann's call because the phone we gave you is tapped."

"The phone is tapped?" Tess couldn't help thinking about the calls she had made home during the day, the embarrassingly kissy-face conversations she had with Crow from the state police barracks.

Major Shields nodded. "The phone is tapped and the computer is set up so we can track every keystroke. We know you've been chasing down all sorts of leads you didn't bother to share with us. We know you didn't go to Spartina the other day, although we don't know where you did go. You want to tell us?"

"I don't think so," Tess said, almost instinctively, guarding what she knew.

"It doesn't matter. We know you went back to see the Gunts family, despite our instructions. Those infractions could have been forgiven because they didn't interfere with the investigation.

"But this girl, sitting in front of us, is key.

Our killer stopped as suddenly as he started. We'll learn his name, one day. But for now the important thing is that he stopped. And death is the only plausible explanation for that."

"Serial killers have periods of dormancy —" Carl began, but stopped when he saw Tess's sorrowful gaze.

"I trusted you," she said. "I thought we were working together."

"We were," he said. "But this isn't important. Really."

"Carl," Major Shields said, "you need help. You ought to think about going back to that place in Havre de Grace, the one where the state sent you last time."

No longer the center of attention, Mary Ann was crying even harder now. "Would he really have killed me? Truly?"

"I hope not," Major Shields said. "It's our belief that something changed his mind. Maybe he was dying, as he told you. Maybe he realized the sickness inside him was as deadly as any cancer."

"Then do you think . . . do you think . . ." Her voice was so choked with heaving sobs she could barely get the words out. She struggled to get control of herself and looked at the major with glistening eyes. "Do you think Lifetime Television would want to make a movie out of this?"

# Chapter 26

Tess moved through the next week in a strange fog. Technically, she was still working, even if she no longer had an office at the state police barracks. After all, the brief career of Eric-Alan-Charlie was perfect for the needs of her contractors. Whitney had whooped with pleasure when Tess told her the bare outlines of what they had learned. The state police were not going public, not yet, but they would eventually give the story to the press. The consortium would be able to make a lot of political hay, once everything was sorted out.

"Especially with this nut, this Carl Dewitt guy, who almost screwed up the investigation because of his own obsession," Whitney had said over the phone. Her bell-clear voice had never sounded quite so hard to Tess, so cruel. "He's practically a walking example of why all branches of law enforcement need training."

"I don't know," Tess had demurred. "I think he had some good ideas."

"How do you figure? He couldn't see the killer had been sitting in front of him — until you came along. Then, once he realized the right guy had slipped through his fingers, he couldn't accept the fact that he might be dead. But why was a Toll Facilities cop investigating a homicide at all? The state police need to be prepared to step in and help these incompetents."

"He wasn't incompetent," Tess said. "Just . . . inexperienced. And the state police were in charge all along. Carl Dewitt kept investigating this homicide on his own time, even after he retired on disability, because he cared."

"Or because he had fucked up," Whitney said, "and was psycho to boot. Look, don't take it so personally. No one's accusing *you* of messing up. The point is, we have reams of stuff to take to the judicial committee next session. You're working for advocates, remember? When you write your report, be sure to gear it to our needs. Who knew that five seemingly unrelated homicides would actually yield such a rich find?"

*Who did know?* Tess wondered as she hung up the phone. She had been so focused on Tiffani and Lucy that she had forgotten about the other three names: Hazel Ligetti, Michael Shaw, Julie Carter. Were they significant in some way? Carl had said it wasn't accidental that their paths had crossed. But Carl was crazy. Well, not crazy, but obsessed.

The day they had returned from Saint Mary's, Major Shields had taken her into his office for a final conversation.

"I want you to know, we don't blame you,"

he said. "You're not responsible for Carl's mistakes."

"Gee, thanks," she said.

"But you are responsible for your own. You were insubordinate. In our organization, we need people to follow instructions. I told you we could overlook your visit to the Gunts family. But you should not have tried to interview the little girl, Darby."

"Why not?"

"Interviewing children is a specialized skill. It requires training." He allowed himself a one-sided grin. "Just like the domestic violence cases that were supposedly your focus."

"Point taken."

Major Shields was not insensitive. He realized that Tess's sourness was not about being cut out of the official investigation.

"Don't blame Carl," he said.

"Why not? You do."

"Carl suffered a breakdown while working on the Fancher case. That's why he's on permanent disability from the state."

"He told me he screwed up his knee in a fall."

"He may have, but that's not why he got early retirement."

"If he's such a nut, why did you let him work on this?"

Major Shields was still wearing his trooper hat, which was disconcerting. It made his eyes harder to see.

"That was Sergeant Craig's idea. He thought it might help Carl. If we made an arrest and he could feel he was part of it, it could have helped him put the whole matter behind him."

"So instead you humiliated him by dragging him down to Saint Mary's."

"That was for you," Major Shields said. "We wanted you to understand how serious this is. And we wanted you to know the investigation is, for all intents and purposes, over."

"They never found a body."

"But that's where you're wrong."

"Excuse me?"

"Several men about the right age have surfaced in the bay since Charlie Chisholm disappeared, including two John Does. Remember, Charlie Chisholm wouldn't come up as Charlie Chisholm, because the real one is alive. We're looking at these drowning victims. We're sure one of them is our guy."

"But if Charlie had surfaced, wouldn't someone have brought Mary Ann Melcher in to make the ID? After all, the DNR police knew he had gone missing because of the float report."

"These bodies were found in such an advanced state of decay that visual ID was — to put it nicely — no longer feasible. But the medical examiner had dental records on file that Mary Ann thought belonged to her boyfriend. She found them in the apartment after he disappeared. Here's the odd thing: The dental records matched the real Charlie Chisholm, the one in the VA hospital."

"How did he get those?"

"Believe me, we're trying to find out. But it explains why they didn't match up to a John Doe."

"But what if Carl is right? What if the killer just faked his suicide and he's still out there? What if he's moved to another state?"

"We've been all over that, Tess. We cannot find a single unsolved homicide that matches. The guy's either dead or he's Houdini. Do you believe in criminal masterminds? Do you honestly think that serial killers are geniuses, toying with law enforcement officials? In many cases, they're the lowest of the low, with barely functional IQs."

"Still —"

"Go home, Tess." His voice was not unkind. "Let Carl be an example to you of what can happen when you get obsessed with something."

*"And what if Carl is right?"*

The question caught her off guard, but only because it was strange to hear Dr. Armistead say what was inside her head. He had a way of sneaking into her thoughts when she least expected it.

She hated it when he did that.

"I don't think he is," she said. "And even if he is — it's up to the police. I don't investigate homicides."

"But you *were* investigating homicides. Or so you insisted when I made the same point two weeks ago."

"I was hired to examine the police work on five — well, four — open homicides. I did that. Game over."

"You think of it as a game?"

"That's just an expression. From video games, you know? You play for ten or fifteen minutes — or, in my case, more like ninety seconds — and then that's what it says on the screen: GAME OVER."

"Are you angry at Carl?"

She sighed. "That word's never far from us, is it?"

"It's the reason we're here."

"No, I'm not *angry*, although he undermined me when he didn't tell me everything he knew. I feel sorry for him. He did the best he could. He had his reasons. They were the reasons of a damaged man, who can't think things through very well, but they were reasons. I'm sad about Carl. I liked him. I liked working with him. I didn't want him to be a nut."

"So someone who spends a few weeks in a mental hospital as the result of a situational trauma is a nut? Or is it the fact of Carl's obsession that makes him — again, I'll use your term — a nut?"

"Sorry." Except she wasn't. She liked mocking his work, liked being politically incorrect about mental illness.

"Whether he is right or wrong, Carl believes the killer is still at large. What if he's right?"

"He's not."

"But imagine if he were. In his mind, he was in a position to try and prevent another woman's death. How do you think you'd feel if another woman died now?"

"No one's going to die. The killer's dead. Are you saying Carl was right?"

"I'm not saying who's right or who's wrong. I'm asking you to show some empathy for this man you claim to like so much. Even if the supposition is false — or even somewhat self-aggrandizing — how would you feel if you thought there was even a chance you could have saved someone's life if you had done something differently?"

Dr. Armistead's deep, rumbling voice was extremely mild. He was learning, Tess realized, that she was quick to take offense if he was too sharp, too pointed. Tyner Gray hadn't mastered that trick, despite knowing her for almost a decade.

"I would feel awful," she said, "but I would get over it."

"The same way you got over the death of your boyfriend, Jonathan Ross?"

"How do you know about that?"

"You mentioned it, at one point."

Had she? She couldn't remember. She thought she had kept Jonathan to herself, even here.

"I wasn't at fault in Jonathan's death. I didn't cause it, I couldn't stop it."

"Did that keep you from feeling guilty?"

"No."

"So imagine if you *were* at fault. How would you feel? That's all I'm asking, Tess. Imagine how you would feel if you believed someone's death was on your hands, as we used to say."

"There are no deaths after Lucy Fancher's. So Carl doesn't have to feel guilty about anything."

"Then maybe he feels incomplete."

"If you use the word *closure* I'm going to get up and walk out."

"You can't walk out," Dr. Armistead said serenely. "You're here under court orders. You're mine for five more months. Do you realize today marks our first-month anniversary?"

The syntax bothered her. It bothered her quite a bit. *You're mine for five more months.*

"I'm not yours," Tess said. "I'm not anyone's."

"My apologies. I didn't mean it the way it sounded. All I'm trying to do is get you to be more empathetic. You say you liked this man, Carl Dewitt. Why can't you see he may have had reasons to do what he did? Why can't you try and understand him?"

"You're saying that, even if he's wrong, his conviction that the killer is still at large would explain why he did what he did."

"Something like that. I don't know anything

about Carl other than what you've told me. But it seems to me that a man who couldn't solve one woman's murder might feel better about himself if he could at least bring the man to justice. He's been denied that. And imagine how he would feel — how you would feel — if someone else were to die now?"

The various minute hands of the various clocks made their way back to twelve and Tess went on her way, her stamped card a reminder this was, in fact, probation, a punishment. Five more months. She'd make it. She was sure of that much.

She was also sure she had no use for the doctor's theoretical questions. *How would you feel if someone else were to die now?* It was just the usual psychoanalytic, hypothetical, hyperbolic crap, she told herself.

And so it was, and so it remained — for the next twenty-four hours.

Things are not going according to plan. He is not used to that. Everything always goes according to his plans. He has been so thorough, so careful, ever since — well, since he had to be. And now, to be undone by a single man, a stupid man. He knows it must be that stupid Barney Fife's fault. How did this happen? He's not sure, he can't be sure, he can't get close enough to be sure.

But the fact remains, she is no longer going to Pikesville every day. She is barely leaving the house, as best as he can tell. And yet there has been nothing in the papers, no announcement of any discoveries. He wonders if the men are cutting her out. Yes, of course. He has once again underestimated the perfidy of his own sex. He has been spending so much time with women — thinking about women, listening to women, catering to women — that he has forgotten how men operate. Their methods are clumsy, barbarous, even — but effective. He wishes he could teach those state cops a thing or two. But he has to hold himself in check, stay in control. It's all about control. Ego must be held in check.

Tonight, for example. He has to be precise yet restrained and remember the objective. A lesser man would be tempted to make some sort of grand flourish, to call attention to himself. But he has always prided himself on his subtlety, his modesty, his ability to keep souvenirs without attracting attention.

He pulls his van into the alley and waits. The city's grid of criminal activity has shifted slightly in the time since he last roamed these neighborhoods in search of her. The cops closed down the old markets, but new ones have opened just a few blocks away. God, junkies have so little imagination. They use all their ingenuity to procure the substance they need to destroy themselves. He knows she'll be here because it's Friday night, and she likes to score on Friday night. Besides, he left a little message on her pager, one guaranteed to bring her here. He knows what she wants.

True, he doesn't know her as well as he knew the others. He didn't have the time to study her. But he knows her tastes, her weaknesses, what motivates her. He knows she is lazy and sly, in equal measure.

But the main thing he knows about her is she fooled him. He can never quite forgive her for that. When he left, he told himself he was done with her. Yet in the back of his mind he must have always suspected this wasn't true. Even before this unexpected contingency arose, he had a score to settle with her. He doesn't like being played.

It's nine o'clock and the spring night should be completely dark by now, but it's never truly dark in the city's worst neighborhoods. She pulls her car into an alley and walks out to the street, where the touts wait, singing the praises of their poisons. She's no crackhead; her taste runs to methamphetamine and heroin. And she won't make a buy on the street, she'll visit the rowhouse where a dealer waits, happy to resell the heroin he bought just that afternoon. Why not, if there's money in it? If the cops gave a rat's ass, they could make her six blocks away, and not just because she's white. She's so small, so obviously out of place. Once she's gone down the block, he rolls his van into the alley behind her car, blocking it in. Now all he has to do is wait.

In less than ten minutes she's heading back, her walk almost a run now. She'll take her treasure home or to her new boyfriend's house — assuming she has a new man, and she usually does. In her mind, waiting for her blast means she's in control, not a junkie. "It's no different than going out and having a beer on a Saturday night," she had said in her defense, the first time he caught her shooting up. Maybe. But when your girlfriend went out for a beer on Saturday night, she didn't spend Sunday through Friday robbing you blind.

He still likes that walk, that silhouette, the side-to-side roll in her slender hips. Given the chance, he'd pick her out again. And again and again. She was his type. It kills him, admitting that. But you have to know your weaknesses. You have to be honest about the things that defeated you in the past if you hope to succeed in the future. She was his one mistake. Well, second, although you couldn't call Saint Mary's a mistake. More of a detour.

Here she comes, almost skipping, like a little girl on her way home from the candy store. The only difference is that she's holding a bag of heroin cut with baby laxative. God, she was such a drag high: stupid, insolent, useless. He hadn't given up on her right away. If rehab had worked, if he had gotten her straight, she might have been his most satisfying transformation ever. But she had only pretended to clean up because it kept his money flowing. Cunning, that was a word for her. Cunning cu— but he promised his mother he would never use that word. It was crude.

She gets into her car and starts the motor, assuming he'll move so she can get out. Dumb bitch. She honks. He cuts the engine, as if he has no intention of moving. She honks again. He shrugs. She gets out, stalks up to his van, fearless because she's stupid. Fearless because she's avid for her treat. She slaps the side of his van, as if it's a horse she's trying to shoo from a pasture. But he still doesn't move, so she marches up to the front of the van. Objects in the mirror, he reminds himself, may be closer than they appear. Still he waits, patient as time, until she's pounding on his door, calling him all kinds of names, too crazed to realize she knows that profile. He listens to the familiar voice on the other side of the glass, waiting to see if he feels any-thing, even a trace of the usual wondrous sorrow he brings to his chore. But all he wants to do is get it over with.

Her voice keeps coming, at once hoarse and shrill. "C'mon, you jerk, move this piece of shit. Move, move, move." She is beating, pounding, slapping the van door, as if she could push the vehicle back with her own im-pressive energy. She's that desperate to get home. Oh, yeah, honey. You don't have a problem. It's no different than a few drinks on a Saturday night.

He lets her go on for a few more seconds. Then, calmly, always calmly, he lowers the window and shoots the dumb bitch in the face. She doesn't have time to register what's going on. If her life passed before her eyes, her only thought was a flicker of regret that she would never enjoy her last dime bag.

He has to shoot her in the face instead of the chest. He hopes that won't throw anyone off. Because this one — this one he doesn't love.

# Chapter 27

Tess was coming off the water late Saturday morning when she saw Whitney on the dock. A former rower, Whitney knew better than to stand in the middle of the boathouse's morning rush hour, creating an obstacle for the college teams staggering beneath the weights of their fours and eights. Yet there she was, in everyone's way, arms folded across her chest. When Tess pulled parallel to the dock, Whitney ran to the side and grabbed one of the Alden's oars so forcefully she almost flipped the shell with Tess still in it.

"Whitney, I've been getting up on this dock for years without your help. I think I can manage."

"We need to talk," she said. Whitney always considered all her needs urgent.

"Fine. Just let me get out and rinse the boat off, put everything away. And if I were you, I'd want me to shower first. It was steamy this morning, almost like summer." Tess indicated the patches of sweat on her chest and back, beneath her arms.

"We need to talk *now*. You're the last one in; it's not as if you're blocking anyone."

Tess glanced around and saw this was true. There were no other boats coming in behind her.

"Let me get out. I feel odd sitting here, with you looming above me."

Whitney looked as if she were going to fly apart from nerves. Her usually smooth hair was almost standing on end, her pale face was white and drawn in a way that Tess had never seen. But she nodded her assent, jaw muscles twitching, and waited for Tess to climb out and carry the boat to a pair of saddle horses in preparation for its daily bath. Hosing down the shell was an essential step for those who rowed the filthy Middle Branch of the Patapsco.

"Did you read the paper before you came down here this morning?" Whitney was sitting on the grass now, digging through the voluminous leather pouch she used as a purse.

"Glanced at the front page, read my horoscope. And the dogs' horoscopes, which they seem to enjoy. Esskay's apparently due for a favorable business transaction." Whitney didn't smile. "Jesus, what's up? How bad could it be?"

Whitney continued to dig through her bag, removing all sorts of strange and wonderful objects — a Swiss army knife, a leather journal, an antique ivory bracelet — until she found a piece of newsprint ripped from what appeared to be an inside page of that morning's Maryland section.

"The name didn't mean anything to me at

first — to tell you the truth, I was reading it over breakfast, laughing at the *Beacon-Light*'s naïveté, because it's so clearly a drug deal gone bad. But she's white and she's from the county, so they turn it into one of those 'sweet suburbanite mowed down in inner city' stories, as if she were a random victim. Granted, they were on deadline, and they were probably trying to find an angle to make it fresh, after it led all the late-night newscasts —"

"Whitney, slow down and start over. You're not tracking."

"Julie Carter was killed last night. Shot in an alley in Southwest Baltimore."

Tess's legs were often quivery and weak after a good workout, but not in this way. She sank to the ground next to Whitney. If she had anything in her stomach, she might have felt sick. But there was never time to eat in the morning. No time to eat, no time to read the paper properly. . . .

"My Julie?" she asked, but that didn't sound right. "Our Julie?" That didn't sound right either. "It's a common name. Common enough."

"This Julie Carter lived out near Beckleysville. Near Prettyboy Reservoir. Ring a bell?"

"Holy shit."

"Yeah."

Tess sat on the ground, hers legs splayed out like a Raggedy Ann. Whitney crouched next to her, looking as if she wanted to sprint away, if she could only figure out where to run. The humidity was burning off as the sun rose. It was going to be a beautiful day, for those privileged enough to wake up alive. The blue skies, the subtle spring smells — Tess and Whitney could have been college roommates again, sitting on the banks of the Chester River after a workout. Tess wished they were. To be twenty-one again, to be free of the knowledge she had gained in the last ten years, or even in the last ten minutes, seemed an excellent idea.

Julie Carter had been twenty-one. Just. But hers had been a hard twenty-one, with hints of more troubles than Tess had ever known.

"It could be a drug deal," Tess said. "She clearly had some problems in that sphere."

"Could be," Whitney said. "Could be just the biggest fucking coincidence to ever come down the pike."

"We have to call Major Shields, over at Pikesville."

"I did. Paged him immediately."

"And?"

"And he said that's exactly what it was. Just one big co-inky dink."

"Did he say co-inky dink?"

"He might as well have. He considers me part of the problem, you know? Me and the board. Thanked me very kindly for the tip, as he termed it, and said they would consider it, but they're still working under the presumption that the man who killed Tiffani and Lucy is dead."

"Unless he didn't die. Unless Carl's right."

"Or if there's another someone and has been all along."

"Who? No one knows who was on that original list, except for your own board members."

"I don't know. Someone who knows what the other guy did?"

Tess was no enemy of coincidence. It permeated life, it powered the daily newspaper, and, as even Mary Ann Melcher knew, made for the best television movies. Most of the stories worth telling, even the smallest anecdotes, begin with a coincidence. You don't tell people about the 364 days you got on the number 11 bus and didn't run into your best friend from grade school. You tell them about the one day you did.

But Julie Carter's demise was a chronicle of a death foretold. Whoever made up that list knew she would join the others as a homicide. Even the cause had been right, a gunshot to the head. That made her death just violent enough to warrant mention in the morning paper, arriving like a sinister greeting card sent by a secret admirer. *Here's another body. Thinking of you.*

"Whitney. Did we ever learn the name of the volunteer who put the list together?"

"We know it now. After I talked to Major Shields, I called that jerk attorney for Luisa O'Neal's foundation. Would you believe he tried to claim privilege? I told him I couldn't decide if I was going to come to his home with

366

my shotgun or go to the state's attorney's office and file a complaint against him."

"What kind of complaint? It's not illegal to be a sleazy dumb-ass in Maryland."

"I was bluffing. That's why I put in the part about the shotgun. He decided the person in question wasn't exactly a client, at least not in this capacity, and he was within his rights to tell me."

"Who gave the board the list, Whitney?"

But even as Tess asked, she knew. Somehow she had always known whose elegant fingerprints she would find on this case.

"Your all-time fave Baltimore philanthropist, Luisa Julia O'Neal herself." Whitney dug her fingers into her forehead, as if she felt a headache coming on or wanted to claw a memory from her overactive mind. "It was her idea all along, Tess. Looking into these cases, hiring you to do it. She was behind the whole thing, and I never knew. I'm as big a dupe as you in this, maybe bigger. Because I never understood why you thought she was so horrible."

"But not this horrible," Tess said.

Whitney lifted her face from her hands. "What do you mean?"

"I hate Luisa O'Neal, but this isn't her style. She's been used as surely as we have. Besides, she's in a nursing home, right? Maybe she didn't do it. Maybe she's someone's fall guy. Where did you say she was?"

"Keswick, I think."

"Let's hope they have Saturday morning visiting hours."

The nursing home on the hill, looming above Baltimore's pricey Roland Park and not-so-pricey Hampden, had acquired a newer, blander name. But old-timers and old families still knew it as the Keswick Home for Incurables.

That seemed right to Tess. She didn't know the exact nature of Luisa's physical ailments, but she had never doubted the rot in her soul was beyond repair.

Luisa was in the clinic, the last stop before the mortuary. Her decline must have been a rapid one to put her there less than a year after taking her own apartment in the residential wing. Tess and Whitney signed in on the depressingly blank visitors' log for the health care center. The attendant then wrote down three numbers on a sheet of paper and passed it to them.

"Her room number?" Tess asked.

"No, it's the daily code."

"Code?"

"To get out." He gestured to the control pad by the double doors, which had locked behind them. "Our residents aren't allowed to leave on their own."

"Grim," Whitney said.

The atmosphere only got grimmer as they took the elevator to the second floor. Their youth was an affront here, an obscenity. The women they passed in the halls — all women, nothing but women — looked up from their walkers and wheelchairs with undisguised envy. Tess heard a voice calling, weak and empty, a voice with no expectation of a reply.

"And this is the top of the line," Whitney whispered. "Can you imagine what the bad ones are like?"

Luisa had a private room, which was little more than a glorified hospital room, although she had been allowed to add a few pieces of her own furniture — a chest, a small table, a flowery chintz chair that Tess remembered from the O'Neals' sunroom. Luisa had sat in that chair when she explained to Tess just what she had done to keep her only son from facing criminal charges for the murder he had committed.

But she didn't sit in her chair anymore. A large white-uniformed nurse overflowed in it, eyes fixed on the television in the corner. Red-haired and freckled, with olive skin, the nurse would have stumped any census taker who tried to guess her race. Luisa was in a hospital bed, propped up. A hand-lettered sign above the bed reminded the night staff that she was to wear cloth diapers, not plastic, because she was allergic to the plastic ones.

Tess had never thought anything could make her feel sorry for Luisa O'Neal, but that sign came close.

"Money not only can't buy you love," she said to Whitney, out of the side of her mouth, "it apparently can't even guarantee you a dignified old age."

Luisa's pale blue eyes narrowed. She picked up a large sketch pad and a black marking pen. **I cannot speak,** she wrote, **but my hearing is fine.**

"She's such a liar," said the nurse, one of those stoic, placid souls well suited to the profession. "She can talk, but she won't, because she sounds funny, and she won't do her therapy."

Luisa turned to a fresh page. **I do not like to do things if I cannot do them well.**

"Big surprise," Tess said. "But you could at least fill up a sheet of paper before starting on a new one. It's wasteful, what you're doing with that sketchbook."

She shook her head, but it might have been a spasm. Then she wrote, **Donna, would you leave us alone, please?** The request clearly bothered the nurse, but she didn't talk back. She heaved herself out of the chair, switched off the television, and marched out of the room. The nurse had a wonderful, insolent walk, her large backside swaying slowly back and forth.

"Do you know why we're here, Luisa?" Whitney asked. They had decided Luisa might be more responsive to one of her own, another moneyed blueblood.

She hesitated. Tess knew she would lie to

them if she thought she could get away with it. At last she wrote, **I have my suppositions.**

"You forwarded a list, through your foundation's attorney, to a consortium of nonprofits interested in the issue of domestic violence."

Luisa nodded.

"You decided which other nonprofits should be invited — and you made sure I was included. Your idea, your list, your project. My family's board doesn't have much experience with social issues. But you knew I'd jump at it, didn't you? And you knew that Tess and I were old friends and I'd put her forward as the private investigator."

Luisa had no response to any of this, no denial and no affirmation.

"In fact, it was your lawyer who suggested we hire a private detective. And it was your lawyer who said, 'Don't you know someone like that, Whitney?' "

She wrote slowly, with more care than she needed. **I cannot speak to things that happened when I was not there.**

"Where did you get the list, Luisa?"

**Research,** she wrote. **We have an excellent library here.**

"Research?" Whitney had reached the limits of her patience — which, admittedly, was never a distant boundary. "With your palsied hands? If there's a computer on the premises, it's a cinch you don't know how to use it."

It was a great advantage, refusing to speak.

Luisa simply stared at Whitney. The partial paralysis of her face made it particularly difficult to read. The stroke had left her with an Elvis-like sneer.

Tess turned to Whitney and mouthed, *Leave.* Whitney shook her head at first, but something in Tess's face convinced her to go. She, too, stomped out to the hallway, shutting the door behind her.

Tess crouched by the bed, so she could speak as quietly as possible and still be heard. "Luisa. I kept your secret. It's been over two years, and I've never told anyone how Seamon O'Neal arranged for Jonathan Ross to be killed."

Her letters were not as careful now. **I was never sure,** she wrote, **that he intended for him to die.** The revisionism stunned Tess. Here was Luisa O'Neal on what appeared to be her deathbed, and she could not quite admit that anyone in her family was capable of wrongdoing.

"Why resist the truth, Luisa? Your husband is dead, beyond justice for the things he did, even if those things could be proven. Your son remains in the institution where you had him committed. The man who took credit for your son's crimes has been executed for his own. No one mourns him, no one feels sorry for him. All your scores are settled, everyone you love is safe. Why can't you afford me the same privilege?"

Luisa began to turn another page in her

sketchbook but wrote instead at the bottom of the sullied page, **I never wanted anything to do with you. I had hoped never to see you again. I am only a go-between.**

"Whose?"

Still on the same page. **I must not say.**

"Why? What are you scared of?"

Quickly, fiercely, as if she were carving the words into Tess's flesh: **Not death. I want to die.**

"Great, good for you. You're much braver than the rest of us. So what does this person have on you?"

Luisa placed her shaking hand on a silver frame at her bedside. A young woman, a woman who resembled the Luisa that Tess had once known, with luminous eyes and soft dark hair. She was with a handsome if beefy man and a chubby baby boy. The daughter, Tess recalled. Luisa had a daughter in Chicago.

Luisa wrote, **He will kill her. I am sure of that.**

Her own eyes were still beautiful, once you got past their withered casings, the faded brows and lashes. Deep in the damaged face, the eyes were as blue as ever, almost robin's-egg blue. Tess remembered that Luisa Julia O'Neal had been known as Ellie Jay. She had been one of the city's best female tennis players, strong and vigorous, albeit in a ladylike way. Now she was dying by inches. What disease had not taken from her, fear would. Fear was exacting a greater toll on her body now than all her medical problems.

"Luisa, I'll do my best to protect you and your daughter. But I have to know something. If you won't tell me who this man is, you must at least tell me what he wants."

Luisa turned a page and wrote in large block letters that took the entire sheet:

**You.**

She should have been more shocked. But the moment the answer came, she realized she had known it all along. It was the gnat in the ear, the buzzing that had bothered her so many times. What did all these people have in common? Tess Monaghan.

*I am the link. Not geography or cause of death. The five were not connected to one another until I came along.*

The list had been the lure, leading her toward something, to someone. She needed to know who, she needed to know why. But Luisa O'Neal had already refused to tell her either, and who could blame her? Killing her daughter would be nothing to this man. He had killed Julie Carter just to remind Tess that he was not done.

She unfolded from her crouch, listening to her knees crack. She was happy to have her legs at all, instead of the atrophied appendages beneath the blanket in Luisa's bed. She was happy to be alive and wondered how much longer she would be. She heard a furious scratching sound and looked up to see Luisa writing hurriedly. Her handwriting was almost indecipherable now.

**You must not tell anyone. No one. No police.**
"But —"

**My daughter,** Luisa wrote. **MY DAUGHTER. He will kill my daughter if you go to the police. And if you send the police here, I will deny everything.**

With that, she ripped the pages from the tablet and shredded them as best she could. Her hands may have been shaky, but they still had some strength.

"But he wants to kill me, Luisa. Right? So are you saying your daughter's life is more important than mine?"

**Not necessarily,** she wrote — and promptly tore it up.

"Are you disputing my first premise or the second?"

**Both**. This note, too, was torn up. Then: **Go.**

Tess did, feeling as she always had when she faced someone from the O'Neal family — defeated, crushed, decreased. But when she reached the door, a voice called after her. It was a sad voice, slurry and soft, unable to make consonants, but a voice all the same.

"Nushing ish ran'um."

"What?"

"*Nushing . . . nushing.*" Tess could hear the fury in Luisa's voice, could see how she loathed her imperfections. Her face was flushed from emotion and effort as she held up a hand, spreading her fingers the best she could. Her fingers curved, slicing the words into the air.

"Fi—" she said. "Fi—"

"Five? Five what?"

But she gave up, returning to her pad.

**Tiffani Gunts**
**Lucy Fancher**
**Julie Carter**
**Hazel Ligetti**
**Michael Shaw**

Five names. Five homicides. And nothing was random. Absolutely nothing.

# Chapter 28

As soon as they signed out of the Keswick Home for Incurables, Tess called Crow on her cell phone and told him to bring her case files to their local coffee shop, the Daily Grind.

She also asked for her Smith & Wesson.

"You're going to strap your gun on here in the Grind?" Whitney asked, sliding into the back booth with a large coffee and a pumpkin muffin. Tess had no appetite.

"Luisa O'Neal just told me that a serial killer — a man who has killed three, maybe five, people — wants *me*. I'd call having my gun nothing more than prudent."

Whitney fussed with her coffee, adding three packets of sugar and half-and-half until it was more *lait au café* than *café au lait*. "What is it between you and Luisa? Why did you ask me to leave the room?"

Tess hesitated. Part of her mind told her all bets were off. Luisa had helped this man lay a trap. The fact that she had done it out of fear for herself and her daughter was not a wholly satisfying excuse, although it was an understandable one. She had set this plan in motion, indifferent to the fact that Tess was a killer's quarry.

377

But seeing her old nemesis so reduced had changed the nature of their relationship. Where once Luisa had made Tess feel inconsequential and helpless, Luisa was now the helpless one. Tess, who once kept Luisa's secrets out of fear, continued to keep them out of habit.

Besides, she had never wanted to test Whitney's loyalties. Whitney loved Tess, but she also had a fierce loyalty to what Mrs. Talbot would call, without irony, "our kind of people."

Whitney, mistaking her silence for out-and-out refusal, said, "I bet you told Crow."

Tess nodded. He was the one person she had told.

"I can keep a secret too, Tesser."

Her use of the old nickname was strategic, a reminder of how long they had known each other.

"It wasn't just about keeping secrets," Tess replied. "I didn't think you'd believe me if I told you the O'Neal family was capable of murder. But yes, after Crow and I began dating, I told him. I needed to tell someone."

"The first time or the second time?"

"Huh?"

"Did you tell Crow the first time you hooked up — the time you fucked it up and he left you — or when he took you back?"

Whitney must be hurt if she was going out of her way to remind Tess of past mistakes.

"The first time. In fact, I told him before we slept together."

"You are easy. I mean, I always knew you were a first-date kind of girl, but I didn't know you gave *everything* up so readily."

"Look, I'll tell you the whole story right now if you like. But don't argue with me, say it couldn't have been that way, or tell me I must be mistaken."

"I don't argue —"

Tess held up her palm. "You're arguing now."

Whitney settled back, as close to contrite as she could ever be.

"Remember Jonathan Ross?"

"Speaking of being promiscuous — you slept with him even after you stopped dating."

"Thanks for reminding me. Remember how he died?"

"He was hit by a car."

"Luisa's husband, Seamon, arranged that. Jonathan was getting too close to uncovering a true scandal. The O'Neals had paid a man already on Death Row to confess to a murder their son had committed. A go-between was used, a lawyer, so the killer never knew which prominent family he was helping. But there was money in it, which went to his mother. He also assumed his 'sponsors' would keep him from being executed."

"Did they?"

"He got two extensions before he was put to death last fall. Tucker Fauquier."

"The psychopath who wanted to kill a boy in

every county, but only made it as far as the Bay Bridge?"

"The very same."

"And he never knew about the O'Neals' involvement?"

"Not to my knowledge."

Whitney was thinking, chin cupped in her hand. "Could anyone else know about all this?"

"Possibly. But I don't see how. Seamon O'Neal, Tucker Fauquier, his mom, the lawyer who made the deal — they're all dead. As far as I know, Luisa and I were the only two people left on earth who knew this story."

"And Crow," Whitney reminded Tess.

"And Crow."

"I always hoped you talked about me when I wasn't around." Crow slid into the booth alongside Tess and, with one easy gesture, dropped her gun into her lap as he squeezed her left thigh. She looked down and almost laughed out loud when she realized he had wrapped the gun in a dish towel.

"That's why it took me so long to get over here. I couldn't figure out how I was supposed to transport it. You may have a license to carry, but I don't, and I had these visions of me being jacked up on Cold Spring Lane. But I loaded it, per your instructions. So." He surveyed the bustling coffee shop. "A little heist? You picked a good day to knock over the Grind. They do a lot of cash business on a Saturday."

His light mood disappeared when Tess told

380

him everything that had happened that morning.

"You've got to go to the police, Tess. I don't care what she said. You can at least call someone you trust, Detective Tull in homicide. This guy wants to kill you."

"Not necessarily," she said, echoing the words on Luisa's pad. "Besides, how's he going to get to me? His pattern is to insert himself into women's lives, establish himself as the perfect boyfriend, the one who picks up the pieces left behind by some asshole. I already have the perfect boyfriend."

The compliment did not soothe Crow. "You've got to call the state police."

"And tell them —"

"Everything."

Tess knew the advice was right and prudent. Truly, Crow cared only about her and her safety. That was the problem. She wasn't the only person in the world. She had to protect herself, but there were others who had to be protected as well. Whitney, Crow, her parents. Luisa's daughter. A man who would kill a woman just to make a point would kill anyone. She wouldn't be safe from him until she knew who he was and why he did what he did.

"Luisa believes that if this man knows she spoke to me, he'll kill her daughter."

"You can't think about that."

"I have to think about that." The gun was still in her lap, hidden in the folds of the dish towel, a black-and-white gingham print. Seeing that dish towel from her own kitchen made Tess long for everything ordinary in her life, everything she had taken for granted when she awoke this morning: her dogs, her bed, the view from her deck, her toothbrush. The happy sensation of coming home at the end of the day and pouring a glass of wine. A life without fear.

Where was he? Who was he? Had they met? Exchanged a few words?

"He'll kill anyone, for any reason. He killed Julie for me."

Whitney nodded, but Crow was confused.

"You didn't want Julie dead," he said. "She was just a pathetic junkie who tried to shake you down for a few bucks. Why would you care what happened to her?"

"No. He killed Julie because he knew the investigation had stalled, that I was no longer a part of it. He killed a woman to get my attention."

"She was on his list," Whitney pointed out. "Perhaps he always intended to kill her. As Luisa said, 'Nothing is random.' "

"Point taken. But if I go to the state police and Luisa's daughter out in Chicago ends up dead, how do I justify that? She's a mother. Whatever her parents have done — whatever her brother did — she's innocent."

"How will he know if you talk to the police?" Crow asked.

"I don't know. He seems to know everything else about me. He knew how to get to me —

how to use Luisa to set up a project that would be irresistible to me. How to get me to put the pieces together."

"But he's dead," Whitney said. "The wreckage of the boat was found. They're looking at bodies, trying to make a match."

"Sometimes," Tess said, "a John Doe is simply a John Doe. People drown, they don't get identified. Who's to say our guy didn't catch a break?"

"Yes, but you're assuming the only person who could know these five names is the killer himself. What if there are two killers, the man who killed Tiffani and Lucy and a second man, who had entirely different reasons for killing Julie Carter, Hazel Ligetti, and Michael Shaw. Those murders all happened after the apparent suicide, right? And they're nothing like the first two."

Tess rubbed her forehead. "My brain hurts."

"My *soul* hurts," Crow said. "I think I'm going to be sick. I've never felt so helpless."

They sat in glum silence, coffee growing cold, muffin untouched. Together, the three could usually figure anything out. Like Dorothy's companions through Oz, they were three incompletes who made a whole. Crow was all heart, like the Tin Man. Whitney was their Scarecrow, but more like the version in the book, the one whose head was filled with needles and pins so he might be sharp.

This left Tess, by default, to be the Cowardly

Lion, the one who marched forward into battle, bitching and moaning from fear all the while. She was afraid. She had no illusions about herself. If she had a choice, she wouldn't fight this fight.

It would have been nice, having a choice.

# Chapter 29

Even junkies have to be buried.

Tess scanned the Sunday edition of the *Beacon-Light*, looking for the classified obituary notice that would tell her if there was a funeral service for Julie Carter. She knew Julie would not qualify for what the paper's writers privately called the *mort du jour*, one of the lengthier obituaries, reported and written by a staff writer.

You didn't have to be rich or socially prominent to warrant a full-blown *mort*, although it didn't hurt. Getting shot and killed in an apparent drug deal was pretty much guaranteed to keep you off the obituary page, with its soft-focus photography and distilled hagiography.

She found, at last, the tiny paid death notice. For a Catholic, Julie was going in the ground fast. The Rosary was scheduled for that very evening, with the funeral mass and burial set for tomorrow. Tess tore out the information and tried to remember if she had a dark dress that was lightweight enough for warm weather.

She also wondered if she was the only nonrelative who was searching the paper this morning for Julie's obituary, if she would be the only stranger who showed up at the service and the graveside. It was 5 a.m., and she was reading the paper after a sleepless night, her gun lying next to her on the dining room table. Her doors and windows were double-bolted, shutting out the balmy spring air that she so loved. The only sound in the house was the trio of slumbering breaths coming from the bedroom — Esskay, Miata, and Crow, who had finally fallen asleep about 3 a.m.

She had a black linen suit, she remembered, something she hadn't worn for years. Could you wear linen before Memorial Day, or did that rule apply only to white linen?

Julie Carter's people probably didn't make those kinds of distinctions anyway.

Tess had more experience with death than she did with its attendant rituals. Julie Carter's funeral, held in a pretty stone church out in what people insisted on calling the country, was only the third or fourth that Tess had attended in her adult life. She counted them up: Her maternal grandfather. An older colleague from the *Star*, who had died of cancer in her fifties. A service for the grandchild of one of her mother's best friends, killed in a fall, the saddest by far.

And Jonathan Ross.

Sometimes, she thought the scar tissue over that wound was almost too hard, too complete. It was as if her very ability to heal had revealed just how half-assed, how sleazy, their relationship had been. The nightmares came from being an eyewitness to his death, not because he was the love of her life. She had never mistaken him for that. She had envied him, however, in life and death. Jonathan's funeral had been crowded, his legacy as a journalistic star unquestioned. Later, when Tess had faced her own near-death, her first thought was of how skimpy her obituary would be. A superficial thought, but it had helped her fight for her life, and here she was — at the most awkward funeral she could imagine, a service of long silences and stammered clichés. What can you say about a twenty-one-year-old woman who died? That she was a junkie and a con artist.

In the front pews, Julie's family — parents, brothers and sisters, a few elderly people who might have been grandparents or even great-grandparents — appeared sullen and disgruntled, as if they had better places to be on the unseasonably warm day. Julie's friends were scattered among the rear pews, party girls and boys, at once sleepy and restless at 11 a.m. The in-between pews were empty. There was no middle ground in Julie's life. You were either family or you were one of her fucked-up friends.

Tess took a seat in the last pew and tried to study the men. Even from the backs of their necks, she could tell the man she was looking for was not here. These young men were mullet heads, their longish hair straggling over shirt collars that were not as clean as they should be, reaching down to jackets that looked as if they had been dragged from some cramped closet and shaken to remove the wrinkles. They were young, too, these men, not much older than Julie. The parking lot outside, with its Trans Ams and shiny pickups, attested to their youth as well. Tess had known before she walked in that her quarry was not here and probably would not be here.

*Unless,* she thought, *he knows I'm here. I'm the one he wants, after all.* And she slid her right hand beneath her black linen jacket, felt for her holster and her gun. It was hot in the church, and the unaccustomed bulk of the leather and metal beneath her arm felt like some strange tumor. She would have to get used to it.

The young are difficult to bury under the best of circumstances. But Julie Carter presented additional challenges. Her life had not only been short, it had been stupid and shiftless. She hadn't even seemed particularly nice. The priest worked gamely through the service, and it was hard to know if his red face was glistening from the heat in the small church or if he was just covered in flop sweat. Julie's family appeared to be seething, muttering among themselves, shifting in their seats impatiently. The funeral, rather than providing solace, seemed only to remind them of all the ways she had disappointed them in life. Julie had found one last way to humiliate them.

Or perhaps it was merely Julie Carter's penultimate disappointment. For there was no room in the church's graveyard for Julie Carter, although there was plenty of space left in that peaceful tree-lined acreage. When the service finally, thankfully, ended, it turned out that Julie was to be laid to rest in a sprawling antiseptic cemetery on the outskirts of Baltimore. Julie would be happy to be that much closer to the excitement for which she had yearned, Tess thought. At least she wouldn't be stuck out in the sticks for eternity.

Only a few mourners made the trip to the gravesite, which made Tess more conspicuous than she had been in the church. She was standing a few feet back, as befitted a stranger, wondering how to approach the family, when the decision was made for her. An older sister — she had Julie's coloring and the same pert features, although they were congealed in an extra hundred pounds — walked over to her after the casket had been lowered and the final prayers chanted.

"I don't believe I know you," she said. Her tone made it clear that she considered this a bad thing.

"My name is Tess Monaghan. I met Julie recently, through my work."

"What kind of work?"

"I'm a private investigator."

The sister rolled her eyes. "What'd she do,

shoplift something? It wouldn't have been the first time, although I bet she told you different. Did she cry — she could cry on cue, you know — and tell you it would never happen again? Because all that meant is she wouldn't do it again in your store."

"I'm a private investigator, not a security guard."

"Oh." The sister was perplexed, trying to figure out the connection. "Did she have to pass a drug test for a job? Or was she fooling around with some married man?"

"Julie wasn't *doing* anything. She was . . . an innocent party."

This provoked a derisive snort. "That would be a first."

Tess almost wished she could tell the sour-faced sister just how innocent Julie was, how undeserved her death. But how could you ever convey such information? For all the Carter family's anger and fury at their wayward daughter, they had not wished her dead. They were angry because she had not lived long enough to straighten up.

"I liked her," Tess said, and it was true enough, under the circumstances. "It was interesting, actually, how we met. I was compiling some information about domestic violence, working with some local foundations that are trying to figure out why it's so hard for women to break the cycle. Because a lot of women do get out of abusive or unhealthy relationships, only to start afresh in new relationships that are just as bad."

"I'm not sure you could call what Julie had relationships. Men were just a means to an end for her, a way to get money so she could get drugs." The sister sighed. The heat was hard on her, overweight as she was, and she was almost wheezing. A burden years in the making seemed to be escaping her, asthmatic breath by breath.

"She was an addict?"

"She was a pain in the ass. I know I sound harsh, but everyone — my parents, me, my brothers and sisters — we've been cleaning up behind her for six years. Trying to make amends with teachers, then with bosses, getting her into programs. Then she'd come out and start all over again. If anything, Julie was the abusive one. Emotionally, I mean. She destroyed every opportunity she got, and she got more than she deserved."

"Still, I bet she had bad luck with men."

"Bad luck? I'd trade my right arm for her kind of bad luck. There was always someone around she was playing, some guy who was too good for her by half. She had one boyfriend when she was just eighteen who woulda done anything for her. He was perfect."

"Perfect?" It was what she had wanted to hear. It was what she had dreaded to hear.

"Well, maybe a little old for her, but that's not a bad thing. He was steady. Nice and polite, drove a nice car, had a good job, although he had to travel all the time. Selling something."

*Sure,* Tess thought. *He was always selling something.*

"When he found out she was a junkie, he tried to get her into rehab, paid for it even, and stayed by her through it all — and she went back to drugs the first chance she got. He finally just gave up on her and left."

"Do you remember his name?" Not that it matters, Tess thought. It would be another man's name, another fortuitous match of an unused life and a sociopath's inexplicable mission.

"Alan Palmer," the sister said promptly, surprising Tess. It had not occurred to her that he would use the same name twice. But then — he hadn't killed Julie Carter, not then, so he was free to move on, to keep using the stolen identity. "Oh, he was such a nice man. I wouldn't have been surprised to see him here today."

"Has he called?"

"No," the sister said, her voice wistful. "I think he moved out of state. He said something about going west. It was almost three years ago."

So Julie had fallen in the interval between Tiffani and Lucy. Which meant that, for all his planning, the man did not know where he would end up next. He knew only who he would be when he moved on. But did he know, from the moment he met them, that he intended to kill them? Why would he kill women like Tiffani and Lucy, who had never disappointed him, only to spare Julie?

"Where was Julie working when she met" — she had to grope for the name, remind herself which persona would have presented himself in the little town of Beckleysville — "Alan?"

The sister looked at Tess. It was an odd question, but Tess was beyond caring.

"She was working at a High's Dairy Store, and he came in one night to buy a soda. The job at Mars came later. He just kept coming back. Like I said, he was the best thing that ever happened to my sister."

No, Tess thought, the best thing that ever happened to Julie Carter was that he decided to leave. Julie had defeated this man on some level, had driven him away. Her addiction, her fierce self-involvement, had kept him from getting what he wanted.

There was a lesson to be learned in Julie's initial survival — and one from her ultimate demise as well.

# Chapter 30

Tess picked up the tail as she headed home from her office that night. This time it was a dark van, a minivan, which might have struck her as mildly comical under other circumstances. Death by soccer mom. But the driver, although nothing more than a silhouette through the windshield, was clearly no one's mother. The shoulders were too broad, the neck too thick. She first noticed him as she was turning on the Jones Falls Expressway from Fayette. He raced the amber light, risking a ticket in an intersection rigged with those new red-light cameras. Who would do that?

*Someone who didn't lose a lot of sleep over traffic tickets.*

Funny — even as Tess had embraced Carl Dewitt's contention that the killer they sought might still be alive, she had not recalibrated her thoughts about his other conspiracy theories. She had assumed, after the fact, that their close encounters on the highway had been nothing but Carl's paranoia-fueled imagination. Besides, the man they wanted had no need to follow them. He not only knew where Tess had been, he often knew where she was going.

Yet here was a dark van, hanging back a few car lengths on the expressway but keeping steady with her speed, no matter how erratically she drove. And she had begun to drive quite erratically, doing her best impersonation of the archetypal Baltimore driver. Local drivers were not so much aggressive as absent-minded, seemingly indifferent to reaching a destination. The average Baltimore driver gave the impression of a sleepwalker who had regained consciousness behind the wheel, baffled and disoriented.

Tess clicked her turn signal, then didn't budge from the right lane for two miles. She turned off the signal, only to drift into the middle lane, then the left. At the Cold Spring Lane exit, she abruptly veered into the far right lane at the last possible moment, which forced her to brake so hard at the top of the exit ramp that her wheels squealed and the Toyota sent up a cloud of brown smoke.

Still, the van managed to hang with her, lurking in the pack of vehicles stuck at the first light on Cold Spring. Tess still could not make out much of the driver's face and features. He wore dark glasses and a baseball cap. He also had on a windbreaker, suspicious on such a warm day, and he dipped his chin into its collar so the lower part of his face was obscured.

The light had changed, time to make a decision. Tess didn't want to lead her stalker to her home. Yet if he had been following her all this time, he already knew where her home was. If she tried to lead him to a different, neutral location — the Northern District police precinct, for example — he might decide to wait for her at the house. Crow could be in the house, possibly lost in one of the endless renovation projects the bungalow kept demanding, like some possessed house in a Stephen King novel. She felt for her gun and looked around for her cell phone, peeking out of the knapsack on the passenger seat. *Time to break my own rules*, she decided, steering with one hand and dialing with the other.

Shit. The voice mail engaged after three rings, which meant Crow was out. If he had been on the phone, or on-line, the machine would have picked up on the first ring. He was probably walking the dogs. Which meant he could arrive home at any moment, unprepared for their mystery guest.

"You think you know me? You think you want me?" She still had the cell phone cradled to her mouth, so if any other driver glanced at her, it would appear as if she were speaking to someone. "Okay, let's see if you do know where I live."

She shot through the intersection, then dawdled up the hill to the next intersection, knowing it was a relatively long light. Perfect — she had timed it right, reaching the light just as it turned amber. She bolted even as it turned red and, Baltimore being Baltimore, one more car sneaked through the light as well. But the van was stuck several cars back. She would reach her house with at least a five-minute head start.

Home. Normally, she exulted in the semi-isolation of East Lane, which was more alley than street. But in the greenish-gray twilight, her block was too private. The neighbors' houses were dark and quiet behind the evergreens that screened them from the street, and the informal dog play group that met in the park behind her house must have dispersed, for she did not hear the usual barks and yips. She let herself in, calling for Crow and the dogs, but no one came out to greet her. On a walk, she told herself, it has to be a walk. No single person could overcome that trio. Not with Crow's common sense and Miata's Doberman instincts. Esskay's breath alone could fell an attacker.

But if Crow and the dogs came back in the next few minutes, and the man in the van had found his way here, things could get dangerously out of control. She had to figure out a way to keep everyone safe.

Leaving her front door standing open, she went to the rear of the house, unlocking the dead bolt on the French doors that led to the deck off the bedroom, then locking them from outside with her key. Now what? The house was built into a hill, so the ground was a half-story down — less, when one slid from the deck and hung from it before dropping to the ground below. Still, the landing was harder than she expected, sending shocks through both knees.

Tess crawled under the deck until she was as close as she could get to the house while still able to see a slice of the gravel driveway. The ground here never saw the sun, and it was cool where it rubbed into the white shirt she had worn with her linen funeral suit. Her black skirt was hiked up almost to her hips, her low-heeled shoes had slipped from her feet while she was hanging from the deck. At least she had thought to leave the jacket back in the house, flung over a chair in the dining room to help create the illusion that she was inside.

Of course, this meant her gun was no longer concealed. She didn't want it to be. The Smith & Wesson was out of the holster. She held it in two hands, arms extended on the ground, and waited.

And waited. Then waited some more, feeling increasingly ridiculous with each passing second, which seemed to be ticked off by the blood that pounded in her ears. If the van's driver had been intent on following her, he surely would be here by now. She remembered a game she had played growing up, German tanks. They had stretched out on the ground just like this, pretending to shoot the cars moving along the streets of Ten Hills. But then the guns had been fingers and sticks, nothing more. God, she felt like an idiot. Her neighbors already thought she was a strange and somewhat outré addition to the Roland Park zip code. If the local swim club got wind of this, they would never let her join.

Then she thought of Julie Carter and Lucy Fancher and Tiffani Gunts, and she didn't feel quite so ridiculous. If someone had given them a chance, if they had known what or who was coming for them in the final hours of their lives, they would have fought back. Despite her self-destructive habits, Julie was scrappy and tough. Lucy Fancher was beginning to find her place in the world, she had told her ex-boyfriend as much. Tiffani was a mother. She would have done anything to keep Darby from growing up without her. Given the chance, these women wouldn't have worried about whether they seemed strange or odd. They would have tried to live.

Someone's vehicle was pulling up front. It was a dark van, its wheels crunching on the gravel.

Tess heard the door slam, saw a pair of sneakered feet approach her front door. She glanced over her shoulder, making sure Crow and the dogs weren't coming up the path through the woods. If they arrived now, she would have to shout and warn him away and risk losing her quarry. But the woods were quiet. Everything was quiet. She listened for footsteps, but the rock foundation of her house was too solid. Had he crossed her threshold, ventured deep enough into the house? Was he in the bedroom yet, looking for her — throwing open her closet and bathroom doors, trying the locked French doors? She needed him to get as far inside as possible.

Her plan was to lock him in her house by racing to the front door and turning the dead bolt with her key from the outside. She then would call the police from her cell, reporting an intruder. He would be stuck inside and she would be safe outside, keeping a watch for the police and Crow, whoever arrived first.

A board creaked. His footsteps were headed toward her. She inched forward on her stomach, ready to go.

And then she saw a second pair of legs, running up her hill in a strange hobbled step. Khaki'd legs, with nerdy dress shoes and no octet of doggie legs alongside them. In other words, not Crow legs. So where had these come from? Who was this? She had not heard another car door slam, and there had been no passenger in the van that she saw. Two men? Why would there be two men? Yet the second man was now in the house, he had just crossed the threshold. If he heard her coming, he would have time to get out, ruining everything. She would have to lock them both inside, ask questions later. She wiggled a few more inches up the hill, gun still extended, wondering how fast she could move. She wasn't built for speed, as the old blues song said. Adrenaline was going to have to power her through.

But even as she catapulted herself forward, a muffled shout came from her house, followed by what appeared to be the sounds of a scuffle. Had a well-intentioned neighbor seen the open door and gone to confront the stranger? Tess only knew that she heard objects falling, something shattering on the floor.

Then a terrible scream, a man's scream but high-pitched, as shrill and pain-filled as anything Tess had ever heard.

She surged up from the ground and sprinted toward the door, still prepared to lock the intruders inside and let them sort it out. Then she saw Carl Dewitt writhing on the floor just inside the foyer, holding his left knee and moaning. Another man stood over him, his back to her, a baseball bat in hand. Unsteadily, he began to raise it over his head, as if to bring it down on Carl's ginger-orange head.

"Stop it!" Tess screamed.

The man with the baseball bat froze for a second, then shrugged, almost as if he could not help himself, as if the bat were alive and had a will of its own. She aimed her gun at the small of his back, but she could no longer find her voice, could not tell him what she needed to say. It was like one of those nightmares where you cannot find your voice to scream or call 911. Only she wasn't going to die. This man was.

Carl caught the bat in both hands as the man swung it toward him. The swing was weak, halfhearted, easily stopped, but the man pulled the bat out of Carl's hands as if he meant to swing again. He stepped back, stumbling a bit. Tess thought about how her shots at the range tended to end up high and right. She adjusted her hold, so her gun was level with the man's hamstring, slightly to the left. She had never fired a gun this close to her target before. It was only a .38, it probably wouldn't kill him if she didn't jerk up the way she often did —

"Jesus Christ, put down the fucking bat and put your hands above your head or you're going to lose most of your large intestine. There's a gun on you."

But it was Carl who had spoken, not Tess. Surprisingly, the man did as he was told. But he still didn't step away from Carl, and his weaving posture made him seem more dangerous, not less. Was he on drugs? Psychotic? Tess had expected to find a calm stone-cold killer in her house. This confused, shambling man was much more terrifying. It was impossible to judge what he might do next.

So she ran straight at him. Ran at him as if she were one of the defensive stars on the Ravens and he was one of the hapless quarterbacks they intimidated. She threw her shoulders at his knees, wanting to hear them crack, wanting the tendons to shred and pull from the bone.

All she accomplished, however, was to knock

them both to the floor. The force of the tackle sent his cap and dark glasses flying, but his flesh was disappointingly silent and whole beneath the weight of her body. He didn't scream, as Carl had, or yell. He landed with a thud and a sharp exhalation of air, nothing more.

She jerked him by the shoulder, rolling him over so she was staring into a pair of watery blue eyes. She was so close to the man that her chin brushed the straggly beard he was trying to cultivate.

But the hair on his head was more interesting than the hair on his face. The intruder's scalp was covered with short sprouts of fluffy hair, interspersed with a few pale pink scabs that would soon disappear.

"Mickey Pechter," Tess said. "My computer buddy."

It took him a few more seconds to catch his breath. Once he did, all he said was: "I hope you know that Judge Halsey and the Baltimore County State's Attorney's office are going to hear about what you've done."

Then, with surprising force, he pushed Tess off him and stumbled toward the door.

# Chapter 31

"What *you* did? He actually said that?"

"Yes," Tess said. "And without apparent irony."

She was at the dining room table, watching Crow as he straightened and cleaned the so-called great room, the combination living and dining room that had been created by knocking out the walls in the front of the house. He was unusually manic, as if he felt the house had been defiled by the afternoon's events and needed some sort of symbolic cleansing.

Crow and the dogs had arrived home just as Mickey Pechter made his mad dash. Unfortunately for Mickey, Miata thought he was running toward Crow and had responded accordingly. She growled and snapped, fur bristling on her neck, penning Pechter in a corner of the house until he seemed on the verge of wetting himself.

If he had been crouched on someone else's wood floor, Tess would have rooted for just that outcome.

But it was her floor, her house, and Mickey Pechter was a problematic presence, wet or dry. If she called the police and made a report, she could end up before Judge Halsey, her probation extended because she was clearly making no progress on the anger front. She didn't worry about additional criminal charges — home invasions went to grand juries, which seldom indicted homeowners. But she didn't want to come under Judge Halsey's falsely benevolent gaze again, didn't want to hear his droning pronouncements on the violence that flowed between men and women. She was tired of explaining herself, tired of asking for permission.

She called to the dog. "It's okay, Miata. Down, girl."

The Doberman retreated, but then the greyhound surged forward, anxious to get in on the action. Esskay, however, had no instinct for combat. Once she confronted Mickey Pechter, her only move was to hook her nose in his armpit, looking for a pat. She ended up knocking him back on his ass. He yelped with pain — a phony, exaggerated cry. *What a whiner*, Tess thought. Crow, meanwhile, had turned his attention to Carl, who insisted through gritted teeth that he would be just fine if he could elevate his knee and ice it.

"What the fuck were you thinking?" Tess asked Mickey. She was suddenly weary, adrenaline draining from her body and leaving her with nothing but a bruised flulike feeling.

"I wanted *you* to know what it's like to be scared and jumpy all the time. It's a joke, what that judge did. You assaulted me. I woke up in intensive care. Then I go back to work, and I get fired. They said it was because of the downturn, but I bet it was because they heard about what happened."

Tess smiled. So she *had* exacted a punishment of sorts. Out of work, Mickey Pechter would have more time but fewer funds to stalk underage girls.

He did not miss her look of satisfaction. "If I were a woman and you were a man, it wouldn't have ended with you in counseling. You should be in jail, you bitch. I have nightmares because of what you did."

"I know. I heard your victim impact statement. So if you're so scared of me, why have you been following me?"

"I saw you with this guy down on Guilford Avenue one day. It got me to thinking."

Guilford Avenue? That was the day they visited the private mail service, where Eric Shivers had once kept a box. What was Mickey doing there? Baltimore was small enough for such a coincidence to be plausible, but Tess had assumed Mickey Pechter was the kind of suburban boy who never ventured downtown.

All she said was, "Got you thinking what?"

"That maybe you and he were fooling around and I should follow you and see if I could get the goods on you, blackmail you, fuck up your life the way you fucked up mine."

"You thought Carl and I were having an affair? Don't be ridiculous."

He wasn't listening, he was wound up in his own logic, illogical as it was.

"Then I thought it would be better just to scare you, make you feel unsafe all the time, vulnerable-like. I tried hang-up phone calls at your office — only I kept getting the machine. So then I started tracking you. I *wanted* you to see me following you. I wasn't planning on doing anything more, but today, when I got here and saw the door open —"

Now even Mickey Pechter seemed to be having trouble understanding how his mind had worked, how he had reasoned himself into almost getting killed. Yet Tess knew. After all, it had happened to her. *All I wanted to do was scare you, get you to stay away from teenage girls. I never set out to strip your clothes off and apply a depilatory.*

She would have told him as much. Mickey Pechter, however, did not strike her as a man who would appreciate that irony.

Instead, she said, "So you came to my house with a baseball bat in hand — just to scare me."

"I'm on a softball team. We had a game today. The bat was the only thing I had in my sister's van. I was gonna come in, wave it around. I thought I'd pretend to be like, you know, some guy in one of those drug movies who's looking for a stash but goes to the wrong house."

"Sounds like a good way to get killed."

"I didn't know you had a gun. And I didn't

know this guy, your redheaded friend, was going to jump me from behind. He was trying to kill me, swear to God. I only swung at him to get him off me, and then he was so angry, I thought he really would kill me if he got the bat out of my hand. It was like I was outside my head. I couldn't stop."

Tess looked at Carl, who had struggled to a seated position with Crow's help and had a dish towel of cracked ice pressed to his knee. His face was pale beneath his freckles. She wondered if he could go into shock from pain.

"Carl, you want to press charges against him?"

"God, no," he said, his voice tough, if a bit faint.

"You sure?" She wouldn't have minded Mickey Pechter facing his own felony assault charges. But this was the city, not the county. There was no Judge Halsey here, no time for such penny-ante antics. Besides, she didn't want any official record of Pechter's visit.

"Positive," Carl said, between clenched teeth.

She waved her gun at Mickey, just for effect. She was suddenly aware of how bizarre she must look. Much of her hair had come loose from her braid and was flying around her head, her white shirt was crusted with dirt and dead leaves, her black linen skirt was still halfway up her hips, displaying the full glory of her now-ripped pantyhose, cut-rate DKNY purchased in bulk at Nordstrom Rack. The Preppie Avenger.

"I'm the one who almost killed someone today," she said. The catch in her voice, almost a sob, caught her off guard. "Do you realize that? I almost shot you in my home, and no grand jury in the world would have indicted me, not under these circumstances. But it would have fucked up my life, just the same. You want to give me nightmares? You came damn close. Thing is, you would have been too dead to enjoy it."

"I told you I didn't know you had a gun," Pechter stammered, afraid again.

"You *never* know who has a gun in this world. Or who has a concerned family friend who's willing to wreck your life for the sheer fun of it. You can't know anything about anyone. So you shouldn't pick fights, because you may not win. Don't flip people off in traffic, don't pull macho shit in bars. We live in a world where people will kill you for one rude look. How can you not know that? Are you too busy trying to pick up underage girls to read the goddamn papers?"

"I know," he said, "that you are one crazy fucked-up cunt."

"Hey, watch your language." But it was Carl who objected to Mickey's rhetoric, not Tess. "You shouldn't talk like that, not in front of a woman. Not in front of anybody."

Mickey began to edge toward the door, unnerved by Carl's intensity, although Carl couldn't even stand, much less go after him. Tess blocked Mickey's way.

"I'm calling my lawyer tomorrow and I'm filing for a restraining order against you," she said. "If I ever see you again — in my rearview mirror, or standing outside my office —"

"I know," Mickey Pechter said, sneering at her, "you'll shoot me. Big talker."

She put her gun on the floor and grabbed him by the collar of the windbreaker with both hands, bringing him nose to nose.

"I'll burn something else off next time. Something that doesn't grow back. Tell that to Judge Halsey if you like. Tell him any fucking thing you like. As far as I'm concerned, I haven't been angry *enough* up to now."

She let go of him as suddenly as she had seized him and he staggered backward, hands shooting instinctively for his groin. Then he turned and ran for his van in a wobbling stride, hands still cupped in front of him. Tess was pretty sure it was the last she would see of Mickey Pechter.

"Of course, Mickey wasn't the only one following me. Was he, Carl?"

Carl had moved to an upholstered mission-style chair, which had cost Tess the approximate bluebook value of her thirteen-year-old Toyota. His left leg was stretched out on a matching ottoman, a second dish towel balanced on his knee, where the first had left a dark wet spot. Tess had poured him a shot of Jack Daniel's, feeling like some saloon proprietress tending to an injured cowboy. Now she replenished his glass and poured herself a little more white wine while she was up. She asked Crow if he wanted anything, but he just shook his head and went back to his obsessive cleaning.

"What do you mean?"

"You've been watching me too. I know it wasn't coincidence that you stopped by today. Were you parked at the bottom of the hill so you could watch the entrance to my little street? Or have you been everywhere I've been today? The funeral, the cemetery?"

The only sound in the room was Crow's dust mop going back and forth across the floor. *Swish swish swish. Swish swish swish.* Tess's mother had given Crow this new kind of mop, a Swiffer, for Hanukkah, and he loved it, the way men often love things for their sheer novelty. He had the wet cloths for the kitchen and bathroom floors, the dry ones for the wide-planked pine floors that ran through the rest of the house. Their floors always gleamed.

"I wouldn't say *watching*," Carl said. "Checking in, from time to time. I've been worried about you."

Tess knew there was good reason to be worried about her. But Carl didn't, or shouldn't. He didn't know what Luisa O'Neal had told her.

"I saw the thing about Julie Carter in the paper," he said, as if anticipating the question. "I remembered her from your original list. Let me guess. She was small, with light eyes and dark hair."

"Yes."

"Lucy. Tiffani. Mary Ann. He's definitely got a type. Although I think Lucy was the prettiest. Even dead —" He did not finish the thought.

"Major Shields said you're obsessed with Lucy."

"It's as good a word as any, I guess." He sighed. "I liked to think of myself as Dana Andrews in *Laura*, only she never comes through the door in a raincoat, still alive. But when I dream about Lucy, she's whole. In my dreams, her head is with her body. She's not the way I found her."

"You dream about her?"

He nodded, his face doleful. "Every few nights."

"Is that why you cracked up on the job, got disability?"

"I got disability for my knee."

"That's not what Major Shields told me."

"Then he's a liar."

"So you didn't have a nervous breakdown at work?"

"Oh, I cracked up." Carl's tone was mild, as if he were telling a funny story on himself. "But when I cracked up, I screwed up my knee, and that's why I had to take disability. You see, I really did slip on the ice in the parking lot, in January the year after Lucy was killed. I was out a month. By the time I came

412

back to work, the state police had pretty much taken over the investigation. They didn't need me. As Sergeant Craig was quick to point out."

"But you didn't stop, did you?"

"I just couldn't stop talking to people, thinking about it. They warned me, told me to back off, and maybe if I had kept going the way I was going, they would have disciplined me."

"So what happened?"

"One day — I'm still in a brace, on pain medication, walking like Walter Brennan — I drove to the bridge where I found her. I started walking. I crossed the Susquehanna: about a mile, I guess, no more. I turned back and did it again. Then again. About the fifth or sixth time, I'm in so much pain I keep thinking I'm going to pass out. Apparently I was talking to myself too, muttering like some old man on the street, although I don't remember that part. I was trying to figure out how the head came to be there, how he had slowed to leave it there, without anyone seeing him. Even in the middle of the night, another car could have come along. He was risking so much —" His voice trailed off.

"What happened?"

"One of my old co-workers called our supervisor. I was admitted to the hospital in Havre de Grace that night. They released me forty-eight hours later, although they recommended I try some post-traumatic stress counseling. It's not like I was nuts. But my knee was so screwed up I had to get replacement surgery, young as I am. I was out the rest of the year."

"Carl, if that's not obsessive, I don't know what is."

"Well, why shouldn't I be obsessed? I found a severed head on a bridge. I think I've come by my obsession pretty honestly."

"Yet when Mary Ann Melcher called the tip line and tried to tell you her ex-boyfriend matched the description of Alan Palmer, only he was dead —"

Carl shook his head. "I knew more by then. I knew the guy we were looking for wouldn't kill himself. He might be dead, but not on purpose. I was just stalling for time, trying to figure it out."

"But it did make sense. There were no killings after Mary Ann, no evidence of any activity on his part." *Until Julie Carter was shot and killed.*

"Everything always makes sense with this guy. What's the one thing we know about him? He plans things out in advance, in minute detail. I think he decided to stop, for some reason, and he wanted to cut off his own trail if the cops ever came looking for him. I don't think he's dead *or* reformed." He gave her a level look. "And neither do you."

"So why does he make sure I get this list? Why draw attention to himself?"

"He's decided he wants to be found, for some reason. Found by you."

The words might have chilled Tess more if she hadn't repeated them to herself, over and over, since the death of Julie Carter. She stared into the bottom of her glass. She was drinking wine as if it was water, and yet she couldn't feel its effects. Fear was a great sponge for alcohol.

"Let's go back to that original list," Tess said. "There are three deaths since Mary Ann Melcher's boyfriend 'disappeared' at sea. Julie Carter, shot and killed this past Friday night. Alan Palmer once dated her, although he left when she wouldn't kick her drug problem. Okay, that makes sense. But the other two don't. Hazel Ligetti, a forty-something spinster, burned up in a house fire. And Dr. Michael Shaw, hit by a car while jogging. Not young women, not gunshot victims."

"Doesn't sound like our guy, does it?"

It made her feel safer, somehow, to have Carl back, to have him speak as if they were partners. Carl, after all, had seen this man in person. With Carl at her side, how close would he dare to come?

"No, it doesn't. Then again, maybe he knew he had to change the pattern. Or maybe these were people who could have identified him, who knew what he had done."

"So where do we start?"

"The emergency room at Union Memorial, to make sure you haven't screwed up your knee again. You're no good to anyone if they put you on crutches."

★ ★ ★

"Can I ask you one thing?"

They were driving through Tess's neighborhood, the passenger seat pushed back as far as it could go, so Carl's left leg was more or less extended and he could still hold the makeshift cold compress on it. Night had fallen, and there were no streetlamps here, so Tess could not see the expression on his face.

"Sure."

"Why would it have been ridiculous?"

"What?"

"That guy said he thought we were having an affair. And you said, 'Don't be ridiculous.'"

"Oh." She understood what he was asking. Was it so impossible to think she might be interested in Carl Dewitt, with his freckles and his orange-red hair and his bowlegged stride? Yes, actually, it was. Only not because of the freckles and the orange-red hair and the bowlegs, but because of something else, some ineffable lack, the thing that people called chemistry.

But she did not think he would find that reason particularly comforting.

"I meant I wouldn't cheat. Not on Crow."

"How can you be so sure? Have you ever cheated?"

The simple thing was to say no. Tess did not owe Carl Dewitt that much honesty. After all, he had not always been truthful with her. But she felt caught on the question, as if she had stumbled into a bramble bush and needed to pull away with great care, separating herself one thorn at a time.

"I had a boyfriend who ran around on me. A lot. We broke up. But when he got engaged to someone else, I became the person he cheated with. I justified it at the time — I was his first love, I was his real love, blah, blah, blah — but there's not any justification for what I did. To make things worse, he was killed one night. After we were . . . together. And I saw it. He died right in front of me."

"Some people would see that as a fitting punishment."

"Yes, I suppose they would. But Jonathan didn't die because he was sleeping with me. It was . . . just a dumb accident."

She lied because the story wearied her, she did not want to tell it again. Every time she told it, she ran the risk that it would be waiting for her when she closed her eyes. Assuming she ever closed her eyes again.

"So he died, and that made you decide you would never cheat again."

"Yes." No. Crow had left her once, when her yearning for another man became so pronounced that she told him about it for fear she would act on it. Carl didn't need to know this either. "It's complicated, being in a committed relationship that falls short of marriage."

"So why don't you get married?"

"I have a hunch that marriage becomes an

excuse for people to start taking each other for granted."

"I wouldn't know. I never made it to marriage."

"Scientists are beginning to say monogamy isn't natural to *any* species. Not even swans. It's a struggle, something you have to work at every day."

"I never had to work at it when I dated. I didn't date much, but when I did, I liked being with just one person."

"Well, then, you're better than most people I know. Crow and I have agreed to talk, if we start having feelings for someone else. That's the best we can do — pledge to be honest about our weaknesses."

"And so far —"

"So far, we're doing fine."

"I did have a girl once." Something in Carl's voice made it sound as if the *once* referred not just to a time long ago but to a literal number. He had a girl. Once.

"And?"

"She said I wasn't ambitious enough. It made her mad that I was happy where I was, being a Toll Facilities cop, living in the town where I grew up. She said I should want more. So I tried. When I found . . . Lucy, I thought maybe this was my chance. I'd be a big guy, I'd be *more*. Then she broke up with me because I worked all the time."

"Shit."

"Yeah. If I had to do it over again, I'd go back to being me. The me I used to be. Then I'd find a girl who liked me just the way I was."

"You still might."

"Except I'm not that person anymore. Whatever happens, I'll never be that person again." Carl sighed. "I miss him."

The conversation was unsettling. It was too delicate, too fraught. Tess felt as if she could make a million mistakes with a single syllable. What should she say? What did he want her to say?

"You should cut your hair," Carl said.

"What?"

"Or not wear it in a braid. I saw this show, on A&E, the Criminal Justice files. A woman with her hair pulled back is too easy to grab. You jog, right?"

"Sometimes."

"Well, imagine how easy it would be for someone to come up and —" His left hand caught her braid at a spot low on her neck. "You'd be in someone's trunk."

She saw the lights of Union Memorial up ahead, the white-pink blossoms of the cherry trees rippling in the wind.

"Al Capone donated those trees," she said, hoping to change the subject and hoping Carl would let go of her hair. "It was in gratitude for the treatment he received here when he was in the throes of syphilis."

"I know," Carl Dewitt said. Of course he did.

It was just the kind of thing he *would* know: gangsters and gangster films. "Al Capone. Now there was a guy who knew how to use a baseball bat. 'We are all members of a team.' From *The Untouchables*. And they caught him because of tax evasion, not for murder or racketeering. Tax evasion."

"You know," Tess said, "I bet that's how we'll catch our killer."

"For tax evasion?"

"For something small, some trivial detail he overlooked. No one manages to get everything right, all the time. God is in the details."

"Really? I thought it was the devil."

He should kill that guy, that Mickey Pechter. That creep, that pervert. He's trouble. She handled him beautifully — of course — but the man should be taught a lesson. And it would be nice to demonstrate his loyalty to her even as he keeps his distance. The problem is, if Pechter is found dead, the police might focus on her because of her connection to the pervert, and that would be inconvenient. He cannot risk it, satisfying as it would be. And the thing is, it never *is* satisfying, not quite. The release can come only in the context of true intimacy. He has learned that the hard way.

Besides, Pechter was an unwitting accomplice, he owes him. Her adventure with him, and its legal consequences, provided the entrée he needed. He has never counted on luck, but neither has he spurned its opportunities. The first episode with Pechter had confused her, softened her up, opened her up in a way he never could have anticipated. The sook is ready for her jimmy. The rush is on.

It's all about redemption, darling, all about redemption: yours and mine.

He always knew this part would be hard, but he also knew that waiting was his own peculiar talent. Now is the time to pull back, and not only because his picture is out there, floating around. Clean-shaven, his hair color altered, he is not that recognizable. But the point is to see if she can do it on her own. She has to negotiate the final part of the maze alone. He is not sure yet how she will do it, which is part of the joy. But he knows she will find her way. He has chosen well. At last.

He pulls his patchwork pillow to his face, inhales deeply, and thinks about Becca. What would she have been without him? Did she ever ask herself the same question? He likes to think she understood in the end, that she recognized her debt to him even as she reneged on it. She was young and, for all her seeming sophistication, not yet ready to accept the gifts he brought her. If only they had had more time. She would have understood how rare his love was, that it was a once-in-a-lifetime gift.

Funny, he always thought the only person capable of understanding his love for Becca was her father: Harry Harrison, mildly alcoholic, bumbling through the island, offending everyone and never knowing it. Becca's senses were more acute, she was not fooled by the bland smiles of the Notting Islanders. But neither was she cowed. The locals came to respect her, if not accept her. Harrison was the perennial outsider, so outside he didn't pick up on the mockery beneath the polite faces.

Once, when she was late coming back from her voice lesson, he had been desperate enough to go to her house. Harry Harrison, drink in his hand, met him at the door and insisted he come in for a little chat. He feared the father would demand to know just what he did with his daughter, all those times they went off on the bay. Worse, he feared he would tell him. He loved Becca so much that he yearned to speak of it to someone, someone who would understand.

Of course, you couldn't tell your girlfriend's father how it felt to make love to her. But Harry Harrison struck him as someone worldly, someone who had loved and lost. He would know that it wasn't about the heat, inside and out, that it wasn't the mere physical sensation. It was Becca. She was extraordinary, otherworldly. Her voice proved that. No earthbound woman could produce those sounds. When he was — with her, joined to her, he sometimes thought he might reach the source of that voice.

He also found himself wishing there was a switch, a way to turn it off, so it belonged only to him. Because he knew, he knew without knowing, that her talent was his enemy. As much as he loved her and worshiped everything that came out of her, the voice would take her away from him one day.

So he had gone to her house, seeking a different kind of kindred spirit.

"You miss her, don't you?"

"Sir?"

"Call me Harry. You miss Becca, when she's away for even a day, don't you? I do too. She's all the company I have."

"Well, we had a date, that's all. Nothing special." He pretended to a coolness he didn't feel. If Becca hadn't missed the boat, they would be heading out now, in his skiff. He would have his hand in hers, and soon she would have him in her. He had never been with anyone before Becca, but he knows this is as good as it's going to get. He sees the people around him, the grown-ups. The dried-ups, as he thinks of them. Even his parents, as much as he loves them — what's the point? How could you settle for such day-in, day-out ordinariness if you've known the thrill of loving someone like this? He'd rather die than be without Becca. He really would.

But all he said to Mr. Harrison was, "Is that your computer? Is that what you're writing your book on?"

Almost no one had computers then and this one was huge, a clunky beast that took up much of the dining room table.

"Yes. It's a pretty good machine, but the power outages on the island seem to have fried something inside. You wouldn't believe how much work I've lost. I have to back up my files practically every five minutes, and it's still not good enough. I should go back to a type-writer. They were truly portable. I had one typewriter that went with me from Italy to Cuernavaca to Vermont. But I bought the computer when I decided to live here."

"Why did you go to all those places?"

"Because I wanted to. I'm a writer. And I make just enough money to live where I please and do as I please — as long as I don't get too extravagant. I wanted to try island life because I remembered visiting Tangier when I was a boy. I didn't count on Becca suddenly deciding she wanted to be an opera singer. If she gets much more serious, I suppose we'll have to move again."

His heart lurched, even as his mind raced through the calculation. He is a junior, seven-teen. Becca is a year ahead of him in school. He knew she would go to the mainland at the end of this school year, that he would have to wait a year to follow her. But he counted on their having the next year. He's not sure he could survive two years without her.

"And you could do that? Just pick up and go anywhere you want to go?"

"As long as it's reasonable. New York is too expensive. Of course, Becca has her heart set on Juilliard. I keep telling her there are other good music schools. Peabody in Baltimore, for example. She's got New York fever."

*No, she doesn't,* he wanted to say. She yearned to sing, yes. But she wanted to be with him too. They had spoken of it endlessly. She wouldn't go to New York, not without him.

"And when I tell her I don't think New York is going to work out, she says maybe she'll run away, go to Italy or somewhere else in Europe." Harry Harrison shook his head, sad and bewildered. "She's always threatening to leave me if she doesn't get her way. It's hard for a man alone to raise a daughter. She seems to think it's my fault her mother is dead. As if, having divorced her mother, I didn't care when she died. But I did. And I didn't want to be a single dad. Taking a four-year-old girl into my life wasn't what I had planned, either. She says I drink too much. But alcohol is just . . . the lubricant. A writer has to shed his inhibitions, get naked. I have to enter a place where I don't care what people think."

He thought, Well, you've ended up in a place where people don't care about you at all. If you knew what they thought of you, you'd probably never get a word on the page.

"I heard," he said instead, "that you're writing a book about us."

"Who told you that?" Harrison's voice wasn't loud, but it was harder, and the sudden change scared him.

"I . . . . I don't know." Big-mouth Aggie

426

Winslip. "It's just something I heard. Becca must have mentioned it."

Harrison switched back to genial host. "She did? I didn't even know Becca listened when I spoke about my work. She seems to find it boring. She calls me a cut-rate Michener. Becca's a terrible snob, if you want to know the truth. Keeps talking about 'high art' and 'low art.' With high art being whatever she likes — opera — and low art being everything else. I'll tell you something about Becca." He leaned in to share his confidence, his breath sour with gin. "She's got the diva temperament, but I don't think she's got the acting chops to be a great singer of any range. She'll have to play parts that are close enough to her own personality to get by. She'll never sing Mimi, she'll always be Musetta."

"I . . . I'm not sure who they are." This was true, despite Becca's endless chatter about what she did and what she sang and what she was learning. When she spoke, it was often as if she were still singing in a foreign language. He was so caught up in joy he couldn't hear the distinct sounds.

"You don't need to know," her father said, clapping him on the back. "Can I get you something?"

But he made his excuses and wandered out, still thinking about what kind of job would allow him to go wherever he wanted. Every job he knew was tethered to a place, whether it was waterman or C&P lineman or school-teacher. He wanted a job that would allow him to go anywhere, because that's what he would need to be with Becca.

Later, years later, he would find himself wondering if there was a different meaning to her father's words. *You don't need to know.* He thought Harry Harrison was being kind, saying these things were unimportant, they would not impede his love. Now he thinks that Harry Harrison assumed this was a high school romance, destined to fade.

This realization made him feel much less guilty about what he had taken from Harry Harrison — who had, it turned out, drunk himself to death in a fashion. When Becca disappeared, Harrison did too, and he spent the rest of his life in pursuit of his wayward daughter. Of course, he never found her. But liver cancer found him.

Everybody dies. He adjusts the pillow beneath his cheek, so he's no longer pressing against one of the more wiry seams. His mother's handiwork improved over the time she was making this pillow. As did his. He sighs, hollow from anticipation. Everybody dies.

# Chapter 32

It took one phone call the next day to determine that Michael Shaw's partner was a real person, now living in California — and not particularly happy to have a stranger call him out of the blue and remind him that his lover was dead.

"Of course I live where I told the police I live," he said when Tess explained, in a smooth-as-silk lie, that she was going over open case files for the Anne Arundel County police and needed to make sure he had provided a correct telephone number and address. "But what about the case? Have you made any headway?"

"We're pursuing it with due vigilance." She thought that was something a cop might say.

"Have you learned anything, anything at all? It's been six months, and when I call your detectives they act as if I'm a gigantic pain. Are they ever going to make an arrest in Michael's case? I understand that accidents happen, but a hit-and-run — a person should have the decency — you can't know whether someone's dead or not unless you stop —"

Shaw's former lover began to cry.

"I'm sorry," Tess said, and this was not a lie.

"But we may have a break in the case soon." She hoped that wasn't a lie.

"I could have told you that the doctor's boyfriend isn't one of our guy's personas," Carl said when she hung up the phone. Esskay had allotted him a small portion of the office sofa.

"How so?"

"Our guy's not queer."

She gave him a look.

"Sorry. Gay, he's not gay. He'd be appalled you even thought to check."

"And how do you know that?"

He tapped his forehead. "I just do."

"Uh-uh. You're the one who said you didn't want to get into that mind-hunter shit."

"I'm just saying I know he's not a — not gay."

"It's still a supposition. Let's keep to facts. Here's one: Michael Shaw's partner, unlike the other boyfriends in our various cases, didn't disappear off the face of the planet. Too bad. Shaw's death would be a more obvious part of the overall pattern if he had. So what else do we know about Shaw?"

"He was a shrink."

"Right. Is it possible our guy ever went to him?"

"Not of his own volition. He wouldn't want to be in analysis."

"What if it were court-ordered?" Tess couldn't help thinking of her own situation. She reread the obituary in her file. Shaw had been a doctor in Hopkins' famed sex clinic. Serial killing had a strong sexual component. If EAC — the shorthand she and Carl had started using for Eric-Alan-Charlie — had committed a lesser crime in yet another persona, he might have been ordered into therapy. But wouldn't an arrest have outed his identity scheme?

Carl was on the same train of thought, even farther down the track. "We'll never get the doctor's client list," he said. "It would be hard enough if we were real cops. As amateurs with no legal standing, there's no way. Besides, why kill your shrink? He can't tell your secrets to anyone."

"That's not exactly true. If you blurt out your intention to harm someone, the doctor does have an ethical obligation to alert the authorities. A psychiatrist has to make a clear distinction between delusion and true intent, but he couldn't sit there and listen to a patient describe his plan to commit a criminal act and just shrug it off."

"Okay, but Michael Shaw is, chronologically, the last on the list. He was killed in December. So what did our guy tell him that was so bad he had to kill him?"

Tess chewed on her pencil, looking at the list she had long ago memorized. The first victim was Tiffani, killed six years ago. Lucy had died eighteen months later. EAC — then in Alan guise — had met and courted Julie Carter between Tiffani and Lucy, dropping her, possibly because of her addiction. He staged his own death the summer after he killed Lucy. Hazel Ligetti's house had burned down a few months earlier. And then — nothing for two years, not until Michael Shaw the past December.

"I bet anything he was the doctor's patient," Tess said. "But I don't know where to go with that. Where does Hazel fit in?"

"Got me. What did she do?"

"She worked for the Department of Health and Mental Hygiene in Hagerstown, in some low-level paper-pushing job. You know, all the other women — the ones he killed and the ones he didn't — they all had some joy in their life, even if it proved to be false. They got to have the illusion of being happy. But Hazel Ligetti had nothing. According to her landlord, she lived alone and seldom went out."

"A paper pusher?"

"Yep."

"What kind of paper do you think they push at the Department of Health and Mental Hygiene?"

"I don't know. Insurance claims?"

"Yeah, among other things. Also" — he paused, to give his words more weight — "disability programs."

"So? He's disabled, he sees a psychiatrist, he kills the doctor and the woman who sent him there. We're back to where we started."

"You don't know much about disability programs, do you?"

Tess shook her head.

"Well, I do, sad to say. When I had . . . my problems at work, they tried to get me to apply for SSI — Supplemental Security Income. That's the federal program. But to get that, you almost always have to go through the state and qualify for some sort of temporary support first. Nobody gets SSI the first time out. What do we know about our guy's second two identities?"

"They're men in hospitals who have suffered catastrophic injury."

"Right. Which means their case files could have passed through the hands of a DHMH worker in Washington County. There's a rehab hospital out there, but it's short-term. What do you want to bet that the real Alan Palmer and Charlie Chisholm were hospitalized there before they found long-term care?"

It took Tess a few seconds to work it through for herself. Of EAC's myriad identities, only the first alias belonged to someone who was dead, Eric Shivers. He had died as a teenager, old enough to have a driver's license on record — and young enough not to have anything else on record. Frederick cops would have run Eric's name and the date of birth and the Social Security number through the computers, but they wouldn't have found anything suspicious. It never would have occurred to them to check Vital Records to see if Tiffani's boyfriend was dead. After all, he was living and breathing, right in front of them.

She booted up her computer and plugged the next two names, Alan Palmer and Charles Chisholm, into a phone directory that searched every listed number in the nation. Dozens of hits came up, unusual names were harder to come by in this day and age. So if there ever was any confusion — if anyone ever said, "Hey, I knew an Alan Palmer back home" — EAC could laugh and say, "Yes, I've met a few Alan Palmers in my time too."

*Did he laugh? Did he smile? How normal-seeming was he? Very, according to his last girl-friend, Mary Ann. The perfect boyfriend. Until he killed you.*

"He needs relatively common names," Tess said, thinking out loud. "Names of people who have no connection to him. The men also have to be a certain age — they all had the same birth year — and have a physical description he can more or less fit. Caucasian, around six feet, light eyes. Hazel helped him get those. Why?"

"Beats me. If she knew what she was doing, it made her an accomplice to some pretty awful stuff. And from the way you said she lived, it doesn't sound as if she was blackmailing him or anything."

Tess chewed the inside of her mouth. "We can't just sit here, speculating. We need to drive out to the office where Hazel worked, find out what records she had access to."

"Same problem we have with the shrink. Why would anyone talk to us?"

434

Tess rummaged through her desk, finding letterheads from an insurance company, one that happened to exist only in her imagination: S&K Fire and Life, named for the greyhound. She loaded a sheet in the printer and began typing.

"To Whom It May Concern —"

"What are you doing?" Carl demanded.

"Lying."

"I don't think I can be a party to —"

"Carl, you're not a cop anymore, remember? You're never going to be a cop again. But you could be a private investigator, if you wanted to, or a security consultant. So step back and watch how it's done."

He walked over to her desk, looking over her shoulder at the template on her screen. "This works?"

"Fake letterhead is amazing. The thing that really sells it, however, is the motto."

"Motto?"

She opened the printer tray and pointed. "There, under the name: *Serving Baltimore families since 1938.* For some reason, that clinches it. It's the little extras that make a lie work, the superfluous details."

"Did you always think like a criminal, or did you learn on the job?"

Tess stopped to think about this, fingers hovering above the keyboard. "I believe there was always a criminal in me, waiting to find a noncriminal way to express itself. So far, this arrangement is working out nicely."

The letter, backed up by Tess's real business card and license, worked its usual magic. Hazel Ligetti's supervisor in Hagerstown had only to hear the words "possible Medicaid fraud" to pull the files requested by the two earnest investigators from the insurance company. After all, Tess had the men's names, DOBs, Social Security numbers, even the Soundex numbers from their Maryland driver's licenses. She knew the hospitals where they were now being treated.

She also knew it didn't hurt that the person suspected of wrongdoing was dead. The department might have closed ranks around a living employee. But if giving up a dead one could make trouble go away, why not bend a few rules?

"Did Hazel have ready access to these files?"

The supervisor, Alice Crane, was a pale thin woman with frizzy bangs that belied the effort that had gone into straightening the rest of her highlighted hair. Or perhaps her hair was naturally straight and she tortured her bangs into those crimped waves. Tess found the things women did in the pursuit of beauty oddly endearing.

"Hazel had access to all the files. She entered the dates of each hearing, as the case moved from the state to the federal rolls. Once someone got SSI, the case was closed, but we kept the files. Part of Hazel's job was transferring the paper files to computer."

So Hazel sat there, her fingers moving over the keys as she recorded the particulars of hundreds of lives that had been interrupted or derailed. The medical files wouldn't tell her everything she needed to know to find the right identities for her friend, but quick calls to the Motor Vehicle Administration and Vital Records would have filled in the gaps.

"What was Hazel like?"

"Oh, she was a good worker. Quiet. Put in long hours. Whenever I had jobs that meant overtime, I always gave Hazel first crack. After all —" The supervisor blushed.

"What, Mrs. Crane? What were you going to say?"

"Hazel didn't usually have plans in the evenings. You could kind of count on that. She . . . kept to herself."

But Tess had known that. Hazel's landlord had told her the same thing, with bland cruelness. At least Hazel had a nice boss.

"Didn't she have any friends here in the office? Or photographs on her desk? Did anyone ever visit her here?"

Mrs. Crane shook her head. "I boxed up her desk myself after the fire. There were just a few things. She had a vase of silk flowers. And a paperweight, I think. She didn't leave a will and, boy, was that a mess. Set me straight about what you have to do, even if you're a single woman. Would you believe we had to put her personal effects in storage, wait to see if anyone came forward to make a claim? In a way, it was almost a godsend the house burned to the ground —" She caught herself, put her hands to her mouth in horror. "I didn't mean that the way it sounded."

"I know," Tess assured her. "What happened to Hazel's things?"

"We were allowed to get rid of them after a year went by, so we did. Except for some silk flowers — I have those on my desk. But if no one came forward for the money, I can't see how anyone would want some flowers."

"Money? I thought it took all Hazel's life insurance just to bury her."

"Her life insurance? Oh, yes, the little state policy we all have. That's about all it would cover, for sure. But we have a good 401(k) plan through the state, and Hazel was a saver. Someone must have told her the value of compound interest because she started putting those dollars away early. There was over a hundred thousand dollars in her account when she died, and it's still drawing interest. They advertise every year, but the beneficiary never comes forward."

"Beneficiary?"

Carl straightened up, like a hound dog catching a scent, while Tess found herself reaching for the edge of the table, to still a suddenly shaking hand.

"Well, she wrote down someone's name on

the form, but there's no address and she didn't put down his Social Security number. Sometimes, I wonder if she just picked the name out of the phone book. Hazel told me one time the only time she felt lonely was filling out forms. She had no kin, but she didn't think of herself as solitary unless she had to fill out a form."

"But there was a name —"

"Oh, yes. Not that it did any good. As I said, they put it in the legal notices in Hagerstown and Baltimore and even DC. But that money just sits and sits. I guess the state will get it, which seems a shame to me. It's not as if the state needs Hazel's money —"

"The name, Mrs. Crane. Do you remember it?"

"I wrote it down someplace, in case he ever calls or comes to look for her." She flipped lazily through the Rolodex on her desk and then through the pages of a date book. It was all Tess could do not to grab her hand and make it go faster. Carl caught her eye and mouthed "Eric Shivers." She nodded, worried about the same thing. If the killer had come to Hazel already disguised, they wouldn't know anything more than they did now.

"Here it is — William Windsor. I'd love to know what he was to Hazel. Imagine, leaving over a hundred thousand dollars to a stranger. He must have done something really nice for her."

Tess managed a mouth-only smile. "Something memorable, at least."

She had Carl call the name in to Dorie Starnes as they drove back to the city. Even from the driver's seat, Tess could hear her mercenary friend's voice booming over the cell phone's unsteady line.

"Remind Tess that I charge extra —"

"I know what she charges for a rush job. Just tell her to do it. Pull out all the stops."

They were ten miles outside Baltimore before the phone rang. Tess grabbed it from the well beneath the radio, forgetting again her principles about using a phone while driving.

"There's a bunch of William Windsors in the MVA records," Dorie said. "You go nationwide, you're looking at hundreds."

"Start with Maryland and worry about the rest of the nation later. And narrow the search to someone who's in his early thirties. Also, this would be a license that's dormant, hasn't been renewed for a while, but is still in the system."

"Dormant licenses aren't in the system."

"Yes, they are, Dorie. I know someone who moved out of state and came back twelve years later, and there was still a record. Had to take the written test again, but her records were still there. Look again."

Silence, then more costly little clicks as Dorie strolled and scrolled through her computer records.

"Here's a William Windsor, thirty-one. No, thirty-two — he just had a birthday. Got his license a few months after his sixteenth birthday but never renewed it."

"What's his address?"

"It's kind of screwy. I've never seen one like this. There's no street — well, there's no street number. In fact, I think it's a typo."

"They don't make typos on driver's licenses."

"Oh, yeah? Then how come I once had a license with an expiration date that predated the issue date? Caused me all kinds of trouble when I tried to renew. This one, I think they just left the number off, or maybe it's a real little street or in one of those gated communities where you don't need a number —"

*"What does it say, Dorie?"*

"Yelling like that is going to cost you," Dorie said. "It says Hackberry Street, Harkness."

"Harkness? Where's that?"

"I don't do geography," Dorie said.

Carl was already looking for the Maryland map in Tess's crowded glove compartment, unfolding it with what seemed to be almost elaborate care, turning it around and around, searching the index, finding the grid on the map, turning it again. It seemed an eternity before he looked up.

"Harkness is in the Crisfield zip code," he said quietly, "but it's on Notting Island. There are two towns there, Harkness and Tyndall Point. We visited Tyndall when we went

441

looking for Becca Harrison. Harkness is on the north side of the island."

Tess glanced at Carl, then turned her attention back to the road just in time to brake for a tractor-trailer that was merging into the right lane, heedless of her little Toyota. Carl's stubby index finger was stabbing at the map, punching it again and again. As if this map were to blame, as if the place were to blame.

Perhaps it was. Perhaps if the bay had succeeded in breaking up Notting Island years ago, this native son, this monster, would never have made his way into the world.

# Chapter 33

On their second approach to Notting Island, Tess imagined the residents watching them, waiting for them, laughing at them. It was a gray day, rain threatening, the bay choppy and rough. May had never been as moody as it was this year. Their old friend, the semi-ancient mariner, had been reluctant to rent them his boat, even at double the price. He quizzed them about tides, asked if Carl knew where the shallows were. But in the end he allowed them to go.

"Don't know why anyone wants to go to Notting Island on a day like this," he said, pocketing Carl's driver's license and credit card as insurance against their return. "Don't know why anyone wants to go to Notting Island at all."

The trip out seemed to take forever, now that they knew what they hoped to find. It couldn't be more than fifteen miles, Tess calculated. But fifteen miles in a boat that vibrated if it went above 30 mph was a thirty-minute journey. Despite the overcast skies, the day was muggy and warm. She shrugged off her denim jacket, but she was still warm in her T-shirt and jeans.

"You going to go around like that?"

"Like what?"

"With your gun showing?"

She glanced down at her holster. She was getting used to its feel. After all, she wore it all day, up until dinner, when she placed the weapon on the table in front of her as she ate. At night, it sat on the bedside and waited, its barrel staring into the darkness like some one-eyed creature, for Crow to come home. The gun then watched, as they made love. And they made love every night these days, at Tess's insistence.

Crow eventually fell asleep, but Tess didn't, not really. She was untroubled by her insomnia, had no desire to fight it or cure it. She believed her body knew she could not afford much more than catnaps, like the one she had allowed herself this morning, on the long drive to Crisfield.

She would sleep again later, when she was safe.

"Why don't you have a gun?" she asked Carl.

"I'm not a cop anymore, as you like to remind me all the time. I had a service revolver. I turned that in." He looked wistful. "It was sweet, a nine-millimeter. I'm surprised you use a thirty-eight."

"It's what I'm used to. Look, I think you should get a gun. There may even be a provision to get the waiting period waived, or we could drive down to Virginia, pick one up there. They're a lot looser about these things in Virginia."

"I don't need a gun."

She sensed something beneath his words. Not machismo or mere contrariness. He had thought about this.

"Why not?"

"For one thing, he doesn't kill men."

"What about Michael Shaw?"

"I don't think he wanted to kill him. And he did it with a car, not a gun. Killing men — it's like *The Leech Woman*, you know?"

"Is this another movie reference?"

"Well, yeah." Carl's voice was stiff, as if she had hurt his feelings, but he kept going. "A woman, a vain woman, learns about this potion that keeps her young. The only drawback is it requires blood, a man's blood. Like a junkie, she needs more and more. The effects don't last as long. Finally, she kills a woman — only it turns out that makes her go the other way."

"She becomes a lesbian?"

Carl blushed, as she knew he would. She loved baiting him. "No, she starts aging, really fast, and she's so horrified she throws herself out the window."

"So William Windsor didn't kill Michael Shaw because that would — well, what would it do, Carl? I'm not following you at all."

"I'm just saying it didn't give him pleasure. He only did it because he thought he had to, for some reason. Hazel too, I bet. He shoots his girlfriends."

"He shot Julie Carter."

"She was an ex-girlfriend. Besides, that's how a junkie is going to die. He tailored the deaths to fit scenarios that seemed possible — a jogging doctor gets killed in a hit-and-run, a spinster dies in a fire, a junkie gets shot in a drug burn."

They bounced along the water, absorbed in their own thoughts. Tess finally broke the silence.

"Do you think he gets confused?"

"What?"

"About his names. He's had at least three in the past thirteen years, probably four, maybe more. He has to memorize different birthdays, birthplaces, remember where his Social Security number was issued."

Carl thought so hard his face puckered.

"My best guess? He's probably a very quiet guy who listens more than he talks. He doesn't trip up because he doesn't speak about himself. Doesn't tell stories on himself, turns the conversation back to others. I think he says things like *Tell me what you were like as a little girl,* that kind of stuff."

It was just what Tess had decided, en route to Saint Mary's.

"So he woos these women, loves them, takes care of them. Then one day, without warning, he kills them. Why?"

"I don't know," Carl said. "Maybe the answer is up ahead."

Notting Island had come into view.

"Saying the name William Windsor around here," Carl said an hour later, "is like farting in front of a duchess."

Tess knew what he meant, although she might have expressed it differently. The locals' faces had frozen at the mention of the name, and while a few said yes, *Billy* Windsor had lived in Harkness once, they offered little more. The family was gone, he had no kin here, no one knew what had become of him. One older man, who appeared to be hard of hearing, pointed out the Windsor house, but it was clearly vacant and had been for some time. Someone was keeping the lawn trimmed at the white clapboard house, but the snowball bushes at the front had not been cut back for years. Bursting with heavy blue flowers, they almost blocked the front windows.

When Tess tried to follow up with questions about Becca Harrison, the older residents of Harkness said pointedly, "She lived down to Tyndall. We didn't know her *at all*."

If Tess had been alone, she might have given up. But Carl wouldn't let her. They had come too far, literally and figuratively.

"Remember the old lady down at the general store in Tyndall Point?" he asked, as Tess slumped on a splintery old bench on the dock.

"Sure."

"At least she admitted to knowing Becca

Harrison. Maybe she'll tell us something about Billy Windsor, too."

"It's worth a try."

The distance between the two towns was no more than three miles, and they thought about starting off on foot or trying to convince one of the local teens to drive them. But there was no road that went all the way through, begging the question of why people here bothered to have cars at all. The only way to get from Harkness to Tyndall was by boat. No wonder those who lived in Harkness felt so separate from the residents of Tyndall.

The old crone was alone today, listening to a shortwave radio that crackled with watermen calling back and forth to each other as they worked. She seemed bored at first, indifferent to her visitors. But something flickered in her eyes at the mention of Billy Windsor, something bright and hard.

All she said was, "Ah, half the people in Harkness were named Windsor once upon a time. But they weren't a hardy lot. Billy's long gone, his father longer gone, and his mother lives with you."

The syntax confused Tess. For a second she thought it was meant literally, that she was harboring Billy Windsor's mother without knowing it. Then she realized the woman meant only that the mother lived on the mainland.

"But there must be people here who remember Billy. No one in Harkness seemed to know anything."

"Of course they remember him. But why should they speak of him to you? They don't know who you are or what you're after."

Tess realized that gossip was the most powerful currency at this store, that the woman would give as good as she got. Yet how could they risk telling her the truth?

"Nothing bad," she said. "Quite the opposite. He may have come into a bit of money. At any rate, we've been asked to find him."

"By who, Becca Harrison? I'd like to see her face when you tell her he drowned himself over her all those years ago. But she was cold then, and I suppose she's cold now."

Tess hesitated, but Carl picked up the lie, sure and confident. "She didn't tell us why she wanted to find him. Just to find him."

"Well, it's an old story, probably not worth telling." The woman was being coy. At first Tess thought she was teasing for money, a bribe. But she was just trying to stretch out the encounter, enjoying this variation in her usual daily routine.

"Please," Carl said. "We'd really like to know. Becca hasn't told us why she wants to find Billy Windsor, only that it's important to her."

"It's a short story. Becca Harrison and her father moved here when she was thirteen, maybe fourteen. Billy Windsor fell for her so hard he was never the same again. Swagger die,

449

it was like he had a killick around his neck. And that's probably how he ended up."

Tess had no idea what a killick was, although she could infer from context that it was inappropriate neckware at best. But Carl seemed to understand, so she let it go. Now that the woman was talking, she didn't want to get in her way.

"At least, we always s'posed that's how he done it," the old woman said. "I think he was being considerate of his mother, in his own way. More considerate than she was of him, I'd have to say. He could have used a shotgun, but no, you wouldn't want your mother to see you like that. Pills would have been hard to get around here. Even over to Crisfield, word would have gotten back. So he must've weighted his body down. He knew no matter how much he wanted to drown, his lungs would have fought it. The body tries to live, even when the head wants to die."

"So you think he tied a killick around his neck," Carl prompted. "But you don't know, because his body was never found."

"They searched near Shank Island, where they found his skiff drifting, but there's no guarantee that's where he went over. My guess is Billy picked a deeper spot. He knew the bay, all the boys here do. He'd pick a good place to go in. His mother never admitted he was dead, though, and no one dared speak of it in front of her. She stayed here for a few more years.

Then, come five years ago, she upped and moved. Still owns the house but keeps it empty." The crone narrowed her eyes. "So for all her grief, I guess she had an insurance policy on the boy, and it finally paid off when she had him certified as dead."

She had skipped over something. A piece of the story was missing.

"What does this have to do with Becca Harrison?" Tess asked.

"Didn't she tell you? Maybe she doesn't know. After all, she was gone." The woman lighted a cigarette, a generic one. "Well, apparently she wanted to get away from here real bad. Went to Audrey Windsor for help. I think Drey — we called her Drey, although I can't remember how that started."

"Ma'am?" Carl prodded. She gazed at him over the haze of her cigarette smoke. Tess realized the old woman saw herself as Notting Island's Lauren Bacall, even if no one else did.

"Drey Windsor helped Becca Harrison run away. She let people think it was because she felt sorry for the girl, but I think it was because she didn't much care for her son being so over the moon in love. She thought she'd kill two birds with one stone: help the girl get away from her father and get her far away from Billy. So it's her conscience she has to live with."

"What do you mean?"

"She was the one took Becca Harrison to Smith Island, to catch the ferry that goes to

451

Point Lookout, over t'other side. But when Billy Windsor realized his girlfriend was gone, he was never seen again. I guess his mother didn't count on that."

Point Lookout. Tess glanced at Carl, he had caught it too. Mary Ann Melcher's boyfriend had disappeared from that spot in just the same way Billy Windsor had. A boat was found but not a body, not a body that could be proved to be Charlie Chisholm, because Charlie Chisholm didn't exist. And Billy Windsor, if that was the man they sought, was not shy about repeating successful tricks. He had used his parked van to create alibis in the two homicides, driving all night in rental cars to return home and kill the women he said he loved.

"Where does Mrs. Windsor live now?"

"I couldn't tell you for sure. I don't have her address, but she left me her number. She likes to keep up with the local gossip. She likes to know" — the woman narrowed her eyes until they almost disappeared into the tortoiselike wrinkles of her face — "she likes to know if strangers come around looking for her."

Again, Tess felt there was a way to get her to tell them more, but she could not figure out what this woman wanted from them. She had to rely on Carl, whose instincts were sharper here, surer.

He leaned across the counter. "Can we take you into our confidence?"

Her lashes were practically nonexistent, but

452

she fluttered them at Carl. "Of course."

"You'd do us a tremendous favor if you didn't speak to anyone of this, but we probably should talk to Mrs. Windsor. If we had the number, we could make an appointment to talk to her face-to-face, tell her what we know about Becca Harrison."

"So where is Becca?" The woman leaned forward, a little breathless. "I never thought she was much. She told people she was going to be famous one day, but I read the magazines when they come in, and I've never seen her, not once. I bet she married a rich foreigner, and that's why her father never found her. She's over in Europe, going parlez-vous. Some place where they think it's a big deal to sing in that loud way."

"Actually," Carl said, "Becca Harrison's life is not what you'd call charmed. She's had some hard knocks."

"Can't say I'm sorry to hear that. She broke Billy Windsor's heart — and her father's, too, though no one cared about him. She was a senior in high school, just turned eighteen, when she ran away, so there wasn't a thing he could do about it. Billy was younger, a year behind her in school. I always thought that bothered Drey, too."

Tess was confused. "That Billy was behind her in school?"

"That she was an *older woman*." She made little hash marks in the air to underscore the irony. "Let me tell you, Becca was eighteen going on forty. She was a hard girl, out for herself. I can't blame Drey Windsor, in the end. She paid a high price. A high, high price."

With that, the woman handed them the phone number. Carl's hand shook a little as he reached for it, but he was otherwise nonchalant. It was a 410 area code, which could be either side of the bay. Tess hated to head all the way back to her office and the crisscross directory, only to discover it was a Crisfield number.

"Where did you say she lived?"

"I didn't. But I know it's on the Western Shore."

Tess and Carl turned to go, trying not to hurry, or seem agitated in any way. But this gave Tess time to think of one more question.

"Becca Harrison — what did she look like?"

"Well, you've seen her, ain't you? You work for her, you said." The old woman was cagey. Not much got by her.

"Yes, but — people change so over the years, and it's rude to ask Becca what she looked like before she was fat." The lie was calculated to please the old woman, and it did. She preened a little, aware her leathery body had no extra weight on it. "What did Becca look like as a teenager?"

"Small, to have such a big voice. Dark hair and light eyes. And because she was so little, she had a way of looking up through all that hair and her eyelashes. I was surprised when she cut it off, real short, because she was always flipping it and poking at it. She was a flirt, although I don't think Billy knew the half of it. Oh, he was crazy in love. But then, you'd have to be, to do what he done."

"Becca's dead," Carl said, once the island was well in the distance. They had not spoken since leaving the store. It was as if the residents of Notting Island could eavesdrop, as if the breeze would carry their words back. "If anyone's at the bottom of the bay, a killick around her neck, it's her."

"I know. I knew even before she told us what Becca looked like. The question is whether Billy Windsor's mother knows."

"She could be the one who called me. Remember? He had some woman call me and Sergeant Craig, to tell us that Alan had been admitted to that out-of-state hospital."

"Her or Hazel. Why kill Hazel, if she doesn't know what's going on? He cut off his own supply of fake names. What's a killick, anyway?"

"Small anchor, used for oystering."

"How did you know that? You never went oystering."

"I lived on the shore, Tess. Upper Shore, but part of the shore. We understand one another. After all, we've got a common enemy."

"You mean Baltimore and the rest of the state?"

"Yep. It's us against you, and we don't ever forget it. Among ourselves, we may note the tiniest distinctions. But when it comes to the big picture, we're in this together. Remember when the governor called the Eastern Shore a shithouse?"

"The *ex*-governor, Carl. And he's always been a few milligrams light of a Prozac prescription. Everyone knows that."

"No, he was on to something. You don't like us, and we don't like you. He's the only one who dared to say out loud what everyone thinks. We think you're nasty, decadent people who live in filth and don't understand what it's like to be dependent on the water and the land for your living. You think we're ignorant hicks who aren't good for anything but putting food on your table."

"So Billy Windsor isn't a serial killer, he's just a resident of the Eastern Shore who murdered these people as part of some complicated eco-political agenda?"

"I wouldn't go that far. But I am saying I have a few insights. And I think his mother doesn't have a clue what he's been up to, okay? He's kept her pure. She's his mama."

"Fine," Tess said. "I'll put my jacket back on when we visit her tomorrow. But I'm not going without my gun."

# Chapter 34

Drey Windsor lived in a retirement community called Golden Shores. A mix of high-rises and town houses south of Annapolis, it was built far enough inland so the term "shore" was strictly euphemistic. But the developers had been serious about the gold, sprinkling cheap gilt on everything they could find.

"Maybe you can see the Severn River from the top floor of that big building," Carl said as they navigated the look-alike cul-de-sacs early the next morning, trying to find Mrs. Windsor. She lived on Golden Meadow, but all they had found so far was Golden End, Golden Bay, Golden Way, and Golden Knoll. They had lied to get past the front gate, unwilling to announce their arrival. Tess was now worried that the Golden Shores security force would be on them if they kept driving around in such aimless fashion.

"There, on the left," Carl said, and she made a screeching turn that drew disapproving looks from those who were out walking on this fine day, strolling along the Golden Loop.

Drey Windsor lived in a duplex bungalow at the far end of the cul-de-sac. A black Buick was parked in the driveway of the attached garage, and the yard was neat but impersonal. While other residences here had decorated their look-alike doors with wreaths and banners, her dark-red door held nothing but a brass knocker.

Tess picked it up, feeling slightly queasy. She felt for her gun, then let the knocker drop. She and Carl listened for the telltale signs that someone was inside — a few reflexive steps, a television or radio. There was nothing. Tess lifted the knocker again, but before she could drop it she heard a small, frightened voice from inside.

"Who's there?"

It was a simple enough question, but they had no answer. Who were they, after all? How would they identify themselves to this woman? Before Tess could figure out what to say, Carl had stepped forward and shouted into the door, as if it were hard of hearing.

"Police, ma'am. From Baltimore."

Tess looked at him, wide-eyed. Of all the lies she had told, she had never *ever* pretended to be a cop. Utility worker or secretary — absolutely. Someone's long-lost relative, disinterested passerby — why not? There was no law against those impersonations. But pretending to be a cop could get you arrested.

"I *was* a cop," Carl whispered to her. "And we were working with the state police. It's not such a big lie if you think about it."

She shrugged. Big lie or not, it was out there. She couldn't take it back.

It seemed to take Drey Windsor forever to come to the door and open it. Yet when she did, she was much younger than Tess had expected, barely in her fifties. She must have given birth to Billy when she was all of twenty.

Still, it was a hard fifty-something. The sun had left her face scored with deep lines, and Tess guessed she had been a smoker as well. She had those telltale lines around the lips, the ones that come from drawing hard on a butt end. Her hair was the flat noncolor that comes from a bottle, a minky brown. But it was arranged neatly and she was dressed in a pair of flowery cotton pants and a bright T-shirt. She was one of those older women who kept their hourglass figures.

"Police?" she asked. "Has something happened?"

Tess looked at Carl: *It's your lie, go with it.*

"No, ma'am, quite the opposite. We think we might have some good news. Could we sit down?"

The bungalow was built in what Tess thought of as the new ass-backward style, with a small formal living room at the front, a large kitchen–family room across the back. She understood why this floor plan was desirable to families with children, but she didn't see why a retirement village had decided to ape it. Older people should be encouraged to move away from television sets, to have meals at tables, to entertain in formal rooms. With children grown and gone, this should be the time of life to eat from fine china, not from a television tray set up in front of a Barcalounger. If not now, when?

Mrs. Windsor took a seat in just such a Barcalounger, perching on the edge, folding her hands in her lap. Tess and Carl dragged two wooden chairs from the low counter that separated this room from the kitchen.

"You believe you have good news?" she asked, her voice cautious, almost skeptical. It seemed to Tess that she found it all too credible for police officers to be on her doorstep but was less convinced that they might bring glad tidings.

"Possibly," Carl said. "I don't want to overstate it or get your hopes up. There's still a lot of work ahead of us. But, Mrs. Windsor — do you think it's possible your son is still alive?"

Mrs. Windsor swallowed hard and blinked her eyes rapidly, as if trying to fan back tears. "Billy? My Billy's been dead for almost fifteen years."

"Well, technically he's been missing, right? They never found him."

"Under the law, I could have him declared dead. But there's never been any reason to do that."

"Really?" This was Tess, remembering the old crone's statement that Audrey Windsor had probably done just that, to collect the insurance that enabled her to live among the rich at Golden Shores.

Or maybe she had merely allowed people to assume this was where her newfound wealth came from.

"If he had been my husband — but he's not. Or if there had been life insurance — but there wasn't. What seventeen-year-old boy needs life insurance? There didn't seem to be any point to it. Besides, I didn't want —"

She broke down, quite convincingly. But it occurred to Tess that Audrey Windsor could have finished that sentence in any of a number of ways.

"You didn't want to make his death official?"

She nodded through her tears, face downcast so her expression was unreadable.

"I suppose a mother can't help feeling that way. You'd want to hold on to the hope that he was alive, as long as his body was never found."

Mrs. Windsor nodded again. Tess thought she saw a cunning glint at the top of her eyes, as if she were studying them, trying to figure out if they were buying her act.

"Well, that's the possible good news," Carl boomed. "You see, there's a man of Billy's age and description, up in Washington County Rehabilitation Hospital."

He paused. Tess realized he was gauging Audrey Windsor's reaction to that piece of information. After all, it was a temporary home to at least two of Billy's various personas over the past few years. But all she showed was genuine concern and even more genuine confusion.

"He's been in a car accident and there was a lot of head trauma. He has short-term memory loss and what he does remember about his past is kind of scattered. But he says his name is Billy Windsor. Now, that's not an unusual name. Could be any number of people —"

"A bad car accident?" There was no doubting the fear in Audrey Windsor's voice. "When?"

"Oh, six–eight weeks ago."

Her body relaxed. So she had seen her son since then. She knew he was okay more recently than that. "And you think it's my Billy?"

"It's a possibility."

"What does he look like?"

"Blond. Hazel eyes. About five-ten, with a small frame." Carl, who had the advantage of having seen Billy Windsor once, was flipping the information, describing the man's polar opposite.

"Oh." Audrey Windsor's voice was almost a purr. "Well, that's not my Billy, I'm afraid. He was brown-haired and hazel-eyed, and he grew to be much taller than that. I mean — even at seventeen, he was already six feet."

"I'm so sorry, ma'am. As I said, it was possible good news. Now I feel as if I got your hopes up for nothing."

"No," Drey Windsor assured him. "I know my Billy's gone. I know. He made sure of that."

"A suicide," Tess said, hitting the word hard, and the woman recoiled a little bit, as if no

462

one had ever dared to speak that word in her presence.

"Yes."

"That's why he never came up, right? He weighted himself down with something."

"Most likely."

"What a jerk."

The contradiction was swift, automatic. "You shouldn't say that."

"Why not? I think suicides are selfish. When Billy decided to drown himself, he was thinking only of himself. What about you? Didn't your feelings count for anything? If someone I loved did that, I'd hate them forever. On some level, he was trying to hurt you, to punish you. What was that about?"

"You have no right to talk about Billy that way. He was a good boy. He tried to do right in every way. That girl broke his heart. He couldn't help himself."

Tess shrugged. "If you say so. But all I know is, it's fifteen years later and you're sitting here, unable to have your son declared officially dead. I think that's because you don't want to admit he is dead. And maybe that's because he isn't. Is that possible? He faked his death, just to get away from you?"

Drey Windsor's mouth opened and closed, like a beached fish trying to breathe. Finally, she said, "Are we done? Is that all you wanted to ask me?"

Carl looked at Tess, unsure of what was

going on. But Tess just nodded. "We're done. But Mrs. Windsor — we do have some bad news for you."

She stood up and leaned over the woman, as if to whisper in her ear. But her voice was clear and cold. "Billy is dead to you now. He can't come back here ever again. Do you understand that? He can't visit you or even risk calling you here because we're going to have you under surveillance. If Billy tries to see you, we're going to have him arrested. We know what he's done. Tell him that, if he calls. We know what he's done and we're coming for him."

"Something come up, didn't it?" Mrs. Windsor was crying now. "I always said something would come up, that it was only a matter of time they'd find a piece of bone or something. But he didn't mean to do it, you have to understand. It was an accident. And it was so long ago. A boy shouldn't be held accountable for such things."

"What about a man, Mrs. Windsor? What about a man who keeps doing this, over and over again?"

She shook her head. "I don't know what you're talking about. Billy made a fresh start, that's all I ever wanted for him. What he does for a living — well, what else is he to do? At least he's responsible. Really, he's protecting the rest of us, don't you see? It has to go somewhere."

Tess looked back at Carl, but he was as baffled as she was by Drey Windsor's sobbing confession.

"What are you talking about?"

"You're DNR, aren't you? Not real police, but the damn DNR. Well, I've never talked to you folks before and I'm not going to start now. You get out of here unless you have a warrant or a reason to take me in. And I don't think you do."

"Why do you think we're from the Department of Natural Resources, Mrs. Windsor?"

Something shifted. Tess had betrayed some ignorance and Drey Windsor had regained control of herself. She knew something they didn't, and that gave her power. Her tears slowed. She drew herself up, proud and closed off.

"We may very well come back with a warrant," Tess said, knowing they could never come back, that they had pushed this lie too far already. "For you and your son, because you clearly knew all this time what happened to Becca Harrison and that makes you an accessory. But remember what I told you, Mrs. Windsor. Billy is dead to you now. Your only hope of seeing him again is turning him in to the police. At least that way you'll be able to visit him in prison."

"Billy won't go to prison," his mother said. "He could never live so confined. He'll kill himself before he lets you take him."

"He'll probably pretend to kill himself. But I don't think he's brave enough to die, more's the pity."

# Chapter 35

"You went too far back there."

Carl had beaten Tess to her own accusation.

"*I* went too far? Pretending to be a cop is stupid. It's something you can get arrested for."

"I *was* a cop."

"*Was* being the operative word. I noticed you didn't say you were a Toll Facilities cop."

"A cop is a cop."

"If you are a cop. But you're not, not anymore. We agreed to pretend to be social workers from the hospital. Which would have allowed us to be warm and friendly, gain her confidence. The moment you said *police* she was on alert, looking for traps. She may not know everything her son has done, but she knows something."

"She knows a lot more than she did, thanks to you. Billy Windsor's going to run now, because of you. He's out of here, we'll never find him. When you're in an investigation, you play your cards close to your vest."

"From what movie did you pluck that cliché?"

Carl ignored the taunt. "All we had to do was wait, and he would have come back."

"Do you seriously believe the two of us were going to pull off surveillance in a gated retirement village with a private security force? They would have thrown us out in the first fifteen minutes. True, Billy Windsor won't be able to go near his mother, may not even dare to call her at home. That will make him more desperate to accelerate his plan, whatever it is. And speeding up might make Billy sloppy."

Carl was driving for the first time since Mickey Pechter took batting practice on his knee four days earlier. He suddenly wrenched the steering wheel to the right and pulled into the parking lot of an abandoned restaurant.

"Let me ask you something. When did we decide you were the boss? I thought we were partners on this, but you're always calling the shots, the one who's always right. Is it because I didn't tell you about what happened to me, or because I didn't tell the cops about Mary Ann Melcher? Well, I'll remind you that I was right — he isn't dead. I'll also remind you that I saved your life."

"Saved my life?"

"When that creep broke into your house."

"You saved me from the hellish inconvenience of killing him, but he wasn't going to hurt me."

"Still, I was there for you. I had your back. And yet you talk to me in that — that mommy voice, as if I'm your little boy and I have to do what you say. Well, I'm not your little boy-

467

friend, okay? I'm not pussy-whipped like that dust-mopping, dog-walking sissy you keep around to service you. I'm a real man. A real man!"

Tess felt the conversation getting out of control, saw it heading toward a place where horrible things would be said, things that could not be forgiven or forgotten. She wanted to fling herself out of the car and run away. She wanted to hit Carl in the stomach or hurl insults at him that would cut even deeper than his rude comments about Crow. She wanted to plug her ears and chant so she could no longer hear his voice.

*Count*, Dr. Armistead had told her once. *It really works.* She counted to ten. Then twenty. Then thirty. Halfway to forty, it was as if the needle on a blood-pressure gauge had started to fall, and she said, "I'm sorry."

Carl, with the look of a man who has been dangling on a cliff's edge, beat his own hasty retreat. "I'm sorry too. It's just that I want you — I want everyone — to listen to *me*, to realize I have something to say, something to contribute."

"I know. I want the same thing. I want people to —" What did she want, anyway? What button had Carl just pushed? Mickey Pechter and Major Shields had found it too, almost without trying, provoking the same odd mix of rage and shame. Now Billy Windsor was playing her, taunting her. He wanted to be found. He wanted to escape.

"I'm tired of people underestimating me," she told Carl, who nodded. "And condescending to me. When I get stuff wrong, I'm stupid. When I get it right, I'm just lucky. If we find this guy, people are going to say it was all luck, that we wouldn't have stumbled on his name if it weren't for your gimpy leg and your knowledge of the disability system. If we screw up, we'll be the fall guys."

Carl looked out his window, so she couldn't see his face. "Do you want to go to the state police, tell them what we've found?"

"No. Because they'll take it away from us."

"Take it away from *me*, you mean. I'm the one with no standing here."

"We're a team on this. If they don't want to work with you, I don't want to work with them."

He turned back, his smile so broad that his eyes almost disappeared in his freckled face.

"They say it's smarter to be lucky than it's lucky to be smart," Carl said. "Frankly, I've never been accused of being either."

"It's one of my favorite sayings. But, truthfully, here's the real luck, the only luck. You get born to two nice people who can provide a comfortable life for you, who don't abuse you —" She broke off, embarrassed.

"That's okay. Keep talking."

"Who are kind to you and to each other. Your DNA doesn't carry any time bombs. You do all the dumb shit that teenagers do, and you come out unscathed. Then you're a grown-up and you make your own luck. You know what word I really hate?"

"What?"

"Overachiever."

Carl looked puzzled. "I thought that was a good thing."

"It's the most subtle insult in the English language, because it implies predestined boundaries and limits. You're supposed to stay in this little box, only you're too stupid to realize it. When people tell you you're an overachiever, they're really saying they could do so much better than you if they ever lowered themselves to giving a shit."

She felt her anger rising again, at some nameless faceless enemy, and she wondered what Dr. Armistead would think about this diatribe. Dr. Armistead — she glanced at the dashboard clock. "Shit. I have thirty minutes to make it to therapy, or I lose a hundred and fifty bucks."

"Physical therapy?"

Funny how Carl, who knew both kinds, who knew she was in anger management, still assumed a doctor's visit had to be for a physical ailment.

"No, you know, it's the guy the judge ordered me to see at Sheppard Pratt. Because of what I did to that guy who broke into my house."

"You told me you had been accused of assaulting him, but I never got the particulars."

She gave him those, even as they raced across the narrow two-lane roads that would take them to the highway and back to Baltimore. It was gratifying to see Carl laugh at certain points in the story, to be reminded that it really was a prank — except for the part where Mickey Pechter had ended up in the emergency room with that severe allergic reaction. She began to laugh too, thinking about how he looked in the parking lot, like one of those hairless cats. Really, the whole story did have a certain comic element.

But it was probably better not to share that insight with Dr. Armistead, who thought she was making so much progress.

There were twenty minutes left on the faces of the multiple clocks staring at her when Tess ran out of things to say to Dr. Armistead. Until she had sat down in the frayed wing chair, she had not realized how much she wanted to withhold from him, at least for now. She could not speak of Carl's reentry into her life, for that would take her to the subject of Mickey Pechter, which should be avoided at all costs. But if she told him she believed Billy Windsor had laid this elaborate trap for her — using a powerful foundation, passing a list of his victims to her, even killing a woman — Dr. Armistead would probably ring for an orderly and lock her up in one of the dormitories.

"What are you thinking?" he prompted, after

she had stared into her lap for several seconds.

"I thought my face was supposed to be so readable," she said, trying for a light tone.

"Not always."

Now other professionals who charged by the hour — a lawyer, for example, or a plumber, even a private detective like herself — would be satisfied to end the hour early. But Dr. Armistead clearly didn't bill by the part-hour. He just continued staring at her, his bushy brows drawn down as low as they could go. Tess met his gaze with what she hoped was a blank face and guileless eyes.

"What are you thinking, Tess?" he asked again.

"Nothing, really."

"Which is, as you know, impossible."

"Well, I'm thinking about how I have nothing to say." Which was absolutely true.

Funny, she wouldn't have minded speaking about the quarrel with Carl, which had surprised her in its heat and fury. Carl struck her as someone whose strengths and weaknesses were inextricable. He was dogged, but dogged quickly became obsessive. He was blunt, yet hypersensitive when it came to his own feelings, collecting slights the way some little boys collect rocks and rubber bands. Where had all that stuff about Crow come from? If a woman had made such a speech, she would be called catty. An unfair characterization — to women and cats.

But even if she could speak of Carl, how could she really explain him to Dr. Armistead? He would need to know Carl's history: the town of North East, his violent father, the mother he had saved. He would have to be able to see Carl, with his squinty eyes and bow-legged walk. How did therapists work without all the day-to-day context of real life?

"Are you sure you have nothing to say? Or is there something you very much want to talk about but don't know how to begin?"

Tess almost started at the sound of Dr. Armistead's voice. She knew he couldn't read her mind, but he did seem to divine how much was popping and jumping inside her head. There was so much to do. Not that she had a clue as to what it was. All she and Carl had achieved today was their successful tyranny of a sad, isolated woman. It was June 6. How much time did they have? Where should they go? Carl was waiting for her outside, coiled in one of the Adirondack chairs that dotted the broad parklike lawns of Sheppard Pratt. She needed to have some plan of action when the hour ended.

"I guess I'm distracted. I've actually been working very hard."

"Really? I thought you had finished your work on that case. We spoke of it last time. You told me that the man you were looking for turned out to be dead, and your partner had proved to be unreliable."

473

"Right. Right, right, right. This is something new."

"What are you working on now?"

"Oh, nothing interesting. This is a desk-bound project, lots of computer time. Securities fraud."

"I didn't know you did that kind of work."

*Neither did I.* "The boring cases pay the bills, actually." She yawned, largely for show, but it was a mistake. Even a yawn was fraught with meaning in Dr. Armistead's lair.

"Are you not sleeping well?"

"I'm a little restless. It's gotten so hot, but I hate to turn on the AC before summer truly starts. It feels like such a defeat."

"Insomnia."

"I'd call it . . . wakefulness. I fall asleep." Once Crow came home. "I just don't stay asleep."

"Are you having the nightmare you spoke of in a previous session? The one in which you see your friend die?"

How did he remember so much? It's not as if he had notes in front of him. Was he taping her secretly? Did he write things down after she left and then read them later? But there were always appointments on either side of their hour together, so he didn't have time to make notes while his memory was fresh. Although the day and hour of their appointments changed weekly, she always saw the same sad, older woman in the hall, the one with the yellowish skin and bluish hair.

"No, not that nightmare."

"Another, then? A new one?"

"I meant, no nightmares at all."

But, despite her best efforts, tears welled in her eyes. His question had taken her back to the alley, to the morning that Jonathan had died. They had made love the night before. Well, they had sex. He was excited, certain of the glorious future that awaited him when he broke his big story. She had been a little depressed, as if Jonathan's upward progress ensured her downward path.

The lights of the cab had come out of nowhere. They should have heard the engine when they left her apartment, should have noticed the sound of the chugging motor. But they didn't have time to notice anything. Jonathan did take a moment, however, to push her to the side of the alley, so she was not in the taxi's path. The driver probably didn't care if he killed her too, but she was not important enough to come back for.

The inevitable question: "What are these tears about?"

"Nothing. It's a bad memory, okay? I *should* cry when I think about it. A man died."

"Surviving," Dr. Armistead intoned with a self-impressed solemnity, "exacts a price. In dreams begin responsibilities."

"We always come back to poetry," Tess muttered. And not particularly apt poetry, she yearned to add.

"Poetry? It's the title of a prose work by Delmore Schwartz."

"Schwartz took it from some French poem. Villon, I think."

Another awkward silence. Tess studied the degrees on the wall. It seemed a little show-off, to her, all those degrees, a half dozen in all. There was George Washington, Wisconsin, two from Johns Hopkins. Of course. Johns Hopkins, the ultimate Baltimore pedigree. If you could claim any link to Hopkins — if you just had your appendix out there — the detail would probably appear in your obituary.

*Obituaries. Johns Hopkins.* Maybe she could get something out of this hour after all.

"Did you know a psychiatrist named Michael Shaw?"

For once, Dr. Armistead was caught off guard. "By reputation. I'm sure we met at some point, but I have no distinct memory of him. Why do you ask?"

"He's connected to a case I'm working on."

"The one on security fraud?"

"Sure. Yes. He may be one of the investors who was swindled in this derivative scam." Derivative scam? She wasn't even sure what a derivative was. "My client is another victim, but he would like to file a class-action suit, so I'm trying to find others, so he can sue the brokerage."

"What brokerage?"

"An out-of-state one." Her eyes were still focused on the diplomas looming over Dr. Armistead's shoulder. "Washington Securities."

"And you think Shaw —"

"May have treated the man who ended up ripping him off. Is there a way to find out?"

"Of course not." Dr. Armistead looked offended. "Confidentiality would not be breached in such a matter."

"But he's dead, and a crime may have been committed —"

"Michael Shaw is dead, not your quarry. And being a suspect in a securities fraud does not mean one suspends the usual doctor-patient confidentiality."

"Oh." She slumped back in her chair, running her fingers through the unraveling fringe on the arms. She had thought she was on to something.

"If it's any comfort, I doubt Shaw treated the man you're investigating."

"How can you be so sure?"

"Before he went into private practice, Shaw worked under a mutual friend at Hopkins. He treated rapists, the hard-core cases — repeat offenders, pedophiles."

"Really?" As Carl had told her, over and over again, serial killings had a sexual component.

"He started with the program as a young resident, back in the 1980s. You may have heard of the study. About a hundred and fifty offenders were given Depo-Provera."

"I thought that was a contraceptive."

"It's derived from the female hormone progestin and is used as a contraceptive, yes. But it also was employed for what is known as chemical castration. The program was somewhat misrepresented in the press, I'm afraid. Depo-Provera was only one component, along with traditional therapy and behavior modification. But the media focused on one patient, the so-called ski-mask rapist, who volunteered for treatment. Unfortunately, he stopped taking the drugs and was arrested a few years ago for raping a three-year-old girl. Very sad."

"But this program was up and running twenty years ago?" She did the math in her head. Billy Windsor had "died" at age seventeen, but that had been fifteen years ago. Could he have disappeared in order to enter the program, or a subsequent version? Had Becca Harrison's murder been a sex crime? No, they were boyfriend and girlfriend, suitably puppylike in their devotion, according to the old woman on Notting Island. Yet Michael Shaw was on Billy Windsor's list. No coincidences, Luisa O'Neal had said. No, that was Freud. Luisa had said nothing was *random*.

What if Billy Windsor had sought treatment from Michael Shaw in order to control his impulses? Could he have been that self-aware, that analytical? It seemed impossible, yet that would explain why the deaths had stopped, why there was the long gap between Hazel Ligetti's murder and Dr. Shaw's hit-and-run.

And it would explain why they had started again. Billy Windsor had given up on modern psychiatry.

"Why are you smiling that rueful little smile, Tess?"

"Am I?" A half-dozen minute hands snapped to twelve, signaling her freedom. "I'm just thinking about what I want for lunch, now that we're done."

"Do you see yourself as a godlike figure?"

The question comes back to him, unbidden. Why is he thinking about that now, when he has so much that he must fix, so many unanticipated problems, so much that has gone wrong?

But he doesn't even have time to track that thought as he normally would. He's vigilant about his own mind, knows it as well as he knew the marshy inlets back home and navigates it with the same delicacy. Only two people have ever known him as well as he knows himself, and one is lost to him forever.

As for the other — he cannot believe they went to his mother, frightening her so that she walked three miles, crossing two highways, until she found a pay phone where she felt safe. "What was she talking about, Billy? Are they DNR? Do they know what you're doing?"

He was at once relieved and horrified. At least they had not revealed all his secrets to his mother; at least she was still safe, still innocent. He told her that the visit meant nothing: The girl was a little crazy, maybe even a pathological liar. He would take care of it. In the meantime, his mother was not to open the door to anyone without asking for a badge or ID, and she was not to talk to anyone without a lawyer present.

She began to cry, telling him she couldn't do this again, couldn't go without seeing him. He reminded her that they had managed in the early years, when she was still on the island, and they would manage now. No one could keep them from seeing each other.

But beneath his soothing voice and calm assurances, he was furious. How dare she go to his mother? How had they found his name, the one thing he had kept for himself? Who had betrayed him? Luisa O'Neal would not dare speak his name, even if she had known it. But they knew whom they sought when they visited Notting the second time. Fuck June Petty, with her big yapping mouth, her love of gossip, and her never-ending rivalry with all the women on the island. She had dined out on this story — the expression had never been more apt — for years, smacking her lips and shaking her head in mock sympathy for a woman she had never liked. He supposed June Petty would say it was ironic, if she knew what irony was: Drey Windsor helped her son's girlfriend escape her terrible father, only to see that son kill himself in despair over her disappearance.

But it had been his mother's idea — he appeals to some invisible jury — a brilliant idea, at that. After all, she had not needed to be a particularly good actress to portray the grief of a mourning mother. He was dead to her all those years — the "good" years, as he thinks of them now, the years of going to school and building his business and finding release with the occasional prostitute. Strange, it was just before his mother joined him on the mainland that the pull began. Not because of her, but because things were finally settled. Anchored at last, he was free to search for the love he craved, to create the love he needed.

But when he persuaded his mother to leave Harkness, it was as if he took her away from the source of her strength and power. On the mainland, she is weak. She is dying. Not physically but emotionally. His father's accelerated death had shown him how a parent can disappear before one's eyes, and he knew he would someday have to face this with his mother. But he had expected that her mind would be unchanged, that she would always be sharp and shrewd, capable in a crisis.

After all, she was the one who knew what they must do when he came home sobbing, overwhelmed by what had happened. It had been her idea to weigh Becca down, let his boat drift on the tide, and then take him across the bay dressed in women's clothes. If anyone had noticed the boat that arrived at

Saint Mary's that night, they would have seen two women on the dock. She had put him ashore with all the cash she could manage to find, hugged him, and headed home to wait for the knock at the door and the announcement that her son's skiff had been found with a note, indicating he had killed himself because Becca Harrison had told him she was running away to be an opera singer. Which was all true, after a fashion. Becca was gone, and he couldn't live without her.

The thing is, she's right, his new girl, his oh-so-clever girl, she's gotten to him. Whatever happens, he cannot risk seeing his mother for the time being. So she has taken something from him, punished him. He who has given her so much. Doesn't she know her debt to him? The others didn't understand, but then the others were not capable of accepting his gifts. He knows that now. He chose poorly, time and time again, and finally despaired of ever getting it right.

He had tried to explain this once, not in so many words, but the doctor had proved to be even dumber than the women he had tried to help.

The doctor. That's why the stupid question is ringing in his ears, after all this time. "Do you see yourself as a godlike figure?"

"Of course not."

The doctor had persisted. "Do you think of yourself as superior to others, better?"

"No," he had said. "Not at all. Are you listening to me? I identify with Pygmalion. He's a mortal."

"It's a Shaw play. I've always been partial to Shaw." The doctor gave a self-conscious, meant-to-be-deprecating smile. "For the most superficial reasons, I admit."

"Yes, I know all about his *Pygmalion*. The basis for *My Fair Lady*, unfortunately."

"Unfortunately?"

"I don't like musicals."

His voice had been too vehement and the doctor pounced. He pounced on everything, without discrimination.

"You like plays but not musicals? Why?"

"Actually, I don't like plays either. They're phony: all that emoting, all those big gestures and voices. I like film. Once sound was developed, the idea of people standing on a stage, reciting lines, became ridiculous."

"Sound was developed quite some time ago."

"Theater has been ridiculous for quite some time."

An uneasy silence fell. He knew he had punctured the doctor's professional shell. The doctor probably liked theater. And opera too, of course, which he loathed to this day. Poor dumb bastard. How could this man ever help him, stupid as he was? He had done his research so carefully, looking for someone with the experience he needed.

He wasn't used to making mistakes.

"The theater has its moments, I suppose," he said, trying to make amends. "I prefer film, however."

"What kind of films? Are there certain genres or directors to your liking?"

"Bertolucci," he said, and instantly regretted it, for the doctor seemed to sit at attention. Oh, everyone knew *Last Tango*, with its silly, obsessive sex. Nothing could have interested him less. He was thinking about *1900* and *The Last Emperor*. The latter was his all-time favorite, because it was about a boy born to greatness — and the world he lost. "I like all the Italians, for some reason. Fellini. Sergio Leone."

"You have sophisticated tastes."

"Sergio Leone? He made spaghetti Westerns."

"Ah, Westerns. You like those? Classic tales of good and evil, a huge underpopulated landscape. And very few women."

"Most people like Westerns." He looked pointedly at the doctor. "I'd be skeptical of the man who didn't."

An awkward silence fell. He did this now and then, reminded the doctor that he knew all about him and what he liked. Who was the doctor to say who was a man and who wasn't?

"Shaw," the psychiatrist said, "was a vegetarian. And a friend of Harpo Marx."

He shrugged. The doctor often produced such self-referential non sequiturs when at a loss.

"I'm sorry, we've wandered away, haven't we. We were talking about . . ."

"Pygmalion. The myth, not the Shaw play."

"Yes, I don't know that so well. A man makes a woman —"

"A man sculpts a statue of the perfect woman."

"And asks some goddess —"

He could not bear to hear the story told in such inept, unknowing words. "He makes the perfect woman, only she's a statue. He prays to Aphrodite, who makes the statue real."

"Aphrodite?"

"The only god on Olympus without parents. She rose from the sea, perfectly formed. You may know her better as Venus. But I've always been partial to the Greek names. They're much prettier. Zeus, Poseidon, Hades — they're a thousand times better than Jupiter, Neptune, Pluto."

"Ah. So is he contented, Pygmalion, with his perfect woman?"

"What man wouldn't be?"

"I mean, is that where the story ends?"

"Yes. They live" — he knows enough to take on the protective coloration of irony — "happily ever after."

"Yet you haven't had much luck with women."

"That's why I'm here."

"You seek an . . . extreme cure."

"I know my limitations. All I ask is that I be allowed to live happily. Ever after." His tone is arch, yet he has never been more sincere.

"It is up to me to decide if you should have what you want."

"I understand the rules. I didn't expect you to let me . . . plunge right in."

"No? Well, we are used to even more extreme things in my field. There are people who want to remove their limbs. Did you know of this? Some see it as a natural continuation of what we call gender reassignment. To me, it lays bare the problem. We can alter our bodies only so much. But our real selves will reclaim us. We see that every day, with boys who were born with incomplete genitalia. They cannot be made into little girls. That's a hard lesson, especially here. Johns Hopkins was once at the forefront of gender reassignment."

"I'm not asking to become a girl."

"No, but you're asking to become something almost as odd — a eunuch. You want to thwart your own masculinity, but you need a chemical crutch to do it. It would be irresponsible of me to authorize this treatment without intensive counseling. Why are you adamant about this? You show no signs of being a sexual predator or of being sexually dysfunctional. A couple of failed relationships are not reason enough to give up. Everyone has failed relationships, you know. One needs to be right only once. Then you realize everything else was part of the journey."

He had reached into his pocket, found his lanyard key chain, squeezed it. "Have you gotten it right, Doctor?"

He blushed. "I don't talk about my personal life. Surely you know that."

"But you've gotten it right, or so you think. For how long?"

"Well, it's been two years —"

"My parents were married for twenty years. It would be forty now, if my father had lived."

"Most admirable. That should bode well for you, assuming it was a loving marriage."

Sharply, instantly. "It was."

"So why are you here?"

"I know what I need."

"That is still to be determined."

In the end, they had to agree to disagree. Dr. Michael Shaw, who had heard so much but listened to so little, had become another loose end to be tied. As Billy waited in the rain that day, he imagined his mother, narrowing her eyes at a piece of thread, snipping it and licking it until she could force it through the needle. The Bible said it was easier for a camel to pass through such a hole than it was for a rich man to go to heaven. But Dr. Michael Shaw, in his brief ride on the hood of that borrowed car, had passed through this life without a whimper. He couldn't guarantee that Dr. Shaw went to heaven, but wherever he went, he went easily, without a sound. There was only the rain and the quiet beneath it. No one heard a thing.

# Chapter 36

"Michael Shaw was part of a program that treated rapists."

Tess had begun babbling as soon as she found Carl, perched on the edge of one of the Adirondack chairs that were scattered about the grounds. He listened intently, managing to make sense of the jumbled details about Depo-Provera and chemical castration.

"That's why he had a dormancy period," she said. "He *stopped*."

"Or tried to," Carl said. "He must have understood enough about his own behavior to know there was a sexual component to what he was doing. He assumed the treatment would kill his sex drive and he would stop killing."

"But the original program had been disbanded, so it's possible he never received Depo-Provera at all, just traditional therapy."

"You told me earlier that a psychiatrist has to tell authorities if he thinks his patient has committed a crime or is a genuine threat to someone. Why would Billy Windsor kill Shaw if Shaw didn't know anything?"

Tess, who had been pacing back and forth, sank into the chair opposite Carl, leaning back in its broad arms until she was staring through the trees and the smoky blue sky overhead. It was a Code Red day, unseasonably warm, a harbinger of how horrible Baltimore's summer might be. The air was thick, almost chunky.

"I have a theory," she said.

"Shoot."

"But I don't want to have theories, I want facts. Theories are for shit."

Carl shrugged. "What else do we have at this point? A name, a mother."

"No one really gets close to this man. His mother, the women he professes to love — they see only one side of him. But in order to get the treatment he wanted from Dr. Shaw, Billy Windsor would have had to reveal some part of himself he normally conceals. He wouldn't have confessed to murder, but he might have told the doctor other things, made revelations that he came to regret. He let Mary Ann live because they didn't reach that point of no return, for whatever reason. He gave up on her."

Carl nodded. "I've been sitting here thinking about Hazel Ligetti. Why kill her unless she's an accomplice, unless she's started making noise about blackmail? But a woman who meant to blackmail someone wouldn't list him as a beneficiary."

"She'd write a letter," Tess said, remembering how she once did the same when she feared Luisa O'Neal and her husband might harm her. "Put it somewhere safe."

"He got rid of her because she knew him. Really got rid of her — burned her place to the ground, wiped her off the face of the planet."

"Which also took care of any incriminating paperwork she might have taken home with her from work," Tess pointed out. "Oh, *shit*."

"What?"

"The first time I went to Sharpsburg, I looked for Hazel's grave. She was Jewish, which isn't something a casual friend would have known. The name is a classic Ellis Island screw-up, Italian by way of Hungary. But someone had been to her grave, left a small stone."

"A stone?"

"Jewish custom. At the time, I thought it was just a passerby, someone who felt sorry for one of the few Jewish headstones in the cemetery."

Carl understood. "He was marking the trail for you. He wanted a day to come when you would make that connection."

"But why does he want *me*, Carl? I don't look like the other girls. I'm not working in a convenience store, waiting for Prince Charming to sweep me off my feet and set my life right. My life is fine."

They both looked north, to where bulldozers had begun ripping up a huge portion of the parklike campus. As Dr. Armistead had told Tess at their first meeting, Sheppard Pratt could survive only by selling off its one asset, its land. The mentally ill no longer spent their

492

lifetimes here; the hospital no longer needed all this acreage. But the trees that were being uprooted had long screened the hospital from the world. Now the world was looking back, if one could call this exposed fringe of suburbia a world.

"Did you see anything in the cemetery that day?" Carl asked. "Another person, a car? It would sure help if we knew what he drove. Even a partial description —"

"He doesn't have a vehicle. His last car was titled to his last girlfriend. Remember? Mary Ann Melcher bawled just thinking about him putting that van in her name. The state police ran all his identities through the computer. Nothing came up."

"Still, he's gotta have a car. And it would be risky, titling and retitling a vehicle to himself. Creates a paper trail of links, which he's managed to avoid. He's never put two of his names in the same place. You had to make that leap, when we were looking at the rental car records in Spartina."

"Are you suggesting he has yet another identity, one that he uses exclusively for vehicle registration? Or an out-of-state car?"

"None of the above. Did you notice that Drey Windsor lives in a pretty swanky retirement home for a waterman's widow? Someone's paying her bills. Someone's taking good care of her. I bet she returns the favor, however she can."

"So his mom buys him a car," Tess said, saying it out loud, testing it. Then she shook her head. "No way. The first time he gets stopped — and everyone gets stopped eventually — he's hosed. How's he going to explain he's driving a car titled to some strange woman?"

"Well, here's where having been a Toll Facilities cop comes in handy." Carl smiled, and Tess realized it was his way of showing he had forgiven her that insult. "All he needs is a letter, signed by Audrey Windsor. Something like, *To Whom It May Concern, so-and-so has my permission to drive this automobile.* As long as the insurance is current and the vehicle doesn't come up as stolen, no one's going to raise an eyebrow. If someone had ever gone so far as to call her, she would have vouched for him."

"Let's go," Tess said, getting to her feet and pulling him out of the deep-seated chair. His knee was still giving him trouble; he winced when she brought him to his feet too fast.

"Motor Vehicles Administration?"

"No, I want to visit my friend who does computer work for me. Because even if we confirm your hunch that Drey Windsor has more than one car titled in her name, where are we going to go from there? I want someone who can hack her way through all the state's databases if necessary."

Technically, Dorie Starnes worked at the *Beacon-Light* as a systems manager. But finding

494

reporters' lost stories and tinkering with the company's balky e-mail software took up only 50 percent of her time — and brought in only 30 percent of her income.

The rest of the time Dorie used the powerful machines at her disposal to do computer-assisted reporting for a few select customers — clients such as Tess — who could be trusted not to betray her hobby to her employer of record. Dorie had a few cards up her sleeve if the *Beacon-Light* ever turned on her. On a regular basis, she hacked her way into the company's e-mail system. Her stash of private correspondence conducted by several high-level managers provided her all the job security she needed.

Still, she wasn't happy when Tess breached their usual protocol and showed up at *Beacon-Light* downtown headquarters.

"You know you're supposed to call me on the cell if you want something."

"But I'm not sure what I want. I don't know everything you can do, and I didn't want to wait."

"Who's the guy?" Dorie was not shy about pointing, and she all but poked Carl in the nose with her stubby index finger. Round, with an upper body that appeared to be all chest, and short hair that was full of cowlicks, Dorie looked like a pigeon who had been caught in the rain.

"My new partner."

She offered this explanation because it was less complicated than the truth. But Carl smiled as broadly as if she had just given him an equity stake in Keyes Investigations. Well, he was welcome to it. There was no money in this enterprise. The only thing at stake was Tess's life.

Dorie took them into her office, an almost eerily neat space hidden in an alcove far from the newsroom. The *Beacon-Light* had undergone an expensive renovation since the last time Tess had crossed its threshold, but the building had an innate shabbiness that no decor could defeat. Newspaper people were notorious slobs, and the reporters had quickly trashed their shiny new spaces, piling papers and files around their desks, leaving food and drinks out to rot.

"Do you still have mice?"

"Yeah," Dorie said. "They're getting better at poisoning them, but the mice have a bad habit of crawling off into these little crannies to die, and they can't find them until they start to stink."

It took her less than ninety seconds to establish the fact that Audrey Windsor currently had two cars in her name: the black Buick that Tess remembered from the driveway and a van, a blue one, that had been purchased two years ago.

"So he got a new van after he left Mary Ann," Tess said. "Maybe he gets a new van after every relationship. Because the vehicle created his alibi with Tiffani and Lucy, he wouldn't risk using the same one twice."

"He needs a van," Carl said. "It's perfect for transporting your girlfriend's body after you've chopped off her head."

"Who *is* this guy?" Dorie asked in an uncharacteristic fit of curiosity. Information was just something she sold, and the facts she dug up might as well have been in Hebrew. "He chopped a woman's head off and he's still at large? Get *out*."

"He's just some guy who's killed at least five people," Tess murmured absentmindedly.

"Six," Carl corrected. "The five on your original list, plus Becca Harrison. Seven if you count Eric Shivers, and what do you want to bet he had a hand in that, too? Serial killers start young."

"Jesus Christ," Dorie said. "Why aren't the police looking into this?"

"They are," Tess said quickly, shooting Carl a look over Dorie's ruffled head. "We're just helping. So where else does a vehicle show up? What traps should we check next?"

"Well, there are no holds on the registration, but that doesn't mean he's never gotten a parking ticket." Dorie began typing rapidly, and within a matter of seconds a list of the city's parking scofflaws was on her screen. "Lookee there, the editor of the editorial page seems to have trouble feeding parking meters on her hundred-thou-a-year salary. That sporty little Saab of hers is one ticket away from a boot. I could get it booted today with just a few keystrokes."

Her fingers hovered over the keyboard, greedy for mischief.

"The guy we're looking for isn't stupid enough to get a parking ticket," Tess said. "He doesn't make mistakes like that."

"*Everyone* gets parking tickets," Carl said, his eyes bright. "The Son of Sam got parking tickets."

"*What?*" Tess and Dorie chorused.

"That's how they caught David Berkowitz. A woman saw a Ford Galaxie get a ticket for parking by a hydrant near the scene of one of the murders. It was Berkowitz's car. Cops went to his house and saw it parked outside, with a weapon and a Son of Sam note visible on the seat. Our guy wouldn't be dumb enough to do *that*, but chances are he's gotten a few parking tickets over the past seven years."

"That's true," Tess said, thinking of how many $24, $48, and $76 fines she had kicked back to the city for the privilege of parking beneath its broken streetlamps. "What time is it?"

Carl checked his watch. "Almost four."

"Good, we have at least thirty minutes."

"To do what?"

"We're going to the Wolman Building to insist on paying a ticket that our sweet little aunt, Audrey Windsor, remembers getting in Baltimore one day last month, but it got all wet in the rain and the ink ran and she couldn't figure out how to pay it. They don't get a lot of people at Wolman who want to pay tickets they haven't gotten. They should be very helpful."

Tess's hunch was right: Going to the city's municipal offices and insisting on paying a parking ticket for which there was no record was a sure way to get prompt, courteous attention. It didn't hurt, having the registration information and Audrey Windsor's name and address. It also didn't hurt that she kept pulling out fistfuls of bills and waving them around, desperate to put them in some employee's hand. Just the sight of those ATM-crisp twenties made the clerks perk up.

"You see, she's afraid that, even though you say there's no record, she's going to find a hold on her registration at year's end. She's scared to death to come to the city again. She thinks you're going to boot her. She thinks there's a warrant out for her arrest."

The overworked clerk clicked wearily through the computerized files. "I just don't see . . . there isn't. Wait, here's something. Your aunt's van got three tickets in this one block of Lancaster over the past two years. That part of Lancaster's in a residential zone, but a lot of people miss that, because one block over, there are no restrictions. We get a lot of complaints, believe me. Like there's not a sign saying it's permit parking. Like people who drive can't *read*. But your auntie paid promptly, every time. She's free and clear."

"Residential zone?" Carl asked. Tess couldn't speak. Her chest was tight. She knew where Lancaster Street was. She knew all about the parking restrictions in that neighborhood.

"In some of the busier neighborhoods, like Federal Hill and Fells Point, you need a residential permit to park for more than two hours. Otherwise, the people who live there could never find a place. You can imagine what it's like, fighting the bar traffic or the Orioles traffic to park within walking distance of your own house. But like I say, these tickets were *paid*. We keep those records, because they're often in dispute. Although, usually it's the other way. Your auntie paid it within the twenty-five-day window. Didn't even have interest on it. I can't believe she got a notice. Look, if she gets another one, come back. I'll give you a printout of this, just in case."

"Sure thing," Carl said, shaking her hand and taking the sheet of paper showing the van's brief history of parking fines.

Tess was edging backward out the door, smiling and nodding, her chest still so tight she wasn't sure she could draw a breath. As soon as they were out of the woman's view, she ran for the stairway and to the front doors. Once on Holliday, she spun in a circle, as if she expected to see someone waiting for her on the busy street.

"What's wrong?" Carl asked, panting from trying to keep up with her. "It's only three parking tickets, spread out over two years. It's a lead, but I wouldn't get too excited."

"I'm not . . . excited," Tess said, "but I know that block of Lancaster."

"So?"

"It's about six blocks from where I lived, up until eighteen months ago."

# Chapter 37

They drove straight to Lancaster from the Wolman Building. Normally, Tess might have detoured by her office and crisscrossed the block first, compiling a list of longtime residents. Older people were more prone to notice who came and went or to complain about parking. But she didn't want to waste a single minute of the late spring light. Tess knew she didn't like to see anyone's shadowy figure on her doorstep past dinnertime, even if it was just a Jehovah's Witness or a child selling band candy.

And she had felt that way *before* she knew someone wanted to kill her.

"You take the south side of the street," she told Carl. "I'll take the north."

"We only have one photo," he said, unfolding the enlarged driver's license, the one that showed "Alan Palmer" with a heavy beard and shaggy hair.

"It's the van that counts. On a narrow street like this, people will remember that behemoth because it takes up so much space. When you live in a neighborhood where parking is hard to come by, you find yourself cursing the big vehicles."

"Okay, but don't go into anyone's house alone," Carl said. "Wave to me, and I'll come over."

"What, do you think our fellow is a mad genius who has a hidden dungeon beneath his Baltimore rowhouse?"

Tess was trying to make a joke, but Carl's sheepish look made her realize that he had not quite outrun his cinematic fantasies. That was exactly what he feared, some subterranean lair beneath the city streets, with bottomless pits and Gothic implements of torture.

"We'll be no farther apart than the length of the street," she assured him. "As for either one of us going inside — this is East Baltimore, hon. We'll be lucky if anyone unlatches the screen door."

Architecturally, this block of Lancaster was hit-and-miss, its partial gentrification arrested by the latest dip in Baltimore's perpetual boom-and-bust cycle. About half the houses had been redone — the brick repointed, the doors painted striking Colonial colors, wooden shutters refastened to the windows in defiance of the damp harbor breezes that would require the owners to repaint them every year.

The others, however, still had painted screens and Formstone siding. No self-respecting yuppie would leave this fake stone siding on his or her house, Tess knew, although she supposed a few artistic types adored it for its pure camp value. Still, her money was on the Formstone as a place where Billy Windsor might have lived, or at least visited on a regular basis.

She was wrong. In less than thirty minutes, she and Carl had worked the entire block, from west to east. People had been helpful, especially when they heard that Tess and Carl were city employees who were assigned to evaluate the efficacy of parking regulations. Many a resident had leaned into the doorjamb and complained long and loud about the interlopers who parked on Lancaster. People from well outside the residential parking district. *People from the other side of Ann,* said one older woman, her head bristling with the kind of wire curlers that Tess hadn't seen in years.

"Or even" — the woman paused, lowering her voice as if she were about to say something truly slanderous — *"Wolfe Street."*

But no one remembered the van as a standout among the block's repeat offenders. After all, it had been several months since the vehicle had received a ticket. Maybe Billy Windsor had moved on — as Tess had.

Tess and Carl met on the corner to compare notes. The sky overhead was shot through with pink now. They had maybe thirty minutes of light left.

"See, Tess?" Carl said. "He didn't live around here. Probably came down to have a meal or something. I mean, lots of people come to Fells Point. This would have been a good place to meet women, if you think about it."

"Not for our guy. He couldn't make the connection he needed in a bar, shouting over the
din of music and other people. He moved
slowly. He courted his women."

"At any rate, he didn't live here."

"Not on Lancaster, no." Tess sighed. "But
maybe on one of the surrounding blocks, outside the parking district."

"It's getting late, Tess."

"Then let's hurry."

This time, however, they decided to go door-
to-door in tandem. They worked Wolfe, moving
north, then turned onto Eastern. The farther
out they went, the less hospitable people were
— and the less likely to speak English. A lot of
Dominicans had settled in the neighborhood,
and they spoke a rapid staccato Spanish that
Tess couldn't begin to follow. They thrust INS
documents at her and Carl, assuming they were
from immigration. Just the sight of strange An-
glos made them nervous and defensive.

Which was why the seventh Spanish-speaking
man stood out. His Spanish was equally rapid
but smooth. He wasn't scared, Tess realized, he
was just trying to build a wall between them, so
they would go away. He was shaking his head,
chanting, *"No sé, no sé,"* before they asked a
single question. When they showed him the license number for the van, he didn't bother to
look, just pushed the paper away and continued
shaking his head. *"No sé, no sé, no sé."*

Only someone who knew something he

shouldn't would be so quick to claim ignorance.

Tess thanked him politely, turned to Carl and
said, "Well, I guess we're done."

"I thought we were —"

"No," Tess said. She was speaking directly to
Carl, as if her words were meant only for him,
but she used a clear ringing tone that was much
louder than her normal speaking voice. "We're
not going to find that van tonight. But we'll
find it eventually — and we'll tow it when we
do, and then he'll have to pay us what he owes
us."

She smiled at the man over her shoulder.
"We did tell a white lie. We're skip tracers, and
this guy's been giving us the slip for a long,
long time."

Nothing in his face betrayed comprehension.
But Tess didn't doubt that he understood every
word she had said.

She tugged Carl away by the sleeve and retreated, heading east. When they reached the
cut-through to the alley, she glanced casually
over her shoulder to see if the man had come
out on the steps to watch them leave. Good, he
wasn't on the stoop. She ducked down the alley
and worked her way back, counting so she
could match the rear of the house to the front.

"Look," she told Carl, craning her neck, "it
has a rooftop deck."

"Not much of a deck, more a platform."

"That's how you build a deck if you have a

506

rowhouse down here. It's not like you've got a backyard. But the point is — that shitty little rental house has a deck, no more than a year or two old, judging by the lumber, and the workmanship looks pretty sound."

"So?"

"He has a view of the water, Carl. Remember? Wherever he goes, he lives in sight of the water."

"You think he lives here?"

"Or stayed here on and off, when he wasn't living with a woman. Illegal aliens aren't inclined to call the police, so it would be a safe place for him to come and go. Señor No Sé is probably calling him right now, telling him of our visit."

"Then he won't come back. Not tonight, at least."

"No. But his landlord may go to him. Chances are, Billy Windsor has stuff he can't afford to have found."

"Like what?"

"The handgun he used to kill Julie Carter, for example. Anything that links him to Tiffani Gunts and Lucy Fancher. If there's a single incriminating item in that apartment, he needs to get it out now. He can't risk the fact that we might go to the cops and they'll come back with a warrant."

"You think —"

She handed him the keys. "Go get the car, Carl, and I'll meet you at the corner of Eastern and Wolfe. You get your wish. We're going to do a little surveillance."

"Isn't it safer if you get the car and I stand here?"

"I'm the one with the gun, remember? I'll be okay."

And she would. Because she was going to press her back against the rear of the rowhouse on the far side of the alley so no one could sneak up on her.

It seemed like forever, it seemed like no time at all. They didn't speak while they sat in Carl's car, didn't listen to the radio, didn't notice how their bodies stiffened in their long-held positions. Tess's stomach was empty, her mouth was dry, and she felt she could hear tiny discrete sounds that were normally lost in the buzz of daily life: the ticking of her watch, a can bouncing along the gutter after it was thrown from a passing car, the blood in her eardrums. She wondered if Carl was experiencing the same sensations. But she did not want to speak, did not want to move, did not want to do anything that would risk this willed vigilance.

She realized they had been going all day, with virtually no break unless one counted the hour at Sheppard Pratt. Haste makes waste. But Billy Windsor was a moving target and she had a feeling he was moving faster and faster, so they had to keep up with him.

Finally, about 8:30 p.m., Señor No Sé left

the house and, with a quick glance around the street, climbed into a faded blue El Camino that needed muffler work. He headed east, toward the interstate.

"He'll be easy to follow, at least," Tess said. "You could almost do it with your eyes closed."

"If you ask me, he's almost too easy to follow," Carl said. "Do you think he's leading us somewhere?"

The thought had occurred to Tess as well. "He could be. Then again, if he thinks we're gone, this is how he *would* drive, right? If he starts acting more erratic — running red lights or making sudden turns — we'll know he's trying to elude us."

"Yeah," Carl said. "I guess so."

Once on I-95, the El Camino headed south, through the Fort McHenry tunnel. Then he took Hanover Street south, crossing the Patapsco and weaving south along Route 2, then cutting east into the Curtis Bay area. These were roads that ultimately led nowhere and it was trickier to follow him here. In a few blocks, he made a turn into the parking lot of an old industrial park that was surrounded by a high fence with razor wire across the top. He got out, yanking on a padlock that appeared to be unlocked, slid the gate open, and drove through, leaving it open behind him.

"Keep driving, as if we're headed somewhere else," Tess hissed at Carl. She was hunched down, so only Carl's head showed. If their prey looked back, he would see only one silhouette. "We can't pull in there behind him."

They continued a few blocks up, then turned left, parking on a side street. They had gone so far east they were back to the water. The site was off one of the tiny inlets off the Patapsco, Tess calculated, near where she rowed. Quietly they crept toward it, trying to stay in the shadows. It was almost too easy. Two out of every three streetlamps along this abandoned industrial stretch had been smashed.

"I don't see the van in there," Carl whispered, as they approached the open gate. "Just that El Camino."

"Motor's not running, though," Tess said. "What I can't tell is if he's still in his car."

There was a Dumpster near the gate and they ducked behind it as soon as they got through the gate. But they must have been seen, for the El Camino's motor roared on and, before they could react, the El Camino made a quick U-turn and headed out of the lot. The man didn't bother to get out and close the gate behind him.

"Did he see us?" Tess asked Carl. "What was that about? He didn't have time to get out of the car, much less meet anyone."

Carl couldn't crouch as deeply as she did, so he had braced himself against the Dumpster with his forearms. "He led us on a goddamn wild-goose chase. While we're chasing him, Billy's probably back on Eastern Avenue, clearing out his stuff. Shit. We should have split up, left you behind to watch the house while I followed this guy. But I didn't want to leave you alone."

"And I didn't want to be left alone," Tess admitted. "We could have called Crow and Whitney. They've helped me before, but never when . . . never when —"

She could not bear to finish the thought out loud. *Never when it might get one of them killed.* Billy Windsor killed the women he loved for reasons she couldn't fathom. But he killed for sheer convenience too. She had been keeping Whitney and Crow at arm's length for the past few days without realizing it.

Carl straightened up, massaging his lower back as if it were tender. Tess was beginning to feel her body again too, noticing all the tight muscles in her neck and shoulders.

"It took us a few minutes to park and work our way over. Let's look around just for the hell of it, make sure he didn't throw something out of the car before we got here."

They glanced into the top of the Dumpster but saw nothing but mounds and mounds of bagged trash, black and wet-looking in the moonlight. They began to pick their way through the littered parking lot, scuffing their feet through the broken bottles and smashed cans, looking for something that might have recently come to rest there.

The old industrial park appeared to be abandoned, a series of vacant warehouses with bay doors rusted shut. They went up one aisle, down another, turning into the third and final row without finding anything.

"We could come back tomorrow," Tess said. "Look in the daylight."

"If we found a weapon, I suppose the state police could use it to shake our Dominican friend down. Assuming he's still on Eastern Avenue come tomorrow."

They were halfway up the last aisle when they realized a bay door was open. They picked up their pace, heading toward it. But as soon as they got there, they heard a motor engage and saw two huge headlights snap on, drowning them in light. Then a van burst from the bay, heading straight toward them.

Not again, was Tess's first thought and she may have screamed it out loud. *"Not again."*

*"Run,"* Carl shouted, as if she needed encouragement. He was moving with surprising speed, given his bad knee.

They gained ground at first, for the van had to turn sharply out of the narrow bay. But once they were in the parking lot, with a long straightaway between them and the gate, the van had no trouble picking up speed. If anything, it seemed to be toying with them, holding back so they would run harder.

Within yards of the gate, Carl veered to the left, intent on making it back to the Dumpster they had used for cover when they were hiding.

Tess had thought they would be better off getting out of the parking lot and closing the gate behind them, but she saw his logic: Once behind the Dumpster, she could get her gun out of the holster and set up for a shot. She picked up speed and was even with him, just inches away from reaching the haven they needed, when she felt the van on top of them, smelled its fetid exhaust.

Carl shoved her, knocking her down, but the momentum of his push carried her along the pavement. She felt something bite her left leg, nothing more than a minor scrape, although it was strong enough to tear the fabric of her jeans. She was there; she had made it. Now all she had to do was shoot at the van's windshield, forcing it off course.

She tried to stand, only to see blood seeping through the hole in her pants. Through the hole in her *leg*. Shit, there was a gaping wound, deep enough to see a bit of bone staring back at her. *Why did you have to push me so hard, Carl?* She turned to ask him this, expecting to see him behind her. But Carl didn't have the advantage of someone shoving him from behind. He had stayed in the open, drawing the van away from her. And now it was going to hit him.

It was just as she remembered when the cab struck Jonathan. The van seemed to hesitate, for a moment, rearing back, like a bull taking aim, and then impaling Carl on its flat snout,

513

flinging his body through the air. What did a van weigh — 3,000 pounds, 4,000 pounds, 5,000 pounds? How fast was it going? ten miles per hour, twenty, thirty? It didn't matter. It wasn't a physics equation. Carl was dead, he had to be. Strangely, crazily, she remembered the moment they had shared in the Suburban House. *Noodles, I slipped. Noodles, I slipped.*

But she was alive — and she had a gun. Even if she couldn't seem to walk very well, she could shoot. She pulled her gun from the holster, steadying it in two hands and aiming toward the blinding headlights.

"I have a gun too," came a voice from inside the van. "And I can see you clearly, while you have only a general idea of where I am. Throw your gun down, or I'm going to run you over. That's not a nice way to die, let me assure you. I have some experience in these matters, as you probably know by now."

She fired off one round, hitting the windshield.

The voice came back, mildly exasperated. "Tess, don't be foolish. Put the gun down, or I'll drive straight at you."

If she could get to the gate and pull it shut behind her — and she had a chance, adrenaline alone might carry her that far, that fast — she could get away. He'd have to get out of the fucking van then, and she'd be in position, she'd have a shot.

"If you run, I'll shoot you in the back," the

voice said. "It's not what I want, but if I have to, I will. Also, you can't see it from here, but I think your friend is alive. He's breathing, Tess. Put your gun down and I'll call for help. Don't you want to save his life? I have a cell phone right here." He pushed a button, and its ringer sounded, a chirpy little song in four notes: dee-dee-*dee*-dee. The tune was familiar. It was the one clocks played, in imitation of Big Ben. *Oh, lord, our guide.*

"Your gun, Tess. It's your only chance — and his."

She threw it, but not at the van. Instead, she threw it behind her, into the shadowy recesses along the razor-wire-topped fence.

"I guess that will do," the voice said.

She heard the passenger door open and close, saw the figure come toward her, backlit in his headlights. It was a man, nothing more than a man, a man of average height and build, a man of average looks. But she had known that. She had known for some time how ordinary-looking Billy Windsor was.

He knelt alongside her, squeezing her left knee. She jerked back, but he pressed harder. He was trying to stanch the blood. Whatever she had fallen on had taken a neat crescent-shaped chunk out of her knee, almost like a bite.

Billy Windsor leaned his face close to hers. He wore a baseball cap, but he was no longer bearded and the hair visible at the edges was light brown, curly. He placed his palms on her cheeks, indifferent to the blood he left on her face. Her blood, from her knee.

"Well," he said. "We've certainly come full circle."

# Chapter 38

Inside the warehouse, he ripped the torn leg of her jeans and pressed a clean rag to her knee — but only after tying her to a wooden chair, a battered bentwood.

He fastened her to the chair's curves with a jump rope. Her own, Tess realized, the one she kept in the trunk of her car. She hadn't even noticed it was missing. It had been there in Sharpsburg, the night she checked into the Bavarian Inn, but she hadn't thought to look for it since. There had been so little time for jumping rope. Or for rowing, for running, for long walks with her dogs. There had been so little time for everything, and now there might not be time for anything ever again. When had he taken her jump rope? Figuring out this one thing suddenly seemed crucial. Had he taken it as she slept that night in West Virginia and then continued to the graveyard to leave the stones on Hazel's grave? How long had he been a part of her life, how long had he been watching her, waiting for her? She had been so easy for him to follow.

But then, he had mapped her course through Maryland. He knew where she was going because he had sent her there.

When he tightened the knot on the leather rope, Tess tried to swell her chest as much as possible, so there might be some slack when he was done, but she was weak and light-headed. Had she lost that much blood? Was she in shock? He wore a denim work shirt over his white T-shirt and he took it off, tying the arms around her leg to make a bandage. All this time he had not spoken, but he had removed his baseball cap, so she could finally see his face. He had a nice build, not unlike Crow's: slender but muscular. He looked to be her age, but then that was one of the few things they had known about him. He was thirty-two. From identity to identity, Billy Windsor had been consistent about his age. He picked men with the same birth year as his, which gave him one less lie to keep track of.

Did he live here? There was a cot, neatly made, with a lightweight blanket and a pretty patchwork pillow. There was an old card table, and he had rigged up electricity and hung a floodlight that threw a circle of light over them. But there was no sign of a bathroom and the rest of the space was stacked with canisters and boxes.

"Shouldn't I be lying down? In case of shock?"

"Possibly," he said. "But that would interfere with what I have to do."

Even now, with her trussed up, he was taciturn about his motives.

"Carl's not really alive, is he?"

He considered her question. "I doubt it. If he is, it won't be for long. He's probably busted up good, inside. But I didn't want to kill you out there."

Again, she tried to divine his intentions. Did he not want to kill her? Or was it simply that he didn't want to kill her *out there?* He had never tortured his victims, she had that faint consolation, and his witting victims — Tiffani, Lucy — had been granted the quickest deaths. He was good to the women he loved.

"Still, you can't be sure he's dead. People do survive getting hit by cars."

She wanted him to go back outside and check and — well, then what? The jump rope was leather and leather had some give, even when knotted. But Billy had grown up on the water, knew his way around boats. He was probably excellent at tying knots.

"It's a method that hasn't failed me yet."

"You mean with Michael Shaw."

He smiled. It was a fond smile, warm and affectionate, as if he knew her. She thought, for a moment, that he might reach out and tousle her hair. "Not just Dr. Shaw."

"Who — ?" But she knew the answer. It was the answer that explained everything, or began to. Jonathan Ross. She was sitting opposite the man who had killed Jonathan Ross. *Billy Windsor had driven the Marathon cab that foggy morning.* Tess had told herself that only Luisa and Seamon O'Neal knew how Jonathan had been killed. But of course they had hired someone. They had hired Billy Windsor, and he had used that tit for tat: to blackmail Luisa O'Neal into being his accomplice when he decided to track Tess down. Even with Seamon dead and her own life almost over, Luisa O'Neal would not want anyone to know what her husband had done.

"How did you and the O'Neals ever meet?"

"Seamon O'Neal helped me out of a jam. It was a little more than two years ago, and I was trying to turn over a new leaf."

"After you burned down Hazel's house."

He let that pass, but he didn't protest or deny the fact. "I got picked up for criminal trespass on a job. And it turned out the name I was using, Ben Colby, had a prior for robbery. I don't know how Hazel missed that. I told her to run criminal checks."

"Is that why you killed her?"

He didn't rise to the bait. "So what was I going to do? I couldn't say I wasn't Ben Colby because then I'd have had to say who I was. But the prior meant I might serve time, and I'd never survive that. O'Neal was my lawyer."

"O'Neal didn't do that kind of petty criminal work. He represented asbestos manufacturers, big firms involved in civil suits."

"We had a client in common, O'Neal and I. A local developer who cut some corners — hired kids to haul asbestos away, wasn't careful about the way he stripped lead paint from old buildings. He didn't want me going into court, telling why I was found on private property. Because I was there on his behalf, and I knew too much about how he did business. He got me O'Neal, and O'Neal got me off. But O'Neal knew I was keeping secrets. So when he asked me to make one of his problems disappear, I had to return the favor. It was business."

"Killing Jonathan Ross was business."

"Yes. I didn't like it much. But it had to be done. I do unpleasant things, sometimes, in my work."

"And in your life."

"It's not the same. Don't confuse what I do for money, or out of necessity, and what I do for love."

Billy Windsor walked over to the small card table by his cot and began rummaging through an old canvas bag. He pulled out a black leather case and unzipped it, revealing a pair of scissors and a razor. They picked up what little light there was, giving off a shine that was almost blue.

"It's better wet," he said. "But I can do it dry, if I have to."

Tess worked her mouth, but no words came out. *This was not what he did,* she reminded herself. He did not slash throats, he had never done any ritualistic cutting or stabbing. Lucy Fancher's head had been removed postmortem.

He looked at her, perplexed by her expression. Then he understood.

521

"Don't be so melodramatic, Tess. I'm just going to cut your hair."

If her arms had not been pinned by the coils of rope, her hands would have flown to her head. As it was, she felt her arms strain against their bindings. There was a little slack there, but not much. Not enough.

"Don't worry. I'm quite good. I cut my mother's hair as a boy. Then Becca's. I had to talk her into it — she liked tossing her curls around. But she was much more beautiful with her hair short. I cut all their hair, and they were all more beautiful for it. You will be, too. Women's faces are like flowers. When you cut their hair, they open up."

"But they" — she did not want to characterize them as his girlfriends. Such normalcy seemed obscene. "They didn't all have short hair."

"Not when I met them, sure. But you must not have looked at the autopsy photos. I cut Tiffani's hair three days before, Lucy's about a month before. I left Julie before we got that far. As for Mary Ann — well, she said she'd rather be dead than have short hair. And I thought, No, you wouldn't. But I didn't give up on her until I found out she wasn't raising her own child. I found that unnatural. That was over two years ago, and I decided I'd never have what I really wanted, that I had to live a different kind of life. Then I met you."

He came around behind her. She flinched at

his touch, but it could not have been more gentle. Apparently, he really did intend to cut her hair. He was unbraiding it, sectioning it, running his fingers through it. Soon enough, she heard the scissors' husky rasp and saw a hank fall to the floor. The brown locks looked so alive, so vital, so much a part of her. It was going to take a long time for him to cut this unruly mass.

"I don't really understand you," she said. "What you've done. Why you do it. You get so close you're ready to start a family. And then you leave."

"I'm used to women not getting it. The important thing is, I understand *you*."

"The way you understood Becca? And Tiffani? Lucy?"

His touch roughened. He pulled hard enough on the next section to bring tears to her eyes.

"I loved them," he said, his voice even. "I loved them more than anything. I invented them. Especially Becca. My love gave her the confidence she needed to discover her gifts."

"Her gifts? You mean her voice?"

"Exactly."

"But she couldn't be an opera singer on Notting Island." She groped for a name, but couldn't begin to think what she should call him. Billy? Charlie? Alan? Eric? The names were all so boyish, so innocent. "She had to leave if she was going to do anything with her talent."

"I know that. I was prepared to go with her. But she wanted to study at Juilliard, the one place I couldn't go. I might have survived a few years in a city like Baltimore, if I had to. Or even Boston. But not New York, never New York."

*Smart Becca. She had probably chosen Juilliard for just that reason.*

"So you killed her."

"It wasn't like that. It wasn't like that at all." He sounded exasperated, in a mild way. "I tried to get her to stay, yes. But she was the killer, she was the one who wanted to destroy a human life."

"What do you mean?" But even as she spoke, Tess thought of the calendars, the careful records he had kept for Tiffani and Lucy. "You got her pregnant."

"We conceived a child." He was leaning in close, his breath warm on her neck. "She asked me to take her to the mainland for an abortion. When I said I wouldn't, she said she'd go without me. When I said I'd stop her, she said it might be another boy's, so I had no say in it."

"Eric Shivers."

"She threw that name out. I was never convinced, though. She may have flirted with him but she loved me. She wouldn't have betrayed me."

"Still, you killed him."

He had moved around to the front of her face and was working on creating a fringe of wispy bangs, high on her forehead. "You have a widow's peak," he said. "I never noticed that."

"Did you kill Eric Shivers?"

He sighed. She wanted to wrinkle her nose at the feel of his warm breath so close to her face, but she willed her features to stay still.

"It was more of a prank, really. I was working the grill for the Kiwanis Club. It was easy enough to put a chunk of crab in the burger I made for Eric. I meant to scare Becca, to show her how weak Eric was. I didn't know she would run away and he would die. At any rate, it didn't work. For some reason, it just made her more determined to leave the island, to get rid of our baby."

Of course it did, Tess thought. Her baby's father was either dead or a killer. What kind of choice was that for an eighteen-year-old girl?

"So what happened?"

He was on her left side now, his breath tickling her ear. "We were out on my skiff. We quarreled. She said she would do what she had to do without my help. She jumped out of the boat, as if it were some big dramatic scene, as if it were one of her damn operas. There was a big piece of driftwood and I grabbed it, held it out to her, meaning only to pull her in. But the water was rough and she was flailing. She bobbed up suddenly, where I didn't expect her, and it caught her on the head. I got her out, took her to Shanks Island, tried to work the water out of her lungs, but it was too late."

Good story. Tess didn't believe a word of it. But he seemed to.

"You weighed her body down so it wouldn't be found. Then you faked her disappearance, with your mother's help, and your own death. It all sounds pretty calculated for a teenage boy who's supposedly beside himself with grief."

"Mother helped me . . . arrange a few things. She knew no one would understand that it had been an accident."

*Because it wasn't.* But Tess didn't bother to say this out loud. Billy Windsor had spent his life arranging and rearranging these facts into a myth he could live with. Deprived of his true love by a cruel fate, he wandered the earth, alone and rootless. But how did he rationalize the deaths that had followed?

"I got the impression your mother never knew about the others you killed."

Several pieces of hair fell before he spoke again.

"I wouldn't want to burden her. But if I told Ma everything, I think she would understand."

"She would have to, wouldn't she?" Tess took a deep breath. "You pay for her place."

"Yes."

"How? That's a pretty expensive development."

"There's a lot of money in what I do."

"Which is — ?" She still didn't understand how he made a living.

"Hauling and transporting. I take what I like

to call *unfriendly* substances and find them homes. This is a temporary holding place, sort of my distribution center if you will. These canisters are filled with various things, things you wouldn't want to touch or inhale. I will relocate them later to more permanent resting places. It can be expensive, doing this kind of work by regulation, getting the proper permits. It's very burdensome for small businessmen. So I help them out."

"By illegally dumping toxic substances."

He allowed himself a one-syllable laugh, not much more than a snort. "It's not as if a lot of the earth isn't already spoiled, Tess. Take Baltimore, for example. The people here live like pigs. They breathe dirty air. They live in houses with lead paint. Or, like you, they row on that filthy water. They don't care how they live. Why should I?"

"I saw your home, Notting Island. It's not a pristine sanctuary. There were rusting appliances and cars in a huge pile."

"Trash is different on an island. It's much harder to haul away. What's the excuse here, where they come to your door and pick up your trash twice a week? Just think. If people were neater, if they didn't litter and throw their garbage on the ground, you wouldn't be in the predicament you are in now."

He gestured toward her leg, pointing at her wound with the scissors.

"Besides, I had to find work in a cash business. Once I was dead, I couldn't make money the way most people do. I was just trying to get by."

"But you kept dying. After you killed Tiffani, you took another identity. Then a third identity, and now, presumably, a fourth or a fifth. Hazel gave you those. Why?"

"Hazel and I became friends," he said. "I don't expect you to understand that, but I genuinely liked her. And she liked me. I told her I had made a mistake as a young man, but I had paid for it, and all I wanted was a chance to outrun my past. She believed me. She wanted to believe me. She often said I was the most interesting thing that ever happened to her."

Hazel didn't know the half of it.

"Hazel led us to you. She put your name — your real name — as her beneficiary."

"Really? Well, that only proves how much she loved me. I didn't want to kill her, but I was turning over a new leaf. I needed to break with my past. Out with the old, in with the new."

Tess's hair kept falling in shining clumps — on the floor, over her shoulders, in her lap.

"You killed her because she knew too much."

"No. I needed a fresh start, and Hazel was part of my old life. I didn't want to keep doing what I was doing. That's why I went to Dr. Shaw. But he never understood. He thought I was just another guy who couldn't find a relationship. Which wasn't my problem at all. It was easy to find women. But it was horrible, discovering how inadequate they were. They weren't ready for my love. They refused it."

"But they didn't refuse — except for Julie, and she was an addict. They loved you. They told everyone you were perfect. You changed their lives, you were their Prince Charming."

"But it was never quite right. I picked poorly, I admit. They were too young, or too dumb, to appreciate what I was offering them. They would come so far, so quickly, but then their development would stop. They wanted such ordinary things, they dreamed such tiny dreams. I had been looking for a physical type, but it's the spirit that matters. You're more like Becca than any of them, even if you don't look like her."

Tess felt something on the back of her neck that she had not felt for almost twenty years — a breeze. Then the battery-powered razor whirred on and began nipping at her skin. She had grown her hair long in protest of just this kind of barbershop cut, which she had been forced to wear throughout grade school because her mother hated trying to work a comb through Tess's snarls and tangles. She had worn her hair in a braid since high school, getting two inches cut from the tip every six months or so. Which meant that the hair on the floor wasn't that old, in all likelihood. But it felt that way. It felt as if Billy Windsor had just cut much of her life from her head.

Finished now, he stooped to gather armfuls of her hair. Then, to Tess's amazement, he carried these tendrils to his cot. He took the patchwork pillow, removed the cover, and unzipped the inside casing. The pillow was stuffed with hair, masses and masses of dark hair. From Becca, perhaps. Almost certainly from Tiffani and Lucy. And now from her. So Carl had been right about something else. Billy Windsor had kept trophies after all. He had just collected them while his victims were still alive.

"Now let me even up the front," he said, coming at her with scissors in hand, peering so closely at the fringe of bangs he had given her that he seemed almost cross-eyed in his concentration.

"Why?" Tess asked. "Why me?"

He drew back, so he could make eye contact. "Why? Because I made you. Even more than the others. You're my *creation*. I've read the papers these past two years, I've seen how successful you've become. None of it would have happened if I hadn't killed that man."

His logic infuriated her as much as it sickened her. How dare he? She was not his creation. She owed him nothing. It was just the kind of condescension she and Carl had discussed earlier that day, which now seemed a lifetime away. Blood rushed to her face and she yearned to protest.

But she should agree, she knew she should agree. Perhaps the others had argued with him, rejected his counsel. He had built up Tiffani and Lucy until they were strong enough and smart enough to have their own opinions about who they were and what they should be. Then he had killed them, for the sin of thinking they knew themselves.

"The others weren't properly grateful, then, for all you had done for them."

"I put them out of their misery. They were imperfect, malformed. They knew just enough to know they didn't measure up." He put the scissors on the concrete floor, then stepped back to admire his handiwork. "Did it ever occur to you that Epimetheus hurried, while Prometheus was guilty of nothing more than having the patience to get it right?"

"What do you mean?"

"It's a Greek myth —"

"I know Greek mythology. Epimetheus made the animals and finished before Prometheus, who made mankind. That's why he had to steal fire from the gods, because his brother had given all the best gifts to the animals. But he didn't destroy his creations, far from it. He loved them. He risked everything for them."

"As far as we know," Billy Windsor said. "But what if part of the reason that Prometheus took so long is because he started over again? And over. And over. I've come to believe he made several attempts, destroying his earlier work, until he got it right. That's why Epimetheus was done first. Because Prometheus had the integrity to strive for perfection."

"You think you made us? That you're our creator?"

"Not exactly. But you would be less without me. Can you deny that?"

"I'll concede you set some events in motion," Tess said.

"I set everything in motion. I *am* motion. We're soulmates, Tess. You can live with me or die with me. If you want to die, I'll kill you now — and join you in death. One quick shot to the heart, and it will all be over. But if you choose life — if you choose me — it will be a love like no one's ever known. I'll hold you forever, the way the jimmy holds the sook, floating on the tide. We'll be beautiful swimmers. Together."

He was leaning in so close she wanted to shut her eyes. His breath was surprisingly sweet, minty, as if he had rinsed with mouthwash before she arrived. The Dominican man must have called Billy Windsor on his cell phone after she knocked on his door. Billy Windsor had told him to come here, knowing she and Carl would follow, improvising this plan. He could not plan everything in advance.

"You have to admit, I took advantage of those events you set in motion. I built up my own business. I got better at what I did. You don't get the credit for all that."

"True. But without me, you never would have crossed the starting line. What would have happened if I hadn't killed that man?"

"His name," Tess said, struggling for control of her voice, the one thing left for her to control, "was Jonathan Ross."

"I know. But he didn't matter to me. Neither did you, at first. But when I realized how you were blossoming, how you began to thrive — then I knew you were ready. And I knew what I had to do."

He leaned toward her, his mouth open, as if he meant to kiss her. Tess swallowed hard, then parted her lips. She had no choice. She had to do what he wanted, had to stay alive every second she could. She opened her mouth, opened herself, allowed his lips to fasten on hers. His kiss was shockingly familiar, not unlike Crow's — probing but polite, not gnawing greedily as some men did. He was waiting for permission. She opened her mouth wider still, drew his tongue inside — and then she bit him.

She drove her teeth into his lips with all the force she could muster, biting through the lower lip until his blood spurted into both their mouths. She bit down and she held on the best she could, until she tore a strangled scream from his throat, shocking him in her betrayal as he had shocked woman after woman in his. She used her teeth like knives, but the human face was surprisingly resilient. She was not strong enough to rip another person's flesh, although she was bearing down so hard she felt a sharp, metallic pain in her molar, the one that was tender because she ground her teeth at night.

But she was strong enough not to let go, to fasten on his mouth like some vicious parasite, sending wave after wave of pain into his face, his head, his body. He slapped her, boxing her ears until they rang. Still, she didn't let go, just kept holding on to his lip with her teeth even as she raised her right leg, the one that wasn't hurt, and landed her knee exactly where her eighth-grade gym teacher had told her to kick a man if she was ever in real trouble.

It worked, it actually worked. He fell back, writhing. Tess calculated she had bought herself ten, maybe twenty seconds at the most. She rocked on the legs of her wooden chair, tucking her chin to her chest, hoping she didn't lose consciousness. The chair fell backward with a thud that knocked the breath out of her — and, as she had hoped, cracked its wooden frame, so the rope was now slack and the chair in pieces. She struggled free and looked around the room. He had a gun, he had said he had a gun. Where was it?

But she was out of time. He was on his knees, those strange guttural sounds still coming from his throat, his eyes slitted in pain and revenge. She saw the glint of the scissors on the floor and dove for them. He grabbed her left leg — high, on purpose, on the very bandage he had made for her — and the pain was searing. Now he was on top of her, he had her left arm, but not her right, which she held away from him, like a kid in a game of keep-away. Her right hand had the scissors.

She didn't want to do it. She knew the nightmares over this act would eclipse everything she had ever known before, would make her yearn for her old night terrors, where she was only a witness, not a player. But this was a nightmare too, and there was only one way to wake from it.

She drove the scissors into his left eye, plunging the blade as far as it could go. New blood — richer blood, thicker blood — flowed over her and into her eyes. He was still making those horrible noises. Which meant she had not driven the scissors deep enough. He was breathing; he was alive. But she was free, she was crawling away from him, her hands sliding along the blood-slick floor.

She stood, her legs shaking. She couldn't run, she could barely walk, and he showed no signs of dying. He was tougher than she was, a cockroach, a scavenger. He had come back from the dead twice so far, and he would come back again if she let him. She staggered to the card table, to the gym bag from which he had pulled the scissors and razor. A 9-millimeter was on top, loaded.

Billy Windsor was sitting up, blood spurting from his face, the scissors jutting out, his voice full of pain and outrage as he screamed incomprehensible threats at her. She watched in a kind of sickened admiration as he took a deep breath, grabbed the scissors by the handle, and pulled them from his eye, releasing yet more blood. She couldn't believe he had any blood left in him at this point. He didn't look real to her. He didn't look human. Good. She couldn't afford to think of him as human.

Tess picked up the gun, held it in two hands, aimed carefully at Billy Windsor's midsection, and fired. The 9-millimeter had more kick than her .38 and it jerked up, so her first shot tore through his throat. She held tighter with her trembling hands and the shots that followed hit him at chest level, again and again and again. She shot him first for Becca — whose only crime was to think well of herself, to believe she had a say in her own future. For Tiffani, and for Lucy. She shot him for Hazel and Michael Shaw and Eric Shivers. For Julie, the stupid little drug addict who had almost escaped him. And for Jonathan, who had been nothing to him but a shape in the morning fog, a means to an end, another person to be sacrificed for Billy Windsor's survival. The gun had ten shells; she had two left. She shot him one more time. For Carl.

Done, she stuck the gun in her own empty holster and limped out to the parking lot. She found Billy Windsor's cell phone in his van. She dialed 911 as she made her way to Carl's body. He was lying faceup under the stars, his eyes still open. She tucked the phone under her chin as she waited for the dispatcher to answer, placing her hand on Carl Dewitt's neck. For a moment, she thought she felt a pulse, but it was her own thumb, sending the news of her beating heart back to her. She was the only one who was still alive.

# Epilogue

"Congratulations," Dr. Armistead said. "I see the stitches have come out."

He gestured toward her leg, which was still a little stiff but otherwise back in working condition. Tess had even rowed that morning, for the first time in almost two months. But she had been wearing shorts all that time, sitting in a lounge chair by the Roland Park Pool, so there was a white stripe where the bandage had been. The cut had required thirteen lucky stitches, two inside and eleven outside, and the scar on her left kneecap was still red and angry-looking. It was as if a begrudging teacher had scrawled a checkmark on her knee: *good work.*

Now Dr. Armistead was saying the same thing, in effect. Congratulations. Good job. But was it?

"Are you congratulating me for being no-billed by the grand jury? I told you they always do, when self-defense is alleged."

"Alleged?" His bushy eyebrows shot up. "But it *was* self-defense."

"Officially. The newspapers didn't report the detail that I used nine shots out of a clip that held ten."

"I don't understand the significance."

"The homicide detectives did. And the state police." She had left one bullet in the gun to show them she was in her right mind, she hadn't lost control. She wanted them to know the deliberation she brought to her task. She had chosen to take a man's life. But she had told Dr. Armistead that much.

"How do you —"

"Please don't finish that question. I feel fine. I did what I had to do."

Or had she? The cops considered her a hero, but she didn't feel like one. Carl was the hero, and he had been given a proper hero's funeral, although she was too numb at the time to appreciate it. Later, his name was read at the annual memorial service of law officers killed in the line of duty. Tess wasn't sure she believed in an afterlife, but she hoped Carl had made it to one, if only because he would have been so pleased by his posthumous glory. She liked to think he and Lucy Fancher had met at last, and Lucy finally had her body back. Maybe her hair, too. If hair and fingernails can grow after death, they should grow in heaven as well.

Tess's own hair was now just long enough to be impossible. She had forgotten how much curl it had when it was short. Her mother said, almost hopefully, that it would never grow back, that Tess should settle for a grown-up cut. But Tess was determined to reclaim her braid if it took five years, ten, twenty. Unlike

Billy's other women, she didn't have the delicate features to carry such short hair. Whitney, being Whitney, had told her she looked like shit. Crow, being Crow, had said she was beautiful.

Neither one was right. But neither one was wrong.

"What are you thinking?" Dr. Armistead asked.

She sighed but told the truth. "About my hair."

"Ah, yes. Your hair. I suppose you've thought about the inherent irony — how you were sent here because you decided to denude a man, like a modern-day Delilah, only to have another man do the same thing to you."

"Well, *duh*." She still couldn't help tweaking the doctor at times. "Although your analogy falters. I didn't lose my strength when my hair was gone. I was stronger than ever."

"Yes. But have you stopped to consider the true source of your strength? Do you credit anyone, or any process in particular, with the fact that you were strong and resilient in the face of danger? That you used your anger properly?"

"Me." He actually looked hurt. "Well, you might have helped."

She wasn't sure if she believed that or not. She knew having Dr. Armistead as a sounding board had been instrumental over the last several weeks. But she never forgot that her visits here were probationary, the result of another man thinking he knew what she needed. *Three months to go, three months to go, three months to go.* She was halfway to the end.

"Have you stopped to think that, if Billy Windsor hadn't fixated on you, he might have continued killing these small-town girls who had the bad luck to look like his first love?"

"You're trying to make me feel better that Carl's dead and I'm alive. But I can't rationalize things that way. I don't think that's what Carl wanted."

"Do you think Billy Windsor was evil?"

They had been here before. "No. He was sick. He even tried to get help, but I don't think he really wanted to be helped. He wanted to *matter.* From the day he killed Becca and faked his own death, he sentenced himself to a shadow existence. Killing was the one way he asserted his reality, strange as it sounds. Restored to his true identity, placed in a hospital for the criminally insane, he might have gotten better."

"Yet you didn't give him that chance."

"No. I killed him."

"One might even say you executed him."

The more he pushed her, the more she felt compelled to defend herself. Perhaps there was a method to Dr. Armistead's madness.

"When I'm feeling charitable about myself, I think that I put Billy Windsor out of his misery. He wanted to stop what he was doing, but he couldn't. He was going to keep killing because no woman was ever going to satisfy him." Tess tried for a light tone. "Not even me."

She felt the dreaded thickness in her throat. She always blinked back her tears when they started in this office because she hated the automatic question, "What are those tears about?" Besides, she didn't want to cry anymore. She didn't want to be anyone's hero, she didn't want to talk to true-crime writers, from the sleazy to the sober, who kept leaving messages at the office she hadn't visited for the past seven weeks. She didn't want to spend all her time assuring solicitous friends and family members that she was fine, really fine, just fine, damn it. But mostly she didn't want to cry, and she found she was crying quite a bit — in her car, at the grocery store, and every time she watched *The Wild Bunch*. The mere sight of William Holden and that damn scorpion was enough to make her break down.

This was the one place she had managed not to lose it. Until now. She began to cry so hard that she had to grope for the box of Kleenex like a blind woman.

"Tess, I know you still don't like coming here. And maybe you never belonged here, maybe the judge was wrong. But you've been through a lot. It's a propitious time for you to be in therapy."

"But doesn't this whole thing prove how angry I am, if not downright psychotic? Aren't you and Judge Halsey going to use this as an excuse to extend my term here? I fired nine shots at a man I could have allowed to live. Isn't that wrong?"

"You were fighting for your life. In hindsight, you see that you had choices. But you were weak, you couldn't outrun him. You had to use the gun."

"So why nine shots. Why not just one or two?"

"You tell me, Tess. You say you left one bullet in the gun to show you were in control. But what's the significance of *nine?*"

Eric, Becca, Tiffani, Lucy, Hazel, Michael, Julie, Carl — and Jonathan. But only the first eight names had been reported in the media. Tess had never spoken of Billy Windsor's twisted motive, never explained how they had met. She had found, much to her amazement, a tiny flicker of sympathy for Luisa O'Neal, faint but true. Let her die with her family's reputation intact, if it meant so much to her. Luisa didn't have much left, lying in a hospital bed beneath a sign advising that she wore cloth diapers. The only thing she had to look forward to was her own glowing obituary. So be it.

Besides, if Tess could forgive Luisa, she might also begin to forgive herself.

She chewed her lower lip. "One day I might tell you. Not yet. But one day."

"If it's any comfort, I think you're doing extraordinarily well. You've begun to sleep through the night without medication. You tell me your appetite is back, and it does look as if you've gained some of the weight you lost. I don't expect we'll go beyond the court-mandated term — which ends in October."

"October twenty-eighth, to be exact. Not that I'm keeping track or anything." But she smiled, and he smiled back.

Finally, all the instruments agreed that the hour was over, and Tess was free, at least for another week. She walked out into an already-searing morning, the seventh in an oppressive heat wave. Now that it was August, every day was a Code Red day. Crow and Whitney waited in the Adirondack chairs, flanked by a panting Esskay and Miata. They followed her almost everywhere she went these days, in some combination. Whitney and Crow, Esskay and Miata. Sometimes Tess wanted to remind them of what could happen to those who got too close to her. But they would not be deterred, and in the end she did not want them to be.

She realized Crow was sitting where Carl had sat just seven weeks earlier, on another Code Red day, a day when sheer momentum had carried them too far and fast. They should have stopped in those increasingly manic twelve hours, should have paused for breath, taken a moment to think things through — but they hadn't. They simply hadn't. In hindsight, she could pick apart what she did, what they did, the mistakes they made.

But at the time, everything had made sense. Sort of.

"We thought," Crow said, "you might like to get out of town for a long weekend, since we didn't do anything for the Fourth this year. Get out of town, get out of this horrible air."

"Where?"

"Ocean City?" Whitney put in. "Or my parents' place at the shore. Or maybe even down to Saint Mary's, to a bed-and-breakfast —"

"No, no, let's head west for a change, toward the mountains. Out of Maryland, even. We could go to Berkeley Springs or somewhere else in West Virginia."

Whitney wasn't fooled. "Don't let Billy Windsor keep you from the places you love, Tess. Don't give him that power."

"I'm not. I just want . . . a change of scenery."

She could not tell them about the new nightmare, the waking one, where Billy Windsor waited for her everywhere: in every small town, along every hidden inlet of the Patapsco, in every industrial park glimpsed from the highway, behind the wheel of every van that tailgated her on the Jones Falls Expressway, beneath the bill of every baseball cap on a brown-haired man of six feet or so. Billy Windsor had finally forged the lasting bond he wanted with a woman. Just her luck, it was her. They would be together for quite some time. Not forever, but longer than it took a knee to heal, and she needed to confront that unhappy fact.

But not today. Not now.

"Let's go," she said. "West. Away from the water."

# About the Author

**_Laura Lippman_** was a newspaper reporter at the Baltimore *Sun* for twelve years. Her previous Tess Monaghan novels — *The Sugar House, Baltimore Blues, Charm City, Butcher's Hill,* and *In Big Trouble* — have won Edgar, Agatha, Shamus, and Anthony Awards, and her most recent novel, *In a Strange City,* was a *New York Times* Notable Book of the Year. Lippman lives, of course, in Baltimore, Maryland. Visit her website at www.lauralippman.com.